IMPERIUM

MATTHEW ROMEO

IMPERIUM

THE OUTRIDER SAGA BOOK 2

Edited by: Katherine D. Graham
Formatted by: D. M. Sonntag
Cover Art by: Nadia at MiblArt
Published by Matthew Romeo

Ebook ISBN: 978-1-7341039-7-7
Paperback ISBN: 978-1-7341039-8-4

To the Maestro and Arnisadors who showed me how to weave in mind, body, and spirit.

CONTENTS

PREFACE

Book number five. Wow! I spent a lot of time this year in denial that this was going to be my fifth self-published novel. It's been a year full of imposter syndrome. Every so often, I question this path of storytelling, especially when 100% of the production process rests on my shoulders. But equally as often, I'm reminded of the story I want to tell, which pushes me forward.

Imperium has been a unique challenge, because the story changed drastically from when I first started writing it in May 2022. I ended up completely scrapping the original plot and tone in favor of what resides in the coming pages. It may be a pleasant surprise for you, or it might be a disappointing subversion. I promise, it's not meant to be the kind of "gotcha!" bait-and-switch that's typical these days. No disdain, no malice. This was the story that spoke in my jumbled mind, so I had to write it.

There were a few lessons I took to heart after *Erinyes*, especially on the character arc front. Feedback was unified in wanting more development from Aelec and Riza, and I do heed most criticisms. That's part of the reason why this story changed; it's much more character driven than the first. As a fan of George Lucas, a key lesson I learned from *Star Wars* is that every story should feel different. Pierce Brown did this between his two *Red Rising* trilogies; one is a young adult resistance tale, the other is a full adult apocalyptic opera.

Erinyes was a fast-paced, heist adventure, and *Imperium* is... Well, you'll soon see.

To my fans and new readers alike, this book is chock-full of Easter eggs, so I hope you have fun finding them. As always, thank you for giving this indie sci-fi author your time.

IMPERIUM

THE OUTRIDER SAGA BOOK 2

MATTHEW ROMEO

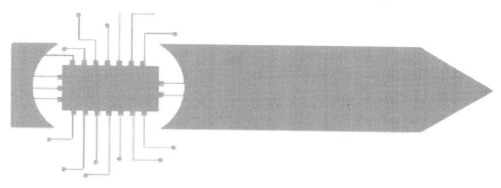

PROLOGUE

Protesters were parasites, and it was Milli Spectre's job to make sure they didn't burrow into the heart of her city.

The ruckus of chanting protesters filled the air within the dockyard's hub as dozens of people crowded the cramped hallway leading from the city to the starport terminal. Narrow corridors, long forgotten cargo crates, and a steady stream of blistering air spewed onto the crowd of people winding their way through the claustrophobic city. If she could eliminate one of those things, it would be the hot air that kept blowing in her face from the vents.

"We will not be silenced!" cried a protestor, and a dozen more echoed the ironic sentiment.

Milli groaned. She also wanted to be rid of the protesters.

She'd gotten an anonymous tip earlier in the day that indicated that these activists might be smuggling E-weapons to the protest in hangar bay L330. Fearing for the safety of an incoming Imperium politician, Milli had volunteered to observe the event closely so that she could subdue any aggressors. The Capital Bureau of Investigation needed to show their effectiveness at even the slightest indication of threat.

Leaning against the corner of a walkway intersection, she watched the chanting group with a keen eye. It was her job to keep a close watch on factions that caused civil unrest, and it was her duty to enforce the law by any means necessary. She didn't want to kill anybody if she could avoid it, but if this radical group made one wrong move, there'd be no hesitation.

She had to set her personal reservations aside in spite of what these protestors had done in past months.

"End the fascism!" another protester roared. "End Sessani's term!"

That got the crowd going. Their shouts grew louder, their words had more bite to them. Milli could feel the viciousness behind their voices. Some of the protesters grew rigid as their aggression buffeted.

With a practiced eye, she noted the various vests, satchels, and terminuses adorning the protesters. A tattered leather vest could conceal a pulseknife. A satchel over a shoulder could carry an E-pistol or a couple flashbang grenades. A sophisticated terminus decorating an arm in the crowd could activate a bomb.

Yet she waited vigilantly as the crowd continued their protest.

Milli was on assignment in the western docks of one of Oais' largest cities: New Skyline. Beyond the glass windows of the hub's walkway, Milli could see the numerous buildings and skyscrapers that made up the city as it spanned over a hundred kilometers in each direction. Swirls of dark clouds blotted out the russet-colored skyline, and the iron dust in the air tickled her throat sometimes.

It's not as bad as it used to be, she thought. *At least kids today won't have to endure breathing difficulties like I had to.*

Despite how much Oais had improved, plenty of young adults

enjoyed complaining and demanding entitlements. Oftentimes, such people would get caught up in radicalization groups. They weren't gangs, per se, because most criminal activity was efficiently weeded out of the Capital Worlds and pushed towards the Fringe Territories. But factions like the Far Syters often dug their greedy little claws into the impressionable minds to mold them into fleshy loudspeakers.

Milli's eyes scanned the crowd again; there was a mix of men and women, predominantly human but with a few Vitrax in their midst. Most donned simple, mesh-fiber clothes of dull gray, white, or black, though some wore vests or jackets—only for style, since the hub was thick with heat. A few of the protesters held up holographic signs with their slogan graphics cycling through them while others had temp-tattoos on their faces.

Their chants were frequently drowned out by the roaring engines of passing ships or the blaring alarms in the hangars that indicated vessels were landing or taking off. Milli narrowed her eyes at the crowd. She couldn't stand protesters or activists; they were parasites complaining about the smallest inconveniences. They didn't stop to think how much better they had it here than the poor nonhumans in the Fringe.

As long as they don't incite violence, she thought, let them shout and stamp their feet. Doesn't make them right.

Tensions were high between the activist group and the various law enforcement agencies, because there was always some hothead eager to stick it to "the system", as they said. Milli herself had dealt with the brunt of vicious harassments from the Far Syters, further stoking her hatred of the group nearby.

Milli kept her arms folded under her breasts, her hand occasionally brushing against the E-pistol holstered inside her mesh-fiber jacket. The desire to disperse the protesters clawed at her mind like an itch.

Any time she saw a protester getting vehement or putting their hand in their pocket, Milli's grip tensed on the pistol's handle. She was far enough away from the crowd that she could drop at least six before they could draw a beat on her. Then, she could rely on the wall's corner for cover if any returned fire. One wrong move on their part, and she would end them.

Still, the last thing she wanted was a firefight to break out. It would mean a lot of terminus work, reports to file, families to apologize to, and even the risk of injuring herself. The cerulean LED light from the hub's hallway reflected off the wedding band on her left ring finger. She had a husband to go home to, and she often had to remind herself that she couldn't go in guns blazing anymore.

All Milli could hope for was that the protesters would remain peaceful, and that her anonymous tip had been wrong.

Part of why this specific post irked her was because it was interfering with her vacation time—time she had intended to spend building model structures with her husband. She'd just gotten him a new set replicating the Starlane Express tower, and he was as giddy as a child to build it with her.

Milli smiled at the thought of her husband. He was what helped her get through these stressful days working for the C.B.I.

Out of the corner of her eye, Milli noticed that the terminus beneath the left sleeve of her jacket was flashing yellow. Rolling up her sleeve, she noticed it was a comm request from the bureau office.

Putting her back to the wall, Milli swiped a finger along the holographic display, and a face appeared on screen. Dark-skinned and bald with a trimmed, black goatee, the man's brown eyes stared into the space over her shoulder, the image hovering above her arm. She could vaguely see a collar on a white mesh-fiber suit.

The man blinked, his eyes finding her own, and cleared his throat. *"Agent Spectre, how's it going down there?"*

She kept the volume of her terminus down as he spoke, hoping the protesters wouldn't hear over their chanting and the cacophony of the docks. Regardless, she peeked out from behind the corner to check. Once she was assured that no one was looking in her direction, she turned back to her terminus.

"Oh you know, got a bunch of windbags and dustflakes complaining about how good they've got it in the Capital Worlds," she replied with a scoff. "No signs of E-weaponry yet, Director Cormack. I'm keeping my distance."

Cormack nodded, the light in the office reflecting off his smooth scalp. *"Let's hope it stays that way,"* he said. *"The last thing we need is to show High Chancellor Sessani that we're incapable of securing the docks."*

Milli rocked her head from side to side. "Gee, if only we could provide the overseer of the entire Picon system with a solid arrival escort. Wouldn't be surprised if Veritas Nova pulled enough strings to prioritize his protection."

Since Sessani spent most of her time on Diivoro, most of Oais' agencies didn't have the same loyalty to her as they did Nova. That, and there were only so many C.B.I. agents on this planet.

While numbers in the Imperium armada and reserves were at a record high, the C.B.I. wasn't as well-staffed as other military agencies. Their training regimen was difficult, the hours were long, and the pay wasn't as grand as you might expect. Milli joined because of her dedication to Oais, but not all former Imperium reserves felt that way.

"Don't start," Cormack said, bringing her attention back to the hologram. *"We need to show competence if we're to get more funding and expanded operations. More personnel means you get to see Ferris more often."*

"Yeah, I know, sir," she admitted with a sigh.

Cormack was quick to change the subject. *"Where did you place your droid backups?"*

She inclined her head in the direction of the opposite corridor. "Two hubs north from my present position. Didn't want them pinging any sensors. I've got them on standby mode. If a fight breaks out, they'll be here in ten seconds."

"Good," Cormack said with a nod. *"Once things wrap up in the Yukai District, I'll send Ithica and Aeros to back you up. Droids are good, but having partners is better."*

"Thanks, sir," she said, peering around the corner again. "I'll keep a comm blackout until the Imperium shuttle arrives."

"Stay safe, Agent Spectre."

The call ended and her terminus screen showed the normal applications. She decided to double check on the status of the riot droids, just as a precaution. Pressing a finger to the hologram button, a small screen displayed over her terminus that showed the photoreceptor feed of three droids. Each feed looked like it was hardly a centimeter off the carbocrete floor.

She was about to check their battery status when the LED lights in the hallway went out with a soft *thud*. Not only that, but her terminus shut off as well. Everything around her had lost power.

No, that wasn't right. Her terminus relied on fuses for power, and she'd charged it that morning. A shutdown of this sort could only be caused by an electromagnetic pulse.

Milli's eyes darted around as she pulled her EMP-hardened E-pistol from its holster for just such an occasion. The ceiling lights in the hallway nearby were still lit, and nothing changed in the ship traffic outside the windows. Only her section had lost power.

Her heart started thumping faster as her skin went cold. She had to grip the E-pistol with both hands because her palms were sweaty. Milli slowed her breathing. Her nerves calmed, dispelling the fear and allowing her to focus.

She watched the darkness of the hallway, her eyes scanning for any sign of movement. There was nothing. Just blackness.

An unseen force abruptly smashed against her E-pistol, ripping it from her grip as she felt something wrap around her neck. Her air was cut off, and she gasped for breath. Milli's hands frantically clawed at her throat.

Milli collapsed to her knees, her lungs screaming for air as frantic wheezing escaped her mouth. A pair of hands grabbed her wrists and pulled her arms behind her back. She felt some metallic binders click onto her wrists, and the assailant pulled the rope tighter around her neck as she was dragged further into the hallway.

Milli's eyes grew dark. She felt the familiar sensation of unconsciousness taking over. Terror gripped her heart. The face of her husband flashed in the darkness before it swallowed her.

Ferris... I love...

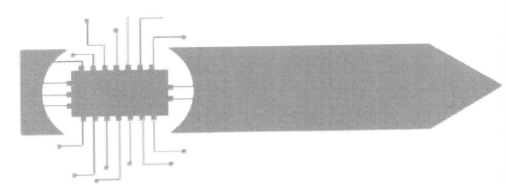

CHAPTER 1

4509.0826 / FT Star System: Sol / 4,760,639.6 kilometers from the planet Terras / GST: 14:15

The *Erinyes*, large and imposing, siphoned considerable amounts of energy and fuel to drop out of the voidstream tunnel and into normal space. The swirling blue lights faded as the ship entered the planetary system. Countless stars twinkled in the blackness beyond the cockpit's viewport, the light from the nearby sun making him squint despite it being lightyears away. A musical *hum* emanated from the rear of the ship as the voidstream drive started to power down.

Aelec Xero was on a mission. It was different from the heist jobs he'd been performing for the past two years. There was more direction to it, more stakes to remind him that he couldn't afford to screw this up. If you messed up on a heist, you could always adapt, and if it came down to it you could abandon the job altogether.

But on a mission, there was no safety net. You would either

succeed or you would fail. His last mission he failed, witnessing the deaths of unarmed prisoners and his fellow Outriders. This time... this time he would succeed.

I won't lose another family to Kuvan, he vowed. *I can't.*

Aelec and his crew had spent the past three days traveling through the interdimensional tunnels that connected each known planet in their galaxy. Khorrus, the planet they'd come from, was a hub for travel in the outer regions of the Fringe Territories—the world was the closest to the border of the Capital Worlds. But where Khorrus was closest to the Capital Worlds, the planet Terras was the farthest from it.

The Fringe Territories were a vast expanse of space with numerous planetary star systems. Lawlessness and crime predominated that part of the galaxy, making it the perfect place for Aelec to make a living as a thief. A noble thief, as some called him. Aelec made it his business to steal from the rich scumbags and slavers in the Fringe, showing the galaxy that they weren't as invincible as they seemed.

However, some planets weren't as lawless as others. Biiras, Khorrus, and Terras were some of the few worlds in the Fringe that upheld a planetary governance untethered from the Sol Imperium.

Aelec used to find it odd that they'd chosen to remain independent. Joining the Imperium would result in a vast amount of resources, knowledge, and weaponry. It wasn't until the past few decades that the taboo restrictions on Terras were lifted, and the planet was deemed habitable and civilized once more. Yet for nearly forty years they had resisted all attempts by the Imperium to join.

After seeing what a corrupt Imperium governor was capable of, Aelec couldn't completely blame Terras' current political state.

The crew of the *Erinyes* were on a mission to bring one such planetary governor, Veritas Kuvan, to justice for his crimes against the Outriders. Against Aelec's clan. Two weeks ago, Aelec had recovered the incriminating footage that Kuvan sought to bury, and the former Outrider was now on a quest to capture him. It was no easy feat capturing a planetary Veritas, and Aelec had to pull a lot of strings for this to happen, which involved obtaining a program directly from an Imperium terminal.

Touching several holograms along the cockpit's dashboard, Aelec helped guide the *Erinyes* through the vast blackness of space. A moment later, the distinct shape of a planet loomed into view. Still a few hundred thousand kilometers away, Aelec couldn't miss the singular massive continent floating in the planet-spanning ocean. Beyond the wispy clouds, he could see grassy plains, harsh deserts, snowy mountains, and volcanic lands all intermixing on the continent like an abstract painting.

"Stars above," Myra breathed in amazement. "Terras sure isn't what I expected. I've never seen a continent so diverse."

The pink-skinned Vitrax had both of her slender hands on the control yoke that steered the ship. She was slouched slightly in the chair, and her arms moved with a leisurely grace, something that was common for her species.

Aelec paused, glancing at his screen to read a few lines of text before replying, "Imperium records call the continent Pan'gea, and it's broken up into multiple nations. It's all pretty vague, though."

"Anything on the scanners?" Myra asked.

Reorienting his attention, Aelec observed the holographic screen to his right to check for any objects lingering in the space around Terras. For a moment, the scanner showed nothing alarming—just some stray satellites and the moon orbiting the planet.

A faint alarm emanated from the ship's systems. The scanner pinged a large object in low orbit above the planet's eastern hemisphere.

"Got something," Aelec said as he turned the alarm off. "Large fusion signature."

Swiping his fingers through the hologram, he expanded the image of the detected object. Flickering into holographic view was

10

an elongated vessel shaped like the eels native to his homeworld; the long body was slender, while the "head" of the vessel was bulkier. Dozens of viewports lined the sides of the ship, while sensory antennas protruded along its top like a spine.

Though it was a newer model, Aelec recognized the design within seconds, and it was precisely what they were waiting for.

"Imperium scout frigate," he said. "Right on schedule."

The prehensile, purple tentacles sprouting from Myra's head twitched as she asked, "How many life forms are aboard?"

Aelec made another scan of the frigate and read the display aloud, "Forty total. Twenty on the upper deck and twenty on the lower deck. The ones on the lower deck seem to be consolidating near the armory."

Myra's violet eyes widened. "In response to us?"

"No," Aelec replied, shaking his head. "Imperium protocol dictates that all starship security guards report to the armory in the event that there's a threat planetside. They've likely been in the armory for the past five minutes, way before we exited voidstream."

The Vitrax raised her hairless eyebrows. "Something's going on below on Terras?"

He shrugged. "Terras is an independent system. I don't imagine they're too happy about the Imperium being here. Make sure to fly casual so that they don't blast us into space dust."

She snorted. "I'm going to pretend that you didn't just tell me to 'fly casual,' Aelec. Did you forget you're co-piloting with the best pilot in the Fringe?"

"Of course not, Best Pilot in the Fringe."

"Damn straight."

He grinned in amusement. As Myra guided the ship towards the frigate, Aelec activated the ship's commlink and spoke to the rest of the crew.

"We're entering geosynchronous orbit now, folks," he stated. "Make sure to stay calm and refrain from making any loud noises."

A basso voice came over the commlink. *"Loud noises like this?"* A metallic banging echoed through the ship.

Dylis Wyri, self-proclaimed master actor and head of mischief, often liked to keep the crew on their toes.

Aelec rolled his eyes. "How old are we, Dylis?"

"Inside or outside? Because I still feel twelve on the inside!" Dylis laughed, pounding twice more.

"Well your face screams thirty-eight, old man. Stop pounding your fist against the wall. Myra will have your head if you don't."

"Mark up my ship, I'll mark up your hide!" the Vitrax affirmed with a smirk.

"I like the sound of that," Dylis' voice echoed from the speakers. *"I've been a bad boy, Myra."*

"Gross," a soft, feminine voice came in through the commlink. *"I don't need that image in my head, Dylis."*

Aelec snorted in amusement. Though walls separated them, he could envision the rigidly prim posture of Riza Noxia. Shifting in his chair, Aelec's posture was similarly as sharp as a nanoblade. Growing up in the Capital Worlds caused such things.

The Vitrax's violet eyes stared coldly out the cockpit's viewport, her lips drawing into a thin line, and her grip tightening around the controls. Aelec knew she was still pissed at Riza for her actions on Caavo.

With ulterior motives unknown to the crew, Riza had almost upended their entire operation. But after apologizing and pledging herself to the *Erinyes*, Aelec had accepted her back. That's what clans did.

"Pipe down," Myra said, her voice lacking any playfulness. "We're closing in on the frigate. They'll be hailing us soon, and I don't want any distractions."

The coldness in her voice brought a chill to the already cool, recycled air of the ship. Aelec sighed. He'd need to have a talk with Myra and Riza when they were done here. A discordant crew was guaranteed to be ineffective on a job like this, and he couldn't risk it being sabotaged.

As the *Erinyes* flew closer to the lumbering frigate, Aelec sat back in the chair and waited for the communications system to light up. Seconds later, the holographic panel along the front dashboard flashed yellow and he pressed two fingers on the display. An image displayed across the viewport of the cockpit, though it was transparent enough for them to still see outside the ship.

The facial profile of an older man displayed on the viewport. A mixture of wrinkles and scars patterned around the man's beady black eyes, becoming more pronounced as he squinted.

He pursed his lips under his salt and pepper mustache and spoke, *"This is Commander Ifan Dextan of the I.S.S. Carthage. Identify yourselves."*

Aelec cleared his throat and sat up straighter in his chair. "My name is Captain Jaxon Shaw of the *Oberon*. Former Imperium captain in the armada, deployed in the Sigma star system. My ID code was C-one-four-eight-six. This is my pilot, Nyri."

Dextan looked at someone offscreen, likely signaling them to run a facial scan and identity check on them. Aelec trusted that his contacts had properly forged a new ID for him and the ship prior to this venture.

"What brings you out here, Captain Shaw?" the older man asked, looking back into the cam.

Aelec brushed his fingers through his long, silver hair and replied, "Well, commander, my crew and I just escaped a Cerata raid near M'ras and are in need of a supply rendezvous. We burned much of our fuel in the escape and only had enough to make the voidstream jump to Terras. We were hoping the locals could help us, but thank the Sol that we found you here instead."

Dextan snorted, his hooked nose wrinkling as he did so. *"Haven't heard of any reports about the Cerata being in this star system. Are you sure it wasn't a local pirate gang or a terrorist cell?"*

"No, commander," Aelec affirmed, shaking his head. "I know

the Cerata when I see them. Only their frigates would look like a cross between a casino and a battleship. That and the H-twenty-twos that pursued us through the asteroid field."

The commander looked offscreen once again, clearly waiting for someone to speak. After a moment, he nodded his head and turned back to speak to them.

"*Understood. Your Imperium code and ship ID check out, captain,*" Dextan said. "*You're cleared entry into hangar bay three. We've got a reserve of fusion that will be just enough to help get you back to the Capital Worlds. I'll have my men meet you in the hangar. Please begin standard landing procedures.*"

"Copy that," Aelec said. "Thank you, commander."

The image of Dextan vanished and the holographic panel stilled. Myra kept one hand on the yoke while her free hand swiped across the dashboard in front of her. Her slender fingers moved with an inhuman dexterity as she diverted the engine power and lowered the landing struts.

The Vitrax looked over at him, her tentacles twitching. "Nyri?" she queried sardonically. "Really? You couldn't find any other Vitrax name? I have at least three cousins named Nyri!"

He shrugged. "I didn't want you to stand out. This won't be like our jobs on Biiras or Caavo. Stealing something from the Imperium is dangerous. I'll need to be extra thorough getting our faces purged from the holonet after this. Next time, I'll let you pick your character's name."

She scoffed but didn't press the matter.

Myra guided the *Erinyes* towards the starboard side of the Imperium frigate, where a rectangular opening connected to one of the inner hangars. Blue energy fields pulsed as the *Erinyes* passed the rows of Imperial snub fighters docked within the hangar and slipped between the light that kept the vacuum of space from pulling the occupants to their deaths.

Aelec performed a quick scan of the fighters and noticed that their fusion engine cores were warming up. Pilots situated in their cockpits sat in idle while awaiting instruction from the frigate's bridge. Coupled with the gathering security force, it confirmed that the *I.S.S. Carthage* was about to see some action from the planet.

Adding to the risky nature of this mission, they were now on a timetable.

Great, he thought. *Nothing is ever as simple as it should be.*

The *Erinyes* hovered through the energy field and entered the wide hangar bay, lights from the freighter's exterior reflecting off the glossy, black morristeel floor. The walls were concave, reminiscent of a hexagonal tube with towering wall lights of pale sapphire. A few engineers were already bustling to retrieve some of the fusion coils that pulsed with an amber glow.

Touching down with a soft *thud*, the *Erinyes* settled into the hangar while a prolonged *hiss* emanated from the airlock as the ship depressurized. Myra flicked her fingers across the hologram panels to power down portions of the ship.

It was almost as good as an Outrider's dexterity. Almost.

Aelec unstrapped his safety harness, stood, and pressed his finger to the commlink.

"Alright everyone," he called. "In and out. Quick and easy."

If they did their job well, they wouldn't need to make an emergency escape, but all the same, Myra remained in the pilot's chair. The Imperium could lockdown the hangar bay in under a minute, but luckily Aelec knew the protocols; he could find chinks in the armor.

Aelec made his way from the cockpit through the winding halls of the freighter before being deposited in the cargo room just outside the airlock. The room was lined with neat rows of racks which secured their cargocases, supply containers, and emergency ration packs. Orange lights outlined the ceiling and reflected off the dark green metal of the floors.

Lacing up her boots atop a cargocase, Riza Noxia's bright blue eyes met his own for a second longer than they needed to before falling back to her hands. She gave her laces a tug, stray strands of dark hair falling like curtains around her face. Aelec blinked and attempted to redirect his gaze from the black pants that hugged her form.

Aelec stopped a meter from her, and she turned to face him fully. Clearing his throat, he asked, "What's your name, rank, and Imperium code?"

Straightening her posture, Riza replied, "Nora Carrin, former science officer aboard the *I.S.S. Sojourn*. My ID code was S-four-seven-three-three."

He nodded in approval. "Very good. And what is our relationship?"

"We're leaders of the Seraphian Fulfillment Retreat Program," she said, planting a hand on her hip. "We were scouting locations to conduct the retreat when Cerata pirates attacked our ship over M'ras. We escaped from them last night."

"Nice," he grunted, the corners of his mouth curling into a faint grin. "You're a natural. You'd certainly fool me... Oh wait. You did."

Riza gave him a nervous laugh.

"Relax, I'm just messing with you," Aelec said, keeping his tone pleasant.

"I'm surprised you're not pissed, Aelec." Riza averted her gaze in shame.

He shrugged. "I'm pragmatic. I can understand why you did what you did, even if I didn't like how it happened. But Outriders are all about second chances. Just look at Dylis. As long as your actions reflect your loyalty, that's what matters."

"It can't be that simple," she said, looking back at him with narrowed eyes.

"We can settle it later, Riza. For now, we need to acquire an Imperium chain code. Let's get it done."

She offered no protest as they walked in unison through the airlock and down the angled boarding ramp.

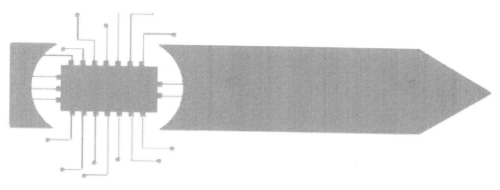

CHAPTER 2

Stepping onto the glossy floor of the hangar bay, Aelec walked beneath the *Erinyes* towards the underside of the cockpit, Riza rushing to catch up. Across the hangar, four security officers wearing form-fitting black and gray armor marched out from a connecting corridor. It wasn't a formal march like the ones conducted in military facilities, but their steps were synchronized with the professional efficiency ingrained into them by the Imperium. The four security officers held their E-rifles in a lowered position; they exuded suspicion.

Aelec's Imperium expertise had certainly not worn off over the past two years; he knew every protocol and every formation. He resisted grinning. This was an acting job that he felt completely at home with. It was a mere extension of himself.

The security officers stopped a meter from him. Their armor was made of overlaid pieces, giving it the look of an exoskeleton. It made their postures rigid.

"Hello my good gentlemen," he said, waving his hand. "I'm Captain Shaw, ex-Imperium. Who's in charge here?"

One of the officers stepped forward, the light giving a sheen to his gelled blond hair. He held his rifle aloft and kept his stark green eyes locked on Aelec.

"I'm Lieutenant Kiiyes, first division aboard the *I.S.S. Carthage*," he said, his voice a bit higher pitched.

"Thank you for receiving us, lieutenant," Aelec said pleasantly. "We're just trying to get some fuel and supplies to make it back home to the Capital Worlds."

Lieutenant Kiiyes relaxed somewhat, though his angular jaw clenched. "We've got our engineers working to retrieve the fusion coils for your ship, captain." He looked over at Riza and asked, "Who is she?"

Her posture went rigid as all eyes went to her. Riza cleared her throat and said, "Nora Carrin, former science officer aboard the *I.S.S. Sojourn*. My ID code was S-four-seven-three-three."

Kiiyes raised an eyebrow and checked the terminus on his left forearm. The holographic displays on the device ran through the Imperium database and showed him the profile on Nora Carrin. The forged profile. Aelec prayed to the Sol that its authenticity would fool the lieutenant. Kiiyes looked from Riza to the terminus and back again, a blank expression on his youthful face.

Aelec's chest tightened in slight panic as the pause lasted for longer than expected. His left eyebrow started to arch. Dammit, he hated his nervous tick. He did his best to make it look like he was raising an eyebrow in annoyance, but it didn't quell the tension in his chest.

His forged identification was accepted, but what if Riza's wasn't? He'd trusted his old contacts with creating the new IDs, and he'd done his best to verify their authenticity. But what if he didn't look thoroughly enough?

"Checks out," Kiiyes said in a monotone voice.

The anxiousness inside Aelec's chest evaporated, and he realized he'd been holding his breath. Exhaling quietly, Aelec nodded to Kiiyes and made a show of surveying the hangar bay.

"Where do you keep your supplies, Lieutenant Kiiyes?" he

asked. "Nora and I can assist in hauling them to the ship while the engineers load the fusion coils."

The lieutenant turned halfway to face the doorway they'd come through and pointed. "Two sectors in the direction of the frigate's nose. We'll escort you."

Aelec nodded, anticipating this level of protocol. Even if they had an authentic background in the Imperium, newcomers on the ship were to be escorted at all times to prevent sabotage or smuggling. Countless pirates and assassins had used forged Imperium IDs to infiltrate starships, so any stray ships were to be kept under strict supervision.

Luckily, Aelec knew one of the loopholes in such a protocol.

Without fanfare, the security officers escorted Aelec and Riza into the connecting hallway that resembled a hexagonal tube. The concave walls were similar to the ones in the hangar but supported smaller, yellow lights for illumination and the morristeel was a lighter shade of gray. In contrast to the curved, winding corridors of the *Erinyes*, the Imperium frigate had rigid, sharp turns.

They followed the hallway before coming to an intersection, the security officers marching into the right corridor. A few meters from the intersection was a circular door of black and gray on the left wall. Further down the hall were other doors of a similar design.

Kiiyes approached the nearest door, a hologram displayed on the right wall, and he input a code to unlock it.

The room beyond was a large storage facility that was twice the size of the *Erinyes*' main hold. LED lights of pale cobalt weaved across the high ceiling, and the air was distinctly cooler—crispier, like that of a larder. Diamonds of matte navy blue patterned along the floor, broken up occasionally by circular, white nanotech ports. Racks of a matching pattern lined the walls which were filled with various containers and crates.

Two of the security officers stood guard at the door while Kiiyes and the other entered the cargo room. The lieutenant beckoned for

Aelec to follow, so he and Riza entered the storage area before the door sealed behind them.

Both agents stood on opposite sides of the room's walkway, and Kiiyes said, "Commander Dextan said you'd be granted one hundred pounds of supplies from our reserves. Select what you need, and we'll help move it to the hangar."

Aelec nodded. "Thank you, Kiiyes. We'll be out of here in a voidjump."

Moving past the security officers, Aelec and Riza followed the racks of containers and kept an eye on their identification placards. Small crests installed onto the sides of each container, the placards varied in size and symbol depending on the product within.

Diamond-shaped placards were on the front containers, which meant that they stored dry goods like grain, potatoes, noodles, and bread. A few rows down were refrigeration cylinders with triangular placards, indicating that they contained chilled goods such as produce or beverages. At the end of the supply room were cases bearing circular placards, meaning they contained parts for E-weapons, fusion clips, or pulseblades.

Aelec stopped between the racks of dry and chilled goods before kneeling to activate one of the nanotech ports. As if materializing out of thin air, a skeletal-looking mechanical arm sprouted from the floor and reached out to grab one of the dry containers. In a smooth motion, the machine plucked a crate the size of a Kygi from the rack and set it down in the walkway.

Riza went over to one of the other ports to similarly retrieve one of the refrigerated cylinders. She nodded to him as her part in the plan came to fruition. Aelec shuffled in the walkway to make it look like he was inspecting the container, but in reality he was blocking Riza from the security officers' sight. Neither Kiiyes nor his companion offered any objections to his movement.

He saw Riza touch her hand to the nanotech machine, and something that looked like a metallic worm slithered out from her sleeve. In actuality it was a large cluster of nanotech that she was manipulating via a basic neural interlace that was clipped to her ear. Similar to Myra, Riza wore her interlace as an earring to avoid detection.

Though Myra and Riza weren't Outriders, Aelec wanted both of them to have some basic control over pure nanoparticle clusters. The Vitrax had been using hers for the better part of a year. Dylis already had his implants leftover from his Imperium days, as did Aelec.

That said, getting an external interlace like this required him to purchase it off the black market, making the ordeal both expensive and extraordinarily dangerous.

If the Imperium ever discovered that Riza and Myra had these interlaces, they'd be imprisoned for life, and Aelec would likely be executed for treason. His drive to bring Veritas Kuvan to justice superseded any reservations. Aelec's faith in the Imperium had been shaken after what happened to his clan, and he wanted to right the wrongs that had been done.

As the nanotech bug coiled around the mechanical arm, it paused briefly before slithering down and vanishing into the port. The bug would follow a few simple mental commands given by Riza, most of which would be limited to "Move," "Access," and "Return." Luckily, the data mainframe they needed access to was on the level directly below them. There were multiple terminals and servers aboard an Imperium frigate, but they just needed one in order to retrieve a security chain code.

Chain codes were only issued to high-ranking members of the Imperium armada, like commanders or admirals. Since Commander Dextan was in charge, he'd no doubt have a chain code stored on his data servers for accessing restricted Imperium sites.

This chain code was the key they needed to infiltrate a high-security Imperium compound. One such compound—the Wasp Nest of Markum—was where they could find Kuvan.

As he and Riza continued to retrieve supply containers, Aelec kept an eye on his wrist terminus—the holograms along the bracer indicated the status of the nanotech bug. The device was on silent mode so that no alerts would draw attention, and the status display looked like any other monitor. Kiiyes and the other officer stood with statuesque postures on the far end of the room.

Just a few more seconds, Aelec told himself.

Pretending to inspect the final refrigeration cylinder, Aelec glanced at the terminus and saw that the nanotech bug had completed its download. Moving his body to block Riza from view once again, he watched as she planted her boot next to the nanotech port and the bug slithered up under her pants leg.

"Alright," Aelec declared, getting the attention of the security officers. "We've got enough supplies to get back to the Capital Worlds, if you gents would be so kind."

Kiiyes nodded, and they approached the gathered containers. The Imperium security officers activated the gravlifts on the larger container and began ushering it out of the storage facility. Aelec and Riza did the same with their equipment, following the officers while dragging the hovering cargo. Upon exiting the storage area, the doors sealed and the remaining security officers followed behind Aelec and Riza.

Though he kept his eyes peeled for any suspicious activity, Aelec felt a bit of tension leave his shoulders. They had the chain code, and their forged IDs were holding up. All they had to do was get to the hangar and they'd...

An inauspicious rumble came from the port side of the ship. Abruptly, the entire frigate shook, forcing Aelec to steady his footing. Riza nearly stumbled, but he held out an arm to keep her from falling. Her azure eyes were wide with a mix of shock and confusion as they reoriented themselves.

Klaxons blared across the ship and the hallway's LED lights changed from yellow to red. Aelec knew the Imperium protocols all too well. The ship was under attack.

Kiiyes and the other officers composed themselves as the ship stopped shaking, their E-rifles were in hand and they adopted battle stances. The barrels of the rifles were aimed at Aelec and Riza.

"Hands where I can see them!" Kiiyes demanded.

Aelec and Riza obeyed, slowly raising their hands. Initially, Aelec assumed that their cover was gone and that the officers were arresting them for theft. But when Kiiyes didn't make a move to pat them down or inspect the cargo, Aelec knew it was something else.

"Let's not do anything hasty, gentlemen," Aelec said, keeping his voice level.

Kiiyes gestured in the direction of the explosion and asked, "Was this the plan all along? Distract us so that the Terrans could attack?"

"What?!" Riza sputtered, genuinely astonished. "No, we had no idea there were problems planetside!"

"It's true," Aelec affirmed, keeping his hands raised. "We have no affiliation with the Terrans. Whatever is happening, it's happening because of your presence in orbit."

Kiiyes' eyes narrowed. "How can we—"

A voice blared over the frigate's commlink system. "*All security officers, we have multiple breaches on the port side. Hostile forces are entering the ship. Report to your stations!*"

The security officers around them hesitated briefly, their stances indicating that they wanted to arrest Aelec and Riza. But as the klaxons blared and more rumbles echoed throughout the ship, the officers began lowering their weapons.

"Dammit!" Kiiyes cursed. "Alright. Jek. Makko. Get these containers to the hangar bay, then rendezvous in sector eleven. Captain Shaw, if there's any funny business we will not hesitate to gun you down. Clear?"

"Clear," he repeated. When Kiiyes turned away, Aelec asked, "Is there anything we can do to help?"

"No," Kiiyes replied firmly. "Just get the Void out of here."

With that, Kiiyes and one of the officers lowered their E-rifles before rushing down the hallway in the direction of the commotion. Aelec and Riza didn't waste any time. With the help of Jek and Makko, they hauled their cargo back to the hangar, where the *Erinyes* was parked. The moment they entered the hangar, the security officers stashed the container near the ship and ran back the way they'd come from.

Once the officers were gone, Aelec spoke into the commlink on his terminus. "Myra, is the *Erinyes* ready for dust off?" Looking up, he spotted the Vitrax through the cockpit's viewport.

She gave him a thumbs up as her voice came over the commlink, "*Ready boss. You got the code?*"

Aelec looked at Riza who proffered the nanotech bug in her right palm. He gave her a faint grin of approval. Plugging the worm-like device into her own terminus, Riza scrolled through holograms of data before finding a line of numeric sequences. She used her fingers to highlight the code and sent it to Aelec's terminus.

"Mission success," she said, looking up at him as they walked.

"Yeah," he said. "Good j—"

Before he could finish, one of the blastdoors on the left wall of the hangar was blown open by an explosion.

Aelec's reflexes kicked in. He issued a mental command and summoned his entire suit of nanotech armor. It felt like cold water rushing over his skin as the armor activated. The nanoparticles covered his body beneath his clothes, the metal solidifying with a white color accented with blue markings.

Leaping forward, Aelec put his back to the explosion and used his body to shield Riza; the nanotech armor solidified a millisecond before the shrapnel hit him. Numerous *clinks* resounded as bits of metal struck him like projectiles. With Riza pulled close to his chest, the last of the shrapnel struck his helmet. The resulting shockwave overturned both cargo containers, spilling their contents.

Smoke blew past him as the explosion dissipated. Turning slightly, Aelec saw the bodies of several Imperial soldiers strewn across the floor, and two silhouettes standing in the hole where the blastdoor had been. The residual fires flickered from a pale crimson to a normal shade of orange as the figures walked through the battered opening.

Aelec's eyes widened in surprise.

The assailants were wearing armor that he'd never seen before; it was something antique and exotic. Unlike most combat suits in the Imperium, these armor sets were bulkier, with swirling designs and wing-like patterns. His nanotech armor was sleek and new, a distinct contrast to these ancient-looking suits; several pieces appeared more ritualistic than functional.

As the figures drew closer, Aelec noticed that one was a man and the other a woman—both human, by his estimation. Terrans didn't mingle with the other species in the galaxy, another reminder of their reclusiveness. Light glistened along their bronze armor, and he saw a few markings of cobalt on their suits.

Turning fully to face them, Aelec formed a pulsecannon in his left hand and raised it threateningly at the incoming warriors.

"We were just leaving, folks," he declared, his voice echoing across the hangar. "We have no quarrel with Terras. Let us go, and we won't impede you."

The female warrior cocked her head to the side, her helmet resembling a falcon's beak.

"Anyone who associates with the Imperium is an enemy of Terras," she hissed, her high-pitched voice grating his ears. "So says the First Sword of Xiön!"

The male warrior snapped his arm forward and unleashed several bright red energy streams from his fingertips. Aelec formed a nanoshield on his right arm. The streams slammed into his barrier with such force it felt like a ship's fusion cannon was blasting him.

To his shock, and horror, Aelec realized it wasn't like a normal E-weapon or pulseweapon attack, because the energy continued to hammer the shield. Most weapons in the galaxy were rapid fire, but only certain starships had energy weapons that could fire a continual beam. Whomever these Terrans were, they were wielding tools far outside the firepower of a standard Imperium E-weapon.

As the ruby-colored energy continued to pummel his nanoshield, he managed to pivot his legs in preparation for a leap to the side. His helmeted head snapped around to look back at Riza even as she crouched behind him.

"Riza!" he called over the sizzling energy. "Get ready to run. I'll keep them distracted!"

Her blue eyes narrowed. "To the Void with that! You'll be outnumbered! Let me help!"

He didn't have time to debate. The Terras woman was already advancing and would be upon him in seconds. Reluctantly, he nodded and Riza was quick to peek out from his side, forming her nanotech watch into a pulsecannon in a quick motion.

Riza fired several shots towards the incoming warrior, the violet waves of energy soaring at a blinding speed. The Terras woman halted in her tracks, raised her left arm to ninety degrees at the elbow, and generated an energy shield of the same ruby color.

The kinetic waves impacted the shield in a shower of violet sparks, but to his surprise, he saw the ruby energy fracturing like a glass pane. Riza seemed to notice this as well and fired another wave from her pulsecannon. The Terras woman's shield shattered like a broken window, the shockwave from the pulsecannon making her stumble backwards.

The barrage against Aelec's arm weakened—the Terras man becoming distracted—so he sprang into action. Transforming the shield into a grappling hook, Aelec fired, and it embedded into the man's bronze breastplate. He pulled. Hard. The man soared towards him, and Aelec fired the pulsecannon into his chest.

The bronze armor dented, but it ultimately protected the man from Aelec's pulsecannon blast. A metallic *clank* resounded across the hangar as the warrior landed a few meters away. To Aelec's astonishment, both warriors arose from their respective beatings— their movements were in an eerie unison.

"Imperium scum!" the woman hissed as she pulled a metal rod from a belt sheath.

Aelec blinked and the rod shifted into a hooked blade of inter-locking pieces. There was a *hiss* as crimson energy enveloped the silver blade, whipping off it like flames. The Terras man did the same thing, but his hooked blade was much longer than the woman's.

As much as Aelec wanted to admire the alien technology of Terras, this was a fight he couldn't risk. Not with his crew in danger.

"To the Void with this!" he snarled, summoning his nanoparti-cles to form pulsecannons on each of his hands.

He raised both arms and fired the pulsecannons simultaneously —the combined shockwave stopped both warriors in their tracks. As they faltered, Aelec dissipated the cannons, grabbed Riza's arm, and pulled her towards the *Erinyes*.

They ran as fast as they could; the Terras warriors quickly recov-ered and pursued them. Riza fired her pulsecannon blindly behind them, the waves rippled across the hangar. His nanotech boots thudded into the glossy floor with such fury that he felt like he was denting the metal with every step. The *Erinyes'* boarding ramp was only a few meters away. Just a few more strides...

A lumbering figure appeared from within the ship and descended down the ramp. Taloned feet like that of a bird's scraped against the steel, and chitinous plates along the figure's form clicked with bony *thuds*. Four insect-like arms moved in a jerking motion, the claws holding an exotic weapon reminiscent of a crossbow.

What looked like a three-meter-tall mix of a roach and a crus-tacean exited the *Erinyes*. The sight would normally be enough to terrify a human, but to Aelec, this was his backup.

Golath, the Kygi member of their crew, got to the edge of the ramp and used two of his hands to pull the emerald fusionfiber strings of his fusecaster. The weapon from Kyg-nor fired multiple streaks of green energy towards the incoming warriors—the arrowhead-shaped bolts whizzing over Aelec's head. Crimson shields sprouted from the warriors' arms, deflecting the Kygi's shots.

Voices shouted over the crackling energy, Aelec's eyes following the source to find a battered Kiiyes and company storming the hangar. Energy exploded from their E-rifles as they ran. The Terras man pivoted, planting his blade to the floor, and a bubble-like shield enveloped him and his companion.

"GO!" Kiiyes bellowed from across the hangar.

The Terras woman leaped through the barrier, energy shield raised. She fell upon the Imperial officers and began cutting them down. The distraction bought Aelec and Riza enough time to get to the ship.

The moment his boots touched the boarding ramp, Aelec shouted, "Myra! Get us out of here!"

Gravlifts on the underbelly of the *Erinyes* hummed as they lit up, causing the ship to slowly hover off the floor. Aelec and Riza continued up the boarding ramp while Golath fired a few more fusecaster bolts before following them into the airlock. The ramp folded into the ship, sealing them off from the hangar bay.

With a mental command, Aelec had his nanotech suit peel away and store itself within the various nanoparticle pucks along his body. Once the suit was fully dismantled, Aelec dashed through the winding corridor connecting the airlock to the cargo bay. He barely made it a few meters when the ship lurched violently, slamming him into the curved wall.

Stunned for a heartbeat, Aelec resumed his pace even as the *Erinyes* jolted a few more times. That wasn't Myra's evasive maneuvers; it was the Terrans outside the ship. Voiddamn, they were using enough energy in their attacks to jolt the ship!

That's settled, I'm never coming back to Terras, Aelec thought as he ran.

The winding, cylindrical corridor deposited him into the cargo bay which had another hallway connecting to the engine room, armory, and main hold. A few seconds later, he was in the expansive main hold and dashing between the cafeteria tables to get to the final corridor which connected to the cockpit. The coattails of Aelec's dust jacket snapped behind his heels as he sprinted into the conical-shaped cockpit.

Myra was strapped into the left side pilot's chair, her slender hands clasped on the steering yoke as she wrestled for control. Electrical *thuds* emanated from the ship's exterior, the hologram panels on the co-pilot's side flashing red. Alarms were going off, indicating that the *Erinyes'* shields were taking a serious beating.

Flopping into the co-pilot's chair, Aelec swiveled the seat and pressed his fingers against a set of hologram panels to divert power to the starboard shields. This left the port side vulnerable, but right now he wasn't worried about someone flanking them. He needed to buy the ship a few more seconds before they blasted off into space.

Outside the cockpit's viewport he could see the Terras warriors extending their hands towards the *Erinyes* as streaks of crimson energy blasted from their open palms. Part of him marveled at the sight of the strange combatants. His kindred Outrider spirit appreciated their effectiveness in combat. The strange energy from their suits unnerved him, however, and another part of him wanted to use the ship's fusion cannons to blast them into subatomic particles.

Yet Myra's piloting prevented him from doing so. In the span of a few seconds, she rotated the ship towards the hangar exit and pressed the accelerator. The *Erinyes* soared out of the Imperium hangar and into the space above Terras.

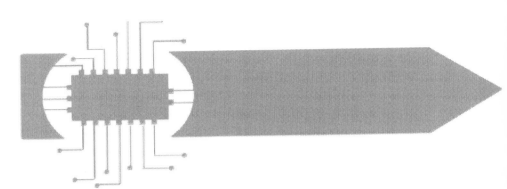

CHAPTER 3

T he chilling surge of dopamine hit Myra's brain as if she'd drunk an ice slushie too quickly. She blinked, letting out a soft groan as her tentacles transferred the chemicals into her brain. It felt like a mild headache at first, but once the initial rush was through, her attention was laser focused. She could track the trajectories of objects in space, plan a tight maneuver from kilometers away, or calculate the exact power the ship would need to escape a firefight.

Presently, she needed to do all three of those things. The headache got a bit worse.

Twisting the control yoke, Myra sent the ship into a corkscrew dive upon blasting out of the hangar bay to avoid an explosion. Just beyond the Imperium frigate, five bulbous corvettes floated like jellyfish, spheres of red energy firing from their surface turrets. Volleys of amber light streaked from the frigate, a ball of fire replacing the spot a corvette had been. Starfighters zipped and dove between the larger ships, and elongated shuttles used the chaos to board the frigate.

The *Erinyes* was caught in the middle of the space battle, and

Myra elected to use the frigate for cover. The hostile ships could target the *Erinyes* if they tried to get clear of the battle. She twisted the controls, evading a few transports which were embedded like ticks, though some were beginning to detach from the Imperium ship.

Myra felt a chill. Streaks of pale sapphire light impacted the sleek hull of the frigate, breaking through the shields and penetrating the morristeel. Bright orange glows caught her enhanced focus, and she saw several holes melted into the frigate's hull.

From one such hole, an amber column of fire erupted like a geyser directly in the path of the *Erinyes*. Time seemed to slow as her dopamine-infused brain watched the flames spew forth. Myra turned the yoke and sent the ship spinning to the side of the explosion, the artificial gravity of the *Erinyes* making her stomach churn.

To her right, Aelec was pinned to his seat. Once the ship righted itself with its belly facing the frigate's hull, Aelec used the holographic panels to raise the power of their shields in the event an explosion caught them by surprise. Myra nodded. Her co-pilot instinctively understood what she wanted.

"Making new friends everywhere we go, it seems," she grunted through clenched teeth. "What in the Void happened here?"

"The Terrans don't like the Imperium near their planet, apparently," Aelec snorted.

"Can't say I blame them at this point," Myra said. "What's the status of the voidstream drive?"

Aelec surveyed the hologram displays to his right and replied, "Calculations will be completed in two minutes. Let's avoid being turned into space dust, shall we?"

Myra scoffed theatrically. "And here I thought you wanted us all to be atomized, boss."

Twisting the yoke to the left, Myra sent the *Erinyes* into another corkscrew as they followed the eel-like hull of the frigate. The *Erinyes* skimmed along the upper decks of the Imperium starship so that they could avoid detection from the enemy starfighters. The scanners blared as they had difficulty pinpointing the hostiles around the *Carthage*, so she needed to rely on her enhanced sight to spot them.

Dodging another explosion along the morristeel hull, the *Erinyes* slipped between two of the communication antennas running along the frigate's spine. As the ship crested the Imperium cruiser, Myra's vision focused as the dopamine coursed through her brain. What she saw made her jaw drop.

From the *Erinyes'* position along the frigate's spine, she could glimpse the temperate world below—they were just above the planet's atmosphere. She could see the expansive supercontinent beyond the swirling, white clouds. Vast plains of green grass and numerous mountain ranges made up the landscape. The topography maps on the ship's hologram console indicated that they were directly above the eastern side of the continent.

Though the landscape was thousands of kilometers away, the Terrans were firing focused beams of crystalline blue energy directly from the surface into orbit. Anti-orbital defenses were not unheard of, but most of them were inaccurate—the fusion blasts often hitting spots where the ships had been rather than where they would be.

But Terras' anti-orbital weapons were constant beams of energy, allowing them to alter the trajectories in conjunction with the frigate. Lines of sapphire cut into the *Carthage*, igniting more explosions and forcing the starfighters to disperse. Based on Myra's knowledge of ship design, the Imperium frigate had suffered damage to its fuel tanks, life support, and voidstream drive. A crystalline violet light was shining through the holes, and Myra understood what such illumination meant.

"Direct hit to their voidstream drive," she muttered, nervousness building in her chest. "We need to get clear before it blows!"

Aelec's gaze snapped to her. "What about those Terras guns?"

"We'll have to risk it," she said, priming the fusion engines for max speed. "Time?"

"Thirty seconds until calculations are complete."

Myra tilted her head to the side, her neck cracking as she repeated, "Thirty seconds. I estimate the *Carthage*'s drive will blow then, if not sooner."

The dopamine surge in her mind helped her plot out a course within a heartbeat; she had twenty-nine seconds to keep the ship from being blasted while gaining distance from the *Carthage*. Chunks of the hull were drifting in the space around the frigate as the beams tore it apart—pieces that could provide cover. She also noted the trajectory of the *Carthage* as it floated limply in orbit; one wrong rotation could send part of the frigate crashing into the *Erinyes*. But as long as she flew along the frigate's spine, they'd be protected as they tried to escape.

Myra pressed the accelerator and the *Erinyes*' fusion engines roared to life with a low *thrum*. The ship rocketed along the spine of the frigate, dodging and weaving through the communication spires. She twisted the yoke and spun the ship beneath a chunk of debris.

As the ship stopped spinning, an azure energy beam sliced through the *Carthage* directly in front of them. A wall of pale blue fire erupted from the impact, and Myra was quick to veer the ship up and above the explosion. Their shields might have taken the brunt of the heat, but she didn't know how the *Erinyes*' deflectors would handle such strange energy. She didn't risk flying through the fire.

Unfortunately, the maneuver caused the *Erinyes* to move out from cover of the debris, leaving them exposed to the starfighters and Terras' anti-orbital guns. A beam of light shot past the cockpit's viewport, the energy mere centimeters from their shields.

"Hang on tight!" Myra called. With one hand, she pulled the control yoke and with the other she fluctuated the ship's accelerator.

The *Erinyes* barrel rolled once before going into a dive towards the atmosphere. Outside the viewport, she could see the landscape below, and a second later she saw a sapphire light erupt from a mountain range. Thanks to the heads-up, she was able to spin the ship out of the way just before the blast hit them. Myra pulled the yoke towards her, and the ship angled itself back towards space.

She eyed Aelec, and he indicated that ten seconds remained before the drive was ready.

The *Erinyes* evaded another slab of debris as the countdown commenced. *Nine, eight, sev...*

The ship rocked suddenly. Alarms blared beside her; something had impacted their rear deflector shields and they were dropping in power. An anti-orbital beam had hit them. Aelec's hands flew frantically over the control panels as he diverted more power, but the shields were dropping at an exponential rate.

Six, five, four...

"Shields are down!" Aelec shouted, his golden eyes going wide.

Something thudded further down in the ship, but Myra's focus was locked on to the clearing in the debris field. She angled the *Erinyes* directly between the floating detritus.

Three, two, one!

Her right hand, which had been hovering over the holographic voidstream lever, moved in a flash. She pulled back on the hologram, the ship's terminal responding to her touch. A loud whir came from the rear of the ship, and the cockpit's viewport was engulfed in gyrating, blue lights as they entered the voidstream.

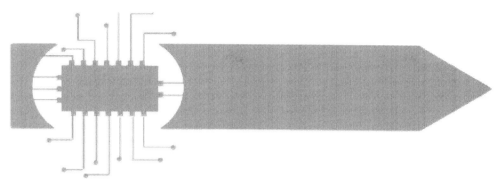

CHAPTER 4

"Oh shiiiiit!" Dylis shouted as a flash of dazzling, purple light pulsed from the corridor with an electric *crack*.

Strapped into his seat, he could do nothing but lock his eyes on Riza. The girl's knuckles turned white as she gripped the straps of her acceleration chair.

"I'm not an expert, but that's not supposed to sound like that, right?!" she called over the high-pitched whine.

"Nope!" Dylis looked around as sweat beaded his forehead. "Rant! Where in the Void are you?"

Like a spider crawling along the walls, the Tarantula Utility droid entered the bronze light of the main hold. His eight legs shifted him from the wall to the floor and his domed head turned towards Dylis. All ten of Rant's red photoreceptors fixated on him, sending a chill down his spine.

"Statement: You called for this unit, Dylis Wyri?" the droid said in a cold monotone.

Dylis pointed towards the pulsing light emanating from the engine room corridor. "Have you not seen that, Rant?!"

The droid's photoreceptors looked from the corridor and back again. "Response: A high energy beam weapon has impacted the hull and disrupted the power lines," he replied. "Pressure seal is still in place. This unit calculates that the power disruption will cause an overload of the voidstream drive, which will cause this freighter to self-destruct."

"No shit, you piece of junk! Can you fix it before we explode?!"

Rant's appendages tittered as he said, "Response: Threat is not immediate. This unit calculates that the voidstream drive will decay in eight hours, forty minutes, and—"

The whirring from the engine room escalated to a roar, the LED lights along the walls flickered, and sparks spewed from open wall panels. Riza cried out in terror and Dylis gritted his teeth.

The droid's head snapped towards the engine room and his appendages scuttled in what looked to be alarm.

"Assessment: Estimated time until decay is now three minutes and fifty-two seconds."

Rant moved faster than Dylis had ever seen as his spider-like legs sprayed showers of sparks before he disappeared down the corridor. Closing his eyes, Dylis offered a silent prayer to the Sol. He still had a wife to see again.

There was also a more desperate aspect to his prayer. The Sol was the god of justice, and Dylis still felt that his past grievances would come back to haunt him in whatever afterlife awaited. His Outrider clan-mark was still tainted from his deeds years ago—deeds that the Sol would surely judge him harshly on.

Dylis didn't consider himself a spiritual man, but he did have faith. Things happened in the universe for a reason; it was the only thing that helped him make sense of everything. Whether he liked it or not, he'd tainted his clan-mark for a reason. He'd joined Aelec's crew for a reason. He'd survived a plasma grenade for a reason.

Now, he hoped he'd survive their current predicament for that same reason...

The ship lurched despite being inside the voidstream portal. Dylis' knuckles cracked as he gripped his safety belts. Vibrations violently wracked the ship, a high-pitched whine coming from the engine room. Panels shook loose from the ceiling, secured containers broke free of their restraints, and more of the LED lights winked out. Dylis was convinced his seat would soon break free of the floor when the shaking ceased.

The whine stopped abruptly; by the Void, there was hardly any noise. The alarms went silent. All he could hear was Riza's panting breath—the girl's face was stark white and sweat glistened on her forehead. Dylis might've looked the same had it not been for his Outrider training. Thank the Sol he kept his cool.

When Riza's breathing refused to slow, Dylis knew she was going into shock.

"Hey! Hey, newbie!" he snapped, getting her attention. "Deep breaths. There's plenty of oxygen. Follow my lead. In. Hold. And out."

They matched motions, inhaling deeply, holding their breaths for a few seconds, and then exhaling. After a moment, he noticed that Riza's breathing slowed, though she still appeared shell shocked. She gazed past him, and he realized she was staring at something behind him. Nervously, he turned his head.

One of the wall panels that had broken off was now floating next to his head. Dylis blinked and his eyes darted around the main hold. Other objects were similarly floating around the cabin. Loose ration packs, droplets of liquid, and even clusters of powder. Though Riza's dark hair was tied into a ponytail, it flowed as if she was underwater.

Artificial gravity is gone, he thought. *Shit!*

"Hey, Dylis," Riza said, "is it just me, or are we in zero-G right now?"

"Nah, this is just some fancy special effects for shock value," he retorted.

Riza drew her lips into a thin line. "I don't need your sarcasm right now, Dylis!"

"I quip when I'm nervous."

Aelec's voice crackled over the ship's commlink system. *"Is everyone okay? Status report?"*

Dylis reached over to the hologram on the wall next to him and pressed the reply display. "Yeah, we're in one piece, boss."

"Golath, Rant, are you two okay?"

A string of rapid clicks came from the commlink, the tone sounding like the Kygi was as cool as a Morrigarian chute. It didn't surprise him; Golath often kept his composure even during strenuous circumstances. Dylis felt a small knell of shame for his outbursts.

Keeping the commlink open, Dylis asked, "What in the Void happened? I thought the voidstream drive was gonna blow."

"It almost did," Aelec replied, his voice bearing a hint of relief. *"Luckily, our seasoned Tarantula got to it in time. Some of the controls and lights are dark, which means Rant shut down most of the ship's power so that the drive didn't draw any excess. As of now, all systems except comms, pressure, and air recyclers are out."*

"I'll take oxygen over gravity," Riza said, her hands still clasped around her safety belts. "Though this is going to get old real quick."

"Just stay strapped in, Riza," Aelec's voice said. *"Get used to the sensation before you try floating around."*

Dylis blinked in confusion. "You're planning for us to float around, boss?"

The comm was silent for a moment. When Aelec's voice came back, Dylis could hear a slight tinge of uncertainty.

"Yeah, about that. I'm going to try and get systems back online up here. We'll need to have a powwow in a little bit. But for now, float carefully."

"Well... Golath and Rant don't have to float," Dylis quipped, trying to lighten the mood. "Talons and appendages seem real nice right now."

The captain paused before adding, *"Speaking of our mechanic... Rant, acknowledge."*

There was silence over the commlink. Dylis felt the blood leave his face. Aelec called for Rant again, but there was no response. Looking down the corridor leading to the engine room, Dylis tried to see if the droid was somewhere in the darkness.

A moment passed, and Dylis heard movement echoing from the opposite corridor. It was the hall leading towards the cockpit, and soon enough Myra floated through the cylindrical passage. Her violet eyes were wide and he noticed her tentacles were writhing more rapidly than usual. The Vitrax had undone the top part of her sage flight suit, revealing her white tank top while the vest and sleeves flowed around her waist.

"Rant?!" she called as she floated through the main hold. "Answer me!"

She floated towards the corridor and the emergency railings extended from panels in the ceiling, allowing Myra to grab hold. Pulling herself along the corridor's ceiling, Myra vanished into the darkness.

The moment Myra left the main hold, Dylis heard the familiar sharp *thuds* of Golath's talons coming from the hall leading to the cargo bay. True to his insectoid form, the Kygi scrambled along the side of the wall as his claws dug into the gaps between panels.

Once inside the main hold, Golath remained perched on the wall as he rotated his head to look at Dylis and Riza. It was difficult to detect emotion on the Kygi's pinched face, especially with the respirator mask covering half of it, but his yellow eyes appeared wide with shock.

A string of metallic clicks echoed from beneath his respirator mask; the Kygi used his four mandibles to tap against his beak-like mouth.

Dylis shrugged. "Sorry, bud. I don't know what those clicks mean. Rant isn't responding, if that's what you're clicking about."

Golath heaved his carapace-covered shoulders, making it look like he was sighing in exasperation. Kygi were able to understand Trade, they just couldn't speak it. Instead, Golath extended one of his four arms and pointed a clawed finger towards the engine room.

Then he made his fingers splay wide, and Dylis faintly understood the gesture.

"Yeah, I'm definitely glad we didn't get front row seats to a void-stream explosion," he answered. "Voiddamn, the little mech spider better be okay."

On cue, movement from the engine room corridor drew his attention. The familiar, glossy black metal of Rant's chassis reflected light from the LED illuminations as it floated into the main hold. Right behind him was Myra—the Vitrax pulling herself along the bars extending from the ceiling before pushing off to float into the main hold.

In one fluid motion, she grabbed ahold of Rant's appendages with one hand, used her free hand to grip the closest cafeteria table, and hooked her legs beneath the bench to stabilize herself. Opening one of the panels on Rant's chassis, Myra flipped some manual switches in an attempt to get the diagnostic holograms to display.

Nothing happened, and the Vitrax hissed.

Riza sat up in her seat as she noticed what Myra was doing and asked, "Is his diagnostics terminal non-functioning?"

Myra didn't bother to look back at Riza and answered tersely, "Yeah. Clearly. I'm trying to fix it."

Dylis looked from the Vitrax to the girl, the tension in the air felt like it could pressurize a ship. To his surprise, Riza was unfazed by Myra's attitude. If anything, it seemed to goad her.

"Myra," Riza said, a firmness rising in her voice. "I can remote access his diagnostics terminal with a program on my terminus. I can help you. All I need is his nanotech port ID."

A prolonged snort came out from Myra's nostrils; Dylis could see the muscles in her shoulders tense as a result of Riza's words. He understood why. Myra was the pilot of the *Erinyes* and Rant's owner; she'd taken it upon herself to be the foremost caretaker of both the ship and the droid. But now, Riza had a way to solve a problem that even Myra didn't know how to fix.

Drawing her lips into a thin line, Myra waved her free hand at the floating droid and hissed, "Fine. Let's see how smart you really are."

Dylis glared at Myra, but she didn't seem to notice. Part of him was glad that she hadn't; Myra was one of the few people he didn't want to get on the bad side of. He'd faced down terrorists, monsters, and all manner of Voidspawned things in his time as an Outrider, but the Vitrax's wrath made him sweat.

He had to hand it to Riza for keeping a level head in the face of Myra's jibes. The girl unbuckled herself and floated up towards the rail extending from the ceiling. Crawling along its length, she pushed off from it when she was above the cafeteria table and drifted gradually down to the bench. Similarly hooking her legs beneath it, Riza tapped her terminus and got to work.

Dylis felt his eyes cross as he tried to watch the painstaking process of reawakening a droid remotely. Technology—apart from E-weapons and nanotech—wasn't his forte, and his brain seemed to turn off the more he stared at Riza's holograms. All the lines of code blurred together, and the girl's constant swiping made it seem like a frantic endeavor.

Still, Aelec hadn't lied when he said she was their best tech applicant.

After a few minutes of working the holograms, Riza flourished her wrist as her terminus flashed green.

With a whir and a few stuttering jerks of his domed head, Rant released a series of beeps as his numerous photoreceptors lit up. A garbled static came from his vocabulator before melding into his normal voice.

"Affirmation: Tarantula Utility unit nine-two-seven-dash-six online," he articulated in a monotone voice. "Analysis: Primary systems active. Appendage tactile status negatory. This unit detects that zero gravity is in effect."

Dylis snorted in response to the droid's analytical nature. He'd been on the verge of permanent deactivation—death for droids— and yet here he was spewing data like nothing had happened.

As the tension eased, Dylis felt comfortable enough to unbuckle himself from the acceleration seat and began floating in the zero-G. Finding a wall railing, he inched his way over to the table where everyone was gathered before pushing off the wall to drift onto the bench seat.

Across the table, Myra hung her head and breathed a sigh of relief, her tentacles calming their anxious writhing. The Vitrax kept her hands clenched on the table's edges, keeping herself anchored in the zero-G.

"You..." Riza stammered, addressing the droid. "You aren't alarmed that you were almost fried by the voidstream drive?"

Rant rotated his head to look directly at Riza, and said, "Statement: This unit prevented the voidstream drive from overloading and destroying I-zero-five-five-two freighter designated *Erinyes*. This unit's primary function is to ensure that the ship remains operable for Master Myra. Deactivation is irrelevant."

Dylis scoffed in amusement. "So, does Rant have a death wish that we didn't know about?"

"Droids don't view death like we do," Myra explained, her eyes on Rant. "When you lack pain receptors, organs, and emotions, self-preservation isn't as important as your prime directives. Still, do warn me the next time you go charging at an unstable voidstream drive, Rant."

Floating in the air between them, Rant raised two of his forward appendages in a saluting gesture, saying, "Acknowledgement: Yes, Master Myra."

"Here," Dylis said, reaching up to grasp one of his legs. "Let's get you back to stable ground, pal."

With a firm tug, Dylis pulled the spider-looking droid from midair so that his appendages could magnetize to the floor panels. Rant teetered on the initial impact, but soon began his customary skittering around like a household arachnid.

Dylis grinned, Riza exhaled a sigh of relief, but Myra was laser focused on the droid. It was as if she deliberately avoided eye contact with Riza. When she finally looked up, the same arctic stare emanated from the violet irises.

He felt his gut being tugged to the floor despite the zero-gravity. By instinct, he leaned away from the tangible tension lingering between the two women.

Movement from the cockpit corridor drew his attention. Aelec glided through the dim lighting like a specter, the eerie waving of his hair and dust coat adding to the effect. Using one hand to grip the ceiling rail, Aelec surveyed them with a stern expression on his angular face.

Aelec's auric eyes narrowed as his gaze affixed on Myra, who was still staring daggers into Riza.

"I'm growing tired of this squabbling," Aelec grunted.

Myra snorted in derision. "I'm growing tired of you saying you're tired of it. It's not something I'm going to forget any time soon, Aelec."

The captain's jaw clenched in annoyance. Dylis knew that look. Blatant insubordination, despite the freedom of their crew, still struck Aelec's nerves. He understood the notion of being raised in the rigid, militaristic lifestyle of the Outriders, but the captain would need to accept the fact that Myra wasn't a soldier.

"We've got bigger problems," Aelec resumed. "I ran some diagnostics, and we're more than a little screwed. That blast crippled the fusion engines and scorched most of the fuel lines. We're dead in the water."

Despite the crepuscular chill of the freighter, Dylis' face grew colder. Without engine power, the ship's inertia could propel them towards a singularity or an asteroid field. While they could use the gravlifts for thrusters, it wouldn't be enough.

"We need to make repairs. Fast," Aelec said, rubbing his forehead with a gloved hand. "The Terrans are less than a ten-minute voidjump from us. We just need to be operational enough to survive another jump."

Dylis' leg twitched as he thought of the Terrans dropping out of a voidstream. They would either be captured or blasted to smithereens. Aelec was right. The *Erinyes* needed to get going.

"Sure do love that you're telling me what needs to be done with *my* ship," Myra muttered, crossing her arms. "Rant, Dylis, we need to get topside to make repairs. Let's get to work."

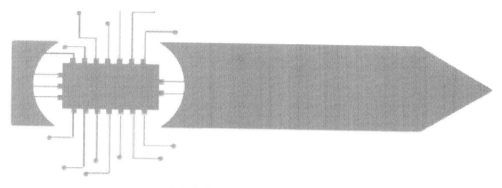

CHAPTER 5

An ocean of blackness expanded from beyond every angle of the ship. It was different from looking up at the sky of a planet. On a world, you looked up and saw the vast canvas sky that was marked by light. In space, however, the canvas was all around. While the *Erinyes* served as a small island beneath his feet, all Dylis had to do was look left and the Void greeted his gaze. It was as if he was trapped in a voidglobe; the singular speck of glowing plasma at the center of enveloping blackness.

To a normal person, this might cause an existential crisis about their place in the vast universe. To Dylis, this was a routine job. After twenty years, he'd performed dozens of spacewalks across ship hulls, space stations, and even asteroids. During an orbital skirmish above Faerius, he and clan-Wyri battled along the hull of an A.I.L. frigate as if they were besieging a ground encampment. It had taken nearly seven hours for them to finally get past the droids, turrets, and shield systems so that they could enter the ship.

It was a strange contrast to how pathetic he felt when flying through a voidstream tunnel. Inside a vessel like the *Erinyes*, you were vulnerable to the mercy of the ship's integrity. You never knew when the ship might decide to break the proverbial and literal seal, jettisoning all occupants into the Void.

Being outside of the ship and enveloped in a vac-suit, while incredibly dangerous, made Dylis feel more in control. Out there, it was on him if he made a misstep or didn't check his suit's integrity. To Dylis, having control over his life was what kept him from succumbing to apathy.

It was why he was so vehement when it came to his tainted clan-mark. Being unable to control the shame he felt at his dishonor was partially what drove him to seek its purification. Cleansing his clan-mark of dishonor would not be a simple task, however.

Dylis had broken one of the laws of Outrider combat, and was required to serve his penance by limiting himself. He would do this until he felt himself worthy to travel to Morrigar and dip into the Fountain of Purity.

Then, and only then, would his clan-mark be cleansed, and he could return to his full Outrider capabilities. Until that time, however, Dylis refused to kill any foe that came in his path. It was the only part of his penance that he could control.

Taking a careful step, he moved along the ship's hull, the fabric of the suit feeling strange against his arms and neck. The vac-suit didn't hug his frame as tightly as nanotech armor did; the deep green, mesh-fiber material bunched up at his elbows and knees.

The helmet was also bulkier, mostly in the faceplate area, which was nothing more than a wide piece of clear plexiglass. It didn't have a HUD, since it was an older style of vac-suit, so he had to use his wrist terminus to monitor its systems. A wide belt—that was more around his stomach than his waist—kept the suit pressurized and had a number of oxygen cylinders to provide him with cold, stale air.

Taking big, deliberate steps with his magnetic boots, Dylis held a large tool kit in his left hand and carried a child-sized fusion coil that was tucked underneath his right arm. Draped over his shoulders was a backpack filled with some of the larger tools and a few quantum cards in the event that their vac-suits needed a recharge.

Ahead of him by a few paces were Myra and Rant, the former was squatting near one of the blasted sections near the engines while the latter scuttled—albeit slower—around a cluster of exposed wires. The loose wires sprouted from the openings and waved like lethargic tentacles. A few other broken parts hovered in various positions from the battered hull, and Dylis knew that this was only a fraction of what probably broke off from the ship. Who knew what else they'd lost in the voidstream tunnel...

Myra turned slightly toward him and waved her hand, beckoning for him to approach. Cautiously, Dylis walked along the scorched hull of the ship, trying his best not to knock any more panels loose. The downside to magnetic boots was that they could pull portions of the ship off if they weren't secured properly. Luckily, Dylis navigated the hull like a Vitrax water dancer.

Stopping next to Myra, he spoke into his helmet commlink, saying, "What's the damage? You know, besides the gaping hole in the hull and the likelihood of our deaths in space?"

Myra rolled her violet eyes. "If I'm to get anything done, I'm going to need less quipping from you." She pointed at the tool kit. "Hand me that. I need the nanoparticle infuser."

Slowly, Dylis extended his arm to hand the kit to Myra, who snatched it from his grasp. She used a few fusionfibers to connect the kit to her utility belt, thus preventing it from floating off into space. Plucking a pen-like device from the kit, she rotated the tip of the nanoparticle infuser so that it glowed a pale blue. Then, as if she was writing, she began injecting the damaged parts with clusters of nanoparticles.

Common nanoparticles were much different from the pure variants that Outriders utilized. For one, common nanoparticles could respond to only a specific command while Outrider nanotech could reform countlessly based on the user's intent. These ones, for instance, would cling to the damaged parts of the ship and wait for a fuse before sealing, reknitting, or mending.

When Myra finished injecting a portion of nanoparticles along the exposed wiring, Dylis used a quantum card to power them with a few fuses. Like waves washing up a beach, the nanoparticles moved in unison to fill the gaps in the frayed wires. It wasn't a perfect repair system, but it would get the job done.

It was a tedious process, especially since Dylis could only stand there and hand her things, but Myra worked to an efficient rhythm. Occasionally, Rant skittered over to assist in areas she couldn't reach, the droid's appendages working like a spider webbing up its prey.

All was quiet for several long minutes. It was an eerie silence— the only noise came from Dylis' breathing as it echoed within the helmet. After what felt like hours, Myra finished her work on the first gaping hole in the ship and started moving towards the next. Checking his terminus, Dylis saw that only fifteen minutes had passed.

He sighed. This was going to take a while.

"So," he said, tired of listening to himself breathing. "Is this the first time the *Erinyes* has been blasted open like this?"

Myra didn't look up at him, but she spoke softly, "Yeah. I've flown her through nebulas, asteroid fields, and clusters of starfighters, and she's never received more than a few dings and scorch marks. I knew it'd only be a matter of time before she took a solid hit, but I never thought it'd be from Terras of all places."

"Yeah," he grunted, staring off into the expanse beyond. "Who knew they'd have ground weapons strong enough to rip a ship open while in flight? I've seen a lot of whack ass weapons in this galaxy, but whatever the Terrans have is on a whole new level. Like magic or something."

Myra snorted. "Magic doesn't exist, you goof. There's always a logical explanation to stuff we don't understand."

Static crackled into Dylis' helmet comm. When it cleared, Aelec's voice echoed, *"Dylis. Myra. We've got a problem."*

"What now?" Dylis groaned.

"Deep space scanners are picking up voidstream drive signatures heading our way. They're coming from Terras."

"Shit!" Dylis met Myra's gaze before asking, "What's our timeline?"

"ETA ten minutes."

Myra licked her lips. "I'll be cutting it close, but I can get us voidstream-worthy in eight minutes."

"That a foretelling?" Dylis asked, his voice raising.

Myra sneered at him. "I can't do that until I'm much older, idiot!"

He felt a pang of guilt as he remembered that Vitrax didn't obtain foresight until they were sixty years old. Biology could be a bitch. The times they needed a seer were of course the times they didn't have one.

From her kit, she plucked another infuser and held it out to Dylis. "It'll be under eight minutes if you help."

Taking the infuser, Dylis followed her instructions. Tension built in his suit, suffocating him like pressure as he thought of the Terrans heading their way. They moved to the engines, where Dylis held the fusion coil while Myra linked it to the external power couplings. Myra and Rant made a few adjustments in the exposed panels, and Dylis saw trickles of amber light flowing from the coil's links and into the ship's couplings.

The familiar glow of the engines crested the rear of the ship like dawn inching over the horizon. Dylis surveyed the *Erinyes'* hull. Portions were still scorched and torn open.

"That'll have to do," Myra said, disconnecting the links. "We've got five minutes. Let's go!"

Collecting their equipment, Dylis and Myra walked as fast as they could back to the airlock. Rant got there first, opening the ramp and scuttling inside. Once back inside, they stripped off the vac-suits and pulled themselves frantically along the emergency railings.

"What's the plan, Myra?" Dylis panted, his arms burning as he navigated the railing.

"We're still in the Sol system," she replied, "which means we're too far away from a solid repair yard like Biiras or Khorrus. The only viable shipyard around these parts is Tog. Ugh, I hate this!"

Dylis felt a pit in his stomach. *Oh jeez, Golath is not going to like this.* He swallowed, pushing down the uneasiness.

The warm light of the main hold greeted him, the zero-G let him float to the ceiling, where he gripped another railing. He caught the coattails of Aelec's duster waving in the cockpit corridor, vanishing behind the corner. Rapid *thunks* resounded as Myra pulled herself along the rails, following Aelec to the cockpit. Dylis pushed off the ceiling, floated down into the seat beside Golath, and pulled on the straps.

Rapid, high-pitched clicks came from the Kygi, his triangular head bobbing up and down. Dylis patted him on his carapaced shoulder, and the clicking grew slower. Across from him, Riza looped her arms through the safety straps, her eyes kept glancing towards the cockpit.

"Where are we at, boss?" Dylis called, the wall commlink blinked green in response.

"*Drive's charging,*" Aelec answered. "*Scanners show—*"

Klaxons blared throughout the ship, the LEDs in the hallways flaring with red light. Dylis felt the *Erinyes* lurch, his head pressing into the padded buffer.

"*...that company's here! Everyone, hold on tight!*"

Grasping the straps over his chest, Dylis squeezed his eyes shut as the *Erinyes* soared into action. The dull rumble of the fusion engines was complemented by the building whine that came from the voidstream drive. Though distinctly softer than usual, Dylis didn't have enough time to worry before the ship jolted with a bombastic *thud.*

The alarms ceased, the LEDs stopped flashing, and a soft vibration filled the cabin.

"*We're in voidstream, folks,*" Aelec huffed through the comm-link. "*We're safe.*"

Dylis mumbled, "For now."

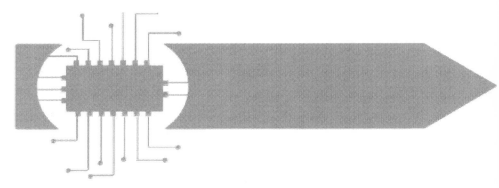

CHAPTER 6

4509.0827 / FT Star System: Aeron / 3,867,656 kilometers from the planet Tog / GST: 17:00

The *Erinyes* practically tumbled out of the voidstream portal, groaning in protest as it dropped into normal space. Riza's thoughts were muddled, confused. She couldn't help but think of all the ship's problems and the consequences they'd bring. Muscles in her shoulders tensed as she considered it.

Riza was strapped to the main hold's couch, a crimson hue cast a bloody light from the emergency LEDs. Her entire body ached from sitting in the same position for nearly eight hours. Nausea rose and fell within her guts like an ebbing tide. Across the main hold sat Dylis, his eyes closed and arms folded tightly across his broad chest.

Was he sleeping or trying to meditate? Dylis' jaw clenched and he groaned as the ship rumbled. *Nope, definitely not asleep.*

Riza sympathized with him, she worried that her hair would

turn gray from all the stress. The events over Terras had reminded her of the horrors of space travel—how one small thing could send them all to the Void's cold embrace.

Well, my ass is going to be feeling that for a few days, she thought.

Their repairs had been quick and shoddy; the *Erinyes* was basically held together by fusionfibers and some smelted metal. Riza's lips moved as she muttered a prayer to the Sol, hoping that the universe would see fit to keep their ship in one piece.

Aelec's gruff voice echoed over the commlink, every other word crackling from power fluctuations.

"We're approaching Tog's spaceyard now, folks," he said. *"Hold on tight. This is going to be a bumpy landing."*

"Ugh if I hear the words 'bumpy' and 'landing' in the same sentence again, I'm spacejumping into the nearest star," Dylis groaned, his face stricken.

The commlink went silent. Violent shakes wracked the *Erinyes,* making Riza's teeth clatter. Dylis retched, but luckily no vomit came from him. Metallic rattles echoed across the ship, and a soft whine emanated from the engine room. She squeezed her eyes shut, trying to escape the grating chorus of pandemonium.

The whine grew louder, growing with Riza's dread. Sol above, if the voidstream drive was broken again, they were certainly doomed. Her muttering to the Sol continued as everything reached a fevered pitch.

The shaking stopped, the whine faded, and the rattling quieted. Riza opened her eyes cautiously and was surprised to see an optimistic look on Dylis' tan face.

"What happened?" Riza asked, more loudly than expected.

Aelec's voice came over the commlink once again, explaining, *"Security tractor field. Standard issue for spaceyards. Helps them maneuver ships in and out of the station."*

He paused, then added, *"The ship's stabilized since they're reeling us in. You want to come see the sights?"*

Riza's eagerness—coupled with her aching body—was enough

to make her move quickly. Unbuckling her safety straps, Riza floated off the leather couch and grabbed the emergency railing. Pulling herself along, she moved into the curving corridor leading to the cockpit. The zero-G took a lot of getting used to, but she had plenty of railings to keep her steady.

Floating through the cylindrical doorway to the cockpit, Riza used the nearest seat to halt her momentum. Her eyes were drawn to the forward viewport. Sunlight from the nearby star illuminated the planet below, and Riza felt her breath catch.

Like an enormous sapphire rotating in the void of space, Tog's crystalline waters shone with a brilliance that made the oceans of Nidal seem polluted. Squinting in response to the bright reflections, she noticed landmasses of deep green and white spiraling in beautiful patterns.

Two moons peeked over the horizon—one much larger than the other. Unlike the fully-populated satellites orbiting Seraphi, Tog's moons were barren of artificial lights, leaving no hint of colonization. Everything appeared purely natural.

Curious of this, she asked, "How in the Void have the Togrians kept their planet so clean? This makes vacation spots like Nidal seem like cheap resorts."

Aelec glanced back at her and replied, "Most of their structures are beneath the surface. Tog's landmasses have high amounts of crystal in them, and history says that their ancestors didn't want to scar the surface."

He pointed towards something beyond the viewport and continued, "They also prefer to do their work in orbit."

Leaning forward, Riza saw an expansive network of space stations linked together like a mechanical spider web. Countless tunnels of gray steel connected the globed stations, and pallid lights gave a glossy sheen to the structure.

A rumble from above stirred her attention, and her heart skipped a beat. A larger ship glided past them, docking in one of the massive open spots along one of the station's arms. The spot next to it had the skeleton of a similar vessel, smaller ships buzzing around it like flies around a carcass.

After a moment, the *Erinyes* was pulled in the direction of the nearest arm. It was a slow process, each minute passing achingly slow. When a *hiss* finally emanated from the boarding ramp, Riza's body heaved in relief.

Artificial gravity was restored, and her feet touched the floor—her nausea vanishing.

Cracking her back, Riza groaned, "That was a thrilling ride, but let's not do that again."

Aelec snorted in amusement. "We don't plan on it."

After securing most of their supplies and prepping the ship as best they could, the crew of the *Erinyes* set foot on the white floors of the Togrian space station.

Riza felt an initial shock of claustrophobia because the hallway looked like the inside of a shell. Craning her neck, she noticed the ovular design with a distinct arch in the ceiling. Though Riza's was enthralled by the sight, Myra and Aelec possessed the jaded expressions of people who'd seen sights like this countless times.

Dylis surveyed the space station with curious eyes, but eventually scoffed in amusement as he glanced up at the chocolate-colored ceiling. Movement in her peripherals drew her eyes to the long viewports on the curving walls, where she saw a vessel being constructed. The air had the distinct smell of salt water, reminding her of the beaches from her homeworld.

A low, guttural clicking came from Golath as he displayed a level of fury that Riza never thought the Kygi capable of. His yellow eyes burned with disgust, his shoulders hunched defensively. Each of his four hands were balled into fists, and Riza could see he was breathing heavily.

She gulped.

It was common knowledge that the Togrians and Kygi had bad blood between them ever since the former conquered the latter. Golath didn't talk much about what the Togrians did to his people, but with this level of animosity coming from him it was certain that those wounds would not heal any time soon.

Continuing into the space station proper, they had to push their way through crowds—many of which were Vitrax and Togrians. Riza accidentally brushed against the white and teal fabric of a Vitrax male, his sculpted muscles accentuated by the clothes. Backing away, she then bumped into the bejeweled shell of a Togrian, eliciting a throaty grumble from the nonhuman.

Threatening clicks drowned out the Togrian, Golath bucked his head towards the tortoise-looking nonhuman. The crowd grew quiet, the Togrian leering at the Kygi with his beady, black eyes. Luckily, the Togrian backed away, and no one protested as Golath made his way through the crowd. Dylis walked next to the Kygi and patted him on the back.

Breaking free of the sea of bodies, the group approached one of the check-in offices on the far side of the central hub. Once at the office entrance, Aelec ordered for Dylis, Golath, Rant, and Riza to remain outside while he and Myra got everything squared away. At first, Riza was confused as to why Aelec didn't want them all inside, but she quickly understood that it was an office exclusively meant for captains and pilots.

As they vanished into the office, Riza set up her cargocases along the nearby wall before sitting in one of the cushioned seats. Dylis and Golath remained standing, the human folding his arms across his chest as he watched the Kygi pace back and forth.

Seeing how disturbed Golath was, Riza asked, "Are you going to be okay, Golath?"

The Kygi clicked aggressively, and Rant chimed in, "Translation: I am unable to find respite with all the foul Togrian smells entering my respirator. I will not be able to relax until we are far away from this Empyrean-forsaken planet."

"Such a great tourist you are, Golath," Dylis said, scratching at his beard. "Remind me to never take you to Nidal. It might be too vacationy for your tastes."

Golath flashed Dylis an indignant look, and the latter held up his hands innocently. A group of Togrians walked by and made sure to give Golath a wide berth. The nonhumans clucked as they passed.

"Seriously, Golath," Riza said, "why do you despise the Togrians so much? I know they conquered Kyg-nor in the past, but weren't you all equally taken under the Comitor's yoke? Shouldn't they be your common foe?"

A dark look came into Golath's yellow eyes as he met her gaze. "Translation: Just because the Comitors enslaved both of our races does not erase the travesties they enacted upon my people. Both Comitors and Togrians will face the Empyrean's judgment. Neither is worse than the other."

Before Riza could utter a response, Golath continued clicking, "Translation: The Togrians targeted many of our spires where the Matriarchs, soothsayers, and workers resided. Countless resources we had gathered were annihilated, along with those who provided them. In our culture, a Kygi who can provide is a Kygi that ensures our future. Losing a Matriarch is like losing an entire food center on your human worlds. It was a loss that cut us deeply."

Riza's eyes widened in shock. "You mean, they didn't attack your soldiers?"

"Translation: Only when we offered an effective resistance or took the offensive." Golath hung his head, his eyes staring at the floor as he continued, "The Togrian invaders had no honor, no rules of engagement. Even the Comitors had more sense than to slay our Matriarchs. So, ever since the Togrians displayed that level of brutality, they will always be seen as barbarians in the eyes of my people. And I have not seen anything to dissuade this."

Riza gestured to the space station around them and asked,

"What of this spaceyard? This offers countless people mechanical aid and shelter out here in the Fringe."

Golath clicked angrily, and Rant hesitated before intoning, "Translation: It is nothing but a Togrianitarian stunt; a gem to distract the galactic populace from the foul deeds of their past."

She noticed some nearby Togrians glaring at Golath, their stubby fingers curling into fists. Dylis turned, met their gaze, and parted his jacket to show off his holstered E-pistol. The nonhumans walked away, disappearing into the crowd.

Riza felt her cheeks growing hot from embarrassment, and she wanted nothing more than to shrink into obscurity. While she hadn't been the one to say such things, she felt responsible for prodding Golath into such a vocal denouncement of Togrian society. She could only hope that the space station's inhabitants tolerated free speech as the Capital Worlds did.

Before the conversation could continue, Aelec and Myra exited the office and rejoined the group. Myra leaned against the wall and folded her arms beneath her breasts. Aelec scratched the back of his head, ruffling his long hair.

"What's the damage, boss?" Dylis asked.

Aelec didn't say anything, instead nudging Myra with his elbow. The Vitrax glanced at him irritatedly and gave a deep sigh.

"There's good news and bad news," Myra announced, though her voice didn't indicate anything good about it. "Bad news: It's going to cost us sixty thousand fuses to get the *Erinyes* back in shape."

Riza felt her stomach drop. Dylis groaned in annoyance as he ran a hand along his wide forehead. Golath simply shook his head.

Sixty thousand fuses, Riza repeated to herself. *That's half of what we made back on Caavo. Sol above, that's nearly the cost of a small yacht!*

"That's theft!" Riza declared.

"Welcome to the Aeron system," Aelec grunted. "We're far from the other industrial planets, and the only neighboring planets are

Kyg-nor and Caavo. And since Caavo secures the majority of the Fringe's income, Tog has to resort to other means of earning a profit."

Dylis chimed in, "The Comitors tax all Fringe planets. I bet the Togrians are willing to do anything to make money. Overcharging for ship repairs seems pretty viable."

"Good news," Myra said, her voice drowning out their conversation. "They'll have it done by oh-six-hundred GST. That just means one night of room and board here. Probably for the best anyways; we don't want to be seen this close to Caavo for too long."

"Can't argue with that," Dylis snorted. "Wouldn't be surprised if our faces were already circulating."

"Why?!" Myra snapped, placing her hands on her hips. "Why would you say that? We don't need any more shitty luck, Dylis!"

The older man shrugged. "Luck's got nothing to do with it. We're here, so now we've got to adapt and stay on our toes."

"Dylis is right," Aelec affirmed, looping a thumb into his belt. "If there are any Comitor spies here, they've likely already reported us to the big shots on Caavo. But until the *Erinyes* is repaired, we've got nowhere to run to. So, we bunk up so that none of us are alone for the night, we sleep in shifts, and we get to the docking arm at exactly oh-six-hundred tomorrow morning."

Riza chimed in, "What if the spies try to sabotage the *Erinyes*?"

Aelec nodded to her in acknowledgement and explained, "I've still got a few thousand fuses to spare. A bribe to the right official will keep things running smoothly."

Myra cocked her head to the side and queried, "And how do we ensure that they'll do as ordered?"

Touching his chin in thought, Aelec turned fully towards Riza and asked, "Would you be able to connect your terminus to the docking arm cam feed?"

Riza grinned at him. "It'll be easier than a Novent sorority girl on graduation night."

Dylis laughed. "Nice! You got her contact info, newbie?"

Aelec sighed, shaking his head. "Marriage, Dylis. It's supposed to be treasured."

"And I do," the older man said, showing his palms. "I would never break my vow of fidelity."

"Yet, you asked for a sorority girl's contact info."

"Technically, I didn't break it. I haven't done anything except ask for contact info. Whether I use it or not is between me and the Sol."

"And Fiona," Riza quipped back. "She has a big say in this."

"She'll have my back," Dylis said, holding out his left arm and displaying his terminus. "Want me to call her and show you all how much of a power couple we are?"

"Nope," Aelec grunted firmly. "No calls until we're in void-stream. Can't risk someone here tracing the transmission back to her."

Despite the moment of levity, Riza felt her chest tighten as she thought about being stranded in the Aeron system for the next eight hours. The Comitors could arrive at any moment. A shiver ran down her spine as she thought about falling into the syndicate's hands.

They needed to be vigilant, cautious, and on guard the entire night. Riza's hands shook as she thought about having to fight off the Comitors—sure, she could fire an E-pistol but she didn't know hand-to-hand combat. Her expertise was in using technology to win her battles.

She took a breath, focusing on her job. All she had to do was hack into the station's security system and keep an eye on the *Erinyes* as it underwent repairs—a simple enough task.

Venturing further into the station, they came across numerous motels built into the space station. Steam filled the air, generated from the various leisure pools between each suite. A few Togrians floated like tortoises within the teal pools, their heads poking up from the water. The earthy smell of palm trees drew her attention;

they were imported from Nidal and potted in automated planters that ringed around the courtyard.

After checking in with a Togrian concierge, they were given passcards to two suites directly next to one another. Approaching the white doors outside of each suite, Aelec stopped and turned to face them.

"Same rules," he said, "Males in one suite. Females in the other."

Myra hissed. "I am not sharing a room with Riza by myself, Aelec! Stars above, I don't want to be in the same suite with her at all."

"Myra, come on," Riza said quietly. "Can't we get past this?"

The Vitrax glared at her but kept her words towards Aelec. "You can impose your archaic military rules on the ship all you want. But not here. Find me another room, Aelec."

Riza shrank back from Myra's scathing presence. The Vitrax seemed to grow even more spiteful because of their situation. Despite her attempts to mend their relationship, Riza was far from obtaining Myra's trust and forgiveness. She suspected that it was something deeper, but she knew better than to press Myra.

Aelec's golden eyes looked from Myra to Riza, a deep frown forming on his marble-like face. Riza could tell he wasn't angry with her or Myra—he just seemed exasperated.

Letting out an irritated sigh, Aelec said, "Fine. Who do you want to share a room with?"

"Rant and Dylis," Myra said all too quickly, her eyes narrowing at Aelec. "At least with them I won't be too pissed off."

Golath bowed his head and clicked innocently, his hands clasping together. Myra's eyes widened in shock, and she tenderly touched one of his arms.

"Of course I'm not mad at you, Golath," she admitted. "But you and I could both give our sensory organs a break from one another." To punctuate this, her tentacles writhed like aggravated serpents.

Golath clicked in what Riza assumed was appreciation, and he relaxed. Her heart felt heavy, ladened by guilt as she saw the discord she was causing. The group was fracturing. She couldn't let that happen. Perhaps giving Myra some space would be beneficial.

"Fine," Aelec grunted, "I'll room with Golath and Riza. Keep your terminuses active and be alert. Check in at the top of every hour. We'll meet out front by oh-five-thirty."

With that, they split into trios and entered their respective hotel suites. Her boots brushed against the velvet carpet, its burgundy color making her eyes hurt. Three retractable beds extended from the beige-colored wall on the right side, the sheets were as white as those from a hospital bed.

The low *hum* of gravlifts brought Riza's attention to a tall device on the left wall. That distinct sound brought her back to her time in the Academy's dorms. It was a gravdresser—a device that would automatically unpack all of their belongings and sort them for use. Riza felt a pang of excitement—she hadn't realized how much she missed having one of these.

Near the gravdresser was an expansive viewport, allowing her to watch the sapphire planet rotating below. Sunlight made the planet shine, casting a cerulean light into their suite.

After setting up their cargocases in the gravdresser, Riza used her terminus to remotely hack into the docking arm's camera system and cycled through until she found the *Erinyes*. Once the link was secured and anonymous, she sent the feed to Aelec, Dylis, and Myra's individual terminuses.

When Aelec left to meet one of the station's officials, Riza went into the suite's washroom to freshen up. An hour later, Aelec returned from his meeting; he'd bribed the official to ensure the *Erinyes* didn't suffer any complications. To her surprise, he came bearing a few cartons of takeout.

Opening hers, Riza was surprised to see that Aelec had gotten her a traditional Seraphian brisket and eggs. She smiled broadly, her mouth watering at the shredded vankir beef and poached eggs. The sweet and salty smell made her feel like she was back home.

They ate in silence, the tension of Myra's argument still lingering in the air. When the meal was over, Aelec was quick to coordinate a watch cycle between the six of them. Rant would remain on alert the entire night and keep his scanners active between both suites. Aelec wasn't taking any chances.

Riza had to admit that despite the dire situation, she felt safe because of Aelec's efforts.

Golath soon drifted off to sleep, and Aelec volunteered to stay up so that she could do the same. Riza changed into her nightwear which was nothing more than some high, mesh-fiber shorts and a tank top.

Washing off her makeup, Riza put her dark hair into a ponytail and exited the washroom. Slipping under the covers of the farthest bed, she tried to doze off, but her mind continued to churn. Unable to sleep, she sat up and looked to the expansive viewport, her eyes gazing out at the planet below.

"Can't sleep?" Aelec asked after a few moments.

Riza turned to look at him. He was similarly dressed down, the dim lighting of the suite accentuating the shadows along his gray shirt, emphasizing his musculature. His firm chest expanded outward with every breath, and his biceps bulged as he crossed his arms.

She averted her eyes, trying not to make it obvious that she'd been staring. Her feelings for Aelec were still muddled. For two years she thought he was the man who murdered her sister, Arenia, and it had only been a few weeks since he'd proven his innocence. Aelec was a good man, yet she had her reservations.

Could she ever move past those early preconceptions? If they grew closer, would she and Aelec actually work together?

"Yeah," she replied softly, looking away from him. "I'm still wired from the last few hours. You know, with the ship almost exploding, on the radar of the Comitors again, and Myra's whole thing. I probably won't sleep until we're back in voidstream."

Aelec paused for a moment, then grunted, "I'm sorry about Myra. She's got a lot of baggage from her time under Sire Dalin."

"If I could go back and undo what I did, I would," Riza admitted, bowing her head. "I didn't have many friends in the Academy, and my home life was... difficult. Arenia always caused unrest and division. Of course I still loved her, but there was always a rift between us. But with you guys, I felt like I was actually part of something. A family that got along. It's why I want to stay."

"This is your second chance, Riza. This is our clan. As long as you're loyal, you have nothing to fear."

She nodded. "Did I mention that it was such a stupid plan? Trying to capture an ex-Outrider with his crew still in the system? I should've looked at the bigger picture. I got blinded by my need for justice."

A hand gently rested on her shoulder, and her breath caught in her chest. Glancing up, she realized that Aelec was right next to her. Though his marble-like face was as stoic as ever, she saw a glint of compassion in his bright, aureate eyes.

"It happens to the best of us," he said. "Everyone gets that void-tunnel vision when it comes to our needs. It's what reminds me that I'm still human. As it should you."

Aelec snorted in amusement, continuing, "And if it's any consolation, I did the same thing. I was so blinded by wanting the truth that I broke into the securest place in the Fringe, owned by the worst people in the galaxy. Now that sounds insane when you think about it."

Riza laughed quietly, trying not to disturb Golath from his slumber. She met Aelec's gaze and found the warmth of his hand on her bare shoulder as comfortable as if she was curled up next to a fireplace. His mere presence helped her relax now that there weren't any secrets of identity between them. Riza could be herself, as could Aelec.

Aelec let go of her shoulder and returned to his perch, pulling up the hologram footage of the *Erinyes*. Riza managed to drift off as she stared out into the void of space, only to be awoken a few hours later by Aelec's gentle touch.

"It's oh-five-hundred," he said softly. "Get dressed and grab your things."

Riza blinked away her grogginess, and she realized that Aelec had let her sleep through the remainder of the GST night cycle. She wouldn't complain. Once they were all packed, they regrouped with the others outside the suite and made one last survey of the *Erinyes*.

While the ship was intact and most of the major damage was repaired, it looked like it was fixed with scrap parts. The holes were plugged with bulky, domed pieces that looked like barnacles. Various missing panels disrupted the sleek black and chrome color of the *Erinyes*. Riza wasn't a mechanic, but this was a shoddy repair job.

"Those slim-shelled assholes!" Myra seethed, baring her sharp canines. "Sixty thousand fuses for that?! Oh they are so lucky we're in a rush to get out of here."

"We'll get a refund later," Aelec said.

"Speaking of getting out of here," Dylis said with a yawn. "Any word on the Comitors?"

Aelec looked to Riza, and she swiped through the screens of her terminus to view the other docking arm cameras.

"Only two new ships docked since we've been here," she announced, pausing on one of the feeds. "First one arrived thirty minutes after us. It's an S-twenty-four asteroid hauler. I doubt that's carrying any Comitors."

She swiped the screen and continued, "The second one arrived an hour ago. TX-eleven gunship. She's docked in sector fifty-one."

"That's on the other side of the station," Myra declared, her eyes darting around. "If they landed an hour ago, they'll be upon us soon."

"Then let's hustle!" Aelec ordered, his pace quickening.

None of them offered protest, their walking speed increased enough to remain inconspicuous. The urgency to leave was still present but running headlong into a possible ambush wouldn't be smart. Instead, their pace was fast enough to get them to the *Erinyes* quickly while still being able to keep an eye out for suspicious activity. Working in the Fringe for so long was bound to make you extra cautious.

Her eyes constantly darted around as she walked, looking for the slightest flinch or dirty look from one of the bystanders. The Togrians gave scathing looks whenever Golath passed by, adding to her worry.

What would happen if a group of Togrians decided to impair them? It was their space station, so they could do whatever they wanted. There were no Imperium security guards, no C.B.I. agents, and no Veriti here.

Riza held her breath in anticipation as they reached the entrance connecting the main hub to the docking arm. No one in the crowd made a move against them. They didn't have much further to go. Just a bit more...

"Six o'clock," Dylis whispered, keeping his gaze ahead. "Three guards have been following us since the hotel. Let's pick this up."

"Togrians?" Aelec asked, hardly glancing at Dylis.

"Yeah. Station security. We could take 'em, but I doubt that would go over well with the higher ups."

This was going to be a close call. If the Togrian security caught up to them, they couldn't fight back without bringing the entire station down upon them. But they couldn't just let the Togrians arrest them on some trumped-up charges and deliver them to the Comitors. An idea sparked in Riza's mind.

"Once we get through the next sector, prepare to run," she said, pulling up a display on her terminus. "I'm going to seal off the sector behind us. I'll change the unlocking sequence, which should buy us a few minutes."

Aelec turned his head just slightly to look back at her and asked, "You can do that?"

Riza nodded. "Isn't this what you hired me for?"

Aelec's eyes widened by a fraction; he was clearly taken aback by Riza's initiative. He raised his eyebrows, and he looked impressed with her plan. Dylis and Golath similarly offered no qualms. Myra, however, narrowed her eyes.

"Don't screw it up," the Vitrax hissed.

A flash of anger surged within Riza, and she had to resist snapping back at Myra. No, she had to be the bigger person. If Myra doubted Riza's abilities, then it was her duty to prove the Vitrax wrong.

Making some adjustments on the holographic screen, Riza kept her finger over the necessary holokey as the crew stepped through the threshold that separated each sector of the docking arm. Once clear, Riza pressed the holokey.

An alarm blared and the hallways lights turned red as the blastdoors sealed with a loud *hiss*. A few small crowds on their side of the blastdoors cried out in confusion, some rushing towards the doors while others tried to call the station's services.

"Go!" Aelec called.

The crew rushed down the corridor and approached the umbilical linking the station to the *Erinyes'* boarding ramp. Unsealing the blastdoors, they went one by one into the connecting tunnel. Myra dashed in first followed by Rant and Golath. Riza took a step forward but hesitated. The same mechanical *hiss* came from back the way they'd came.

The blastdoors were already unsealing. The Togrian security guards stormed into their sector. They carried rifles with long, rectangular barrels that were at least a meter long. An angry, orange glow emanated from the ends of the barrels, the metallic pieces separating slightly as they prepared to fire.

"Halt, humans!" bellowed one of the Togrians, his voice rumbling like thunder.

"Oh shit!" Dylis groaned, raising his fist towards the Togrians. "Plasma carbines!"

"Haven't seen those in a while!" Aelec said, similarly raising a fist.

Simultaneously, the pair harnessed portions of their nanotech to form tall shields. A bombastic *thud* came from the Togrian carbines as they discharged. Orange light flashed from behind the nanoshields. Sparks erupted from the impact; the Outriders took a faltering step backward.

Her jaw dropped at the sight. Shaking off her shock, Riza hauled her cargocase back into the ship as Aelec and Dylis backed into the connecting umbilical. They kept their nanoshields active until they got into the *Erinyes* proper, the boarding ramp sealing tightly behind them.

"*Boss!*" Myra's voice called through the commlink. "*Get your ass up here!*"

The nanoshield melted back into his arm, and Aelec dashed through the winding corridors of the ship. Riza and Dylis rushed to the main hold, strapping themselves into the necessary seats. The ship rumbled beneath her feet. Golath pulled multiple belts to keep himself in his seat, and Rant clung to one of the cafeteria tables.

The ship lurched just as Riza fastened her safety strap. The familiar whine emanated from the engine room as the voidstream drive came to life, and she felt her breath catch in her chest. She thought she heard a flutter in the charging sequence. A spike of anxiety stabbed into her.

It didn't matter. Within a few moments, the voidstream drive was fully charged and Myra announced that they were clear of the space station. Riza forced herself to breathe through the tightness in her chest. She closed her eyes, and the *Erinyes* entered the void between worlds.

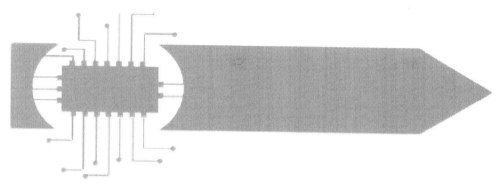

CHAPTER 7

A elec leaned back against the headrest of his seat and let out a prolonged sigh. The tunnel of gyrating light greeted his vision, the swirling colors of blue, white, and violet forming a tempest beyond the viewport. While the notion of the *Erinyes* breaking apart in voidstream still haunted him, the muscles in his shoulders relaxed and the tenseness in his neck abated. They were safe, for now.

Still leaning against the headrest, Aelec stared up at the cockpit's ceiling as the thrill of the chase abated. It had been a long time since they'd suffered so many problems all at once; even the Golden Spire heist hadn't been this stressful. The near loss of the *Erinyes* was a sobering reminder that if they were stranded out in the Fringe, it wouldn't be long before the Comitors found them.

It felt like they were being hemmed into a corner. They couldn't run much further out here in the Fringe.

He glanced over at the panels next to him, each separated by function, making it easier to identify issues with the ship's integrity. Various holographic bars indicated shield readouts, power distribution, fuel levels, and hull integrity.

Scanning each display, Aelec saw just how shoddy of a job the Togrians had provided. Their fusion levels were barely at *50%*, and engine power was fluctuating between *70%* and *80%*, meaning that the ship had only three days' worth of travel. Checking the gravlift readouts, Aelec saw that four of them were still inoperable, which left only six available for stabilizing their takeoff sequence. It wasn't as noticeable while in space, but once inside an atmosphere they'd have a difficult time getting the *Erinyes* airborne.

The voidstream drive was functional, but the quantum field generator was missing calculations every thirty seconds. It wasn't enough to drop them out of the voidstream tunnel, but if it continued missing the calculations, the system might rewire itself to accept the missing variables. That would risk sending them into another dimension of spacetime.

In short, they were screwed once they hit atmosphere. They needed to find somewhere accommodating to land and get the ship properly fixed without the threat of Comitors on their tail. That meant getting the Void out of the Fringe Territories.

It meant returning to the Capital Worlds—to the Imperium.

Aelec felt a profound sense of melancholy as he made the realization. Over two years had passed since he'd been in the Capital Worlds, and while it was his home, he felt like a stranger returning to the refined part of the galaxy. For so long he'd been used to the chaotic rules of the Fringe; stealing for a living, killing without repercussions, and flying wherever they wanted. If they returned to the Imperium, they'd have to adapt to the rules.

He, Dylis, and Riza wouldn't have much difficulty doing so, but Myra's carefree attitude and Golath's quirkiness might not mesh well with the stringent societies in the Imperium. Still, they would be accepted as equal citizens due to the reformed culture, and they'd have no fear of falling into the hands of an alien-sire.

The only problem Aelec could foresee was having the funds to pay for repairs. Repair costs on a Capital World would be exponentially higher than those on Tog. Stealing wasn't an option. Neither was smuggling. Mercenary work was rare but not impossible in the Imperium.

Aelec was getting ahead of himself. First they had to settle on a Capital World, then they could figure out what to do for work.

Myra's voice roused him from his musings. "Our voidstream trajectory is all over the place, Aelec," she said. "We need a destination, and soon. I don't want to waste fuel."

"Set a course for the Picon system," Aelec ordered, making a snap decision. "If we're going to drop out of voidstream, it may as well be in the Capital Worlds."

Myra arched a hairless eyebrow at him and asked, "Why not Khorrus? It's closer."

Rubbing his neck, Aelec answered, "Because I don't want us getting stuck there. We're down to six gravlifts and the voidstream drive is going to need a matrix overhaul. The Comitors still have free reign in the Niramis system, and I bet they'd be on our asses in a day or two."

"Fair point," she said, rocking her head from side to side. "I'll set the autopilot for the Picon system, but we need to settle on a planet within the next hour. I don't want to cause added strain to the voidstream drive by changing trajectories at the last minute."

"Agreed," Aelec affirmed, activating the commlink. Clearing his throat, he spoke into the speaker, "We're stabilized for now, folks. Crew meeting in the main hold."

Unbuckling themselves from the chairs, Aelec and Myra followed the winding corridor from the cockpit to the main hold. Once the others gathered, he cleared his throat.

"Alright," Aelec grunted as he stood at the center of the main hold. "Good news and bad news. Again."

Lounging on the couch with one leg crossed over the other, Dylis groaned, "Here we go." He leaned his head back against the couch.

Riza paced anxiously near the central hologram, but remained silent.

71

"Bad news first," Myra said, crossing her arms. "The *Erinyes* only has enough fuel and power to make a three-day flight."

"Translation: And the good news?" Rant said for Golath, the former skittering around the cafeteria table while the latter perched on the bench seat.

"The ship will hold together," Aelec said, though he wasn't entirely sure if it was the truth. "But in order to ensure that it does, we need to settle on a destination. And fast. We're presently aiming for the Picon system."

Rant perked up, his domed head swiveling as he said, "Analysis: Picon system. Six point five lightyears away from our current position in the Aeron system. Less than one lightyear between its two inhabited planets: Oais and Nidal."

Dylis shifted in his seat and said, "It's been a while since I was on Nidal. Last time I was there was when the Anti-Imperium League was still a thing."

Aelec nodded in understanding. Ten years ago, a small terrorist faction known as the Anti-Imperium League rose to prominence on Nidal, seeking to secede from the galactic governance. Naturally, Nidal was quarantined, Outriders were deployed, and a manhunt began for the terrorist leaders.

"That said," Dylis continued, "Nidal is a prime resort location, and prone to a lot of holonet media coverage. If we're still trying to remain anonymous, it might not be a great idea to go there."

"Dylis is right," Riza added. "There's no way we can get to Seraphi? I'm sure my family would be happy to help us out."

Aelec shook his head; curtains of platinum hair draped around his face. "The Sigma system is an extra day's flight that we won't have enough fuel for. Our options are either Nidal or Oais. And since you've made a strong case against Nidal, it'll have to be Oais."

"Oais," Myra repeated, tapping a finger against her round chin. "It's another educational planet, right?"

"Mostly," Aelec affirmed. "It's a full ecumen with other infra-structures, though it's primarily where our business owners, tech developers, engineers, and politicians go to school. There's no shortage of dockyards, if that's what you're asking."

"Tons of nonhuman businesses, too," Dylis said, raising a finger. "When I was stationed in Iridium Point, the entire Starlane Express office was run by a Vitrax fellow. A bunch of his employees were secretly S.R.A. terrorists, but still."

Myra's violet eyes widened in intrigued curiosity. "That's refreshing to hear." She paused, glancing at Aelec before saying, "Hold up. I've seen you repeatedly make transmissions to Oais. Usually, every time we end a job."

Aelec didn't want to respond, but the other members of the crew leaned forward with keen interest, expecting him to explain. Well, they'd find out eventually anyways.

"My old Imperium contact is on Oais," Aelec explained. "She's the one that repeatedly expunges our faces from the holonet. I haven't seen her in person in years, but she's Voiddamn reliable. She's also our ticket to Markum."

A hush fell over the crew. Golath tilted his head to the side, confused clicks emitting from his respirator. Now that they had the chain code from the *I.S.S. Carthage*, Aelec needed to explain the next part of their plan.

"That chain code from the *Carthage* means we now possess legitimate Imperium access to some of the most secure facilities in the galaxy," Aelec explained, pacing with his arms clasped behind his back. "Places like the Wasp Nest. If we can get Kuvan to seek sanctuary there, we'll have VIP access to pay him a visit."

He paused for emphasis. The Wasp Nest was a military stronghold on the planet Markum, a main proponent in the Imperium armada. It was a place where High Chancellors and Veriti could retreat to when threatened.

"However," Aelec continued, "the code is only a small part of the plan to infiltrate Markum. If the Imperium armada sees a ship like ours using it, they'll know we're phonies. Therefore, we need an Imperium-sanctioned ship to get us to the Wasp Nest."

Riza sat on the edge of the hologram projector and asked, "So, what's the plan?"

"This Imperium ship also needs to have a clean trail," Aelec said. "The new plan is to have my Imperium contact charter us a legitimate ship from Oais to Markum, once she's scrubbed our faces from the holonet again."

"And once we reach Markum?" Myra asked, concern evident on her pink face.

"One plan at a time," Aelec replied, "Before we can strategize our play against Kuvan, we need to have that ship ready. Else we won't be going anywhere near him."

Dylis frowned. "Are you sure your contact is willing to lend us a ship of that caliber?"

"For enough fuses, yes," Aelec answered with a nod. "I can pay what I have left to get our IDs purged, but we're going to need a lot of fuses to get a ship like that. Since we can't steal from the scumbags like we used to, we need to come up with alternative sources of income."

"Why don't we just steal from Kuvan?" Myra asked. "Destroy two asteroids with one blast."

Aelec rubbed his forehead and said, "The idea is to keep a low profile before we attempt the Wasp Nest heist. If we steal from our target, he'll get the entire armada to hunt us down, and I'd rather only be hunted in the Fringe right now."

"So, what can we do for money?"

"I can get us lined up as Private Security Contractors," Dylis announced, pointing to himself, Aelec, and Golath. "We've all got combat experience, and there should be no shortage of protection jobs."

Riza perked up, raising her hand and saying, "I can do some commission work for SunTech. Last time I checked, they had five openings for terminus programmers."

Aelec gave her a soft grin. He appreciated her initiative, and she was trying to stick with her skills rather than applying for something she was not. These moments of genuine honesty made Aelec appreciate Riza's presence more and more.

Myra sighed and tilted her head to one side. "Fine. I'll figure something out once we get there. But everyone pulls their weight in this. No exceptions!"

"Agreed," Aelec acknowledged, clasping his hands together. "Then it's settled. Everyone applies for temporary work once we touch down on Oais. I'll send a transmission to my contact to make sure we're clear. Dismissed."

Parting ways, the group left Aelec alone at the hologram terminal. After the thrill of the last few days, Aelec was willing to give them some much-needed downtime before they exited voidstream.

Typing in the codes for the secure transmission channel, Aelec opened the instant messaging chat that linked to his contact on Oais. The feed showed she was offline, but that didn't stop him. His fingers typed slowly; Aelec wasn't as tech savvy as Riza or Myra when it came to typing in Trade.

Once finished, he closed the transmission channel and stood from the leather couch. He'd give it a few hours before checking to see if his contact had responded. Usually, she would reply within two hours of receiving the message. Until then, he needed to find a way to unwind.

Aelec's bare fist connected with the burnished wood of his target, sending a vibration up his arm. A mild tingling came from his knuckles. The calloused skin had grown accustomed to such strikes after years of practice. He pulled his punches so the wood wouldn't break. It was also useful for keeping his fist accustomed to physical contact.

Inside the *Erinyes'* armory, Aelec sparred with a training droid in the back section of the long, rectangular room. This sparring section wasn't as large as the arenas of Morrigar, but it was enough.

His bare feet quickly swept across the mat-covered floor. The sparring droid raised its arms—the dim, blue light emphasized the dark grooves in its wood coatings.

The droid threw a wide hook at his head, forcing him to duck and weave. Springing up, Aelec jabbed the droid's face twice before hopping backward. Keeping his arms raised and his hands close to his face, Aelec waited. The wood-covered machine moved slowly, bringing its arms up for defense. Cold air from the vents tickled his sweaty skin.

He'd purchased the sparring droid from a martial arts shop on Khorrus during their last visit in the hopes of sharpening their skills. It had been good physical therapy for Dylis after suffering damage from the attack on Asmodum. More importantly, it had been a good method of allowing Riza to learn the basics of hand-to-hand combat.

While Riza excelled at her job as a technician and hacker, Aelec wanted her to be ready for anything. It reassured him to know that she was taking the first steps towards being proficient with E-pistols and self-defense.

For now, he was alone on the sparring mat—wearing nothing more than a sleeveless gray shirt and loose, black shorts. Sweat glistened along his olive skin, highlighting the lines of his muscled arms.

The droid jabbed forward. Aelec stepped off to the left, and smacked its wooden arm aside. His fist connected with its head again. He pivoted behind the droid, raising his arms defensively. Blood thundered in his head, his vision fixing on his foe. He wanted to see how long he could go before performing a takedown.

Minutes passed as he continued the sparring session; his sterling hair plastered to his face. When he finally had enough, Aelec waited for the droid to lunge before stepping into the attack—meeting its arms before they could gain enough momentum. Hooking his leg behind its knee joint, he pressed his palm into the droid's face and pushed. It bent backwards, Aelec swept its leg and pinned it to the floor.

Remaining in the kneeling position, Aelec slowed his breathing as the droid relinquished its combat parameters. His heart hammered for a few beats and then slowed. Standing away from the droid, he allowed it to rise and return to its original perch. He ran his forearm across his brow, wiping away some of the sweat.

A slow clap emanated from behind him, and he spun on his heels.

Riza stood a few paces away, her pale arms sticking out from a loose, sleeveless shirt. She tapped her bare feet against the indigo mat, arching an eyebrow as she surveyed him with bright, sapphire eyes—eyes clear of makeup.

"I know better than to go toe-to-toe with an Outrider," she said, stepping closer. "Hence why I'd just pull an E-pistol on you."

"Correction, you already did that," Aelec snorted, grinning at her.

Riza scowled. "Keep holding that over my head, why don't you," she said.

"I plan to. It's only been three weeks. You're far from being off the hook."

"Well darn. Guess I'll just have to stick around until it wears off. I'm getting quite fond of this side of my captain."

My captain. Aelec went rigid. Voiddamn was Riza good at catching him off-guard.

As Riza stepped closer, her fitted dark pants emphasized the sway of her hips. She raised her arms into a stretch, and her shirt was pulled tight enough to show the neon green sports bra beneath. Aelec quickly averted his gaze, running his fingers through his sweaty hair. The temperature seemed to increase by a few degrees as he stood there, or was that just him?

"Would you be a dear and set Sparman to level five?" she asked sweetly.

Aelec chuckled, approaching the droid and adjusting its settings from *Level 20* to *Level 5*. Stepping away, he watched as Riza continued to stretch her arms and legs.

"The fact that you named him 'Sparman' is ridiculous," Aelec grunted in amusement.

Riza shrugged. "It's already a faceless opponent. I need some personality to go up against."

"You could always use Dylis as a punching bag," Aelec pointed out. "He's got plenty of personality."

"Again," Riza said, holding up a finger. "I know better than to spar with you Outriders. Plus, I don't want to give Dylis an excuse to put his paws on me."

"Fair," Aelec stated, "but Dylis is all talk. He'd never do anything."

"Yeah sure," Riza scoffed, shaking her arms and bouncing on the balls of her feet.

"Arms up," Aelec ordered as the droid stirred and marched onto the mat.

She quickly brought her fists up to protect her face as the droid sent a wide hook towards her head. Most of the blow hit her arm, but it was strong enough to knock her off balance and she stumbled away. Thanks to the lower combat setting, the droid paused, allowing her to recover before pursuing her.

As Riza raised her arms in a defensive stance, Aelec asked, "What should you do when your opponent is larger and stronger than you?"

When the droid was within a few steps from her, Riza kicked its knee joint.

"Target pressure points," she answered, huffing her breaths.

As the droid wobbled, she jabbed at the spot where its shoulder connected to the chassis. A wooden *thud* resounded. She weaved and punched at its elbow joint. Riza struck fast and light, her knuckles were still unused to physical contact. In a real fight, she'd need to dig into those pressure points for the technique to work.

Aelec watched her closely, analytically. Her arms snapped

forward when she punched. Yet, her stance was off—her feet weren't planted. Aelec remained silent. Sometimes the best teacher was learning the hard way.

Sure enough, when Riza punched the droid's chest, the force pushed her backward. The droid took a step forward, delivered a jab, and caught Riza in the stomach—throwing her to the mat.

The droid stopped moving and stood at attention as Riza curled up on the ground, groaning from the impact.

"Oww," she moaned, holding her stomach. "My guts feel like they've been blended."

"It'll pass," Aelec said, walking over to her. "Getting hit is a good thing. It conditions your body. Better here than out in some alley on Asmodum."

"Ugh, if you say so, boss," Riza mumbled, rolling onto her back. "You sure that's not just from your special Outrider skin?"

He grinned, extending a hand which Riza promptly clasped. Gently, Aelec pulled her to her feet, his free hand on the small of her back kept her steady. Mere centimeters separated them as he held on to her for a moment longer than he should've. Riza didn't shy away—he could feel her soft breaths against his exposed skin.

Both of them were covered in sweat, and the heat radiating between their bodies could spark a fire. His head buzzed at the smell of her perfume, floral and heady, goading a familiar hunger to rise in his gut. Aelec pushed it back down, burying it beneath cordiality.

To his surprise, Riza was the first to break their embrace—patting his arm and giving him a thankful smile. A sigh of relief escaped him. Was it relief? His arms felt empty, and he already missed her, even though she was just out of reach.

He cleared his throat and said, "You've improved since last time. Practicing on your own time?"

"A bit," she responded, rubbing her stomach. "I'll sneak in here when most of you are asleep. I'm just glad the armory wasn't torn open in the space battle. Losing Sparman would be a Voiddamn shame."

"Well, Sparman is going to give you a run for your fuses at higher levels," Aelec said, crossing his arms. "Especially if you don't plant your feet."

Riza frowned. "I thought you said I should be quick on my feet."

"I did," he admitted, raising a finger. "But when you throw a punch, the power comes from your hips, and you need firm footing to keep yourself from losing balance."

Dropping into stance, he shifted his weight from one leg to the other. Rotating his shoulders, Aelec raised his arms and stepped forward. The second his feet were planted firmly, he threw a jab and then snapped his arm back to a defensive posture, his weight shifting again.

"Think of it as a striking snake," Aelec explained. "The snake spends a few seconds rearing its head back in preparation, and when the timing is perfect it lunges forward to bite. The bite itself is barely a millisecond, and then the snake recoils."

Riza nodded and glanced at her hand, saying, "Okay. So, something like this?"

Bouncing from foot to foot, Riza quickly set her balance and threw a jab aimed at Aelec's chest. Aelec moved by instinct, his training taking over in response to a perceived threat.

Stepping to his left, Aelec brushed aside the incoming fist with a soft tap from his open palm. Pivoting, Aelec went into stance and was about to throw a counterstrike when he hesitated. He saw the playful twinkle in Riza's eyes vanish. Regret swelled in his chest as he breathed deeply.

It's just Riza, he reminded himself. *Just a playful jab.*

Her blue eyes widened with a mix of confusion and apprehension.

"Sorry," she whispered, moving to a normal stance. "I was just messing around."

Aelec waved his hand, saying, "Don't apologize. It's a reflex. You just surprised me."

Riza tilted her head slightly and pursed her lips, eyes boring into him with a skeptical gaze. Aelec felt her gaze peering right through him, breaking down his walls of gruff stoicism. He didn't mind being open with her, but he still felt uncomfortable when they got too close. When he showed vulnerability.

Backing away from her, he scratched the back of his neck and said, "On that note, I need to wash up and get some sleep. It's been a long day."

A frown tugged at the corners of her full lips, but she nodded. "I'm going to get some more practice in," she declared. "Gotta work off this restlessness."

"I'll leave you to it," Aelec said, turning from her. "Goodnight, Riza."

"Goodnight, Aelec."

Walking to the circular doorframe of the armory, Aelec paused for a heartbeat and glanced over his shoulder. Riza was already sparring with the training droid, her ponytail whipping back and forth as she moved. Soft huffs emanated from her as she jabbed at the wood coatings, creating a chorus of martial music.

Once again, he cursed himself. Riza was gorgeous, intelligent, and compassionate. So why did he have such difficulty in expressing himself to her? He stepped out into the winding corridor as he followed that train of thought.

It was because he was afraid. Afraid of screwing things up, afraid of losing all he'd worked for. Riza was a valued member of the crew, their hacker who could break any digital code. She rounded out the skills of the *Erinyes'* crew.

That's surface level, you idiot, a familiar voice said. Hagen, one of his closest friends in clan-Xero. Somehow, the words themselves were familiar. Even in death, he still hounded Aelec.

Dig deeper, why are you so hesitant?

Aelec knew. It was because he felt unworthy. He was an

81

Outrider, a man bred and built for war. Deep down, he didn't know if he deserved a woman's love. For years he'd battled and killed, oftentimes relishing in the thrill of the mission. Aelec feared that he might never be rid of his need for that thrill. Who could ever look past that and accept what he'd been?

What he still was.

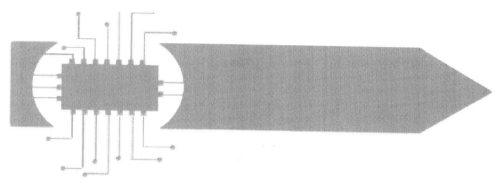

CHAPTER 8

When it came to dealing with inner turmoil, Aelec found solace in his memories. Many people avoided their pasts, but he felt comfortable reliving the nostalgia. If you used a mod-pill, you could see your memories as vividly as if they were a holonet film.

As his mind grew fuzzy and exhaustion tugged at his body, Aelec felt the mod-pill's effects. Lethargy kept him rooted, and his eyes grew heavy, though his cognitive abilities increased tenfold. It was like the pill took energy from his body and transferred it to his brain.

Aelec had grown so accustomed to taking nightly mod-pills that it was routine at this point. Many would see it as an over-reliance, but Aelec saw it as his way of destressing at the end of each day. Perhaps one day he'd be rid of them.

Sitting at his desk in the dark dormitory, Aelec pressed his head against the back of his chair, his eyes closing. Memories flashed by in incredible detail like a sizzle reel. For the past few weeks, he'd been reminiscing about his days in the Imperium, now that he'd gotten closure from his final mission.

But if those memories were now as free as a morcat running across the savannah, other ones felt like they were trapped in a cage. Plenty of other recollections were clawing to get out.

Dread nagged at the back of his mind as he thought about the delayed reply from his Imperium contact. She'd never taken this long to reply to him, and he got the distinct feeling that something was wrong. All the more reason to return to Oais.

Thinking about both Oais and his contact caused him to remember in vivid detail the events that transpired around their first meeting. Distinct smells and sounds triggered his senses as he fell into the memory; the rumble of thunder, the patter of rain, and the smell of wet carbocrete.

4503.0314 / CW Star System: Picon / Planet: Oais / GST: 17:44

SIX YEARS AGO

Rain fell in sheets like a tapestry of rippling water as Aelec's eyes scanned the neon lights of the expansive city below. He gripped the railing above him, his hand practically magnetized to it. Light vibrations emanated below his feet as the gunship hovered in wait. His heart hammered in his chest, mixing with the chorus of pattering rain and humming gravlifts.

Aelec breathed deeply. He focused on the downpour just beyond the gunship's open bay, wishing he could retract his narrow helm to feel the cold rain on his face. It was a strangely soothing thought that eased his heart-rate.

The clear visor was faintly outlined by holographic data, and if he gave a mental command the heads-up-display would focus on what he wanted. Fixing his attention on the street below, his optics magnified the area as if he was standing just a few meters above it rather than a kilometer.

Between the six-story residential buildings was a wide street of dark carbocrete painted with neon yellow street markers. Clusters of abandoned gravvehicles blocked portions of the street—some deliberately placed there as makeshift barricades. Among the neon LEDs came other forms of illumination: streaks of amber energy, flashes of sparks, and raging light from fires.

The tenseness left his shoulders as he analyzed the enemy numbers, tactics, placement, and armaments. Knowing what to prepare for helped calm his nerves. Despite performing dozens of insertions like this, he always feared for the safety of his squad. As a sub-squad commander for clan-Xero, Aelec had to keep the odds in favor of him and his nine subordinates.

Scanning the street, his HUD determined that there were eighteen hostiles spread out along the street as it headed east into the residential district. Most were taking cover behind disabled gravvehicles, but four were hiding out inside one of the residential buildings.

Damn, he thought. *That means we need to watch for civilian casualties and hostages.*

Fusion fire erupted from the west side, and Aelec noticed three standard Imperium gravtanks lumbering over the disabled vehicles. The tanks' cannons arched from the rear like that of a scorpion's stinger, and amber light blasted from the tips. He could hear the rumble of cannonfire, even from this altitude.

A gravvehicle exploded from the fusion blasts, but the terrorists didn't back down from their barricades. While the gravtanks were relatively unstoppable in the face of poorly armed terrorists, their size and speed prevented them from responding quickly. Already the terrorists had occupied parts of the district before the tanks were even streetside, and the initial police force was defeated spectacularly.

It was one of many attacks across the ecumen of Oais. Veritas

Nova had called in the Outriders to help defeat the terrorists—a faction referred to as the Sol's Resistance Army—but even they were having difficulty squashing this insurrection. Targeting a densely populated planet such as Oais made open warfare an impossibility, so the Outriders had to adjust their tactics.

From what he knew, the S.R.A. was trying to indoctrinate citizens with the more archaic beliefs of the Fringe Territories. Extortion, kidnapping, arson, slavery—all the barbaric customs that the syndicates practiced, and the Imperium would not tolerate this. When attempts at negotiation failed, the S.R.A. began openly attacking sectors across the planet, thus prompting a military response.

Aelec's HUD indicated that the terrorists below were entirely focused on the incoming gravtanks, leaving them prime targets from an attack from above. Since the close-set buildings were difficult for gunships to maneuver between, it left one option available.

"Sync HUDs," he ordered, keeping his attention focused on the area below. "Target dropzone is marked. Keep a tight formation."

"Yes sir!" a chorus echoed; their voices tinged with metallic resonance.

"Jumping into the Void again, clan-Xero!" came Hagen's voice.

"Ooh rah!" cheered Ida.

He grinned inside his helmet. The voices of his friends, particularly Ida, always calmed his mind before these skydrops. Confidence surged within him like a growing tempest, yearning to join the rainstorm beyond.

"With me!" Aelec shouted over the howl of the wind as he leaped out of the cabin and dropped into the city below.

Within seconds, Aelec had to use his suit's gravlifts to weave away from the towering skyscrapers. Rainwater splashed against his faceplate as he cut through the downpour, streaking like one of the droplets descending from the heavens. Wind whistled around him as he snapped his arms close to his sides. His eyes squinted in response to the neon lights shining with blinding intensity through the wall of rain.

Navigation data from his HUD told him how much gravlift thrust was needed to arc his trajectory. The motion tracker showed that his nine squad mates were right behind him. Passing by the nearest skyscraper, they swung to the east. He felt the pulse of his gravlifts as they helped guide his fall. His display indicated only four hundred meters remained before they made impact.

Almost there, he mused, narrowing his eyes.

Some of the terrorists below finally noticed the incoming skydrop, turning their weapons skyward to blast the Outriders.

At the last moment, Aelec flipped to allow his boot gravlifts to halt his momentum and he landed on the carbocrete in a crouch. Amber light from E-weapons flashed around him, forcing him to create a nanoshield on his left arm. Thuds of metal on carbocrete reverberated around him as his squad landed in similar poses, each one creating shields to deflect incoming fire.

Behind enemy lines, the Outriders began tearing through the meager defenses; members of his squad leaped through the air to flank each S.R.A. cluster. Pulsecannons blasted apart their turrets, E-pistols dispersed them, and nanoblades cut them down.

This was what Outriders were for: quick insertions to disrupt the enemy defenses. In a normal battle, they would pull back to safety once they disabled key targets, but here with only a few enemies to face, they could end the skirmish single-handedly. A single nanotech-armored Outrider was said to equal the might of fifty men, giving them their reputation as machines of war.

Boosting with his gravlift thrusters, Aelec blasted through the air and smashed into a terrorist—the impact forced him into the side of a gravvehicle. A bony *crunch* erupted as his spine snapped like a twig. Twisting around, Aelec fired his E-pistol at another foe, the fusion bolt burning right through the terrorist's chest.

In a matter of minutes, the Outriders had broken the defenses of the S.R.A. and eliminated most of their soldiers. Aelec's HUD told him that there were still four hostiles left inside the nearest apartment building. Snapping his fingers, he summoned six of his squad to form a perimeter around the building's entrance before ordering three others to scale the structure.

Taking point, Aelec held his E-pistol at the ready and raised his nanoshield defensively as he stepped into the structure. The main doors had been blasted open, and he took slow steps over the various piles of rubble within the lobby. An angry red light pulsed from the lobby's emergency LEDs. Shadows in the room's corners were so dark that even his optics couldn't see past them.

Aelec focused on his motion tracker. Nothing pinged in this area, indicating that the lobby was clear of enemies. He signaled for Ida and Kadir to follow him in, leaving Hagen in command of the others as they quarantined the building.

Just as they entered, he heard the electronic thuds of E-weapon fire from above. Looking up, the HUD scanned and indicated that the discharges were coming from the third floor. Static crackled in his ear as his commlink came to life.

"Sir!" It was Eamon. "Four hostiles confirmed on the third floor. They've got hostages and are blockaded in the hallway. We don't have clean shots."

"What's their position?"

"East gravlift landing," Eamon answered. "They disabled the lift and positioned themselves to cover the hallway and stairwell."

"Damn!" he hissed. "You get a scan of the hostages?"

"Aye. Most are residents, but there are four Imperium reserves in the mix. They look pretty banged up."

Aelec paused to consider his next move. The terrorists were dug in like ticks, and they had leverage against the Outriders. They'd have to move quickly and precisely to get the hostages free without any casualties. An idea came to him.

"Keep their attention on you," Aelec ordered, holstering his E-pistol. "They don't know how many of us are here. When I give the command, fire at the ceiling above them."

Eamon hesitated before replying, "*Yes sir. We'll await your orders. Hurry!*"

Aelec turned his attention to Ida and Kadir. "You two, use the stairwell and take position outside the third-floor exit. On my command, you breach."

Ida cocked her helmeted head to one side. "Trident approach?"

Aelec nodded. "You get clean shots, you take them."

Ida and Kadir dashed towards the eastern stairwell as Aelec approached the disabled gravlift. Summoning his nanotech in both gauntlets, he formed twin, short nanoblades before stabbing them into the narrow crevasse between the lift's doors. The blades easily sank into the gap, and with the combined effort of his suit and enhanced strength, he pried the doors open.

The cylindrical shaft of the gravlift was wide enough to carry at least twelve people, and was similarly illuminated by deep, crimson lights. Devoid of the usual gravlift hum, the central platform remained inert as he stepped forward. Glancing up, Aelec saw the same metal doors leading to the third floor roughly twelve meters above him.

He couldn't use his gravlift thrusters, they'd be too loud. Nor could he magnetize his gauntlets. So, he shifted the nanoparticles into a grappling hook, and Aelec took careful aim at the wall directly above the door. He had to be precise, he couldn't risk alerting the terrorists on the other side.

His heart pounded in anticipation. This had to work.

Firing the device, the nanotech cable sped out from his wrist as the hook embedded neatly into the carbocrete above the door with a soft *thunk*. Aelec prayed that it hadn't been too loud. In a smooth motion, the grappling hook pulled him up the shaft until he was dangling just behind the third-floor door.

Aelec's body moved back and forth as he hung there, his other gauntlet shifting into the next device he'd need.

"*Sir, we're in position,*" Kadir's voice whispered over the comm-link. "*Ready on your mark.*"

"*As are we,*" said Eamon.

"Share your HUD visual, Eamon," Aelec declared quietly.

Eamon's feed blinked into Aelec's HUD. Ducking out from the corner of an apartment door, the HUD footage skimmed from Eamon's E-pistol gripped in his hand to a hallway. At the end of the hallway pulsed with a faint, blue energy shield separating the hall from the landing. Only two meters tall, the deployable shield was effective at covering in a tight space. Behind the shield were four men wearing shoddy combat suits and brandishing E-rifles, their faces obscured by masks.

Sitting on the floor with hands cuffed behind their backs were twelve individuals: six men, four women and two children. The casual shirts on six of the adults indicated they were civilians—as were the children—but three of the men and one woman wore the bulky gray armor of Imperium reserves. The bruises and cuts on their faces didn't look good, but they were clearly still alive.

Noting the positions, Aelec saw that the hostages were grouped in the landing's center, a meter from the gravlift door. Two terrorists were to the door's left guarding stairwell, one knelt behind the hallway energy shield, and the last kept his E-rifle on the hostages.

Aelec dismissed the feed with a mental command. He had his plan.

With a soft *hiss*, the nanoparticles on his right hand transformed into a bulky, rectangular device. Lines along the barrel glowed with an angry, orange hue. A plasma carbine. His suit could technically create most modern weapons, but the more exotic ones would drain its fuses faster than something like a pulsecannon. In this scenario, however, only the plasma carbine could get the job done.

Charging the plasma carbine, Aelec took deep, steady breaths as he prepared his move.

"On my mark," Aelec commanded. "Three. Two. One!"

A sizzling beam of orange energy erupted from the barrel as he pulled the trigger. Hitting the metal doors, the plasma melted them to slag in a matter of milliseconds. With his gravlift thrusters, Aelec soared out of the shaft and landed on the marble tiles of the landing just as a pulsecannon formed on his left arm.

More E-pistol shots streaked from the hallway as Eamon and his team fired at the ceiling above landing, creating a shower of sparks. A few meters away, Ida and Kadir breached the stairwell door and exchanged shots with the two terrorists. Cries of panic erupted from the hostages, fusion bolts flashed in the dim lighting, and the terrorist guarding them staggered.

Aelec moved as fast as the flaring lights. He fired the pulsecannon into the man's chest, the rippling wave sending him crashing into the nearby wall. The body crumpled to the marble floor in a heap. Two more *thuds* behind him indicated that the stairwell guards were eliminated. Spinning around, Aelec faced the last terrorist just as the man raised his rifle towards the hostages.

Aelec snapped his arm up as the pulsecannon thrummed.

A sonic *boom* emitted as the kinetic wave splashed into the terrorist, pushing him backward. The blast felt dimmer, weaker. The HUD beeped in alarm, the outline melding from blue to red. He was low on fuses, and the remaining quantum energy diverted into his armor. Adapting to the development, Aelec dashed forward just as the terrorist got his footing.

His armored hands closed like clamps on the man's E-rifle, he twisted it in a windmill motion, and ripped it from his grasp. A pulseknife spun in his other hand, but Aelec grasped his wrist, twisted with a flick of his hand, and broke the bones. His armored fist smashed the terrorist's face once, twice, three times—cracking his skull. His body went limp and toppled to the floor.

With the last S.R.A. member eliminated, Aelec surveyed the area, ensuring that each enemy was down. When he was satisfied, Aelec motioned for Ida to disable the shield generator while he dissipated his weapons and retracted his helmet.

Squatting down, Aelec began uncuffing the Imperium reserves while Kadir checked their vital signs. Eamon and the others joined them once the shield was down, and the Outriders reassured the hostages that they were safe. They'd need some time to let the shock fade away before ushering them down the stairs.

He disabled the binders on the final Imperium soldier—a pale-skinned woman with pixie cut black hair—and put a gauntleted hand on her upper back. The woman steadied her breathing, meeting his eyes.

It was hard to tell beneath the cuts and bruises, but Aelec surmised she was about his age. Dark blood ran from her nose and over her thin lips. A purple bruise surprisingly brought out the color of her ocean blue eyes.

He blinked, feeling a swell of awkwardness for staring at her. "You alright?"

The woman nodded. "Leave it to Veritas Nova to call in Outriders to deal with these S.R.A. assholes. Sol forbid he trust his reserves to get the job done."

Aelec snorted. "You're welcome, Miss..."

"*Missus* Spectre," she answered tersely. "Milli Spectre. What's your designation, Mister Outrider?"

"Name's Xero," he replied. "Aelec Xero. How'd you end up in this mess?"

"Oh, now you're debriefing me?" Milli rolled her eyes. "C'mon, this can wait until we're out of this Voiddamn apartment building."

"Sure. Though technically I'm a sub-squad commander, so I'm allowed to debrief you."

"Well, technically I'm in charge of these reserves, so I'm allowed to tell you to suck it."

Aelec let out a soft chuckle, and Milli's lips curled into a faint grin. Before Aelec could quip back at her, Milli's eyes widened in alarm, her vision glancing at something behind him.

His head snapped around, and saw the terrorist he'd pummeled rising to one knee and leveling a small E-pistol at the civilians. He tried to summon his nanoparticles, but his low fuses made the suit react slowly. The children shrieked in terror.

An electric *crack* echoed within the gravlift landing.

Just as Aelec's pulsecannon formed on his left hand, he noticed the smoldering spot on the terrorist's combat suit, just above his heart. The man teetered on one knee just before amber light flashed and a fusion bolt struck the same spot—fully burning through. A wheeze came from him, and he fell face first into the marble floor.

Aelec blinked in surprise as he turned his head back towards Milli. The Imperium trooper had her hand on his shoulder, using it to steady herself as she extended her other arm holding an E-pistol. Aelec's E-pistol.

She'd been so quick on the draw that he hadn't noticed the pistol had left his holster.

Impressive.

"Nice save," he murmured in appreciation. "Thanks."

"Don't mention it," Milli said, lowering the pistol and handing it back to him. "It's not every day I get to have an Outrider's back."

It was the first of many saves, on both their parts. The mod-pill's effects started tapering off, but Aelec managed to sift through a few more memories of him and Milli. Scenes of them being debriefed together, breaching S.R.A. hideouts, sharing meals, and being awarded medals passed by like swirling smoke.

Despite not being an Outrider, she'd had been a comrade-in-arms, watching his back and aiding his squad like a true member of clan-Xero. Their bond was deeper than that of lovers or friends—it was born out of respect, cultivated in battle.

Aelec would go months without talking to her, yet she always had his back when it came to clearing his holonet records. He owed Milli a few times over.

Honor compelled him to make good on that debt.

Dizziness greeted him as he came down from the high of the mod-pill. Aelec pinched the bridge of his nose and closed his eyes. Breathing in the crisp air of the dorm, he felt the trickles of sweat inch down his forehead, and shifted to pull his skin from the cool metal of his desk chair. It only took a few seconds for the effects to wear off, but he always felt hyper aware of his surroundings during the cooldown.

Opening his eyes, he blinked away the bleariness and cracked his neck. Aelec thought that after finding closure on Khorrus that he'd no longer need to relive his vivid memories. He'd hoped that he could spend less time dwelling on his past in favor of the promising future he had with the crew of the *Erinyes*. Life, it seemed, wasn't that simple.

With the tension between Myra and Riza, the theft of an Imperium chain code, and his own relationship with Riza... By the Void, sometimes he missed being shot at by Insurrectionists.

The spat between Myra and Riza was a problem, one that might impact their mission. The Vitrax usually burned hot and fast, but Aelec saw no signs of her fuse running out. Perhaps keeping them apart on Oais would be beneficial.

Interacting with Riza was still something of an enigma to him. They got along fine—more than fine—and he could sense that they were bonding in a way he hadn't with Myra or even Ida for that matter.

Laying on the firm mattress of his bunk, Aelec folded his hand across his chest as he stared up at the metal ceiling. He felt the exhaustion tugging at his eyelids, but his mind still churned even with the lingering effects of the mod-pill. It was meant to focus his mind and work through some of his more troubling memories, but now he seemed more frazzled than before taking the pill.

Aelec groaned, a headache forming. Damage to the *Erinyes*, Myra's feud, no word from his contact, and his feelings for Riza all swirled within his mind like a voidstream tunnel. If his hair could get even more silver, then it likely would have due to the mounting stress.

In the muddled sea of thoughts, Aelec found the first glimmer of respite: the mission to bring Veritas Kuvan to justice. He put all of his will into it until it was the only thing predominating his thoughts.

One by one, the stressful thoughts were buried beneath the importance of his mission, serving like foundations of a great statue. It was important to have a personal stake in the mission; it gave you something to fight for. But emotional turmoil had no place on the battlefield. And this was a mission that Aelec could not—would not—let himself get distracted from.

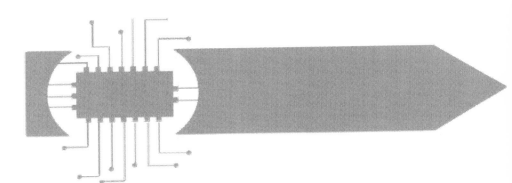

CHAPTER 9

4509.0830 / CW Star System: Picon / Planet:
Oais / GST: 11:10

The *Erinyes* lurched forward, making Riza's stomach churn. Gone were the usual smooth exits from the voidstream tunnel. She was glad for the safety straps that criss-crossed over her torso.

The orbital shipyard above Tog had helped them in a pinch, but the Voidspawned Togrians performed shoddy repairs on the *Erinyes*. The voidstream drive had been fixed to an extent, but most of the salvaged parts weren't compatible with the I-0552. Riza wasn't a mechanic by any means, but she knew enough about tech systems to know that incompatible components couldn't operate properly for long.

Luckily, the hologram displayed over the main hold's terminal indicated that their flight was over. She rolled her shoulders, letting the tension ease. Riza was back in the Capital Worlds, back in a place of law and order. Though she had resentment towards the Veriti, she was grateful for the security brought by the Imperium. Pirates and syndicates couldn't hunt her here; public security was efficient and fair.

Riza leaned forward in her seat, looking closely at the hologram that displayed the planet Oais. She'd never ventured beyond Seraphi to the other Capital Worlds, so she didn't have much expertise aside from what she knew from the Academy. Another reason why she was happy to be out in the galaxy, not working corporate hours on a sole planet.

If Seraphi was the basic, acceptable place of learning, then Oais was the competitive, outstanding schooling system. Unlike Seraphi, Oais was ingrained into the political machinations of the Imperium with courses and trade skills for government agencies, starship manufacturing, galactic shipping, and holonet oversight. Seraphi's Academies could guarantee work after graduation, but Oais' schools would ensure that such work would be prominent in the Imperium.

Her sister, Arenia, had once wanted to get a trade skill in xenoarchaeology, hoping to unearth the secrets of the universe. Riza wondered where Arenia would be today if she hadn't joined the Insurrectionists. If she hadn't...

Riza sniffed. Thinking of her dead sister encouraged her desire to make Veritas Kuvan answer for his crimes. The crew of the *Erinyes* had a sample of the proof needed to bring him down, but it wasn't foolproof. Kuvan could simply pass the HUD data off as a Comitor ploy to smear his image, and he certainly could silence a small-time crew like theirs.

Riza glanced down at the terminus on her arm, considering the chain code they'd stolen from the *Carthage*. If all went according to plan, they'd use the code to bypass the orbital defenses above Markum and infiltrate the Wasp Nest. Then, it was a simple matter of subduing Kuvan and getting a confession out of him while she recorded it for all to see.

The hologram flickered before displaying a map of a city as the *Erinyes* entered the atmosphere. While Oais was an ecumen, it was broken up into countless distinct cities. Riza glanced at the words above the image which read: *New Skyline, Western Dockyard Bay L317.*

A metallic rattle came from above, drawing nervous clicks from Golath, who was sitting across from her. All six of Golath's limbs dug into the seat and floor. Dylis, who sat next to the nonhuman, patted him on his chitinous shoulder. Golath's clicking eased, and Riza couldn't help but smile.

After a few minutes of turbulence, the *Erinyes*' rattling gradually ceased as they landed in one of Oais' dockyards. The second the fusion engines began shutting down, she, Golath, and Dylis unbuckled themselves and stood as if their lives depended on it. Dylis then dropped to the floor, kissing it and murmuring to himself. She arched an eyebrow.

A moment later, Aelec and Myra joined them in the main hold. The captain's russet dust coat hung low, stopping just above his tall black boots. Aelec's silvery hair was more disheveled than normal, and his jaw was shadowed with the first hints of stubble.

Her eyes focused on Aelec, specifically his brilliant golden eyes, which shone with a bit of determination. Aelec met her gaze, and she noticed that his eyes lit up by a fraction. It was subtle and vanished after a heartbeat, but Riza knew that Aelec had an interest in her. Whether or not he would act on it remained to be seen.

By the Void, Riza wasn't even sure how she felt about him. Sure, he'd been fascinating to learn about, but for the two years after Arenia died she'd thought that he was the one who killed her. It was difficult to get that stigma out of her head in spite of what he'd done to prove her wrong.

"Sorry for the bumpy ride, folks," Aelec said. "Good news is, we won't be going back into orbit until the *Erinyes* is fixed. Properly this time."

"Voidspawned Togrians," Myra hissed, crossing her arms

beneath her breasts. "Once we're done with the Wasp Nest, I want to blow a few holes in that space station for the shit job they did."

Golath clicked beneath his respirator, and Rant said, "Translation: I think they did a fine job, Pilot Myra."

Riza and Dylis both jerked their heads towards the Kygi, who remained stoic for a moment before emitting a higher pitched clicking.

Myra's lips parted in surprise. "Golath," she said, "did you just use sarcasm?"

"Translation: Well, they did a fine job sabotaging the Great *Erinyes*. I pray to the Empyrean that they did not use our parts to build those monstrosities they call racers."

Dylis snorted. "Not sarcasm. Just droll Kygi humor."

One of Golath's arms swatted Dylis' shoulder, and the former Outrider chuckled.

"Choose your gear wisely," Aelec ordered, nodding in the direction of the armory. "I want us to be prepared, but let's not draw attention. Dylis, that means no grenades, and seal your E-rifle."

"I hate this already," Dylis groaned.

Following Aelec to the armory, the crew pulled together the necessary equipment for an incursion on a Capital World. That meant minimal armaments and concealable weapons.

Riza pulled on her signature black leather jacket, which concealed the E-pistol holstered on her hip. Golath hid his fuse-caster pieces between his chitinous plates, Dylis set his E-rifle in a weapon case, and Aelec pulled on his brown duster to hide his own holstered E-pistol.

The captain cracked his neck and grunted, "Professional faces, folks. Capital Worlds are nothing like the Fringe."

Upon exiting the *Erinyes*, Riza gazed around the dockyard, her jaw dropping.

Beyond the open ceiling of the hangar bay, a rich russet color stained the skyline. It was such a contrast to the pale azure skies of her homeworld, and she nearly tripped while staring at it.

"Iron dust," Aelec pointed out. "There's still a high concentration in the upper atmosphere."

"Isn't that lethal?" she queried.

"Normally, yes. But keep watching."

On cue, an elongated corvette streaked through the sky above, mist seeming to stream off its white hull. Looking closer, she saw countless more circling like hawks in the russet heavens.

"Air processors," she murmured. "I bet there's no shortage of those on Oais."

"It's warranted," he said, "especially after the incident in thirty-nine-zero-two. The corvettes were attacked by the Bringers of the Void, and within the first hour of the attack over a million people died."

"That's horrible! Did they catch those who did it?"

Aelec nodded. "C.B.I. agents took them out and personally flew some of the emergency corvettes to clear the air. It was centuries ago, but I've always admired the C.B.I. because of that."

Riza smiled but said nothing, her attention wandering to the city beyond the plexiglass windows which had a faint cobalt tint. Walking through the hub connecting their docking bay to the city, she marveled at the smooth and cylindrical structures rising like stalks of bamboo.

"Don't stare too much, Riza," Aelec said, amusement lacing his voice. "Don't want you to get lost in New Skyline."

She sniffed, tapping her terminus. "I could find you all in a heartbeat."

"You willing to bet on that?"

"You ready to lose some fuses?"

A grin spread across Aelec's thin lips, but he said no more.

The familiar sounds of urban traffic hit her ears, and Riza took in a deep breath as she blinked slowly. She was eager to see how their crew would fare on a world such as Oais.

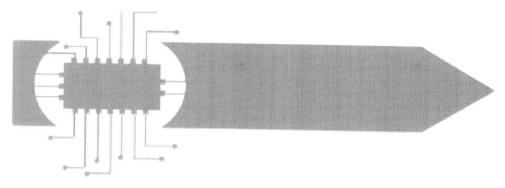

CHAPTER 10

A hundred scents hit Golath the moment he left the Great *Erinyes*. It was like having a Togrian smash him in the face with a pulsehammer; the Kygi couldn't help but recoil. His taloned feet teetered as he descended the boarding ramp, and he used one of his arms to steady himself against the bulkhead. He clicked to the emotion of horror as his senses were assaulted by the new world.

The dockyard reeked of bitter engine fluids, oxidized iron, and stale sweat. Beyond the port, dozens of food vendors secreted potent smells of frying oils, boiling salt water, roasting meats, or searing vegetables. Further in the city, he could detect countless pheromones of humans, Vitrax, Pyrons, and Togrians. Their bodily secretions told Golath that they were alarmed, marking territory, following trails, or signaling mating.

Golath grew woozy as his feet touched the cold floor of the dockyard. His eyes rolled slightly as he clicked to the emotion of disgust. He took a few more steps, and Liberator Aelec placed a hand on the Kygi's shoulder.

"You alright?" he asked, his fleshy voicebox always sounding strange to the Kygi's sensory organs.

Golath, in turn, clicked to the emotion of surprise, at which Translator Tarantula said, "Translation: I was unprepared for setting talon within such a grand human city. The buildings and ships we go to are one thing, but this is entirely different. I can smell everything for the next league. It is... overwhelming."

Liberator Aelec frowned as he looked up at Golath's face. "Do you want to stay on the ship?"

He shook his head in a gesture the human would find as negatory. Golath clicked to the emotion of awkwardness.

"Translation: I do not wish to be left behind. I shall center myself after a time."

The silver-haired human nodded and didn't press the matter, though he kept pace with Golath. He once thought that Liberator Aelec's compassion was rare among humans, but traveling with Warrior Dylis and Hacker Riza had altered that assumption.

Golath lumbered behind the humanoids as they ventured further into the hub. After a few strides, they entered one of the terminal tunnels connecting to the nearest district. The tunnel ended at a gravlift that could hold up to a dozen humanoids and their luggage, but luckily only their party entered the lift. Golath felt a tingling sensation in his legs as the gravlift activated and lowered them to the ground floor, depositing them in a large lobby that opened up onto the street.

Outside the lobby, Golath could see the bustling activity of the human city as sentients walked the streets, gravvehicles sped by, and shuttles flew between the towering skyscrapers. In a strange sense, the activity reminded him of how the colonies of Kyg-nor used to be.

Though the Kygi couldn't fly between spires, they'd developed other methods of travel like gondolas or catamarans that ran on fusionfiber. Colonies that resisted the rule of the Togrians weren't privy to gravlift technology, so the Kygi resorted to fusionfiber cables to interlink their spires. If they couldn't soar over the landscape naturally, then the Kygi would take the next best thing.

It was one of the many differences he noticed when on human worlds. The consistent gravity often took time getting used to, and he ensured his respirator was fully charged. Yet, he was always thrilled to explore these strange planets—ones with whole atmospheres and moderate temperatures.

The only detriment was getting used to the smells wafting through the air. His respirator filtered the gasses he needed to survive, but it didn't protect him from airborne scents. One, in particular, caught his attention. It was metallic and bitter, yet it was faded, weakening. Like a drying liquid.

Or perhaps drying blood.

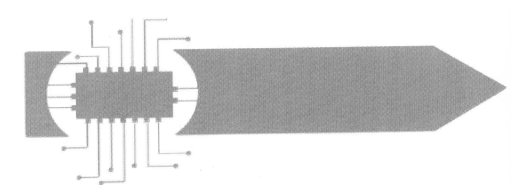

CHAPTER 11

The slick sound of steel sliding against steel resonated from high above, drawing Aelec's attention to the cylindrical towers that shifted sporadically. Russet sunlight highlighted the contrasting metallic colors of violet, dark brown, and black. The bitter scent of cooling metal drowned out the other stenches permeating the walkway.

As he watched the skyscraper's upper wall open, a walkway formed and extended to the tower directly next to it. New Skyline's architecture was influenced heavily by Meridiem designs, which meant they could reshape themselves for ease of access.

Ahead, one of the street's raised walkways rotated to allow a crowd of pedestrians to cross above the lane of repulsor traffic. The air grew oppressive as the crowd closed in, and the mixing scents of body odors and perfumes nearly made him sneeze.

Aelec's right hand kept brushing up against the handle of the E-pistol holstered on his hip. Despite being back in the Capital Worlds, his Fringe sensibilities created a spike of alertness that refused to fade. It didn't help that he was still wary from stealing an Imperium chain code.

A hologram banner weaved across the upper story of a nearby tower, depicting Veritas Nova. He glared at the image.

Veriti, he mused. *Planetary governors that are supposed to protect their people.* His own planetary governor—Veritas Kuvan—authorized a massacre of an entire Outrider clan, all of Aelec's clan, just to bury a secret that Arenia Noxia knew about.

A secret that he had never learned.

He shook his head, sending his platinum hair into a shaggy disarray. Veritas Kuvan would pay for his crimes soon enough. Right now, Aelec needed to focus on finding his Imperium contact and get their faces wiped from the holonet.

"Wow, they sure do like promoting their Veritas, don't they?" Myra noted, her eyes watching a hologram banner high above.

"He's popular among the corporations," Aelec explained. "Veritas Nova is responsible for turning Oais into a full industrial ecumen. His predecessor, Veritas Cahil, spent decades trying to keep the wildlife preserves and natural parks intact. But he died twenty years ago, leaving Nova to govern Oais."

Myra frowned. "He destroyed those reserves?"

"More like he just shipped them off-world," Dylis grunted. "When I was on Faerius, we saw a huge influx of critters in our wildlife parks."

The Vitrax frowned. "It's a shame. This place could use a little bit of nature."

Aelec guided his crew towards one of the surface-level grav-trams that flowed throughout the city, connecting it to the other ecumen sectors. Map booths in the station showed that New Skyline was broken up into five districts: Medina, Egris, Calvetti, Yukai, and Rakto. The Medina was the western industrial park between the dockyards and the rest of the city, the Egris was the central urban zone with governmental facilities, the Calvetti was the eastern residential area, the Yukai was the southern supply distribution center, and the Rakto was the northern university setting.

Government facilities, he thought. *Egris District, here we come.*

Once aboard the gravtram, he gripped the ceiling-rail while the others sat on the cushioned benches. Wide windows along the tram's side gave full view of the city as well as the many other grav-trams speeding between buildings. This one, in particular, would make a stop at a station a few blocks from the base of operations for the Capital Bureau of Investigation, the place where his clandestine contact worked.

Riza was in the seat closest to him. She crossed one leg over the other and kept her hands folded on her lap. As the gravtram began to move, she glanced up at Aelec with curious blue eyes.

"Aelec?"

"Yeah?"

"Do you come to New Skyline often?" She glanced at the window, then back at him. "I mean... did you used to come here?"

Aelec snorted with a faint grin. "To be honest, this is only my second time on Oais."

She raised her thin eyebrows. "Seriously?"

He shrugged, keeping his right hand firm on the ceiling-rail as he explained, "I visited Oais once when I'd begun my tour in the Imperium armada. It was a brief stay."

Riza adjusted in her seat and faced him squarely, her head resting against the wall of the tram.

"Leisure or military stuff?" she asked.

"Outriders didn't have much leisure time," he replied. "It was a simple operation. A terrorist cell—the Sol's Resistance Army—had attacked parts of another Oais city, Merricas, so clan-Xero and clan-Arix were deployed to assist. Coordinating with the C.B.I. and Imperium reserves, we eliminated each S.R.A. cell before subduing their leader, thus preventing more Fringe propaganda from being broadcasted to the citizens."

Riza gazed out the opposite window to watch the passing city, her expression pensive. Aelec still had a hard time reading her when she put her walls back up.

Without looking at him, Riza queried, "Do you think that adds to the stained image of the Imperium?"

"Because it sounds like we were silencing voices?" Aelec asked in kind, turning his gaze to the same window. "Yeah, I suppose. It didn't seem like that when we completed the op. But I can see how it could be construed."

She looked back up at him. "And you still think the Imperium is legitimate?"

"Nothing is perfect," he retorted. "No system is without flaw. I think it's important to be inspired by the good while working to fix the bad."

Riza was silent as she turned back to the window, but a soft smile spread across her pale face as she seemed to accept Aelec's rationale. Her smile was perfect, his heart agreeing as it beat a little faster. He shifted his footing and tore his gaze away from Riza, feeling hot all over.

Apart from Ida, Aelec had never felt this way about anyone—not even Myra. About two years ago, he and Myra tried dating, but it had fizzled out just as quickly as it began. He still considered her a dear friend, but there hadn't been that swell of emotion when he thought of her.

But now, with Riza, he reflected on how he felt every time he saw her, talked with her, or was close with her. Simply put, she brightened his day.

He opened his mouth to speak to her again, but the gravtram slowed to a halt and the metallic intercom voiced that they were in the Egris District. When the tram fully stopped, the doors parted with a low *hiss* and the six of them departed onto the carbocrete walkway.

Past the crowd of humanoids in the street, Aelec looked up and saw an imposing facility made up of multiple cylindrical towers and interconnecting bridges. The violet morristeel glistened in the russet-colored sunlight, and Aelec could pick up the faint smell of cleansing chemicals.

Myra inclined her head to the side as they approached and said, "Yeah, that definitely looks like a C.B.I. building. Not very inconspicuous."

"It's a government building, Myra," Aelec said, "on a Capital World, no less."

As if to punctuate his words, the air around the building shimmered with a blue tinge. The only way past the energy shield was through the entry checkpoint. Approaching the nearest entrance, Aelec paused, the crew halting their stride. Pedestrians continued to walk around them, some giving them irritated glances for stopping abruptly.

Dylis frowned beneath his beard and asked, "What's up, boss?"

Aelec nodded towards the C.B.I. checkpoint and answered, "It's best if only Dylis and I go in. We're the ones with Imperium ties. Plus, it won't attract as much attention if two ex-military guys visit a C.B.I. building."

Riza cleared her throat. "I'm from the Imperium too. Maybe not the military, but still."

Aelec kept his tone level, but remained steadfast. "I'm not asking. It's an order. Dylis and I can pass off as consultants. You might attract attention, Riza."

Riza sighed theatrically but didn't protest. When the others didn't object, he ordered for them to keep a low profile in the district. As they melded in with the moving pedestrians, Aelec and Dylis approached the checkpoint.

A shimmering field of energy connected two, small defense towers at the checkpoint, barring entry. Both towers had narrow doors on the ground-level that were open, revealing a pair of guards sitting in office chairs. When they closed the distance, the guard in the left tower spotted them and exited carrying an E-rifle.

He stopped a few paces from Aelec—the man was a few fingers taller and his pristine, copper-colored combat suit struck an imposing visage.

The guard's clean-shaven jaw clenched before he spoke. "This is a government facility, fellas," he said in a gruff voice. "Civilians are not permitted."

Aelec grinned slightly and said, "Don't worry, we'll let the civilians know."

The guard frowned, his brown eyes reflecting distaste. "I've seen every C.B.I. agent come through these gates for the past year. Never seen your faces before, so clearly you're not agents or officials."

"You're a perceptive one," Dylis noted, "it's a shame they've got you on bouncer duty."

"Someone's gotta do it," the guard growled, his grip tensing on the E-rifle. "If you're not civilians, show me your credentials."

Aelec nodded to Dylis and the latter produced a small hologram puck before handing it over to the guard. Snorting in derision, the guard returned to his office to activate the puck. Upon authenticating their Outrider IDs, he returned and quickly handed the puck back to Dylis. The guard's pockmarked cheeks took on color as he exchanged glances with them.

"My apologies, Commander Wyri," the guard said, standing at attention. "I didn't mean any disrespect to an Outrider such as yourself."

Dylis waved his hand in dismissal, scoffing, "No offense taken, pal. Are we good here?"

"This isn't normal procedure, sir," the guard said, shuffling his weight from foot to foot. "We don't have any op data regarding Outrider missions in New Skyline. Plus, we don't have you scheduled in the data logs. Forgive me, but I still cannot permit you to enter."

Dylis glanced at Aelec and said, "Competent security. Gotta hand it to them."

"We don't really need to enter the facility," Aelec noted, stepping towards the guard. "We just need a message passed along to someone who works here. Old acquaintance."

"Who do you need me to contact?"

"Her name's Milli Spectre," Aelec said, putting his hands in his coat pockets. "Cyber Response Department. Special agent."

The guard nodded, a few strands of his slicked brown hair falling across his forehead. "Give me a sec. I'll ping their department and see if she's available."

Slinging the E-rifle over his back, the guard opened a transmission link on his wrist terminus. The device let out a metallic chime. There was a pause, then it chimed again. Aelec could see a faint image of Milli's profile face on the screen, but the image crackled with static. Strange. She usually answered calls after the first two chimes.

By the third and fourth chime, Aelec knew she wasn't in the office. Something felt off. Milli rarely took off work, and when she did she'd notify Aelec, letting him know that she couldn't get his image scrubbed from the holonet until she returned.

The guard ended the transmission and frowned. "Looks like she's not in today," he grunted. "We can't permit entry without someone to vouch for your visit."

Aelec pursed his lips as he looked up at the towering facility.

"Who is Agent Spectre's superior? I want to talk to him, or her."

"Sir, that's not standard procedure."

"Let me talk to them," he repeated, his voice reverberating so much that he felt his whole body shake in response. "Or at least get them to confirm where Agent Spectre is. Then we'll leave you in peace."

The guard leaned away from Aelec, his brown eyes widening with a hint of uncertainty.

"One moment, sir," he muttered. Swiping through holograms, the guard opened another transmission channel.

After one chime, the profile of a dark-skinned man appeared in the hologram. The text beneath, though backwards, read as *Director Cormack*.

"*What is it, Corporal Jeffyrs?*" Cormack asked in a deep, basso voice.

"Director, we have two ex-Imperium fellas out front asking about Agent Spectre," the guard said. "I tried her terminus but she isn't responding. Is she in today?"

Cormack paused, stroking his black goatee before saying, *"Agent Spectre is on leave and won't be returning for the foreseeable future."*

Aelec felt a chill as the words were uttered over the transmission. Milli was a distinguished member of the Oais reserves and a career agent for the C.B.I. Being on indefinite leave wasn't like her. Coupled with her holonet silence, Aelec knew something was wrong.

Milli Spectre was missing in action.

The hologram faded, and the guard, Jeffyrs, said, "You heard the man. Spectre isn't in today."

"Can you get us in for a meeting with the director?" Aelec asked, pulling out his quantum card. "Fifteen minutes. Tops. I'll make it worth your while."

Jeffyrs glanced around nervously. "Sir, I can't accept bribes."

"The word of an Outrider carries a lot of weight," Aelec noted. "You help us out, I'll put in a good word with the director."

The guard raised his eyebrows. "I do like the sound of Agent Jeffyrs." He blew out his breath, then said, "Alright. I'll get you guys cleared for entry. Fifteen minutes. No more. Understood?"

"Loud and clear," Aelec said with a nod. "Thanks."

He waited as Jeffyrs typed into his terminus, soft beeps emitting after each tap of a finger. A moment later, the shimmer around the entrance faded and the guard waved for them to enter the facility. Aelec strode forward, his steps quickening as he passed through. It was time for answers.

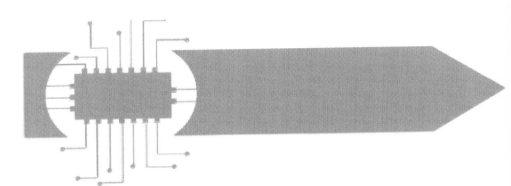

CHAPTER 12

New Skyline: C.B.I. Headquarters, GST: 12:00

Aelec had almost forgotten how orderly an Imperium building could be. For nearly three years he'd been living aboard the *Erinyes*, a ship that—while tidy—had stained furniture, rusty floors, and occasionally smelled like burnt meat. Here in an Imperium facility, everything was pristine, sharp, and mostly devoid of color.

He and Dylis had been ushered through the lower levels of the Bureau's complex after being relieved of their weapons. The administrative assistant, a young man named Zac Lestin, kept a close eye on them as they walked, clearly dubious of their agenda. The central gravlift had deposited them on the twentieth floor, and a distinct hush came over the crowd of agents.

Despite the size of the C.B.I. office, it seemed like the walls were slowly closing in, the air growing thick. The office felt like a cage, but perhaps that was because he'd been spoiled by living on a ship, bouncing from planet to planet. Regardless, Aelec tried not to let it bother him as he traversed the glossy tiles of the office.

He gave a wide berth around a desk with corners so sharp they might cut through nanotech armor. The air was frigid and recycled, giving it a stale smell. Much of the twentieth floor was lined with white desks, which were occupied by the lower-ranked agents, their suits matching their desks.

The receptionist escorted them to one of the open offices at the back, the glass walls permitting them to see everything within. Just as he walked through the office's doorway, he noticed a name projected by a dim hologram: *Milli Spectre, Cyber Defense.*

The glossy tiles gave way to velvet, gray carpet as he entered the office. Sunlight seeped into the room from an elongated window on the far side, and Aelec could see various lanes of gravvehicle traffic above and below. Dylis flopped into one of the cushioned seats near Milli's desk and put his hands behind his head. Aelec paced around the desk, his uncertainty winding him up like a knotted rope, and he found that he couldn't remain still. The Fringe sensibilities came back, his hand brushing towards the holster on his hip. It was empty; it had already slipped his mind that the security guards had confiscated it.

Aelec wrung his hands, a tightness gripped his chest and refused to let go. Minutes passed like hours as they waited. He took a deep breath, glancing at the desk and spotting some of Milli's knickknacks. A plastic model starship caught his eye before his gaze wandered to a few hologram pictures hovering above the pale desk.

One depicted Milli beaming up at a tall, burly man whom Aelec assumed was her husband, Ferris. The picture caught him laughing hysterically, and it surprised Aelec to see such an unceremonious picture on her desk. Directly beside was the image of Milli's old reserve squad as they stood stoically with a squad of Outriders. Clan-Xero Outriders.

Aelec blinked in surprise. He saw himself standing just behind

Milli in that image. He'd forgotten that pictures had been taken after the defeat of the S.R.A.

Someone tapped on the glass door of the office, and Aelec turned to see Director Cormack entering. Cormack straightened his white suit jacket before approaching Aelec with an extended hand.

"Captain Xero," he said, his voice vibrating around the office. "Welcome to the C.B.I."

Aelec shook his hand, their grips seeming to vie for control. Meeting the man's dark eyes, Aelec said, "Thanks for seeing us, Director Cormack."

Cormack arched an eyebrow in curiosity. "Pardon my bluntness, but why are you here? It's unusual for a pair of Outriders to visit a C.B.I. office. What's your interest in Milli Spectre?"

"Milli was an associate of mine back during the skirmishes against the Sol's Resistance Army in forty-five-oh-three. I heard she's on an indefinite leave of absence. Seems strange for an agent of her caliber."

Cormack shrugged. "Agent Spectre wanted to pursue other career paths."

"Really?" Aelec queried skeptically, gesturing towards her desk. "That doesn't look like the desk of an ex-employee. And the last time I talked to her, she said she wouldn't leave the C.B.I. until retirement."

The director ran a hand over his bald scalp. "Alright, fine. We're just trying to keep this quiet for the time being."

"She's MIA, isn't she?"

Cormack was quiet, and he nodded slowly.

"I'm guessing since you want to keep this on the downlow, you don't have any leads."

"Who says we don't have leads?" Cormack countered, his eyes narrowing. "But you're no longer active duty, son. You're not privy to C.B.I. intel."

"Unless we're hired on as Private Security Contractors," Aelec countered, crossing his arms. "We can help each other out here."

Cormack drew his lips into a thin line. "What's your offer?"

"You give me and my crew intel on Milli, we'll track her down. No government insurance. No overtime. No paperwork."

"Why should I entrust a group of civilians with this?" Cormack asked.

Aelec glanced at the hologram picture on Milli's desk, memories flashing by every time he blinked. He remembered one time where Milli had elbowed him between the ribs for not asking Ida to dance at a nightclub. Her expression had been comically aghast, and the thought made him smile. Cormack stepped towards the desk and examined the photo, his dark eyes no longer reflecting suspicion.

"Ah," he murmured. "Not just an associate. A friend."

"Yeah. She was like a sister to me. Saved my ass more than once during those skirmishes. I owe her big time."

Cormack let out a protracted sigh. "Alright, I get it." He glanced around before saying quietly, "Milli was investigating potential terrorist activity in the western docks three days ago when she went missing. Intel stated that a group of activists, the Far Syters, were smuggling weapons to a rally and High Chancellor Sessani was the target. Her last report indicated that the activists were growing aggressive, then her terminus signal went dark."

"Any tracking implants?"

"She had a standard issue tracking implant in her shoulder," Cormack answered. "It's gone dark too. No one should have the tech available to disable those kinds of devices outside of the C.B.I."

"Could it have been another agent?"

"No. Our agents were spread thin that day. All are accounted for. I'd just sent two to back her up, but by the time they got there it was too late."

"Security cam footage?"

"There was a flux in the western docks' power grid that day," Cormack said, stroking his goatee. "She was ordered to stay in view of the cams, but it was disabled for exactly two minutes before coming back on. One moment she was there, and the other she was gone. I'll send you all the reports we've gathered."

Cormack flicked the hologram above his wrist, and Aelec's terminus flashed yellow.

"So, Milli was investigating the Far Syters in the western docks, no backup, there was a power flux, she went missing, and all tracking methods were disabled," Aelec repeated. "Am I missing anything?"

"Just this," Cormack said, "the Far Syters have eluded our pursuits ever since Agent Spectre went missing. We have no intel on the whereabouts of their compound."

Aelec frowned. "So no leads on the would-be terrorists?"

Cormack nodded reluctantly. "No official leads from the C.B.I. But, Agent Spectre and her husband had some run-ins with the Syters before the incident. We tried to question him, but he was too distraught to give unbiased information. Perhaps a contractor such as yourself would have an easier time getting that info."

Aelec rubbed his pointed chin, glancing over at Dylis, who gave him a thumbs-up. It surprised him to see the older Outrider so willing to help him in this cause. Part of him always believed Dylis would run off when the plan deviated; he had a wife and a home to return to.

He grinned at his older friend before turning back to Cormack. "We'll take the job," Aelec declared.

Cormack smiled thinly and said, "Having Outriders assist in this investigation will be greatly appreciated. Just don't do anything outside the law. Mister Lestin will get your credentials set up downstairs."

"Understood, Director Cormack," Aelec grunted. "We'll bring Milli home safely."

"Let's hope so."

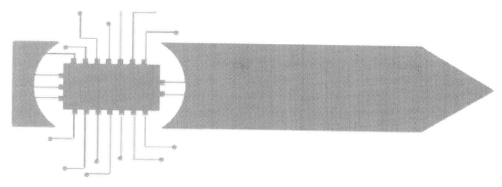

CHAPTER 13

New Skyline: The Egris Trade Center, GST: 12:00

Throughout his ninety-seven revolutions, Golath had only set talon on five worlds, including his homeworld. The asteroids of the Xionic Belt did not count, despite how much they reminded him of home. For ninety-six of those revolutions, he had been isolated to Kyg-nor, where it took considerable effort to make out the various scents on that planet. Only within the past revolution had he ventured out to places with such a variety of scents.

Even still, the locations he visited on Asmodum, Khorrus, and Caavo were tame in comparison to Oais. Golath surmised that it was the scattered nature of the Fringe planets that resulted in less bodies being present. That was a simplistic answer. No, Oais had more life to it than those other worlds—more diverse species, more activities, and more culture.

Here, one could walk down the street and see a Kygi eatery next to a Vitrax soup cart on one side, while the other had a Togrian deli stand directly beside a human grill. Golath's cooking sensibilities made him want to separate them immediately—sweet Vitrax soup did not belong within a hundred meters of a Kygi shellfish spread.

Golath had followed Hacker Riza, Pilot Myra, and Translator Tarantula into the Egris District's trade center, and was now moseying about on his own while they waited for Liberator Aelec's signal. It was Golath's first time on a Capital World, and he wanted to glimpse the proverbial mixing pot of nonhuman chefs and how they operated.

Hacker Riza was watching a tech demo while Pilot Myra and Translator Tarantula were at an astrogational presentation. Though difficult, Golath could still track their specific scents through the miasma of smells with the aid of his respirator mask. It was part of his duties to keep tabs on them for Liberator Aelec.

His eye was first drawn to the Vitrax soup cart, which had a wide countertop where countless biodegradable cups were stacked. Steam plumed from several pots of boiling liquids, and he noticed distinctive hues of yellow, green, and orange. Golath felt his stomach twist as he inhaled the aromas. A Vitrax male wearing a stained apron stood behind the counter and used a variety of ladles to serve specific types of soup.

Moving past a large kiosk, Golath saw rows of thinly sliced meats lined up in intricate patterns along the counter. A Togrian butcher hacked at a slab of meat with a strange cleaver affixed to his hand like a glove. Golath correctly assumed that it was due to the Togrian's proclivity to let things slip between their massive digits. The tortoise-looking nonhuman glanced at him, and he could feel the resentment radiating off the Togrian like a fiery grill.

Golath returned the feeling, clicking to the emotion of disgust as he passed by. With his back to the Togrian deli, Golath gave a soft click to the emotion of sadness as he considered his shameful action. He should not let the old rivalry sway him in a world such as this. But those wounds would take many, many revolutions to heal.

Further along the street, he spotted a Kygi eatery. The familiar layout of separate cooking stands was common among his people's cooks. It was not as extravagant as the kitchen aboard the Great *Erinyes*, but it was quaint. Honing his scent glands, he picked out the delectable, faintly sweet smell of Kyg-nor krill frying in zygnut oil.

Stepping up to the counter, Golath noticed a Kygi female hunched over and filling her claws with more krill. Standing to her full height, she cocked her head curiously upon noticing him.

She clicked to the emotion of surprise, and her intentions became clear in his mind.

"It is always a pleasure to see a fellow child of Kyg-nor in a place such as this," she said in the language of their people.

Golath inclined his head as he clicked in response, "May the Empyrean bestow great harvest upon you. I am called Kuanishu-Zaskari-Aka-Kup-Golath. What are you called?"

"I am called Kabiri-Zakimbi-Zaaliyak-Kup-Skya," she replied, similarly bowing her head.

Her name was a surprise to him. All Kygi names were meant to be an amalgamation of their life experiences and titles. Golath's, for instance, indicated that he was of the warrior-priest caste, a liberated gladiator, a crewmate, and a cook. Skya's name revealed that she was of the soothsayer caste, a former refugee, a former cantina worker, and a cook.

"A pleasure, Kabiri-Zakimbi-Zaaliyak-Kup-Skya," Golath responded as he glanced at the numerous items on display. "I am curious, how did you go from working in a cantina to being an independent street vendor?"

Skya laid out her handfuls of krill, grabbed some utensils, and expertly began peeling the talon-sized crustaceans.

"Humans can be very fickle when it comes to their food," she answered, dropping the krill into a pan of oil. "They require peeled krill or softshell decapods to protect their brittle teeth. I did not know this as the chef of the Seedy Shack, and many complaints arose against me. It was not long before they terminated my employment."

Golath clicked to the emotion of amusement. Not regarding Skya's plight, but because he understood her predicament. It was indeed odd for a Kygi to keep company—let alone work—with humans because of the extreme differences in physiology, language, and culture. Golath had a soft spot for Liberator Aelec and the crew, but he knew that other Kygi were not as lucky as he.

"What brings you to Oais?" she asked.

All four of Golath's claws clasped together as he replied, "I have traveled here with my dear friend, Liberator Aelec Xero. He seeks to meet an old acquaintance somewhere in this city, and left me to explore the area. This is my first visit to the Capital Worlds."

Skya made a gesture with her free claw, saying, "A leisure visit for you, it seems. You are lucky not to have to find work. When I arrived with my brood, I was expected to begin working within a single day cycle."

"I am sorry to hear of this," Golath intoned, eyeing the frying krill. "Though it seems your skills are not going to waste. The zygnut oil is perfect for complementing the krill's salty taste."

Skya cocked her head and clicked to the emotion of adoration. "I was surprised to hear that you are a cook."

"Indeed," he answered, "I was trained by the Matriarchs of our homeworld. The Empyrean smiles upon those who provide rather than take."

Skya clicked to the emotion of amazement as she noted, "An unorthodox practice. Might I gain your opinion on a batch of zygnut fried krill?"

"It would be my pleasure," Golath replied, using his lower left claw to reach into a pouch and retrieving his quantum card.

She waved two of her claws in protest, stating, "There is no need for fuses, Kuanishu-Zaskari-Aka-Kup-Golath. Your opinion would be payment enough."

"I insist." He clicked to the emotion of adoration and continued, "A fellow child of Kyg-nor deserves compensation for the culinary arts. It is a grueling skill to learn. My opinions would not be close to what is owed."

Skya did not offer further protest, and Golath transferred several fuses into her quantum card. As a fellow Kygi, her four claws were able to multitask throughout the entire ordeal; one hand used the quantum card, another notated the purchase on a countertop terminus, and the others prepared a small bowl of fried krill.

Accepting the bowl, Golath plucked a krill from the group and raised it to his respirator. A metallic *click* resounded as a compartment opened, and he placed the krill within. The device processed the small crustacean through the machinery while allowing him to breathe, and a heartbeat later the krill was dropped into his open beak.

Clicking to the emotion of nostalgia, Golath savored the nutty taste of the krill, which transported him back to Kyg-nor. It was strange to think how a mere piece of food could make him feel as if he were in another place. Despite the hardships of their homeworld, Golath missed the towering spires, the majestic catamarans, and the food prepared by the Matriarchs.

Skya clicked to the emotion of satisfaction in response to Golath's display. "I trust it is a reminder of home?"

"Indeed," Golath replied, the flavor still fresh on his tongue. "It was as if I was in my colony spire and feasting with our people. Your work is exceptional, Kabiri-Zakimbi-Zaaliyak-Kup-Skya."

"You honor me, Kuanishu-Zaskari-Aka-Kup-Golath," she intoned, bowing her head. "Are you in need of any other services?"

Golath clicked to the emotion of interest and stated, "I am curious about this world. What can you tell me of it?"

"Oais is a busy world," she answered, using two claws to flip the frying krill. "Far busier than Kyg-nor or even Khorrus. I assume you have had difficulty adjusting your olfactory senses to the scents?"

Golath bobbed his head in confirmation, and she continued, "Sifting through the scents will take time, but it is possible to fully adapt to them. I must warn you of scent bombs used by the authorities. Many protests have been dispersed with such devices, and if a child of Kyg-nor is on the receiving end it will numb your olfactory senses for a lunar cycle."

Golath's eyes went wide as he clicked to the emotion of fear. "That is horrendous. Why would the authorities implement such things?"

"Tensions have grown strong between the Capital Bureau of Investigation and a protester gang called the Farthest Sighters, or some such. This gang has a tendency of appealing to nonhumans and using them as shields against the authorities."

"Using us as shields?"

"The humans of this gang see us as beings without flaw," Skya explained. "They seem to think that we cannot be harmed by the authorities without it being an act of oppression. I do not understand these human hatchlings. We are just as flawed as they are, and we must answer to the same justice as they do."

Shaking his head, Golath intoned, "Humans can be so strange. I will do my best to avoid this gang. Are there any others I should be concerned with?"

Skya clicked to the emotion of anxiety as her yellow eyes wandered off. "I do not know of any others, but that human has been staring at you for a few heartbeats."

She pointed a clawed finger over Golath's left shoulder, and he turned slightly to see what she was referencing.

Sure enough, a human wearing strange robes of gray and white was looking at him from across the thoroughfare. As Golath peered more closely, he noticed that the robes were intermixed with pieces of black armor. A metallic facemask obscured most of the human's face, but he could see the stark azure eyes staring at him.

Golath hunched defensively and clicked to the emotion of anger. The human—now aware of the Kygi's attention—simply stepped back and turned away. Golath blinked and the human was lost in the crowd of people.

Once certain that the human was gone, Golath turned back to Skya and queried, "Do most humans stare like that here on Oais?"

Skya shook her head. "No. That was strange. Most humans are well-accustomed to children of Kyg-nor."

"I think it is time for me to locate my fellow crewmates," Golath intoned, giving a deep bow. "It was a pleasure visiting your eatery, Kabiri-Zakimbi-Zaaliyak-Kup-Skya. May the Empyrean smile upon you."

"May your harvests be bountiful, Kuanishu-Zaskari-Aka-Kup-Golath."

Golath turned away from the eatery and began sifting through the scents of the crowd in search of Hacker Riza or Pilot Myra. He had enjoyed the comfort of nostalgia—of feeling like he was back home—but there was only so much time for reminiscing. Reality would not wait for him.

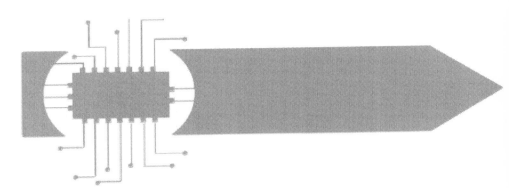

CHAPTER 14

Riza stopped to preen over a display system, one that implemented nanotech rather than holograms. Images and shapes formed from the clusters of dark gray nanoparticles, and she could actually *feel* them. It would do wonders for terminuses that were used for games, artwork, or strategy.

Utterly enthralled by the prototype, she hovered over the table as crowds shuffled behind her in the Egris trade center. In her peripherals, neon holograms shined brightly, making her squint. Applause resounded, drawing her attention to a hovering stage where a man showcased a new exosuit.

The expo event in the Egris District spanned half a kilometer. Hundreds, if not thousands, of citizens crowded the event. An elongated glass terrace rose high above with beams painted to resemble antique wood.

A thin layer of steam wafted through the expo as a result of demonstrating new food or water processors. The familiar minty scent of coolant tickled her nose. Her fingers tapped against the nanotech display, the particles surprisingly warm to the touch.

Effortlessly, she manipulated the display to resemble a checkerboard.

Incredible! she mused. *This would be great for a game night on the ship.*

Riza wondered if there were any models available for sale. She had some spare fuses to spend, and she'd be remiss to purchase a new style of terminus.

Just as she began mulling over the purchase, Aelec called, ordering them to regroup outside the C.B.I. building. For the first time since joining the crew, she wanted to disobey his command and stay at the open trade center. Technology was her life; it was what made her want to get a trade skill in the first place.

Sighing disappointedly, she regrouped with the others and followed them back towards the C.B.I. tower several blocks away.

After ten minutes of walking, she spotted Aelec and Dylis leaning against the glass wall of a navigational booth. Dylis straightened his posture, grinning when he spotted them. Aelec, on the other hand, had his attention fixated on the carbocrete walkway, his aurous eyes cold.

Only when they closed the final meters did Aelec look up, his eyes focusing on Riza and he smiled faintly. Riza recognized that look. It was the mask of contentedness overtaking his consternation, as if to say, "don't worry, I'm fine."

Riza cocked her head to one side, letting her dark hair fall over an eye. Aelec didn't avert his gaze. Something wordless passed between them that Riza didn't have a name for. She would have to bother him later about it. For now, Aelec needed to be the poised, confident leader of the crew.

Gesturing for them to enter, Aelec shuffled into the elongated booth that was big enough to hold a few people. Golath, unfortunately, was too large to enter, and thus remained outside—the Kygi emitted a string of guttural clicks that Riza could've sworn was his method of grumbling.

Once they were inside the navigational booth, Aelec surveyed the interior before deactivating each of the various hologram projectors. Sporadically he would glance out the glass window of the booth, his eyes wide with alertness.

"Whatcha got for us, Aelec?" Myra queried, putting her hands in her pant pockets.

Aelec flicked two fingers to activate his terminus, sending a datafile to the rest of their devices. Raising her left arm, Riza pulled up the holographic file and saw the profile image of a young woman, maybe a few years older than her.

"Agent Milli Spectre," Aelec narrated, "current member of the Cyber Defense Department of the Capital Bureau of Investigation. Three days ago, she was investigating a group of protesters called the Far Syters when her quadrant suffered power loss and that was where she was last seen."

Myra tilted her head to the side. "Is she a friend of yours?"

"She's my old Imperium contact who regularly scrubs our data from the holonet," Aelec affirmed, folding his arms across his broad chest. "And yeah, she's an old friend. She's the only one who can get us access to Markum. Well, the only one I *trust* to do it."

"She's missing in action?" Riza queried as she skimmed the profile.

"Yeah," Aelec replied, rubbing the back of his neck. "My guess is she got nabbed by some of the more ballsy Far Syters and is being held in their compound."

Riza looked up from the image. "You don't think they killed her?"

Aelec shook his head. "If they'd wanted to kill her, the C.B.I. would've found her body after the power flux."

Myra's tentacles twitched as she asked, "Any ideas why they'd capture her?"

"Access, leverage, blackmail... You name it." Aelec let out a deep sigh. "This is one of the few times I *hate* civilians who have nothing better to do."

Riza's gaze fixated on the profile once again, her eyes soaking up the details.

Investigation of possible weapon smuggling, no incident reports during the protests, no distress signals, no weapon discharges... It was too clean. One moment she had been fine on the job, and the next she'd vanished completely. Forensics had found only a small sample of blood, but there were no fusion blast marks in the vicinity. Only Spectre's E-pistol, terminus, and tracking implant were left.

That entry caught Riza's eye. According to the report, Spectre's terminus was shattered in deliberate fashion and—even when salvaged—didn't have any data on what happened. The tracking implant, however, was a different issue. It was composed of standard nanotech particles and had an emergency failsafe to prevent unauthorized tampering.

It was a start.

"Hey, Aelec? Dylis?" Riza asked suddenly, drawing their attention. "What kind of failsafes could a nanotech implant have to avoid tampering?"

Dylis scratched his beard and replied, "Ah you know, the kind where it lunges out of your skin, or burrows into your bones..."

Riza's eyes went wide with horror, and Aelec smacked Dylis on the shoulder.

"He's being an idiot," Aelec grunted, meeting Riza's gaze. "Ones commonly used by non-Outriders in the armada had nanotech that broke down to enter the bloodstream. A small cluster of nanoparticles would break down into something so small that it wouldn't cause any damage to your internal organs, unless you have too many inside you."

Riza cupped her chin, focusing on Aelec's statement about the nanoparticles breaking down into the bloodstream.

"If that were the case," she said, "wouldn't Spectre's tracker have done so if the assailant tried to forcibly remove it?"

"You're right," he admitted, his brow furrowing. "The implant should've broken down during the emergency, which would've allowed the C.B.I. to track her."

Riza tapped a finger against her chin as she considered her next question. She then asked, "Is it possible that there are devices that can negate the implant's procedures? Like how do they remove them when an agent retires, or something?"

To her surprise, Rant chimed in. "Answer: There are two known devices used in medical facilities and autodocs that have that precise function, Riza Noxia. The first is a quantum disintegrator, which emits an ultrasonic frequency that neutralizes the nanoparticles and atomizes them. The second is a quantum scalpel, which generates an electric field that compels nanoparticles to coalesce into a single mass so that they can be extracted."

Riza's eyes went wide.

Myra nodded to the droid and said, "And Milli's implant was found in one piece. Which means..."

"The nanoparticles were coalesced before being cut out," Riza finished.

She glanced at Myra eagerly, but the Vitrax ignored her. Riza had a sinking feeling in her chest; she really hoped that they'd be able to set aside their qualms in the face of this new job.

Rubbing his gloved hands together, Aelec said, "Okay, we've got a lot to cover on this job, so we'll need to split up. I need to visit Milli's husband and get him to talk since he wasn't so keen on complying with the C.B.I. Golath, I could use your tracking abilities if Mister Spectre gives us a trail."

The Kygi clicked in acknowledgement outside the map booth; she heard his chitinous plates crunching together as he shuffled.

"Rant, since you're well-versed with these medical devices, you and Myra will check in with the nearest hospital to find out if any have been purchased," Aelec continued.

"I'll go with them," Dylis interjected, cracking his knuckles. "I can use my status as a Private Security Contractor to get higher authorization, if need be."

"Good idea," Aelec said, looking at Riza. "That just leaves you."

"Guess I'll go with you and Golath," she declared. "I can hack into the security cams over in the western docks. There might be more than what the C.B.I. was able to find."

Riza caught Myra eyeing her. By the Void, she really needed to confront the Vitrax.

Glancing at his terminus, Aelec sniffed and said, "Alright, it's just after twelve-hundred GST. Let's try to meet back at the *Erinyes* by no later than twenty-hundred. Keep low profiles, and don't do anything stupid."

"You telling that to us or yourself?" Myra noted, her violet eyes going from Aelec to Riza.

The captain grunted, "Both, I suppose. Check in when you have updates."

Dylis gave him a lazy salute. "You got it, bossman!"

As everyone shuffled out of the map booth, Myra said, "Riza. Let's chat."

Aelec eyed them but said nothing, exiting the booth. Dylis' eyebrows were almost to his hairline, but he too remained silent as he quickly followed Aelec. Riza's boots felt heavy, the Vitrax's words kept her tethered like a fish on a hook. The biting edge to her voice told Riza that she couldn't brush it off. Closing the door, she faced the Vitrax.

Myra let out a long sigh, putting her hands on her hips. "We need to clear the air," she said through clenched teeth. "So, before we split up, I need to go over a few things."

"I agree," Riza said firmly. She put her hands inside her jacket pockets and leaned against the glass wall, trying to exude confidence.

Myra's eyelids drooped, her expression unimpressed. "What you did on Caavo," she said quietly, "was reckless and stupid. It makes me seriously doubt your ability to think straight. Trust issues aside, if you make another dicey choice that could endanger Aelec or

Golath, there won't be anywhere in the galaxy where I won't find you."

A jolt of alarm stabbed into Riza's heart, and she did her best not to show it. Licking her lips, she said, "Myra, I can't express how sorry I am for what happened. But I know words alone won't atone. So, I'm going to show you that I'm loyal to this crew. This family. I'll use whatever skills I have to help Aelec and protect him if necessary."

Myra's eyes narrowed to slits. "Can you protect him from yourself?"

"I don't know," she admitted. "But I'll have his best interest at heart. Not mine. Myra, I swear!"

She met the Vitrax's deep, violet eyes that were slowly softening to Riza's words. It was impossible for Myra to forgive her after a quick talk, but the tension wasn't as thick in the air between them. It was a start.

"Aelec trusts you," Myra murmured, "So, I'll trust in his judgment. Don't give me another reason not to."

"I won't."

When Myra didn't reply, Riza felt that the conversation was over and turned back to the door. Her hand hovered over the activation panel, and she glanced over her shoulder.

"Be careful out there," Riza said gently.

The Vitrax sniffed, but inclined her head just a fraction. It was enough for Riza.

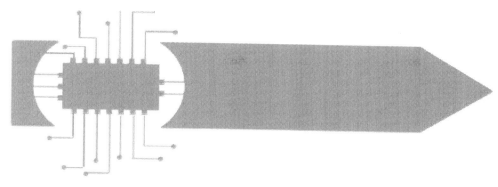

CHAPTER 15

New Skyline: The Calvetti District, GST: 13:00

Alec took a deep breath, but it didn't soothe him. Milli's disappearance had wound its way around his chest, wrapping so tightly he couldn't breathe. Martial training or not, he found that even with deep, slow breaths, the ache refused to recede.

All the momentum he'd felt after the Golden Spire and *Carthage* heists had halted abruptly, and it stung. Milli being MIA had metaphorically thrown an asteroid into the path of their voidstream trajectory.

He had a responsibility to Milli; it was his duty to help her if she was in trouble. She was a fellow soldier of the Imperium—a comrade in arms. As an Outrider, his clan-mark compelled him to come to her aid.

That duty also extended to her husband.

He, Riza, and Golath hopped aboard one of the gravtrams and

traveled thirty minutes from the Egris District to the eastern Calvetti District. One of the largest residential sectors on the planet, the Calvetti was where most of the middle and lower class citizens lived. Nearly thirty million residents were within the borders of the Calvetti District, and it showed.

The buildings of this district had a distinct blocky design, only some bearing a thatched roof. Everything was cramped together; apartments were stacked on top of one another while walkways zigzagged in tight angles. To his surprise, he'd learned that the Bureau—despite having Capital funding—didn't pay their agents as well as he thought. With the costs of food, water, fuel, and technology, Milli and her husband could only afford a two-story townhome in the Calvetti District three blocks from the gravtram station.

A block from the townhome, Riza cleared her throat, drawing his attention. "Everything okay?" he asked.

Riza looked away, taking a deep breath before saying, "Aelec, pardon my bluntness, but why in the Void are we doing this?"

"What do you mean 'why?'" He frowned at her, then said, "We need her to clear our records from the holonet and get us a proper ride. Did I not speak in Trade?"

"There's got to be another way we can achieve those goals," Riza protested. "What about Ko? Why couldn't he get us cleared?"

Aelec sighed. "Ko is good at finding data, not erasing it. Besides, he no longer has credentials to enter Imperium databases."

"Okay," Riza breathed, pushing her hair behind her ear. "Then someone else. Another Outrider? C'mon, Aelec. I don't think we should be spending our time chasing Spectre. We need to go after Kuvan."

"We will," he said simply. "But we have to be smart about it, Riza. Milli is our best chance, and I'm not going to leave her hanging out to dry."

Riza's nostrils flared, and her sapphire eyes narrowed. "So, this is more of a personal thing then?"

"It's not like that," Aelec said, his fingers combing through his long hair. "Milli's a friend, a comrade-in-arms. She wasn't an Outrider, but she was almost like a clan-sister. If she's in trouble, then I have to help her."

Riza huffed, cramming her hands into her jacket pockets. "You're the boss. But this isn't exactly what I signed up for. I thought we'd be closer to bringing my sister's murderer to justice, not taking a detour."

"The path forward isn't always a straight line, Riza," Aelec said with a shrug. "It twists and turns. You never know what allies you might make along those detours."

Riza arched an eyebrow but said nothing as they turned at the block's corner.

Milli's townhome was narrow, with elongated windows on both floors and a small balcony. It was constructed of simple carbocrete of cream and gray colors, though the window and door frames were a burgundy morristeel. The townhome was sandwiched between two others; you couldn't tell where one ended and another began.

Being a former soldier in the Imperium armada, Aelec was quick to spot the smart lock at the front door. It was a small hologram display that linked to the ID signatures of the Spectres' terminuses, relying on signals rather than pin numbers. Such a system would be difficult for the average burglar to trick.

Closing the distance, Aelec paused when he heard a soft buzzing sound coming from above him. He spotted a white-colored drone hovering near the townhome's second floor, its red photoreceptor fixating on him. It was yet another security measure; a drone would deploy if anyone other than the Spectres approached the property.

Not bad, Milli, Aelec thought as he stepped up to the door. *Even an Outrider would think twice before breaking into your home.*

He gently pressed his thumb to the buzzer. The sweet smell of perfume alerted him, and he noticed that Riza had stepped up beside him.

She looked up at Aelec with big eyes and asked, "Have you met Spectre's husband before?"

"I have not," Aelec said, shaking his head. "She talked about him a lot when we worked together, but once the S.R.A. crisis was over I was quickly shipped out to Morrigar. I never had the chance to meet him."

"What did she say about him?"

"He works in maintenance. A contractor, I think. Apparently he's big into building models, and last I heard Milli was getting into the hobby."

Riza smiled. "That's kind of adorable."

A *hiss* emanated from the door as it slid into a wall nook. Within the doorway was a burly man bearing a haunted expression. His eyelids drooped, and his frizzy brown hair looked like he'd just gotten out of bed. Aelec could feel the anguish radiating from this man.

Stepping out from the doorway, the light from the sun illuminated more of his tan face, and Aelec noticed the dark circles under his hazel eyes. He crossed his arms, his biceps bulging through his fitted white shirt. His size reminded Aelec a lot of Dylis, though his musculature was distinctly civilian—only military exercise could achieve certain results.

"Can I help you?" he asked in a gruff voice.

"Ferris Spectre?" Aelec retorted, keeping his own hands within his dust coat's pockets.

"Yeah," he grumbled. "What do you want?"

Aelec took a step forward and lowered his voice. "I'm Aelec Xero. I'm a friend of Milli. These are my crewmates Riza Noxia and Golath of Kyg-nor. Can we chat inside?"

Ferris' eyes narrowed. "The guy who stiffed her last year? You're the one Milli kept covering for. The smuggler!"

"Sol above, Aelec!" Riza said, her expression aghast. "You stiffed her?"

He raised his hands in an innocent gesture. "A robbery job on

Asmodum didn't pay as well as I thought."

Ferris ignored Aelec's explanation, murmuring, "Not sure how I feel about having smugglers in my home."

"Ferris," Aelec said firmly, "let's talk inside. I don't want the wrong ears listening in on us."

To his surprise, Ferris didn't budge—he continued to block the door frame and a snarl crept onto his face. Before either of them could respond, Riza took a few steps in front of Aelec.

"We're here to help," she said, her voice soft and sweet. "Sorry. I know the captain can be a bit... blunt, at times. But we want no trouble. We want to help you."

The scowl didn't leave Ferris' face as he looked from Aelec to Riza and back again. Yet, the man's shoulders relaxed by a degree and his arm muscles stopped tensing as he met Riza's gaze. Shockingly, Ferris' hazel eyes softened as Riza smiled gently at him.

Aelec raised his eyebrows.

Riza had shown herself capable of deception and determination when she lied her way onto the *Erinyes* and got the jump on Aelec during the Golden Spire heist. Her craftiness had made him drop all of his preordained opinions of her, though he still felt that Riza was a good person. But seeing how she effortlessly slipped into a benevolent persona and speaking with such kind tones made Aelec reevaluate her once again.

Either Riza was really, *really* good at acting, or she was simply a kind woman. Aelec wanted to believe in her earnestness, but he couldn't shake the suspicions gnawing at his mind. If she was so effortlessly compassionate with Ferris, did that mean she could still be masquerading around Aelec?

You chose to trust her again, Aelec reminded himself. *Doubts are corrosive to an Outrider's clan.*

Her attitude worked like a charm, and Ferris lowered his arms as he took a step back from the doorway.

"Come in," he snorted. "Let's see how helpful you really are."

Riza looked over her shoulder at Aelec and gave him a playful wink. Aelec rolled his eyes. He followed her into the townhome, and Golath was forced to hunch down just to get through the doorway. A few irritated clicks emanated from his respirator.

The inside of the townhome was a stark difference from the inner areas of the *Erinyes*. Aelec's boots gently thudded against the velvet, burgundy carpet. Pallid white LED lights lined the ceiling, highlighting the pale couch and chair in the lounge room. News footage from the holonet was displayed over an antique wooden shelf at the room's opposite end.

Inside the kitchen Ferris shuffled a few items on the granite countertop. Aelec spotted countless scattered pieces of plastic and a half-built model skyscraper.

Ferris waved his hand at the hovering gravlift seats by the counter, saying, "Sit if you want. Stand. I don't care."

Riza didn't hesitate to sit on the couch, crossing one leg over the other and putting her hands in her lap. Aelec leaned against the wall next to a nearby fusion generator. Golath shuffled toward Ferris, stopped short of the human, and emitted a string of soft clicks. In conjunction with his vocalization, he gestured with his four limbs, pointing from his chest to the kitchen. Ferris arched an eyebrow in confusion as he stared up at the nonhuman.

"He's asking for permission to enter your kitchen," Aelec affirmed.

"Why?" Ferris asked tersely.

"A kitchen is like a shrine to the Kygi," he explained. "He sees it as a holy part of your home and I believe he wants to pay his respects."

Ferris frowned but stepped to the side. "Fine. Just don't touch anything."

Golath bowed his triangular head and moved slowly into the kitchen area as his clicking rose in pitch. Ferris, in turn, leaned his elbows against the granite bartop and eyed Aelec.

"You said you were here to help Milli," Ferris grumbled. "How? You're not C.B.I. or any other Imperium agency."

"As you said," Aelec retorted, "we're smugglers, so we won't be playing by the book. The C.B.I. hasn't had any luck finding her because they've scared off these Far Syter folks. My crew and I are off the grid. Any details on us would show that we operate outside the law."

Riza cleared her throat before adding, "We can get into places the C.B.I. can't. We can pass off as beneficiaries to a lower level gang."

Aelec nodded in agreement. "We just need more information about these Far Syters."

"The C.B.I. didn't give you enough data to go on?"

"Agencies tend to miss the little things that these cases are built on," Aelec retorted, crossing his arms. "Their insight is analytical, not personal. Milli would've talked to you if something was troubling her. From what the C.B.I. did tell me, it seems like she had a run-in with the Syters before."

Ferris sighed, almost in resignation, and Aelec noticed a change in his tone. "You're not wrong, Xero. Milli always tried not to talk shop when she came through the door, but there were some cases that nagged her no matter where she went. This was one of 'em."

Riza rested her arm on the couch's backrest as she turned more to face Ferris. "Why was it bothering her?"

Ferris rubbed the back of his neck and took a deep breath. Now that part of his gruff persona had been chipped away, Aelec could see the worried spouse beneath. The restless anxiety wafted from Ferris like an odor, and Aelec felt a swell of pity for the man.

"The Parasytes... what we call the Syters... had been messing with Milli for a few months," Ferris admitted, looking from Riza to Aelec. "Nothing physical, they're too smart for that. But cyber attacks. Harassment. Altered images of her and myself. It was some messed up shit."

Aelec frowned. "Why would they do this?"

"She was cracking down on some of their threatening posts on the holonet," Ferris explained. "The Parasytes posted anything from video threats, banner burning, and even alleged coordinates for Imperium officials. It got bad enough that law enforcement started arresting gang members on sight. And they weren't gentle with them. Tensions escalated between the gang and government agencies. Then some Parasyte assholes started to harass anyone associated with the Imperium reserves or C.B.I. So, Milli was caught in the crossfire."

Riza nodded in understanding. "The dark side of the holonet," she murmured. "I knew a few people in the Academy that got a taste of how awful those posts can be."

"She put up a good front for a while," Ferris continued, looking at his feet. "But a few weeks ago, she had a panic attack and I had to get her to Calvetti General. The autodoc got her calmed down, but she was still shaken up afterwards. She said she was going to give the Syters payback, but I assumed that meant something she'd do at work."

Aelec's eyebrows raised and he took a step away from the wall. "She confronted them?!"

Ferris nodded. "Off C.B.I. books, too. Said she was having words with a guy named Leonis. Head of the Parasytes, or some such."

Faster than he could have anticipated, Riza ran a search on her terminus, and after a moment she pulled up a profile. With a wave of her hand, she sent the image to the hologram displayed above the shelf. A profile image of a dark-skinned man with graying-black cornrows rotated above lines of text.

"Leonis Ingot," Riza narrated, standing up from the couch. "Current head of the Far Syter guild, and former history professor at New Skyline's Umber Academy. His trade skill specialized in artifact preservation and analysis. Looks like he was let go from his tenure due to inciting protests against the Academy's benefactors."

"Not a bright idea, biting the hand that feeds you," Aelec noted.

He glanced back at Ferris, who was still standing near the bartop and resting his elbows on the granite counter. Behind him, Golath was moseying around in the kitchen, the Kygi's yellow eyes widened as he surveyed the equipment. Particularly fascinated with Ferris' cutlery, Golath cocked his head from side to side as he examined the various knives.

Ferris glowered at the image of Leonis and asked, "Why haven't the C.B.I. taken him into custody?! They have his file, so he should be suspect number one! That son of a bitch is responsible for all this!"

"It looks like he's on their most wanted list," Riza explained calmly, pulling up the search warrant. "But he and all known Syters have been off the grid since your wife disappeared. Reports show that field agents tracked the guild members to the underground gravtram tunnels before losing them."

Shaking his head, Ferris huffed, "Dammit! But it makes sense. Heat in those tunnels is enough to scramble all kinds of sensors. Unless you know where to go, you can easily get lost down there."

"How do you know that?" Aelec queried.

"Because I work for the district's maintenance department," Ferris replied shortly. "Couldn't tell you how many complaints we get about the gravtrain tunnels."

"Now we're talking," Aelec said, rubbing his gloved hands together. "Do you have schematics of the tunnels connecting to the western dockyard?"

"I do," Ferris answered, nodding to the second floor. "The puck is in my work kit."

"Mind if we borrow it?" Aelec asked. "We need to pay a visit to the spot where Milli disappeared and see if we can find some Syters."

Ferris leaned away from the bartop and crossed his arms. "Yeah, I mind. Unless you take me with you."

"What?"

"Take me with you," the burly man repeated. "I know those tunnels, and I can't just sit here on my ass while Milli is missing. Not when I can do something about it."

"Ferris, we can't," Riza said softly. "The Syters know who you are. It'll be hard for us to win them over if we're seen hanging around with you, the husband of a C.B.I. agent. It's better if you stay safe at home."

"But I—"

Aelec raised a hand, cutting him off. "We'll give you updates as often as we can, Ferris. On my clan-mark."

"That literally means nothing to me!" Ferris snapped. "I barely know you and expect me to trust you? Why should I?"

Staring at him with a stoic expression, Aelec said, "Because I care for Milli like a sister, and without her, my crew and I are completely screwed."

Ferris glowered at him with those keen, hazel eyes. His jaw clenched in irritation, and Aelec could see that he was resisting the urge to shout.

"Explain," Ferris hissed through clenched teeth.

"I can't go into explicit details. The less you know, the better. But we need your wife's help, so it's in our best interest to find her and bring her home safely."

When Ferris narrowed his eyes, Riza was quick to lend her voice.

"The details might put you in danger, Ferris," she explained. "Please. You have to trust us."

Taking a long moment to examine them, Ferris let out a defeated sigh.

"Fine," he admitted. "I'll trust you. For now. If you give your word to check in with me on every update, I'll lend you the schematics."

Riza met the man's gaze, and Aelec saw conviction there.

"You have my word," she breathed.

Ferris relented and allowed Aelec to retrieve the hologram puck in his workman's kit. While most people used wrist terminuses for such things, maintenance workers opted to use individual pucks to prevent hackers from tampering with them. Aelec placed the palm-sized puck into his duster's pocket, curtly thanked Ferris, and beckoned for his companions to follow him out.

As he reached the front door, however, Ferris put a hand on his shoulder, and Aelec stopped.

"You bring her home to me," Ferris grunted, a note of pleading in his voice. "I don't care what it takes."

It wasn't the firm hand on his shoulder that gave Aelec pause. It was the words that reverberated from the mouth of a desperate and distraught husband. Aelec knew that desperation; of that incessant need to fulfill a promise.

"I will."

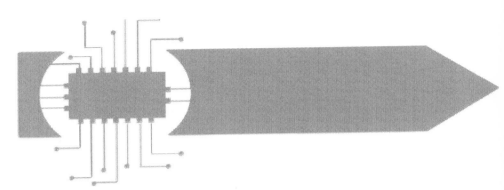

CHAPTER 16

Riza walked alongside Aelec as they followed the street back towards the gravtram station. The heavy *thuds* of Golath's taloned feet came from behind her, and the Kygi's four claws fidgeted with bony taps. High above, the russet skyline was darkening; the sun slowly hid behind a canvass of churning gray clouds. Rumbles echoed from beyond the district, and Riza smelled the first vestiges of rainwater. A storm was coming.

She kept her hands tucked in the pockets of her leather jacket as she walked. Neither she nor Aelec had spoken since leaving the Spectre townhouse, but neither of them were in foul moods. She wanted to process the new information supplied by Ferris, and she guessed Aelec did as well.

Pushing through a crowd of humans and Vitrax, they weaved their way through more pedestrians as they approached the gravtram station. Out of the corner of her eye, Riza noticed that Aelec's hand kept brushing against the grip of his holstered E-pistol. Looking up at him, she saw his auric eyes staring off into the distance.

She hesitated, but then reached out to gently touch his upper arm, causing him to flinch.

"Aelec, relax," she said. "We've got a solid lead. Once I get my hands on the security cams, we'll have a better idea of what happened to her. Then we'll scour the tunnels."

He sighed, and she felt his muscled arm pressing into her hand as his shoulders heaved.

Aelec was well known for being gruff and serious with a dose of wryness, but this was different. He was on a mission to save a friend, and he was doing so with the steadfast determination of a man still rooted in the military. There was an intensity in his eyes that drew her in, even more hypnotizing than before.

Part of her felt slightly irritated at his attention to this mission, this quest to save Spectre. Riza had hoped that she'd be able to clear the air with not just Aelec, but with Myra as well. This could've been her chance to open up to him, and maybe get him to do the same. She wanted more moments like the night they'd shared together before the heist, before she'd screwed it all up.

She'd been given a second chance to be part of the *Erinyes'* crew, but she still felt the wedge of incredulity. Trust had to be repaired, and she felt the intense desire to prove her worth. Weeks ago, she'd embarked on a similar path, but only to manipulate the crew. Lead seemed to fill her stomach as she recalled trying to capture Aelec in that vault on Caavo.

Aelec, despite her betrayal, had offered closure on Arenia's death two years ago. He showed her that it was the Comitors who were responsible for her sister's murder, and that Veritas Kuvan had pulled those strings. That day she'd learned that Aelec Xero was a class act—a true man of honor. Riza wanted to live up to that expectation.

"You might need to relax yourself, Riza."

Aelec's voice snapped her out of her thoughts, and she saw her fingers digging into his arm. Her eyes went wide and she jerked her hand away, promptly shoving it back into her jacket pocket. She felt her cheeks burning as Aelec gazed at her with his keen eyes.

"Sorry," she squeaked. "I kinda zoned out for a second."

Aelec chuckled. "I could see that. Guess that's why we're a team. You tell me to relax, I tell you to relax, and Golath keeps us both in line."

The Kygi clicked in what sounded like a grunt; Aelec looked back at him and smirked. Golath returned Aelec's gaze with a slight bow of the head, a gesture Riza interpreted as his way of saying, "if you say so."

"What's on your mind?" Aelec asked, his eyes surveying her.

"I keep reliving that day in the Golden Spire," she sighed. "It's eating me up inside, Aelec. I want to make it up to you. To Myra. But, I don't know what I can offer."

"You have your hacking skills."

"But that's it!" Her head snapped to look up at him. "All I am is a hacker. But you... you're a warrior, a tactician, a leader. You're... you're incredible. How can I possibly prove my worth to someone like you?"

It was Aelec's turn to touch her arm, his grip firm and warm. Comforting and secure.

His keen eyes pierced into her like twin suns. "Be yourself, Riza."

When she hesitated, Aelec continued, "No lies. No performances. No hidden agenda. Just Riza Noxia."

"And that's enough for you?"

He nodded. "It is."

"Well, alright then," Riza said, looking away. She cleared her throat and continued, "Sorry about that. Time for me to focus. You're still up for scouring the tunnels, right?"

"Depends on what you find in the dockyard," Aelec said, releasing her arm.

"Do you think the Syters are dangerous?"

"If they attacked a C.B.I. agent in broad daylight, yes." Checking his terminus, Aelec continued, "It'll take us an hour to get from here to the Medina District. I want you to analyze the tunnel schematics and see which ones are linked to the dockyard hubs."

Riza nodded. "You got it, boss."

He paused as they entered the gravtram station, then said, "I need to call Dylis. See what they've been up to."

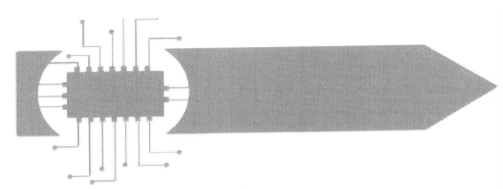

CHAPTER 17

New Skyline: The Egris District, GST: 13:30

Myra always hated the smell of hospitals. The overwhelming scent of antiseptics, cleansing solvents, and healing foams made her tentacles shiver. Her heightened sense of smell was sensitive to the scents wafting through the sterile, cold air of the hospital. Though, it was better her than Golath—she knew the Kygi would be catatonic if he'd ventured into this place.

After splitting off from the others, she, Dylis, and Rant had traveled to the nearest medical facility in New Skyline: Egris General. It was a short gravtram ride from the C.B.I. office, and they'd arrived just after 13:15 Galactic Standard Time.

Swirling clouds blotted out the sun once they'd gotten off the gravtram, allowing the city's lights to become more prominent. Neon LEDs of violet, blue, and gold sparkled across the glossy morristeel structures and reflected off the gravvehicles that passed by. She had to push through a sea of humans, Togrians, and Vitrax before finally getting to the hospital.

Egris General was a massive complex of cylindrical towers interconnected with walkways that occasionally shifted to different levels based on the occupants. The morristeel framework was pallid white, while portions of carbocrete were either black or red. The red and white helped signify this as a medical facility to the common masses.

Well... it signified to the *human* masses.

White for their preferred style of hospital room colors, and red for the shade of their blood. A Vitrax-built medical center would use colors of green and orange, since their room colors had a warm, orange tint and her species had green blood. But alas, humans always had to have things *their* way.

Even with the Meridiem-style buildings, the Togrian-style plating on gravvehicles, the Kygi-style food vendors, and Vitrax-style leisure dens, Oais was still human-centric. Myra could feel it in the air. The humans were much more civil and inclusive on a Capital World, but she could sense a pedigree of elitism in their glances. Whether they knew it or not, the humans carried themselves as if they were the lords and ladies of this world, and the nonhumans were just visitors.

Myra reasoned that it was a fundamental human flaw, one that they couldn't evolve past. No matter how hard they tried to play nice with nonhumans, she felt like humans couldn't truly acquiesce control. They could never one hundred percent trust a nonhuman.

It was for that very reason why Myra still harbored resentment towards Riza. She had been the prime example of a human doing what she wanted without any regard to those around her. Riza didn't care that two nonhumans had put their full trust in her; she had only been using them to get close to Aelec.

Myra suppressed the resentment that was threatening to build up like bile in her throat. She had a job to do.

Standing off to the side in the waiting area, the reception area was massive, large enough to host a few hundred people and not feel crowded. Glancing to the side, she saw her reflection in a wide mirror. In fact, most of the walls were lined with such mirrors. An equal number of patients and medical personnel shuffled around, their murmurs creating a chorus of white noise.

Something that caught her attention was the equal number of humans and Vitrax wearing white lab coats and silky-blue scrubs. A few Vitrax were even giving instructions to the humans, signifying them as doctors.

Myra took a deep breath, shivering at the bitter scents of the medical facility. *You're not on Sath,* she reminded herself. *You're not on Caavo. You're on Oais. And you've got a job to do.*

The trio approached a ring of terminals that served as the reception area. Neon holograms formed a screen-like barrier displaying patient information, medical prescriptions, and account data.

Myra stopped a couple paces from the terminal-desk. Dylis leaned his hip haughtily against the machine and rested an elbow on its top. His arm distorted the transparent hologram, and the nearest receptionist sneered at him.

Myra eyed the receptionist. He was human, likely no older than twenty. His sky blue, mesh-fiber scrubs were pristine, with very few wrinkles. Myra also noticed the cluster of medicinal nanoparticles attached to his belt for emergency purposes.

Before Dylis could utter a word to him, Myra decided to use one of her most effective charms: herself. She stood with her hands clasped before her, a pose which highlighted the natural curves of her body. The form-fitting turtleneck was perfect for this occasion. As a Vitrax of this generation, she was peak perfection among the humanoid species—even a Meridiem would consider her gorgeous.

"Oh, hello there, young sir," Myra said, the words rolled off her tongue like a purr. "How are you today? Hope things haven't been too crazy."

The young man's eyes lit up at the sight of her, clearing his throat before saying, "I can't complain. We've been steady for the past two hours. I'm more than happy to help assist you. Do you have a medical emergency or an appointment, ma'am?"

"Technically, no," she admitted. "I mean, I might be having some shortness of breath."

"Shortness of breath?" the receptionist repeated. "Do you have any underlying conditions, ma'am?"

She rocked her head from side to side. "Does talking with a handsome receptionist count as one?"

The young man's cheeks reddened, and Myra spotted a mix of interest and nervousness in his dark eyes. Humans, especially young males, were so easy to manipulate. A sensual expression, some compliments, and showing a sliver of interest was enough to wrap them around her finger. Dylis rolled his eyes and groaned. Even Myra felt ashamed of what she'd said. It was such a bad line that it felt like her tentacles were shriveling. Yet, it worked.

"That... that doesn't sound like a serious condition, ma'am," the receptionist chuckled.

Myra shrugged. "Well, say if I were looking for something," she said, tilting her head to the side. "Something you might be able to help me with."

He gulped. "What might that be?"

"An equipment manifest," Dylis said quickly before Myra could continue the tease. "Or directions to a hospital that would have what we're looking for."

The young receptionist broke his gaze away from Myra to look at Dylis. "Depending on what you're looking for, I might be able to detail if it's in stock. But, what are your credentials? If you're not patients, who are you?"

"Contractors," Myra said smoothly.

In conjunction with her words, Dylis flashed the Private Security Contractor chain code from his terminus. The receptionist blinked, and Myra could see some of the color leaving his face.

"Of course, of course!" he said quickly. "We're happy to help a few government contractors. We share databases with all of New

Skyline's hospitals, so I'll get all of that to you. I'll warn you that the manifest of equipment is quite extensive."

Myra smiled at him. "That's alright. My friend here can make short work of it." She gestured to Rant, the droid's head jerking around to survey Myra and then the receptionist.

After a moment, the receptionist waved his hand at the hologram before him, and Myra's terminus blinked. She, in turn, sent the file to Rant's nanotech port, and the droid went rigid, a soft beeping emitting from him.

Myra turned back to the receptionist and gave him a wide smile. "Thanks, handsome. And if you could do me a solid and not mention what we were looking for, that would be so sweet."

Some color returned to his cheeks and he nodded his head. "Sure thing, ma'am."

She winked at him, hoping her flirtations would help him keep his tongue tied. It was another tactic she'd learned out in the Fringe. A pretty smile and a little bit of flirting would put you into a man's—or woman's—good graces; it made them feel important. Someone who felt as such was less likely to act against you than someone you'd scorned.

The last thing they needed was for the entire medical community to know that they were investigating their manifests. Even if his superiors saw the data transfer signature, they wouldn't know who he'd sent it to so long as he remained tight-lipped.

Rant's domed head rotated as the beeping ceased, his scan complete. They moved to the back of the waiting area, letting the other patients funnel in like a rushing tide. Myra sat in one of the cushioned seats extending from the wall, and Rant skittered up to her, his appendages clicking against the burnished tiles.

"Statement: Master Myra, this unit has finished the analysis of New Skyline's medical manifest and have noted one oddity," the droid said in a monotone.

"And that is?"

The droid wobbled, responding, "Answer: The medical center at coordinates three-seven point six-three-one-one-seven-three, designation Medina General Hospital, had a private purchase of one standard quantum scalpel on forty-five-zero-nine point zero-eight-twenty-six."

Dylis perked up and met Myra's gaze. "That's four days ago," he said.

"The day before Spectre went missing," Myra concluded, her voice quiet. Looking at Rant's spider-like eyes, she continued, "We need to track that purchase. Is there any quantocurrency data?"

Rant paused, his head swiveling. "Answer: Negative, Master Myra. All medical purchases in Medina General Hospital on forty-five-zero-nine point zero-eight-twenty-six pertained to copays, nanoparticle surgeries, and drug prescriptions."

"Shit," she muttered, her hand tugging on one of her tentacles. "How in the Void can we track that purchase then?"

Dylis snorted. "We can use a time-honored tactic known as *asking*."

Myra glared at him. "And they'll just spill their guts like they've done a round of Void Shots?"

"It's a start," he replied with a shrug. "If they don't talk, I'm good at shakedowns."

"Dylis," Myra sighed, "the whole purpose of this is to *not* draw attention."

"And I won't," Dylis said, frowning. "I've had to shakedown people far worse than a Capital World hospital attendant, you know."

The words lingered in Myra's mind, her tentacles pulsed, and she felt a cool surge of dopamine. Like all of their crew, Dylis had a complicated past, one that he didn't particularly enjoy talking about. Myra had gotten glimpses of what happened before his tenure on the *Erinyes*, but plenty of calculations were still missing.

"That happened a lot on Faerius?" she asked.

Dylis shot her a dark look. "Something like that," he grunted. "C'mon. This thing isn't going to solve itself."

Myra didn't press the matter, following Dylis out of the hospital building and back towards the nearest gravtram station. Rant skittered beside her like a mechanical canine. Once aboard the gravtram, the trio went to the rear of the vehicle as it took off at a steady pace.

She sat in one of the worn seats. There were plenty to choose from since there weren't many people in their compartment. The ride between districts would take close to an hour, and questions still burned within Myra's skull.

"Aelec's never mentioned Spectre before," she blurted, drawing Dylis' attention. "I know this mission against Kuvan is important to him, but why is he so gung-ho to find her?"

"Why don't you ask him?" he replied, crossing his muscled arms.

"I'm asking you. You knew Aelec back in those days. I want an outside opinion."

Dylis glanced away and sighed. "She saved his life. More than once, apparently. And vice versa. He might've been a prime Outrider, but he was still new to being a leader. Imagine being only twenty-one and having to be responsible for nine people's lives."

"I figured he'd always been a capable leader." She cupped her chin, saying, "So, she was like a guardian seraph to him?"

"More like a partner. I watched their debriefings, and even saw footage of their raids. They almost single-handedly wiped out the S.R.A. together."

Myra considered the information. She knew Aelec valued camaraderie, and after witnessing his entire clan massacred, it made sense for him to be overprotective of his friends. But she still found it odd that Aelec had never mentioned Spectre before.

"I always assumed we were his only friends left," she murmured.

"He had a good reason to keep her on the downlow," Dylis said. "Aelec probably wanted to keep her identity a secret in case any of us were turncoats. It's a part of his past he kept hidden, and it was warranted."

Hiding from your past, Myra repeated. Words itched at the back of her mind, and they snuck past her lips.

"Why do you hide from your past, Dylis?" she exclaimed, instantly regretting the words.

The older man looked down at her with cold, green eyes. "I'm not hiding," he hissed. "I just choose not to dwell on it and instead focus on how I'm going to fix it. If you spend your life worrying about a few mistakes, then you'll never find a way to move beyond them."

Myra leaned her head against the headrest, glancing up at Dylis. "Your wife is alive and well. What more could you want?"

He paused and gazed out the same window, watching the city pass by before replying, "It's *how* I kept her alive that bothers me." Dylis snorted in agitation before rounding on Myra. "Could say the same about you. Last time I checked, you're still running from SecuriTrax."

She sneered at him. "That's different and you know it! I was a slave, Dylis! It's not something I'm terribly keen on reminiscing about."

"So why haven't you targeted Sire Dalin?"

The question hit her like a ton of carbocrete. Pax Dalin was her former owner on Sath, and the human in charge of SecuriTrax, a private defense fleet. It was true, in all her years working on the *Erinyes'* crew, she'd never sought to target Dalin for a job. She could've robbed him, sabotaged him, or even tried to kill him. Yet, she hadn't.

When Myra didn't respond, Dylis continued, "We've hit way harder shitbags than SecuriTrax, so what are you afraid of? Unless you have mixed feelings about Dalin."

"You don't know anything!" she snapped. "I shouldn't have brought it up! Forget I said anything!"

"It's a shame you couldn't use clairvoyance to see how pointless this conversation would be," Dylis muttered. "At least I'm trying to fix my past."

She turned away from him, not rising to his bait. That was the thing about Dylis, if you got him riled up he'd hit you where it hurt. She wouldn't show him, but she was disturbed that his words had sunken in.

Pax Dalin and SecuriTrax had been things she'd left behind and never wanted to look back on. But what if they'd never left her? What if her past eventually came back to affect her or the crew? In Dalin's mind, she was still under his employ—under his ownership.

And if she knew anything about the *sires* in the Fringe, it was that they never forgot what was theirs.

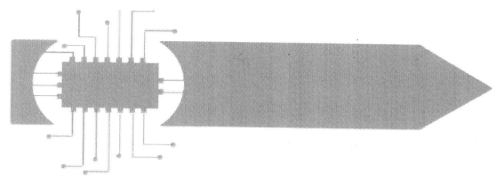

CHAPTER 18

New Skyline: The Medina District, GST: 14:38

Dylis was no stranger to investigative work; a lot of operations clan-Wyri performed involved subterfuge and tracking. Eight years ago, he and a full squad had scoured the forests of Nidal to track an alien-sire who'd tried trafficking several Vitrax girls to the Fringe. They'd followed tracks, analyzed DNA samples, observed heat signatures... all standard methods for finding a human. Within hours, they'd located and subdued the scumbag.

Trying to track Milli was another beast entirely. There was no steady trail or solid proof as to where she was. It was all obscured, messy.

But that didn't mean the trail was cold.

The front doors of Medina General parted with a strained, metallic groan. One of them wobbled as it moved into a wall nook. He blinked rapidly, his eyes adjusting to the dim LEDs. The clacking of Rant's appendages against the floor seemed louder, and Dylis noticed portions of tile were cracked and loose.

A shiver ran down his spine. Hopefully they wouldn't be there long. On a hunt like this, they needed to cover as many starlanes as fast as possible to have any luck with finding Milli.

Approaching a similar receptionist area like the one in Egris General, the trio stopped just short of the ring-like terminal desk. Beyond the wall of holograms, he saw a middle-aged man squinting at the images, his hawk-like face scrunched in concentration. Beady brown eyes glanced up at them, and the man swiped a few of the holograms away to get a better look at them.

"Welcome to Medina General," he yawned. "What brings you in today?"

Pressing two fingers to his terminus, Dylis proffered his arm as the chain code displayed above his wrist. The receptionist, in turn, used a separate device to scan the code, and his eyes stared at one of his terminal projections. Myra crossed her arms, and every time he made eye contact with her, she averted her gaze.

Her lips pursed in a sour expression. They hadn't spoken since getting off the gravtram. After his rather unsavory conversation with Myra on the ride over, Dylis wasn't in the mood for games. The sooner they solved this mystery, the quicker they could continue their mission against Kuvan.

He kept his haughty persona on like a mask—he always did, because there were enough brooding people on the crew of the *Erinyes*. But more, he didn't want to bring any attention to his darker side, the side that he tried to bury.

"Your code checks out, sir," the receptionist declared, meeting Dylis' gaze. "What can Medina General do for a contractor such as yourself?"

Dylis nodded to Rant, and the droid teetered forward to display a small hologram list. Myra turned her attention towards the clerk and cleared her throat.

"My droid found a slight discrepancy in your supply manifests," she said quietly.

"Statement: This unit detected that an undisclosed party visiting Medina General Hospital on forty-five-zero-nine point zero-eight-twenty-six purchased one standard quantum scalpel."

The man blinked rapidly. "That doesn't seem right. It's against policy to sell medical devices or tools to parties unaffiliated with the medical guilds. Are you sure this data is accurate?"

"Without a doubt," Dylis said, his voice a low rumble.

Myra lifted a slender hand to stroke one of her tentacles as she said, "It won't show in the quantocurrency exchange logs. Perhaps they used something else to barter for it. Can you check for anything like that?"

"One moment," the receptionist said as his hands flew across the holograms.

Dylis leaned his hip against the terminal desk, his eyes wandering around the hospital waiting area. There were patients waiting to be seen, families reading terminus articles, children playing with toys, staff gathering supplies... All appeared normal.

He wasn't looking for anything in particular, it was just a habit of people-watching that he'd picked up in the Fringe. It was a type of situational awareness, a way of remaining vigilant even in places that were deemed safe.

A few doctors conversed heatedly with their staff, a nurse rushed through the crowd, a hooded figure stared right at him...

Dylis' attention snapped back to a spot in the crowd. Near the connecting hallway stood a man wearing a gray hood that obscured most of his face and head. The mesh-fiber was stained with dark splotches, portions shredded along the shoulders. The ends of the hood were tucked beneath a suit of form-fitting, black armor.

He stood with an iron-back posture, like a morristeel statue, his chest rising and falling. Normally, Dylis wouldn't think anything of it, but the man continued to stare at him. He felt a chill trace down his back.

The hooded stranger noticed Dylis' gaze, and he casually turned away, weaving through the crowd of people. It confirmed Dylis' suspicions. They were being watched by someone, and he was going to find out why.

"Hey!" Dylis shouted, trying to draw everyone's attention. The more people that were aware of him, the more witnesses there'd be. Also a dense crowd would make it easier to catch up with him.

The hooded figure didn't miss a beat as he looked back at Dylis and went into an all-out sprint. Dylis hesitated, and by the time his own legs started moving the man was a dozen paces away. He couldn't let him escape!

Barreling through the crowd of medical attendants, Dylis kept a tight grip on his E-rifle case. He easily nudged people out of the way, tempering his enhanced strength to avoid hurting anyone.

"P.S.C. here, people!" He pushed through more attendants and yelled, "Stop that man!"

The crowd shuffled nervously, and they began grouping together in a tight formation. A tight formation between Dylis and the hooded man. *Crap!*

His attempt to draw attention to the hooded figure had back-fired, but there was no stopping it now. Losing a few seconds, Dylis sprinted down the hospital hallway, his boots thumped against the floor so fiercely he felt the tiles cracking.

The target was a dozen meters ahead of him and nearing the end of the hallway. Skidding to a halt, the figure opened a blastdoor on the left side and slipped through. The LED sign indicated it was the west stairwell. Dylis skidded to a halt, then dashed into the stairwell.

He glanced up, trying to see where the figure had gone. The familiar hooded shape darted up the stairs. With the practiced skill of an Outrider, he set his weapon case down, opened it, and snapped together the pieces of his E-rifle within a couple seconds before resuming pursuit.

Aiming above him, Dylis shouted, "Stop right there or I'll shoot!"

The hooded figure ignored him, bounding up another flight of stairs. He was almost two floors above him. Dylis couldn't let him gain any more ground. Halting on the stairs, Dylis aimed the E-rifle at the spot where the figure's shoulder would be and squeezed the trigger.

An electric *crack* echoed within the stairwell, and a brilliant, amber-colored fusion bolt exploded from the rifle's elongated muzzle. The energy streaked upward and struck the wall just behind the man with a dull *thud*. His stride didn't slow. It was like he didn't care that Dylis had just fired at him!

A heartbeat after he fired the weapon came the wailing klaxons of the hospital. He winced, the blaring alarms stinging his eardrums. LED lights turned from pale to flashing red. He could hear the panicked shouts from patients and medical staff.

Keeping his E-rifle raised, Dylis advanced up the stairs. His eye caught movement. The hooded man was nearly three floors above him now.

"That was a warning!" Dylis barked. "This is your last chance! Stop!"

The figure ignored Dylis, heading towards the sixth floor of the hospital. Once more, Dylis paused, aimed, and fired the E-rifle. The shot struck the carbocrete mere inches from where the man's head had been.

Yet again, the hooded man moved without a care in the galaxy like he was expecting Dylis to miss. Perhaps that was intentional. Did he know that Dylis wouldn't shoot to kill?

Shit! Dylis swore to himself. *He's good.*

It took some effective combat training to anticipate someone's firing intent like that. Dylis was certain that whoever this man was, he was no stranger to a firefight. But to his surprise, the hooded man didn't return fire. He just kept running.

Six floors above him, his target quickly activated the blastdoor on the ninth floor and went through. Focusing on his nanoparticles, Dylis created a grappling hook, fired at the ceiling, and was pulled up the stairwell. Deposited on the ninth floor, he saw the open blastdoor, retracted his grappling hook, and surged through the entrance—his attention glued on the hallway beyond.

Something struck the underside of his E-rifle and he lost his grip on it. He made a rookie mistake. He'd been so focused on the pursuit that he forgot to check his corners. As his weapon clattered to the tiled floor, Dylis barely got his arm up in time to block another strike.

The hooded man attacked with the fury of a meteor shower, his fists aiming for targeted regions of Dylis' body. Throat, clavicle, elbow, ribs, knees... Dylis felt his body naturally drop into the martial blocks he'd learned decades ago, but despite his enhancements he wasn't as fast as the assailant.

Bouncing off the wall, the hooded man twisted and kicked Dylis squarely in the jaw, spinning his head around as blood wetted his tongue. He tried to throw a punch, but his opponent caught him by the wrist and used Dylis' own momentum to throw him to the ground. The floor came up in a rush, and Dylis' forehead smacked against the tile with a *crack*. Lights danced in his vision, and he felt blood dribbling down his nose.

Stunned, Dylis managed to roll onto his back just in time to see the assailant thrust his arm to the side. An electric *hiss* emanated from the man's hand as a dazzling, blueish-white energy flowed from his gauntleted wrist. The energy coalesced into twin, glowing blades half a meter long, extending from his closed fist like claws.

Dylis' eyes went wide, and the hooded man lunged. The blades stabbed towards his heart. With a shout, Dylis pressed his foot into the man's right shoulder, halting the momentum of the incoming energy blades. The energy was mere centimeters from his chest, the blades radiating a blistering heat that burned his vest.

He looked from the glowing weapon, and he glimpsed piercing, blue eyes peering out from the facemask. The eyes were level with an icy calmness. Dylis was surprised to see such cold detachment in the eyes of a would-be killer. Even as they struggled, the hooded man exuded no irritation, frustration, or desperation. He was merely focused on his task.

Realizing this, Dylis was finally able to clear his own thoughts and issue a mental command to the puck concealed in his left sleeve. His left hand became covered in the glossy, white metal of Outrider nanotech. Grabbing the man's wrist, Dylis twisted it away from his chest while using his leg to kick him away.

His fingers burned as if he'd touched a boiling pot, and his eyes widened in horror. The energy blade had already cut through the gauntlet. A few slivers of condensed nanoparticles dripped from his fingers after being melted away.

"Impossible!" he breathed.

Nanotech armor could defend against most bladed weapons; pulseblades and nanoblades could cut through, but it took considerable effort. Yet this energy weapon had managed to melt his armor within milliseconds!

The hooded man rolled across the tiled floor before coming to rest in a crouch, his blade arm extending out to the side. Dylis rolled to his knees and he saw the E-rifle out of the corner of his eye. It was too far away. The hooded man would get to him seconds before he'd reach it.

He took a deep breath. Focusing, he willed the nanoparticles into a pulsecannon. A metallic scraping emitted as they formed, though pieces were missing. A warm thrum came from the weapon as it charged.

The assailant didn't move, so Dylis didn't hesitate. The pulsecannon fired a shimmering wave of violet energy that rippled towards the man.

Instead of dodging, he raised his free hand, blueish-white energy crackling around his wrist. A luminous gauntlet formed over his hand just as the kinetic wave smacked against his palm. White light flashed before him, followed by an electric *screech*.

The light lingered in Dylis' vision for a few seconds before he blinked it away. When his vision returned, the assailant was gone.

His breaths came in rapidly as he remained crouched in the hallway, the pulsecannon was still aimed at the spot where the man had been. Dylis scanned the hall, looking from door to door for any signs of movement. Down the hall, a blastdoor closed.

Dammit! he thought. *He's a fast son of a bitch, I'll give him that.*

Taking a deep breath, Dylis stood slowly and surveyed the hallway once more. Nothing stood out, all the corners were clear. He willed the nanoparticles into a thin glove that dispensed healing solvents along his injured fingers. The cool sensation soothed the inflamed skin, and a faint tingling meant that the nanoparticles were repairing the damaged tissue. Within an hour, his fingers would be free of burns.

Retrieving his E-rifle, Dylis stepped carefully towards the farthest blastdoor. Focusing his attention, he made sure to check his corners as he went through the opening.

It was a standard medical room with a sterile white bed next to a tall autodoc. Shards of glass were scattered across the tiled floor, drawing Dylis' attention to the broken window across the room. A light breeze whistled through the opening.

Raising the E-rifle, Dylis inched towards the broken window and peered out. The flat-top roof of a residential building was two stories below and several meters spanned the gap between the two structures. Walking towards the rooftop access door was the familiar figure of the hooded man.

The gray hood fluttered in the wind, but remained affixed to his head and face. Sensing Dylis' eyes on him, the assailant turned around and gazed back at the hospital. Dylis' eyes narrowed as he felt the heat of anger bubbling up in his chest. Turning away, the man entered the access corridor, vanishing from sight.

Dylis' arms relaxed, his grip loosening on the E-rifle. He'd lost the hooded man; the chase was over.

For now.

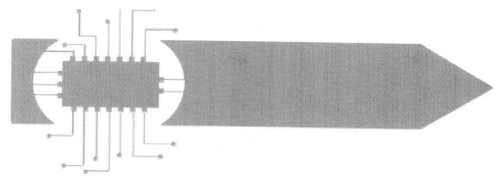

CHAPTER 19

Myra let out a gasp of relief when she saw Dylis return to the waiting area. The tension she'd bottled up beforehand was gone; comfort returning to her as she thanked the stars above for his safe return.

She noticed that his steps were measured, almost hesitant. The older Outrider carried his E-rifle like a briefcase, sweat glistened on his wide forehead, and his cheeks were flushed. It took Myra a second to notice that part of his vest was singed, and a nanotech glove covered his left hand. Whatever had happened, Dylis didn't make it through unscathed.

For the next hour, Dylis gave reports to the hospital administrators and New Skyline's police force. Discharging an E-weapon inside a medical facility wasn't to be taken lightly, even with Dylis' credentials as a Private Security Contractor. Myra and Rant waited diligently while most of the patients were escorted out of the hospital. By the time Dylis finished calming down the administrators, the waiting area was nearly empty.

Breaking away from the authorities, Dylis walked over to Myra, his shoulders sagging and his eyelids drooping. She threw her arms around him, squeezing him tightly even as he grunted in surprise.

"That's," he sputtered, "that's new. Remind me to do stuff like this more often."

Just as quickly, Myra let go of him and punched him lightly in the shoulder. "Are you ever not going to be a jackass?"

"Telling me to suppress my self-expression?" he quipped back. "So anti-progressive, Myra."

She rolled her eyes but couldn't help but smirk at him. "I'm glad you're okay," she said. "When the protocols went into effect for E-weapon discharges, I feared you'd gotten into a firefight."

"I was the only one shooting," Dylis admitted, scratching his beard. "It takes two to firefight. But the bastard had me pegged. Knew all my shots were warnings."

"He knew you wouldn't kill him?" Myra queried. "Did you know him?"

"Void no. Hardly even saw his face because of his hood. He was a trained fighter though, that's for damn sure. Nearly skewered me with an energy blade."

"An energy blade?" Myra's shoulders tensed as she repeated the words, recognition echoed in the corners of her mind.

"Yeah." Dylis ran his fingers through his receding hair, saying, "Never seen anything like it. And I have a sneaking suspicion that this sucker is involved with this C.B.I. shit."

When Myra gave him a quizzical look, he continued, "Think about it. We've been following leads for most of the day, and the second we find a connection to Milli's disappearance, this guy shows up to keep tabs on us. And I've never seen mercs with those types of weapons in the Imperium armada. He had to be working for another party. Perhaps the Syters."

An icy grip tightened around Myra's chest. She'd stolen from dangerous criminals, survived space battles, and escaped ravenous creatures of all sorts. Through all of that, she'd reveled in the thrill of adventure. But this sensation, this pit of dread forming in her stomach, was something new. Myra felt her tentacles flicking nervously as she considered the implications of Dylis' discovery.

Normally, the *Erinyes'* crew was a few steps ahead of their target, and even if said targets caught up with them, they had contingency plans. The Golden Spire heist, for instance, was almost botched by Riza's actions, but thanks to the crew's quick wits they managed to scrounge up a new plan. But in the case of finding Milli Spectre, *they* were the ones several steps behind.

And now, it seems, whoever is responsible knows we're on their trail and can attempt to thwart us, she considered. *Or they can adjust their plans entirely.*

"You said he was carrying an energy blade," Myra said after a moment.

Dylis' brow furrowed. "Yeah. Why?"

Myra paused, her hand instinctively began tugging at her tentacles. "I heard stories back on Sath about such people. Slavers would use them to eliminate rivals, bounty hunters, and even rebellion leaders. My best friend, Seni, told me that when his father tried to formulate a revolt on a spice plantation, he was slain by such a creature. He called it the 'shadow that strikes with the light of a star.'"

Dylis grumbled. "Well ain't that ominous. Did he say anything else?"

"It was mostly stories," she answered. "Some said that they were extra-galactic creatures summoned by the slavers. Others claimed that they were from our galaxy, but no one could pinpoint which world they originated from."

"Well, he was human from what I could tell," Dylis said. "So, unless there's a whole other galaxy of humans, I'd say he's from our neck of the woods. Though that's still unsettling."

She gulped. Myra wasn't afraid of much in the galaxy—she'd witnessed the brutality of the Fringe ever since she was a youngling. But the cruelty of the slavers and syndicates was something she was familiar with. Dread of the unknown stirred the terror within her, gripping her heart.

Letting go of her tentacles, Myra took a deep breath. She reminded herself that Dylis had been able to fend off such a creature, and she felt a modicum of reassurance. Additionally, she was no longer a frightened youngling on a fusion plantation—she was a mature, crafty, and resourceful Vitrax. Myra was far from helpless, and that thought alone subdued the remainder of the fear.

Straightening her jacket, Myra declared, "In any case, just before the alarms went off, we were able to nab the data. Rant explained it to me while you were busy getting debriefed."

Dylis raised his eyebrows and asked, "What did you find?"

"Medina General's accounts revealed a higher amount of mithium four days ago," Myra explained. "Which means that whoever acquired the quantum scalpel paid for it with a few empty quantum cards."

"No cam footage?"

She shook her head. "Must've been done outside the premises or in a blind spot."

Dylis' green eyes lit up. "Makes sense. You want to be off the grid, avoid cams. You don't want a trail of fuse exchanges, barter with an empty card."

Myra nodded. It was quite common in the Fringe to find dealers in the black market exchanging goods for empty quantum cards. These cards were crafted with a small quantity of mithium—a rare metal—and were quite valuable to certain vendors. It was like recycling the casing off a dead battery, it wasn't worth the full amount, but the material still had a fraction of the monetary value.

Normally, such practices were controlled by the banks—most notably the Ruby Dawn Banking corporation based on Diivoro. Mithium was such a high commodity that the banks wanted to control as much of it as possible, so they required citizens to return their empty quantum cards to a R.D.B. kiosk. But out in the Fringe, where the banks had less power, most people would trade their empty cards on the black market.

"So that means that there's likely a used card dealership somewhere in New Skyline," Myra deduced. "If we locate them, we can figure out who visited four days ago."

"And if they won't talk?"

"Oh they will," Myra said, smashing her fist to her palm. "If not, I'm sure you're great at getting people to squawk."

Dylis smirked. "I like where your head's at, Myra. We should check in with the boss first. See what he, Riza, and Golath found."

Raising his left arm, Dylis sent a transmission to Aelec. After a few chimes, the familiar profile image of the captain appeared on screen.

"*Dylis. Myra. Is everything alright?*"

"Just peachy, boss," Dylis snorted, glancing at Myra. "Boy have we got something for you."

Several moments passed as they explained their discoveries at Medina General and Dylis' encounter with the shadow assassin. When they'd finished, Myra saw Aelec's jaw clench and his aureate eyes widen by a fraction.

"*I don't like where this is going,*" Aelec said after a moment. "*Milli's husband said they'd received countless threats from the Syters before she vanished. It's starting to look more and more like they sent an operative after her.*"

"Guess we won't know for sure until we chat with the Syters in person," Myra said.

"*Easier said than done.*" Aelec rubbed his chin. "*We're heading to the western dockyard to look around. What's your plan?*"

Checking her nanotech watch, Myra noted that it was close to 17:00 GST. They still had a few hours left to peruse the city before needing to retire to the *Erinyes*.

"We'll track down the mithium dealer," Myra declared. "See if we can get more info on who purchased the quantum scalpel."

Aelec nodded. *"Good idea. Just keep a low profile. I don't want that operative to catch you off-guard again."*

"You got it, boss," Dylis said. "Watch your six."

"You too."

Sunlight was fading as they exited the hospital, and people crowded the carbocrete walkways as they got off work. Gravvehicles moved sluggishly over the wide traffic lanes, while countless other vehicles soared above with soft whines.

They got a few blocks from Medina General without saying a word, but as they neared the gravtram station, Dylis broke the silence.

"I'm curious," he said as they walked down the street. "When you and Riza spoke privately earlier, did you clear anything up?"

"No," she replied tersely. "I mean... we came to an understanding. I still don't trust her, but I do trust Golath and Aelec. I just warned her to think about her loyalty to the crew."

"It's been weeks, Myra. We've got bigger fish to fry."

She narrowed her eyes at him. "Any human who lies, no matter their reasoning, can never be trusted. It's an addiction for your species. Once you've had a taste, you can never not do it, no matter how hard you try."

Dylis drew his lips into a thin line. "She just wanted justice for her sister. If I thought Aelec had killed one of my clan brothers, I'd have done the same thing."

"That doesn't excuse her actions!" she snapped. "We accepted her into our family. We put our trust in her, and what did she do? She tried to capture Aelec for her own selfish needs. What's to stop her from doing that again?"

"She's got no reason to do that again," Dylis countered. "Our goals align."

"Yeah, for now," Myra snarled, baring her sharp canines. "What if things start going to the Void and she decides to save her own skin? None of us really know her. She could still be playing us."

Dylis sighed, rubbing the back of his neck before saying, "Sometimes you need to have a little faith in people. None of us are perfect, Myra. We've all got our own shit bogging us down."

"I have faith in some people," Myra retorted, looking away from Dylis. "But I learned a long time ago not to put such sentiment in the wrong people."

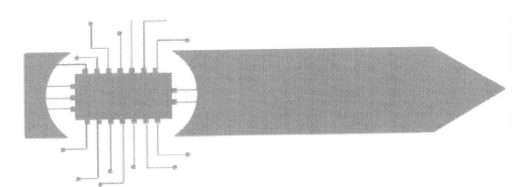

CHAPTER 20

New Skyline: The Western Dockyards, GST: 17:10

Riza felt a mounting dread start to creep up in her chest. Every time they discovered something new about Spectre's case, the more tension she felt in the air like a cord was tightening around her. The fact that such a crime could happen to a government agent directly within the Imperium troubled her deeply.

Oais was like a pristine window, and this case was putting cracks into it. Capital Worlds were supposed to be the pinnacle of prosperity—the utopias craved by humans and nonhumans alike.

Riza squatted next to a nanotech maintenance console within one of the central hubs just outside the western dockyards. It was little more than a large, enclosed intersection that connected to various tunnel-like walkways along the perimeter of the Medina District.

"I really don't like where this is going," Aelec repeated. "Milli could've been taken in any direction."

Riza looked up from her task and saw Aelec kneeling in the left hallway, examining marks on the floor. Yellow fusionfiber cords draped along the corridor's entrance, quarantining it from the public per orders of the C.B.I. Riza spotted several containers casting dark shadows in the hallway—an easy spot for someone to hide.

Golath paced along the pale carbocrete, his talons tapping against the floor. He bobbed his triangular head up and down as he let out a chorus of muffled clicks. She guessed it was his version of pacing and talking to himself.

After a moment, Riza called out, "You find anything over there, Aelec?"

Standing abruptly, Aelec ducked under the fusionfiber cords and approached her. Golath went to the spot where the captain had been, hunching over to inspect the floor.

Leaning against the wall, Aelec finally answered, "The smear of dried blood is still there. Forensics already IDed it as Milli's. Void-damn, if she's dead..."

"Don't think like that, Aelec," Riza said reassuringly. "I don't think the Sol put this mission in our path just for us to come to a result like that. She's out there."

"I want to believe that," he grunted, giving her a hooded gaze. "But if the Sol would allow someone like Kuvan to commit acts against my people, then this wouldn't be a long shot."

"The Sol is the entity of justice, the progenitor of peace," Riza murmured. "I was raised to believe that all injustices in the galaxy will eventually be rectified. It's the only way to make sense of the universe's chaos."

A low grumble emitted from Aelec's throat. "The Sol Imperium. Our galactic governance even includes the Sol's name, as if to claim we're bringing peace and justice. I used to believe that. But now, I'm not so sure."

Riza looked up from the console and met his golden eyes. "Aelec, we'll find her."

He didn't reply for a long moment. Eventually, Aelec tilted his head to examine her work and asked, "How's your progress?"

"I'm almost done figuring out this console's port signature so that I can access remotely," she replied, her eyes scanning the nanotech device. "I don't want to risk a hardlink in case someone bugged the cam. Once that's done, it's a simple matter of bypassing the security network, which I've done like a hundred times."

Aelec arched an eyebrow. "Literally or figuratively?"

"Are you serious?" She gave a soft laugh. "I can count on one hand the number of actual security systems I've hacked into. Believe it or not, I was a good girl before I left Seraphi."

"You're still good, Riza," Aelec said in a gentle voice. "The way you handled Ferris earlier... that was something only a decent person could do."

She scoffed. There was no skill involved in it. All Riza had to do was soften her tone and show a little empathy. Her stomach churned as she considered it, because she didn't know how much of it was sincere. Ever since coming aboard the *Erinyes*, Riza hadn't been certain of what was genuine and what was a façade. Was she a decent woman? Or was she just really, really good at putting up a front?

Glancing at Aelec, Riza felt the familiar swell of regret for her action on Caavo. She'd resolved to work with him to bring down Veritas Kuvan as penance for betraying him, which extended to this quest to find Spectre. Riza wanted to prove to him and the others that she was loyal to their cause, but she wondered what things would be like afterwards.

Would Aelec want her to stick around on the *Erinyes*? Would *she* still want to?

A soft *click* emanated from the nanotech console as her slender finger adjusted it to the right setting, displaying the port signature. Using her terminus, she scanned the signature before displaying the root menu of the hacking system. Inputting a few algorithms and sequences, Riza easily bypassed the network and was able to access the hub's main camera feed.

"I've got eyes, boss," Riza declared triumphantly, raising her arm to display the hologram.

Aelec nodded, his argent hair hanging over one eye. "Let's see what we've got."

Standing, Riza kept her left arm level, the hologram bathing her with neon light. Golath was still doing his weird pacing, and she didn't feel like disturbing him. She cycled through the various recording files until she found one that matched the time Milli Spectre disappeared.

Flicking her index finger, the hologram expanded, and they watched the scene unfold. Despite its size, the camera had an incredible view of the hub and connecting hallways. She could see roughly ten meters down each of the tunnel-like paths.

Down one hallway, she could see a group of protesters—likely the Far Syters—chanting and raising their fists. Their postures were hunched, and they pumped their fists feverishly. The hallway to the right was empty, but standing at the corner of the left hallway was a woman.

Milli Spectre leaned against the corner wall with her arms crossed over her mesh-fiber jacket. She kept her dark hair tied in a bun, and a scowl was on the woman's angular face. In a very agent-of-the-Imperium way, Spectre kept reaching into her jacket, likely to grip her E-pistol in response to the crowd.

They watched the footage for the next few minutes until the cam's feed cut out. An alert flashed across the screen saying: *Main Power Disabled. Rebooting.* This must've been when the grid lost power. A few seconds later, the footage returned to normal and Riza caught the last glimpses of the hub's LED lights coming back on. Spectre was gone from her spot; only a broken terminus and an E-pistol remained in the hallway.

Riza frowned. "No altered footage, boss."

Aelec leaned his head against the wall and let out a protracted sigh. "It was a good hunch, but it looks like the case details add up."

With a flick of his wrist, Aelec pulled up a communication display and said, "I need to call Director Cormack. See if he knows anything about these shadow assassins."

Placing her hands in her jacket pockets, Riza waited as Aelec's terminus flashed with yellow light. After a few chimes, the profile of a man with dark skin emitted from the hologram.

"Captain Xero, have you found something?" Director Cormack asked, his brow furrowing.

"There's a new development," Aelec answered, looking towards the hallway. "I need to ask, what's the possibility of operatives being after Agent Spectre? Any mercenaries or assassins that the Syters might utilize to target her?"

"What makes you think so?"

"Dylis had a run-in with an elite operative while following leads on Agent Spectre's case. I suspect that he was sent by the Syters."

Cormack's dark eyes narrowed. *"An operative, you say. That's news to us, though not necessarily surprising. The Far Syters are rumored to be in contact with possible terrorist organizations on Faerius, though we don't have solid proof. More than a few Syters have been arrested while bearing military-grade E-pistols, shield generators, and surveillance equipment. If it's true that they're in league with an off-world terrorist faction—and I'm confident they are—then having their own assassins wouldn't seem far-fetched."*

Riza and Aelec locked gazes. She couldn't help but tug at her dark ponytail. It was one thing for Spectre to be in the hands of a rogue guild, but a military operative or assassin was disturbing. Stuff like this didn't happen in the Capital Worlds—at least, it wasn't supposed to.

"But that's all I know," Cormack concluded. *"Where are you now, Captain Xero?"*

"Western dockyard," Aelec answered, glancing around the area.

"We just surveyed the hub where she went missing. I'll report back if we find anything else."

"*Keep me posted,*" Cormack said with a nod. "*Good luck.*"

Aelec lowered his arm, his shoulders sagging. Riza continued to stare at his terminus, a question churning in her mind.

"If the C.B.I. suspected the Syters were associated with terrorists," she asked, "why didn't they mention that in the file? Why didn't they act on it?"

Aelec glanced at her out of the corner of his eye and grunted, "They didn't have proof. My guess is that C.B.I. was trying to build a case against the Syters by keeping tabs on their protests."

He turned to face her, his gloved hand cupping his chin as he looked thoughtful. "As for why it wasn't in the file, protocol dictates that we eliminate all possible planetside leads before pursuing an inter-system investigation."

Riza pursed her lips. "That sounds more like an excuse than protocol."

Rocking his head from side to side, Aelec said, "Rules exist for a reason. Despite the circumstances, I've missed the regimentation of the Imperium. Makes me feel more in control."

"Despite having to report to a superior? You were your own boss out in the Fringe. Surely that's a bit frustrating."

Aelec shrugged nonchalantly. "Like I said, I'm pragmatic. No use getting frustrated about it." He glanced around at the hub again and continued, "We need to find a way into the tunnels. You got the puck?"

Reaching into her jacket pocket, Riza produced the palm-sized device. Tapping it with her thumb, a three-dimensional map of New Skyline's underground tunnels hovered above the puck. With a thumb and forefinger, she zoomed the image into their current location, and she noted that there were over three dozen access points in their sector.

She groaned, shuffling her feet. "That's a lot of ground to cover. Where should we start?"

"Where we can," Aelec grunted, glancing back to address the Kygi. "Golath, time to head out, pal."

To Riza's surprise, Golath ignored the captain. A deep clicking emanated from the Kygi, and he walked as if stepping on eggshells. Aelec cocked his head to the side, cleared his throat, and then spoke.

"Golath? Buddy, you okay?"

The Kygi stopped pacing when he reached the entrance to the left hallway, his tall frame hunching over as if he were stalking an animal. Two of his arms raised, and he waved for them to join him. Riza pursed her lips, utterly befuddled at the Kygi's intentions.

As she and Aelec approached, Riza asked, "Golath, is everything alright?" She knew it was foolish to ask since he couldn't vocalize in Trade, but he could at least understand her words.

Rapid, high-pitched clicks came from the nonhuman, and his arms waved urgently. Golath dropped to all sixes and scuttled beneath the fusionfiber cords, entering the hallway where Spectre had been stationed. Riza and Aelec followed, her eyes widening as she saw what the nonhuman was trying to convey.

Still low to the ground, Golath gestured a claw towards a faint, russet stain on the carbocrete. It was dried blood from where Spectre's implant had been cut out. Golath jabbed a digit at the stain, while another one of his claws gestured towards his respirator.

Riza raised her eyebrows and asked, "Do you understand what he's doing?"

Aelec clapped his gloved hands together, a grin forming on his marble-like face. "He picked up a trail!" he exclaimed. "Sol bless the Kygi and their senses!"

"Wait, seriously? He can smell where she is?"

"Not exactly," he replied, patting the Kygi on his carapace-covered shoulder. "Kygi olfactory sensors are enhanced by their respirators when in oxygen-rich environments. Like how a phiraxen shark detects a single drop of blood a kilometer away, Golath can reorient himself to follow a specific scent trail, even if it's days old."

Riza beamed at the Kygi. "Golath, have I told you how awesome you are?"

The nonhuman turned to look at her and emitted a low clicking. With his two right arms, he gestured towards the end of the left hallway which connected to another hub area down the way. His lumbering, carapaced form moved towards the other hub.

"Shouldn't we regroup with the others?" Riza asked, looking from Golath to Aelec.

"No time," Aelec said, following the Kygi. "I won't risk him losing Milli's trail. The scent might be too weak after a few more hours."

Riza moved quickly to keep up with Aelec. "There's only three of us," she pointed out. "Is this smart?"

"An Outrider, a Kygi warrior, and a hacker," Aelec retorted, glancing at her. "I like our odds. If things get dicey, just take cover and we'll handle it. My nanotech pucks are charged and ready. We'll be fine."

Nervousness bubbled in Riza's stomach, and she felt the corners of her mouth tug into a frown. She was confident in Aelec and Golath's abilities, but she couldn't help but feel wary of venturing into the unknown like this. But when she reminded herself that Oais wasn't like Caavo, and that criminals weren't lurking around every alley, the feeling abated.

Her hand brushed against the grip of the E-pistol strapped to her thigh, and she said, "I'll watch your back."

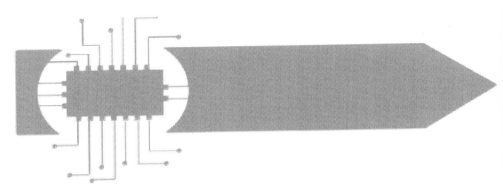

CHAPTER 21

The metallic scent of human blood circulated through Golath's respirator and tickled his olfactory senses. It was a clear distinction from the plethora of other smells in the area. Golath clicked to the emotion of entrancement as he focused on the scent the way he would fixate on frying cephalopods. If one drowned out the outside world, there was no limit to what one could do with the task at hand.

He bobbed his head up and down, the odorant molecules were faint and scattered. A path began forming in his mind. Everything was much more potent whenever he was in oxygen-rich places; the corroded atmosphere of his homeworld forced his species to heighten their senses. The trail led him to the nearest hub area, which connected to another dockyard for incoming starships.

Outside the long windows of the connecting hallways, the dark gray clouds churned as if fighting for control. Pattering sounds from the long widows confirmed it was raining. Neon lights from vehicles shone brightly through the haze of rain and made him squint as he passed by.

He clicked to the emotion of appreciation; the scent was flowing in the indoor sections of the dockyard. If the human female had been taken outside when captured, the trail would likely have been long gone by now.

Golath paused inside the next hub area, raising his head to detect where the odorant molecules were. After a heartbeat, he found it leading into the nearest hangar bay. He narrowed his eyes and clicked to the emotion of anxiety. Golath hoped that the trail didn't end there. That would indicate that the human female was hauled aboard a starship, and only the Empyrean would know where she was now.

There was still hope, though. Liberator Aelec and Hacker Riza were counting on him, and he would not fail.

An expansive, circular structure greeted him as he exited the hallway. An open-top roof revealed the roiling sky above. A faint sizzle came from above as raindrops struck the shimmering energy field. He bent low to the violet morristeel floor, then snapped back in revulsion as he got a whiff of minty engine coolant.

Across the bay was a droid flight control tower like the one on Khorrus. Extending above the bay like a watchtower, the lights along its sides were dim, and its insect-like appendages were folded inward.

Golath raised his head, locating the scent of human blood once again. He followed it into the circular hangar, his taloned feet scraping against the morristeel plates inlaid on the floor.

Liberator Aelec and Hacker Riza were a few steps behind, silently observing him. Without Translator Tarantula, Golath had to rely on primitive claw gestures to communicate with them. Sometimes he wished humans could truly understand the language of his people. The symphony of clicks to each emotion was their way of expressing spirit.

The odorant molecules dispersed once he entered the bay proper—her blood's scent mixed with the smells of bitter oils and musty fumes. Golath paused, his mandibles tapping against his beak beneath the respirator.

Squatting to the floor, he tucked his four arms into his chitinous chest and closed his eyes. His clicking was to the emotion of entrancement as he homed in on the old smell of blood. The olfactory organs on his face siphoned out the odors of the dockyard, separating them one by one until he found his target.

Tilting his head up, he found that the trail was leading to the northern side of the bay. Opening his eyes, he saw the grated cover of a ventilation shaft at the precise point where the scent led. He clicked to the emotion of interest as he stood and approached the vent.

Taking one last inhalation, Golath solidified that the human female was taken into the shaft. Pointing a clawed digit, he gestured towards the vent's cover and clicked to the emotion of excitement.

"They took her into the ventilation shaft," Liberator Aelec said, translating Golath's gesture. "The puck showed a few dozen access points in this area. This is the one."

"And this would be the perfect place to enter unnoticed," Hacker Riza affirmed. "Especially if most of the attention was on the High Chancellor's shuttle that day."

Liberator Aelec nodded and approached the vent; his gloved hand ran over the metal grate.

"There's no sign that this was forced open," he informed them, "nor is this a replacement. Whoever brought her here managed to unseal and reseal it within a matter of minutes."

Hacker Riza's thin eyebrows furrowed. "That's some incredible speed if the blackout was only for two minutes."

"Yeah," Liberator Aelec grunted, "so keep your guard up. Both of you."

With a metallic *hiss*, the human formed a white gauntlet over his right hand. Extending his index finger, the nanotech shifted into a cylindrical tool. A whirring came from the device. He pulled several metal bolts loose, and lifted the grate from the vent's opening.

Setting the grate aside, Liberator Aelec reset the gauntlet, and a light shined from his palm. The pale cobalt light illuminated the vent's passage, showing that it curved downward into the depths below.

Looking back at him, Liberator Aelec said, "Looks like it'll be a tight fit, Golath. You still up for this?"

Golath clicked to the emotion of craving; he was eager to follow the trail, his curiosity belying his wariness. Though the human couldn't understand exactly how he felt, he nodded in understanding.

Flicking his wrist, Liberator Aelec called up his hologram terminus, and a heartbeat later the face of Warrior Dylis melded into the screen.

"What's up, boss?" he asked.

"Golath tracked Milli's scent to a vent in the western dockyard," Liberator Aelec explained. "We're going to follow it. Riza will send you a schematic of the underground tunnels, and my beacon will be active. If anything starts looking fishy, I'll be calling for backup."

Warrior Dylis scratched at his facial hair. *"You sure you don't want us there?"*

"Positive. We need more info on who that shadow assassin might be, and you've got a good lead. We can't waste that."

"Alright. Be careful down there. We'll look out for your beacon."

The neon hologram dissipated, and Liberator Aelec said, "I'll take point." He looked at Hacker Riza. "You follow me in, and Golath will cover our six."

The Kygi always found that phrase odd. There was no numeral of the sixth digit on their bodies, so why did humans say that when asking to watch their backs? Regardless, Golath understood his role and clicked to the emotion of calmness.

Liberator Aelec moved with a lithe grace, ducking into the vent and sliding down the shaft. Hacker Riza followed, her boots thumping against the metal. Golath turned to survey the dockyard, ensuring that no one was watching them before he hunkered down to crawl into the vent.

It was indeed a tight fit; Golath's carapace continually scraped along the sides of the shaft with a bony *screech*. He had to use his four arms to push himself further, a constant clicking to the emotion of anger emanating from his respirator. More than once he feared he would get stuck in the shaft, but he was quick to fold his arms against his thorax or wiggle his shoulders.

After what felt like a solar revolution, Golath pulled himself out of the vent shaft and into the underground tunnel. Hacker Riza and Liberator Aelec helped him to his taloned feet. He blinked rapidly, his eyes adjusting to the dimly lit tunnel before him.

Carved out of russet-colored carbocrete, the underground grav-tram tunnel stretched for endless kilometers in both directions. A beam of gray morristeel was five meters above them and ran throughout the center of the tunnel, attached to multiple supports protruding from the ground.

Only a few small LED lamps hung from the curved ceiling, but Golath's anatomy allowed him keener eyesight in dark caves and tunnels. It reminded him of the inner network of his colony spire back on Kyg-nor. His people had to rely on their vision to navigate the darker paths. During the distal end of the planetary revolution, temperatures on Kyg-nor would reach scorching levels which forced his people to shelter in the spires. Even with their technological enhancements, the Kygi had to dwell beneath the surface until the next planetary revolution started.

Despite Kyg-nor's hardships, he was grateful for his people's evolution. Otherwise, he would be just as limited as the humans.

Shuffling further into the tunnel, Golath tilted his head upwards once more to sift through the scents that hung in the air. To his surprise, the trail was easier to detect, and he pointed a clawed digit.

"They went north," Liberator Aelec said, his eyes narrowing.

Hacker Riza pulled up the schematic gifted by Constructor Ferris. The holographic map shone brightly in the dark tunnel, and Golath had to squint in response.

"That's consistent with Ferris' reports," Hacker Riza said. "Looks like it heads into the Rakto District. Nearest gravtram station is in thirty kilometers."

Liberator Aelec grunted in acknowledgement. "Then we have no time to waste."

Golath clicked to the emotion of calmness, reached into the various plates of his carapace, and started piecing together his fuse-caster. Emerald fusionfiber cords hummed faintly when the weapon was ready, and he set off at a quick pace in the direction of the scent. Liberator Aelec and Hacker Riza followed briskly behind him as they ventured forth into the darkness.

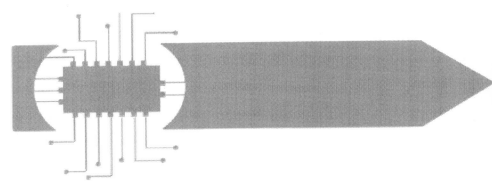

CHAPTER 22

Cold, blue light shone from Aelec's gauntleted palm as he moved through the dimly lit gravtram tunnel. The air was musty with metallic bitterness, likely a residue of the fusion coils powering the tram's gravlifts. One had passed overhead moments before. The gravtram had been moving at such speed that he'd blinked, and it was already on the other side of the tunnel.

Aelec moved with the methodical steps of a soldier who was sneaking up on an opponent, at least that's how his Outrider brain thought of it. He didn't want anyone to notice them traversing the gravtram tunnels on foot.

If the Syters were in the vicinity, Aelec wanted them to be unaware of their presence. That, coupled with Dylis' report of the would-be assassin, had put him on edge. Who knew what kind of defenses the Far Syters had at their disposal. So he kept focus, the nanoparticles ever present in his neural interlace like a fresh memory.

Ever since he'd taken it upon himself to locate Milli, Aelec couldn't shake the feeling that he was being watched. A nagging sensation in the back of his mind kept him on high alert. His hand itched for his E-pistol, his eyes darted around, and his heartbeat increased.

Golath lumbered a few steps ahead of him, the faint glow of his fusecaster silhouetting him. Riza was next to him, her steps cautious, as if she were stepping on shards of glass. He could tell it was her attempt at being stealthy in these tunnels, though he had to admit it looked quite comical.

The slight pang of levity helped keep his mind focused on the task at hand and prevented him from dwelling on what might've happened to Milli. Positive emotions worked in synchronization with his neural link to the nanotech pucks, as long as they weren't overwhelming. Fits of joy, elevated excitement, or passionate love would be just as detrimental as boiling rage, chilling fear, and scrambled confusion. Controlling emotion was one of the keys to being an effective Outrider.

His clan-leader, Tolum Xero, had instructed that emotions were needed to separate people from droids. Outriders already had a stigma for being hardly better than droids, and suppressing all emotion would only confirm that theory. So Outriders were told to let controlled feelings of determination, fear, anger, and love fuel them in combat. It was better to feel something while fighting for the clan, planet, Imperium, or one's life rather than nothing at all.

That was part of the reason he wanted Riza with him on this mission; she reminded him of those feelings that he often tried to bury. Aelec felt at ease when she was present, even if he always seized up in the face of intimacy.

They traversed for another kilometer, the gravtram tunnel curving several times like a winding river. Apart from their soft footsteps, the trio remained silent as they walked. Even Golath refrained from clicking, though Aelec knew it was driving the Kygi to extreme lengths of frustration to subdue his expression. Aelec raised his right hand, the light of his nanotech gauntlet illuminating the russet carbocrete a few meters ahead of him.

Aelec glanced at Riza, who in turn met his gaze as if anticipating his need. Sensing his intentions, she pulled up the schematics, which showed that they were two kilometers from the next gravtram station. This was marked as the "ghost zone", where the Far Syters tended to vanish.

Riza promptly deactivated the puck, her full lips drawing into a thin line as her eyes darted around. Her posture went rigid, and she drew in short breaths. Aelec could sense her fear. Without thinking, he reached out and gently gripped her shoulder. Her muscles tensed beneath his hand, and she inhaled sharply—the noise was extra loud due to the eerie quiet of the tunnel.

Once more, she looked up at him with her oceanic eyes. Aelec unclenched his jaw, and his eyelids grew heavy. Everything in his posture was meant to convey comfort and reassurance. No words escaped him, only the silent song of his intentions.

After a few deep breaths, Riza released the tension in her shoulders and her eyelids drooped by a fraction—faint glimmers of light emphasized her smokey eyeshadow. Her expression almost bordered on a look of sultry intimacy that made Aelec's heart race. His normal reaction would be to shy away and close himself off, but he remained firm. He was helping to calm Riza, and in turn, her presence eased his thoughts.

It was a perfect balance, like finding the flow of a *tajido* kata.

The sound of metal scraping against carbocrete snapped him out of his trance.

Aelec whirled around as his left hand formed a nanotech pulse-cannon, his right holding up the gauntlet's flashlight to see what was behind them. Riza was frozen like one of the marble statues on Morrigar, her face turning pale. Golath emitted a low, guttural clicking.

Aelec instinctually created a helmet, the nanoparticles feeling like cold water running along his scalp. A holographic heads-up-display lit up the interior visor and he sent a mental command to the suit to scan for any activity. The HUD gave him a readout: *Lifeforms Detected: 2*. He took a breath, it was just Golath and Riza.

Narrowing his eyes, Aelec switched the vision to infrared. A cerulean filter came over his visor, numerous splotches of red and orange highlighting the fusion generators powering the rail. Odd. Nothing was showing on scanners or infrared.

A bead of sweat trickled from Aelec's hairline down his temple as his eyes bored into the darkness. He looked for any sign of movement, but even with his enhanced vision he couldn't see farther than a few meters. The silence was broken only by the sporadic dripping of fluids.

The sensation came back into full force, the feeling that someone was watching them. Aelec's heart thundered in his chest as he stood motionless. He'd faced down danger many times before, but this was different. The uncertainty of the unknown rattled him.

Shadows stretched forth from the dim LEDs. Droplets fell into a puddle nearby, creating an echoing *drip*.

Aelec waited, barely breathing. Both of his arms were raised, his mind concentrating on the pulsecannon—ready to fire. He could hear Riza's frantic exhalations through her nostrils, her knuckles white as she gripped her E-pistol.

Light exploded from the other end of the tunnel, followed by the rumble of gravlifts. In an instant, the light sped towards them at blinding speed before passing overhead. A gust of wind surged through the tunnel and sent his dust coat flapping uncontrollably.

It was just another gravtram.

As the vehicle passed by towards the Rakto District, Aelec felt a collective sigh of relief among his companions—well, Golath clicked in relief.

"Holy shit," Riza breathed, her shoulders sagging.

Aelec put his hand on the small of her back, patting her reassuringly. He glanced around once more; the suspicion was still in the back of his mind. But after a moment, he resolved to move onward.

They approached the area where the schematics indicated that the Syters dropped off scanners. With his HUD still active, Aelec looked around for any sign of activity. The scanners weren't as sophisticated as others in the Imperium, but they could detect miniscule things like footprints, fluid trails, fusion residue, and toxic particles.

The scanner beeped softly as it scanned, and after a few seconds, it pinged and zoomed in on a long scuff mark along the carbocrete. The HUD processed the color and width, then indicated the scuff was made from a pure rubber boot sole. Aelec grumbled softly.

The majority of commonwear shoe soles were made from a mix of mesh-fiber and leather. Only military boot soles were made completely from composite rubber—boots like the ones Milli was wearing the day she vanished.

Squatting to the floor, Aelec ran his fingers along the scuff mark.

"What is it?" Riza asked in a whisper.

"Someone was dragged here," Aelec replied quietly. "But the scuff mark runs for only a few meters."

Riza squatted next to him, her eyes glancing from the floor to the closest wall. "That doesn't make any sense," she breathed, "Spectre was taken this way, so why isn't there a longer scuff trail?"

"They could've been carrying her initially," Aelec said. "Perhaps she was only dragged for the last few meters to wherever the Syters vanished to. Or..."

"Or what?"

"Or this might be a different trail." Aelec stood and faced Golath. "Status of the scent?"

The Kygi hunched over, bobbing his triangular head. Golath turned to Aelec and used two of his arms to make his approximation of a shrug. A soft clicking emanated from the nonhuman, almost like a purr.

"The blood trail ends here," Aelec said, dread knotting his stomach. "Something's not right."

His stomach twisted to the point of aching, and his palms grew clammy beneath the gauntlets. Pivoting on the spot, Aelec surveyed the area around his companions, his visor changing colors as it cycled through vision settings. A *whir* came from his left hand, the nanotech forming a pulsecannon.

Riza snapped to attention, unholstered her E-pistol, and glanced around the tunnel. She kept both hands on the grip, the muzzle pointed at the ground. Golath tugged on the fusionfiber cords of his fusecaster, his body hunched defensively.

Aelec scanned and scanned. His eyes stung from not blinking. There was something apart from gravtrams down here, yet he saw nothing.

An electrical *hum* emanated from a spot directly behind him.

Twisting around with the speed of a typhoon, Aelec reacted on instinct and pointed his pulsecannon at the source. At first, only shadows greeted him. But as he looked closely, he saw the air shimmer like that of a heat wave on the horizon. He blinked, and lines of electricity arced around the shimmer, outlining it as a humanoid figure. The *hum* grew louder.

The electricity coalesced in a flash of blue light, and revealed a young man. His smooth, waxy features glowed in the pale illumination of Aelec's gauntlet light. A glint caught Aelec's eye, and he saw the copper frame of an E-pistol pointing right at him.

Time seemed to slow as he came to grips with this newcomer's sudden appearance. No one moved, no one fired. Taking advantage of the pause, he observed as much about the assailant as possible. Worn combat suit, old gloves, dirty boots... It didn't scream organized military.

A silver, metallic sheen caught his eye. Strapped around his waist was a mechanical belt the likes of which Aelec had never seen before. Cylindrical conduits bulged out like lumps along its length, and they blinked with a deep, violet light.

Before he could react, more electrical hums emanated from all around them—a cacophony that echoed throughout the tunnel. Aelec's HUD pinged multiple times, the radar picking up dozens of individuals. They appeared as if out of thin air, a web of electrical energy pulsing around their frames for a brief moment before dissipating. Aelec, Riza, and Golath, were quickly encircled without any cover.

The urge of survival flowed through him like a jolt of energy. His HUD opened a channel to Dylis' commlink, and Aelec practically shouted into the mic.

"Dylis, it's an ambush!" he said, surveying the enemies before him. "Hostiles at my coordinates!" Static crackled in his ear. "Dylis? You read me?!" More static.

The familiar pinging sounds of primed E-weapons brought him back to the scene—each individual raised either an E-pistol, E-rifle, or E-shotgun. Aelec pivoted again, as did Golath and Riza, so that they were all back-to-back. The nanotech of his right arm transformed into a nanoshield, though it wouldn't be enough to protect them all. The ambushers had them at the center of a deadly crossfire, and there was no way he could take them out *and* protect his companions.

These are likely the Far Syters, he thought. *How convenient of them to show up.*

They didn't open fire, opting to keep their weapons trained on the trio in a silent stalemate. Aelec would take it. He wouldn't risk any harm coming to Riza and Golath. He raised the nanoshield an inch higher, his body tense with alertness.

"Call all you want, but that signal ain't going nowhere," a basso voice said from the group.

With a wide stride, a towering man stepped forward from the ring of ambushers, his E-shotgun aiming directly at Aelec's head. Beneath a thick mustache, his lips curled into a sneer, his eyes flicked towards the terminus on his wrist.

Aelec followed his gaze, and noticed a red light blinking on the hologram. A line of text hovered near the light, which read: *Signal Blocked.*

Shit! Aelec thought, his face going pale. *They've been jamming us the whole time.*

The man's emerald eyes locked on Aelec with a mixture of fury and annoyance. "Who are you? Why are you sniffing through these tunnels like a traxi hound?"

With his helmet still active, Aelec stood tall and kept his pulse-cannon aimed at the large man. A few of the Far Syters shifted their footing. An Outrider had a reputation that couldn't be dismissed lightly, and Aelec wanted to keep that edge for as long as he could.

"Skipping the name," he grunted, "but I'm looking for someone. A man named Leonis Ingot."

He let the name linger in the air. Aelec didn't want to reveal that he was working with the C.B.I. in the search for Milli. If he showed his zapaak hand too soon, he might get cleaned out.

One of the younger Syters let out a soft gasp. A few others murmured amongst themselves. *Good, that got their attention.*

The big man scoffed, "And what makes you think your man is down here, in a gravtram tunnel?"

"Because this is where Far Syters tend to hide," Aelec said. "Lo and behold, here you are. That's some fancy stealth tech you've got. Where did you steal it from?"

"You're an Outrider," he said, ignoring Aelec's question. "And not just any Outrider, I reckon. Traveling with a small posse without Imperium backup; you must be the infamous Captain Xero."

A young Vitrax female shuffled next to the man, her eyes widening as she murmured, "Xero? Captain Aelec Xero?"

When Aelec didn't respond, the Syter man said, "You might be a bigshot hero out in the Fringe, but this is our domain. If you all don't keep walking to the Rakto station, you and your friends are going to be seared like a vankir steak."

Aelec didn't back down. "Look, we're not here to fight. We just want to—"

"Gonna be a rare steak it seems," the man sneered, his finger tensing on the trigger.

"We can help clear his name!" Riza blurted.

Her words echoed through the tunnel. All eyes fell upon Riza as if she were the sole performer on a stage.

"What?" the man snapped, his eyes still on Aelec.

Riza took a deep breath and raised her voice. "The C.B.I. says he's Oais' Most Wanted for the disappearance of Milli Spectre. You take us to him, and we can help prove him innocent."

Though her words caught him flatfooted, Aelec decided to play along.

His training wanted him to take the lead, but his gut told him to keep faith in Riza. Her words had the intended effect, some of the Syters lowered their weapons. Many looked to one another in confusion.

The big man remained steadfast, a growl escaping through clenched teeth. His knuckles turned white as he gripped his E-shotgun.

"Joss, they could prove useful," said the Vitrax female. "If they can prove us innocent, we should take it."

Aelec's attention fell upon her. Unlike Myra, she had sharp cheekbones that drew attention to her angular jawline. Shorter tentacles on her head flicked sporadically. Her composure was rigid, straight-backed—the antithesis to Myra's relaxed and often swaying posture. The low-cut shirt told Aelec that this Vitrax still had confidence in her species' natural beauty.

The man, Joss, glanced at the nonhuman and grunted, "It's too risky, Nyri. The boss—"

"Will want to speak with them," Nyri cut him off. "We can't just kill them. We should bring them back to base. See what they can offer."

Joss stared daggers into Aelec, his cheeks flushed with indignation. Yet, to Aelec's surprise, the E-shotgun lowered by a fraction.

"Relinquish your weapons and nanotech devices, and we'll see if Leonis wants to meet with you," Joss ordered.

Letting out the breath he didn't realize he'd been holding, Aelec willed his nanotech back into their puck forms. Unclipping them from inside his dust coat, Aelec handed them to one of the Syters, along with his E-pistol and ammo belt. Riza did the same, but Golath was being very meticulous about how he gave the Syters his fusecaster. The Kygi, per his own traditions, had to decommission the entire weapon until it was nothing but a pile of parts. He then handed the pile to a Syter who nearly collapsed from the weight.

Joss was quick to pat Aelec down for any other items, the Syter's hand smacking and shoving him. Once satisfied, he nodded to his companions who grouped around Aelec, Riza, and Golath. They didn't cuff them, but they weren't about to let them walk without an escort.

From his belt, Joss pulled out a palm-sized disk made from a strange goldish-brown metal. He pressed his thumb to its center. The device's edges glowed violet, and he tossed it to a spot on the ground. The metal disk split into four pieces as a transparent, violet energy screen opened between the pieces. Expanding to about three meters in diameter, the energy screen revealed a passage directly under the floor.

"Sol above," Riza breathed as if she'd seen a divine entity. "That's a phase-shifter!"

"A what?" Aelec asked, leaning his head towards her.

"It can phase matter through different objects," she explained, her eyes wide with wonder. "Makes you able to pass through a wall or a floor. Word on the tech forums indicated those wouldn't be public for another three months! That plus their stealth tech... Who in the Void is funding these people?"

"Guess we'll ask Ingot when we see him," Aelec stated.

As the Syters led them through the phase-shifter and into the passage below, Aelec muttered, "I hope you're right about this."

Riza swallowed. "Me too."

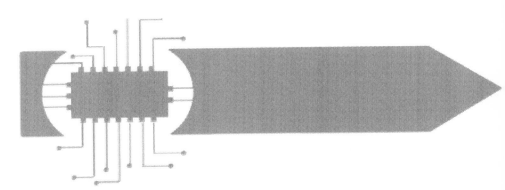

CHAPTER 23

New Skyline: The Medina District, GST: 18:06

I t was surprising how easy it was to locate a black market quantum card dealership on a planet like Oais. Dylis imagined that these kinds of shops would stick to the bowels of the city or be in secret underground facilities. Finding one in the back of a public store made him feel relieved knowing that they didn't have to scour the entire city.

An hour ago, Aelec had called to inform them that they were following a trail into the gravtram tunnels beneath the western docks. Evidently Golath managed to pick up Milli's scent and Aelec wasn't about to let a lead like that slip under the rug.

Dylis continued to check his terminus like a nervous habit. Aelec's tracking beacon was still active, moving north to the Rakto District. He felt a tingling in the back of his mind, as if the shadow assassin was still stalking them.

It was just after 18:00 Galactic Standard Time and the city

bustled with activity as the corporate working hours ended. Hundreds of vehicles clogged the streets, their electronic horns blaring like bellowing oxen. Sheets of water splashed into the city with a soft *hiss* carried on the wind.

Myra was practically skipping through the rainstorm, her pink skin and purple tentacles absorbing the water right on impact. Dylis was always jealous of her race's biology, she was getting hydrated by just walking through rain.

Dylis was soaked through to the bone, and he certainly didn't feel hydrated. After walking in drenched clothes for several blocks, he created an umbrella with his nanotech. He hated how soggy his underclothes were.

The first few shops they'd visited were common dealerships that bought broken nanotech, terminuses, or fusion coils for meager sums of quantocurrency. Often such stores would retrofit the technology into a custom design which—despite looking cool—were always way too overpriced. After a quick look around, they'd left each of the shops, heading back out into the rain.

Eventually, they found a shop that specialized in stripping tech for rare metals—but Dylis saw clear evidence of a back room. A locked blastdoor with a security cam was behind the main counter area, and the shop owner never left his perch at the counter. Since mithium was a rare—and highly coveted—metal on quantum cards, having a back room was a necessity.

"See that security cam?" Myra asked in a whisper, pretending to study a box of kygitite shavings.

"Yeah," he said, leaning his back against the shelf. "Looks to be standard issue. You think it displays a feed to the back room?"

Myra inclined her head. "The interface conduits run into the room beyond rather than to the clerk's counter."

Dylis glanced at the silvery lines beneath the camera, then murmured, "Good eye."

"Someone wants a head's up if the back door is accessed," Myra breathed, setting the small box of yellowish shavings back on the shelf.

Glancing from the cam to the shop owner, Dylis yawned theatrically to throw off any suspicion. It was another social manipulation tactic—if you looked bored, glancing around was seen as a normal coping mechanism. The shop owner looked over at him but snorted and returned to his work, paying no heed to Dylis' wandering gaze.

"So what's our play here?" Dylis asked, facing Myra and resting an arm on the shelf. "Should we play the odd couple looking for thrills? Or the classic 'slap the pig' performance?"

"As much as I love 'slap the pig', we don't need to sell ourselves too much," Myra replied. "I'll try to pass off as someone trying to sell an empty quantum card. You're my escort."

He raised an eyebrow. "Like a guard escort or a... *escort* escort?"

Myra rolled her eyes. "Obviously a guard escort you doof. Stars above, you're carrying a weapon case!"

Dylis chuckled and conceded—clearing his mind to connect with his neural interlace in the event things got dicey. While he had his E-rifle, Dylis knew that summoning a pulsecannon would be faster than trying to assemble his rifle. If another shadow-assassin showed up, he'd have to be quick on the draw.

Following Myra's lead, Dylis puffed out his broad chest and set his jaw. Exaggerated machoness could fool people into thinking you're more threatening than you actually are.

Stopping in front of the counter, Dylis hooked his left thumb into his belt which showed off the bulge of his bicep even through his jacket. He looked at the shop owner, who happened to be shorter than he was, and he could see the man's lips curl into a frown.

The shop owner ran his fingers through his stringy, blond hair as he looked up at Dylis. He was a few heads shorter than Dylis, and he wore an identification pin on the lapel of his gray jacket. At a quick glance, Dylis read: *Olso Reef, Store Manager.*

Myra leaned an arm on the counter, and a sly smile crept across her pink lips.

"Find anything you like?" Olso asked, stroking his pudgy chin.

From within her back pocket, Myra proffered an empty quantum card between two fingers. She made a show of flicking it onto the countertop, as if she were dealing zapaak cards.

"You do trade-ins for mithium?" she asked with a slight accent, which Dylis placed as her overexaggerated variant of Sathian.

Makes sense now, he thought. *She's imitating a Vitrax matriarch, who struts around with a guard or two at all times.*

The shop owner eyed the quantum card on the countertop, his hand twitched like he wanted to grab it. His green eyes narrowed as he looked from the card, to Myra, and then to Dylis.

"Are you police? Agents? Oais reserves?" Olso's eyes locked on Dylis. "By Imperium law, you have to tell me."

Dylis snorted, but said nothing.

"He's just my bodyguard, Mister Reef," Myra said. "Private security. Now, I've got mithium to trade. Are you interested or not?"

Olso's eyes flitted back and forth between the pair. "Fine," he huffed, "but I'll have you know that I've got this interaction recorded, in case you try to pull one over on me."

"I wouldn't dream of it," Myra purred. "Are we in business?"

The shop owner nodded. "Technically speaking, we do trade-ins for quantum cards to personalize them. Now, since it's impossible *not* to shave some mithium off the card to aid in the customization, we *happen* to have a system in place to refund clients such as yourselves for any unintended damage to the card. It's all legit."

Dylis rolled his eyes. Of course Olso was word vomiting the technicalities of their "customization" business, which Dylis knew was code for "yeah we barter mithium cards."

Olso snatched up the quantum card, twirled it between his fingers, and beckoned for them to follow him. As expected, he led them over to the rear security door and promptly input a code into a wall-mounted holopad. The steel slid into a wall nook with a soft *hiss*, revealing the shady backroom beyond.

A short flight of stairs led into a large room about half a floor beneath them. Three long tables were set along a checkered pattern of fake marble tiles. Sitting behind a desk piled with hologram pucks and old leather-bound ledgers was another man, who eyed them keenly.

Entering the cold, blue LEDs of the room, Olso gave a lazy wave to the man. The man at the back relaxed, continuing his work. A chorus of mechanical whirring caught Dylis' ear.

Perched on each table—like some overgrown insects—was a tall, multi-appendaged droid. Their appendages were constantly in motion, the light bouncing off their cream-colored chassis.

Each of the droids performed a different task. The first one was picking quantum cards from a plastic container before using a laser pick to remove any ID strips, engravings, or other customizations.

The card was then passed off to the next droid, which took the "clean" cards and used a grinder to shave the violet metal off the cards. It collected the shavings and deposited them into a small metal case on the table before transferring the card to the final table.

Using a mix of cutting tools, the third droid dissected the remains of the card into smaller portions; each still had bits of the quantum field machinery and were sorted into plastic boxes based on function.

When they reached the end of the stairs, Myra spoke in her most innocent, heavily accented voice, "Quite the operation you've got back here. Are those modified Mantis Accounting droids?"

Olso raised his eyebrows at Myra and replied, "Good eye, miss. I figured you'd know a thing or two about droids, given your Tarantula companion there. But yeah, I modded these fellows myself so that they process mithium net worth by gram instead of quantocurrency."

Myra nodded, her hand absently stroking her tentacles. "I can see the first one is removing ID indicators and the second is taking the mithium shavings, but what's the third doing?"

"Ah, that's a trade secret I'm afraid," Olso chuckled, stepping up to the first droid. "Can't encourage any competition around these parts. I've got a good thing going here."

Dylis kept his eyes on the man at the back desk. His fingers flicked nervously, yearning to have his E-rifle at the ready. This shady shop reminded him of being in the Fringe, his vigilance melding over him like coalescing nanoparticles.

"Do you get frequent customers like us?" Myra queried, looking around the backroom.

"Not like you, per se, but there's a steady stream of people who want to sell their used cards." Olso paused, turning to face Myra before continuing, "Now, on to business. Since your quantum card is in good shape and lacks customization, it'll be pretty standard for us to decommission it. Since that negates a lot of extra work, and standard cards possess two grams worth of mithium, I'd be willing to buy your card for ninety-five fuses."

Dylis grunted, setting his jaw. Olso gave him a sideways glance, irritation flickering in his eyes.

As if sensing Dylis' skepticism, the manager affirmed, "It's more than the banks would give you. Fewer taxes and whatnot. Usually people come in wanting to sell multiple cards."

"What about customers wanting to buy mithium cards?" Myra asked, her eyes meeting Dylis'. "You ever get those?"

Olso was silent as he went to inspect the plastic box of empty quantum cards. The pudgy man's nostrils flared in response to the question, he could see his neck muscles tensing.

That threw him off, Dylis thought as a soft grin tugged at the corners of his mouth. *Let's press a little harder. Time to let the charade slip a little.*

"I heard the penalties are far worse for selling mithium than for buying it," Dylis declared, his voice booming in the room. Olso's head snapped in his direction, his eyes widening as Dylis continued, "Something about the R.D.B. wanting to ensure accurate distribution or whatnot. I hear those bankers can ruin someone's life with the push of a holokey."

"Ma'am, I think your bodyguard's—"

"He brings up a good point," Myra interrupted.

Olso gulped. "Okay, okay," he said, his voice cracking slightly. "Yes, it's best to avoid the R.D.B. That's why most of us have a policy of not selling empty cards. Anyways, for this one card I'll transfer…"

"You said 'most of us,'" Myra intoned.

"I did."

"So," Dylis said, "that means there are some that do, yeah? Who's willing to break those kinds of rules?"

Olso's eyes flashed dangerously, his posture defensive. "You said you weren't police!"

"And we're not," Dylis affirmed. "We're just concerned citizens."

The shop owner sneered. "I thought you were her bodyguard. What is this? Some sort of con? If you're not a matriarch coterie, then who are you? Mercenaries?"

Dylis rocked his head from side to side, a few strands of auburn hair fell into his forehead. "Something like that," he said, "but if we're putting cards on the table, I'm a Private Security Contractor."

With a flick of his wrist, Dylis displayed the proper chain code. Olso's eyes went wide with fear and he sputtered for words. The man at the back desk gaped, frozen to his desk.

"We didn't do anything! I swear!"

"He says in the room full of illegal shit," Dylis scoffed, looking at Myra then back to Olso. "I wonder how much the C.B.I. would pay if we tipped them off to this shop?"

Myra examined her fingernails and said, "A recent posting said at least five hundred fuses for a reward. It's not much, but it's better than a paltry ninety-five."

"What do you want from me?!" Olso sputtered, waving his arms frantically. "Cards? Fuses? I'll pay double what that bounty's worth!"

Dylis took a step towards Olso, his pectoral muscles bulged out from his mesh-fiber shirt as he stood to his full height. Towering over the shop owner, Dylis glared down at him and tensed his grip on the E-rifle case.

"What we want," he growled, "is to know who bought some empty quantum cards four days ago. We suspect it was from this shop, so spill it!"

Olso raised his hands pitifully and stammered, "I... I don't know! There were a few people asking to buy quantum cards that day."

"Did anyone stand out?"

"No!" Olso wiped sweat from his forehead. "I get all kinds asking for my services. Humans, Vitrax, Togrian, Kygi, Pyron... You name it. Unless you know who you're looking for, I don't know what I can do."

Myra raised a finger, drawing their attention. The Vitrax looked back towards the room's entrance and asked, "You keep all footage from that cam?" Olso nodded, and Myra continued, "Pull it."

Obeying, Olso went to the wall terminal, synced his terminus to it, and returned with a recording displayed on the device. The cam footage cycled through most of the day, showing a number of clients entering, meandering, and exiting the shop. A few were escorted by Olso towards the back room.

"Rewind the feed and slow it," Dylis ordered, leaning towards the hologram.

The shop owner did so, and as the feed replayed at a slower rate, someone caught Dylis' eye.

Stepping with the grace of a dancer, a lanky man followed Olso into the back room. Behind him he dragged a small cargocase, and Dylis assumed that he was an off-worlder. Only someone fresh off a shuttle would bring their luggage into a shop with them.

"Freeze frame," he commanded.

He scanned the off-worlder from head to toe. The man's tan skin seemed richer—a shade darker than Dylis'—and had a faint sheen of oil. Though that might've been due to his greasy, black hair. His hawk-like face was cold, statuesque. Ice blue eyes were perfectly highlighted by the hologram's light. Eyes that he would remember anywhere.

"That's him," Dylis murmured, pointing at the hologram. "That's the guy from Medina General."

Myra stepped up next to him; his nostrils flared in response to her perfume which smelled like sweet chilis. She narrowed her violet eyes at the hologram.

"Are you sure?"

"When a man tries to kill you, you never forget what he looks like," Dylis explained, staring at the image. "I only saw his eyes, but I'd recognize them anywhere."

She nodded, then demanded, "Who is this human?"

"I didn't get a name," Olso answered, wringing his hands. "He offered a ton of fuses in exchange for a few empty cards. I figured he was a private investigator or something."

"You have any transaction receipts?" Dylis queried.

Olso gawked and snapped, "You really think I'd keep receipts in this business?"

"Dammit!" Dylis rubbed his hand against his forehead, frustration bubbling up.

They were so close, he could feel it. Spectre's trail had led them to the shady purchase of the quantum scalpel, and when they started making headway the shadow assassin scoped them out. Now it was confirmed that the mithium cards used to acquire the quantum scalpel were purchased *by* said assassin.

He was the one who targeted Spectre, Dylis concluded. *But how does the assassin tie in with the Far Syters?*

A few snaps of metal against tile drew his attention, and he noticed Rant approaching the nearest Mantis droid. Dark crimson photoreceptors twitched on Rant's domed head as he skittered like a spider.

"Statement: This unit would be able to determine the identification of the human in question, Dylis Wyri," Rant said dryly.

"How so?"

"Answer: Based on the data this unit received from Medina General, the mithium cards deposited into their funds will have identification markers on their quantum field generators. This unit will communicate with Mantis Accountant eight-zero-four to determine which account the initial plancks came from."

Dylis cocked an eyebrow. "Plancks? What in the Void are those?"

"It's the technical term for 'fuses,'" Olso corrected softly.

Myra tilted her head towards the black droid and said, "Go for it, old friend. Just make sure to play nice."

Rant's left appendages made a salute as he stated, "Acknowledgement: This unit will proceed with the communication. The command 'play nice' is unrecognized."

The Vitrax rolled her eyes. "It's just an expression, Rant."

Rant moved up to the third Mantis droid, extended one of his appendages, and connected with an interface on the droid's side. A soft beeping emanated from the device, the machines speaking in a language that Dylis couldn't understand.

Dylis blinked and Rant disconnected from the Mantis droid, their frequencies allowing them to talk much faster than humans.

Rotating his domed head towards them, he said, "Statement: This unit has acquired marker of item five-one-two-six, a quantum field generator installed on a mithium card purchased by plancks linked to the quantumbank account of Raheem Na-heema."

Rant displayed a hologram bearing the name, but it was spelled: *Rajim Na-jima*.

Dylis went rigid. Despite Rant's monotone, the droid pronounced the name with a specific Capital World accent. He'd heard names like that before, ones that varied depending on the vernacular of the planet they hailed from. Outriders, for instance, preferred to use 'y' in favor of 'i' in the initial portion of their names.

Yet, there was one accent he would never forget—an accent used by those who'd caused him to take his vow of non-lethality. This man, this Rajim Na-jima, was from the planet Argentia.

A wave of icy terror washed through his body as he made the realization. It was a familiar fear, like what he felt on Faerius the day his wife nearly died. His legs felt heavy, like they were glued to the floor. Apprehension pulsed within him as more and more understanding snaked through his mind.

Dylis spun on his heel and made for the doorway, his heart pounding in his chest. A man from Argentia wielding a mysterious energy blade. The legends were starting to meld together into a cohesive picture. *The shadow that strikes with the light of a star.* It couldn't be...

"We need to find Aelec and the others!" he ordered, his voice booming across the room. "Now!"

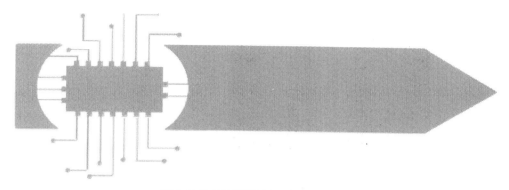

CHAPTER 24

New Skyline: The D.E.F. Access Network, GST: 19:00

Riza didn't have much experience being a prisoner. Prior to her venturing to the Fringe Territories, she'd been an upstanding citizen of the Imperium. No records, no complaints, and no debts. Arenia had been the troubled child.

Yet here she was, surrounded by armed gang members and being escorted through the winding network of hidden tunnels. The air was thick with fumes, mostly minty engine coolant, and heat kissed her skin the deeper they went. She wasn't cuffed, but she no less felt like a prisoner heading towards her cell.

This must be how Arenia felt when she vandalized the dean's grav-car, Riza thought, resisting the urge to smirk.

Before leaving to join the Insurrectionists, Arenia had attempted to get her trade skill in archaeological repair at the Novent Academy. Riza's older sister wasn't much of an academic, but she'd been fascinated with the bygone civilizations of the galaxy. That was before the Imperium armada squashed an attempted secession on Nidal.

Arenia hadn't immediately joined the Insurrectionists, but she began resisting the Imperium in her own ways. Well... the same ways she used to rebel against their parents. A lot of shouting, spray-painting graffiti, and occasionally sabotaging electronics. By the Void, she was a pain in the ass when they were growing up.

Joss, the leader of the Syter squad, shouted something at them, breaking her thoughts. His words were hoarse and grating; he was speaking a language that had a mix of throaty vowels and drawn out 's' sounds. To Riza's surprise, Nyri replied in the same language. They were speaking Vitraxi, likely to conceal their conversation.

Beside her walked Aelec, his demeanor as cool as a chilled glass of tea. His argent hair hung around his chiseled face, the strands tangled and messy. Aelec's aurous eyes stared forward as they marched down the under-underground tunnel.

"How are you this calm when we're being taken prisoner?" she queried quietly, frowning at him. "It's both impressive and frustrating."

Aelec glanced at her from the corner of his eye and smirked. "This isn't my first vankir rodeo. I've played prisoner for far worse groups than these guys. I'm surprised you're not calm, considering this was your idea."

"Yeah, that was all bravado," Riza hissed, "I'm kinda freaking out here!"

Aelec met her eyes and murmured, "Relax, you've got this. You went with your instincts and I trust you. We're going to need that soothing disposition when we meet Ingot."

"And if I can't?" She glanced around at their escorts and whispered, "What happens if I'm not as good of a talker as you think?"

Aelec shrugged. "Then I guess we'll have a few fusion holes in our heads."

The color left Riza's face and her heart skipped a beat. When

Aelec saw the anxiety present on her face, he added, "That was a joke. They'll be in our chests."

"Aelec, I swear to the Sol…"

"I'm kidding," he chuckled, looking ahead. "I won't let anything happen to you, Riza."

Familiar clicking came from behind her, and Aelec clarified, "And neither will Golath."

She pursed her lips before saying, "And I won't let anything happen to you. We're in this together, remember? I can't take down Kuvan without you."

Aelec raised his eyebrows in surprise. "Well, I guess I'm in good hands."

"Yeah, you are," she said.

A grin formed on his pale face, and Riza had to conceal her doubt. In a galaxy of Outriders, pirates, nonhuman warriors, and shadow assassins, what hope did she have of facing them down? She was a rural girl with a fancy education, not a warrior.

I don't need to be a warrior, Riza reminded herself. *My skill—my talent—lies in technology. And having a soothing persona.*

It was different from the personas Dylis informed her about; it wasn't an act to fool someone. No, this persona was a true extension of herself. If Riza could bring a little more comfort to the darker parts of the galaxy, then she'd do a damn fine job of it.

A pentagonal corridor extended into the distance, the end barely visible due to the dim, violet lights. The tunnels snaked through the underground with a rigid flow like they were navigating through a pyrostone maze. Dirt and stone dust crunched beneath her boots. The grayish-brown carbocrete was old—far older than anything she'd seen on Seraphi.

According to Imperium records, Oais was the second planet humanity colonized in the bygone ages of the galaxy, roughly around 1924.1214. That was millennia before the Capital Worlds and Imperium were even founded; the human spaceforce was nothing more than a small exploration fleet.

Since the planet wasn't originally oxygen-rich, Riza could envision the colonists using these underground networks for survival. She was in the ancient depths of Oais, and Riza understood why Arenia was obsessed with galactic history.

The corridor ended at a grand flight of metal stairs that led two floors deeper into the depths. Metallic *clicks* emanated from the Syters as they turned on some flashlights. Down they went, the soles of their boots thumping against the metal echoed in the dark. Bony taps distinguished Golath's footsteps from the others', and the stairs creaked under his weight.

Reaching the bottom floor, the Syters guided them down a short corridor—similarly devoid of LEDs—before reaching a door. Well, calling it a door was being generous. A slab of dark ore stretched from floor to ceiling, barring the end of the hallway. Riza squinted, noticing the glint of a conduit at its center.

Joss pushed past the other Syters and approached the door. Digging through his pockets, he fished out an object and placed it within the old conduit. A resounding *clank* emanated from the door, followed by a *hiss* of old hydraulics. Joss just as quickly pocketed whatever the key was, glaring back at them.

Metal grinded against carbocrete, the door opening slowly, deliberately. Warm light poured into the hallway from beyond, forcing Riza to shield her eyes.

When her eyes adjusted to the yellow light, she lowered her arm and witnessed a scene ripped straight out of a holonet film. The sweeping expanse of an enormous cavern extended as far as her eyes could see. Her jaw dropped at the sheer magnitude of this space.

Carbocrete melded seamlessly into old morristeel—or what she thought was morristeel. The rusted, violet metal bore a millennium's worth of cracks, and black smears pocked the faces of small, blocky structures.

Ahead of the group, Joss waved a hand up at a few guards

perched on outcroppings sticking out from the buildings. High above, the arched ceiling of natural stone rose nearly six stories.

As she stepped upon the ancient metal, she felt a soft vibration. It took her a moment, but she noticed that the metal structures were *alive*—rippling as if they were breathing while small portions broke off to reform on another wall or surface. It was reminiscent of how Meridiem buildings shifted depending on what was needed, but Riza could hardly fathom that such a style would be down here.

Riza's gaze wandered in utter fascination as they walked into the complex, some of the structures resembled massive drills, cranes, and dumpsters. Following the perimeter, she could see that the entire place was lined with mining equipment, like it was a droid with countless appendages.

She pieced it together. *It's not just a complex, it's a machine.*

"Wow," she breathed, her eyes drinking in this marvel of millennia past. "What Arenia would have given to see this place."

To her surprise, Aelec closed his eyes reverently, and when they opened Riza could see hints of regret. "Was Arenia a student of history?" he asked.

"You could say that," Riza replied. "Before the whole Insurrectionist thing, she wanted to get a trade skill in archeology. She wasn't a great student by any means, but she loved learning about our past."

Aelec averted his gaze, his eyes stared down at his feet as he said, "She... err... she seemed like a decent person. Despite the whole terrorist thing."

"Yeah," Riza admitted, tugging on her ponytail. "A decent woman making a few poor life decisions. Runs in the family it seems."

"There's one difference, though." Aelec returned his gaze to Riza, and his golden eyes alight with fire. In a gravelly voice, he stated, "You're here to continue her work. Finding the truth and seeking justice."

"And seceding from the Imperium, right?"

"Heh, good luck with that." Some levity returned to Aelec's voice as he continued, "I don't think anything apart from a full-scale revolution of all nine worlds would break the Imperium. Nor would I want that to happen."

"Why?"

"Because I still have faith in the Imperium, Riza. It can be a force of good in this galaxy once the corruption is annexed."

Riza furrowed her brow as the pessimism rose within her. "And if nothing changes? What happens when we remove Kuvan and his cronies, but corruption still remains? How do you know the Imperator himself isn't responsible?"

Shaking his head, Aelec responded, "I've got to believe that there's still some good in this galaxy. The best we can do is take it one mission at a time. We Outriders have a saying, 'The missions never stop.' Even for ex-Outriders. We'll make that voidjump when we have to."

Riza sniffed. "It's all military comparisons with you, isn't it?"

"Would you prefer some vague Outrider analogies?" Aelec retorted with a shrug.

"Touché."

She didn't realize it until the conversation tapered off, but talking with Aelec helped put her at ease. One of the Syter escorts raised his E-rifle by a fraction, striking a few chords of nervousness in her. Still, she wasn't as scared as she'd been half an hour ago. It was another reminder of why she sought to stay with Aelec. Why she wanted to be...

Nope! she cut herself off. *Not indulging those thoughts right now! You're a prisoner, for Sol's sake.*

Riza remained silent as the Syters escorted them further into the mining complex. Metal structures melded back into the cream-colored stone, many of which were embedded into the rock. Yet, the structures didn't end with the complex; column-like buildings had been carved from the pale stone. Looking further into the cavern,

Riza noted the serrated patterns in the rock, which suggested it had seen multiple mining events.

She frowned in confusion. *Perhaps these structures existed before being discovered by the machine's mining efforts.*

Entering the swath of old buildings, crowds of Syters gathered to herald their arrival, though she felt an aura of misgiving. Countless eyes were glued to them. The distinct nebula-like eyes of a few Vitrax glared at her. A set of black goggles on one individual sent shivers down her spine.

A Pyron? she thought, her eyes widening in shock. *Working underground? That's a bit ominous.*

The natives from Pyron were a sun-worshiping race, cultivated by the harsh desert world that they hailed from. From what she'd heard, the Pyrons felt it was sacrilegious to enter the bowels of the world. It had something to do with their souls being tethered to the sun, or somesuch.

Despite the goggles and sand-colored wrappings, the nonhuman's gaze was more piercing than any she'd felt. She turned her head away sharply.

The thoroughfare continued for a few hundred meters before stopping at a large, granite structure that melded seamlessly into the cavern's walls. Shaped like a spade, the building rose about three stories, its curving roof reminded her of the old monasteries from the Seraph Ridge Mountains. Smooth columns held up the overhang above the main doorway, which was yet another slab of black ore.

Joss approached the door, pressed the key to its center, and it peeled away like the petals of a flower. She could see that the ore was made up of distinct pieces, lines webbed along the surface like a cracked mirror.

A string of high-pitched clicks came from Golath as he wrung his four claws.

"Yeah, this isn't normal," Aelec noted, patting one of Golath's arms.

"What in the Void is this place?" Riza breathed, running a hand along the smooth stone column.

"Beats me. The mining complex was likely ours from the colonization. But this... This is not human-made."

When the door had fully peeled away, the Syters escorted them in. Grayish-brown granite slabs formed intricate patterns along the floor, inlays of ore pulsed with a soft, emerald glow. She blinked in recognition; it was reminiscent of older shrines dedicated to the Church of Sol. It was absent of pews, altars, or inner columns, but the layout tickled her familiarity.

Walking deeper into the monolith, she spotted several triangular obelisks jutting up from the floor like spearheads. Grafted from the same black material as the door, most of the obelisks were intact, though some had chunks missing, the pieces scattered across the stone floor.

Squatting next to one of the broken obelisks was a man in a ragged, orange combat suit. He held a plasma pick in one hand, using it to delicately scrape pieces from the broken obelisk. After a moment, he sheathed the pick in his wide utility belt, keeping his back turned to them.

The escorts stopped a few paces from the man, forcing Riza, Aelec, and Golath to do the same. Joss approached the man, knelt beside him, and placed a hand on his shoulder. He leaned in to whisper, and the man perked up.

After a moment, Joss stepped away from the man, and the latter let out a low grunt before rising to his feet and turning to face them.

Riza's mind flashed with recognition. The warm light of the temple gave a sheen on his dark skin. He raised a hand to brush stone dust from his graying cornrows. Clasping his hands behind his back, he took a step forward, tilting his head to one side.

Examining them with keen, dark eyes, the man said, "I am Leonis Ingot. Welcome to the Syter's Foundry."

"An ex-Outrider, a Seraphian girl, and a Kygi walk into a Foundry," Leonis noted, pacing slowly before them. "There's a joke in there. Still, I wasn't expecting this today."

Riza stood rigidly as they faced the leader of the Far Syters, the escorts were shuffling in formation but remained on guard. She could feel the vibrations of the Golath's guttural clicks run down her back. Aelec looped his thumb into his belt, leaning to one side with the inscrutable swagger of a Fringe thief.

Behind the Syters, the black obelisks rose from the floor like jagged teeth. Nearby was a sage, mesh-fiber tent that was large enough to host a dozen people, and the familiar glow of holograms radiated from its open flaps.

Dirt crunched beneath Leonis' hiking boots as he paced, his dark eyes analyzing them. Upon hearing his words, a wave of curiosity compelled Riza to speak first.

"How did you know I'm from Seraphi?"

"Your jacket style is of the faux variety, which is commonly bought and worn by middle-class Seraphians," he explained. "You also have an aura of inquisitiveness, something that I find common in students."

"You're not a teacher," Aelec snorted. "Not anymore."

"No," Leonis conceded. "No, I am not a professor, you got me there. But I still have enough intuition to know when someone's fresh out of the Academy. How long since you graduated, young miss? Two, three months?"

"Two and a half," she answered, her eyes widening. "A good guess."

Leonis gave her a faint smile. Riza glanced at Aelec and met his stern, auric eyes. She inclined her head, her expression pleading as she made her intentions clear.

Let me break down his walls, she thought, hoping Aelec would understand. *If I can get him comfortable, then we can start questioning.*

To her relief, Aelec's gaze softened by a fraction, and he tilted his head towards Leonis, gesturing for her to continue. Riza's eyes lit up, and she had to resist cracking her knuckles in anticipation for her task.

"What is this place?" Riza asked genuinely. "I've never seen equipment and structures this old."

Leonis' smile widened like that of a child explaining a new project, and he made a sweeping gesture.

"This is a Foundry," he explained, "well, more precisely a D.E.F. —a Domain Expanse Foundry. Millennia ago, when mankind first set foot on Oais, our terraforming techniques weren't yet capable of combatting this world's toxic atmosphere. So, the colonists used these great machines to create a livable environment, mine resources, and expand upward. Records state that it took close to one hundred years before Oais' surface was actually colonized."

Squatting, Leonis ran a hand along the dirt covering the old stone. For a moment, he examined his dirty hand before clapping it free of dust.

"This was where the Church of Sol was born," Leonis stated, pointing to the arched ceiling. "The first light in the Void. Though it was quickly followed by dark times. The Sage priests used the doctrines of religion to seize power from the governors. Their cult, the Furies of Sol, exercised martial law and persecuted non-believers."

Leonis raised a finger and queried, "Did you know that a common punishment from the Furies involved being literally thrown into the nearby sun via gravlift capsules?"

"That's horrible!" Riza said, aghast. "But, this doesn't look like a shrine dedicated to the Sol. It's something else."

Leonis raised his eyebrows. "Good eye, young miss. This structure predates humanity's arrival on Oais. We archeologists can only speculate on what its original purpose was. Suffice it to say, using it as a beacon for religion seems about right. It was a time when mankind was united against a single threat: the darkness of the Void. Survival is what kept us together. But now, avarice and indolence divides us. Complacency. It's where we went wrong these past few centuries."

"How has the Imperium been complacent?" Riza queried, placing her hands on her hips. "We've seen more terrorist activity and secession wars in the past fifty years than in the last millennium."

"Ah, a student of history, are you?" Leonis continued to pry. "What was your main trade? Xenobiology? Archeology?"

"Terminus programming. My sister was the history nut, I'm afraid."

"Wait a minute." Leonis paused, pointing a finger at Riza. "Yes, the resemblance is there. The dark hair threw me off. You're Arenia's sister, aren't you?"

It felt like a punch to the gut, her sister's name echoing throughout the corners of her mind. She always wondered how well-traveled Arenia had been during her time with the Insurrectionists and what kinds of friends she made across the Imperium. Fate, it seemed, had a twisted sense of humor.

"How did you know?" Riza asked, her voice growing hoarse.

Leonis shrugged as he resumed pacing. "You need to have a keen eye for details if you're to unravel the mysteries of the universe. Same eyes, same complexion, same posture... Though you're a bit shorter, and lack purple hair. Arenia mentioned you on more than one occasion."

"I guess that tracks." Riza surveyed the crowd of Syters. "She always had a knack for getting mixed up with the wrong crowd."

The older man chuckled, halting his stride and rubbing his beard. "Oh, we're the right crowd, Miss Noxia. We're the ones who promote autonomy in the face of fascism."

Aelec grumbled in response.

Leonis' gaze snapped to the captain. "Got something to say, war machine?"

Riza's face went cold as she saw Aelec's eye twitch.

Rising to the Syter's bait, Aelec growled, "Don't call me that."

Leonis narrowed his eyes at the captain, then returned his gaze to Riza. "A former Academy student working alongside an Outrider. Forgive me, but how in the great Void did you end up together?"

Riza didn't reply. The Syter escorts expanded their formation into a ring around them, allowing Leonis to get a bit closer. Nyri and Joss stood between them and the Far Syter leader, their hands tightly gripping their E-weapons.

The trio remained motionless, only Golath's arms moved as he wrung his claws nervously. Aelec folded his arms across his broad chest. The Outrider stood a few fingers taller than Leonis, his jaw clenching as if he was biting back a scathing remark. She had to give it to Aelec, even with the odds stacked against him he didn't let it faze him.

Tapping her fingers on her belt, Riza did her best to examine Leonis' disposition. The clasped hands behind the back told Riza that he felt in control of the situation—he didn't need his hands to be at the ready. The faint grin and heavy-lidded eyes indicated that he was perhaps amused or curious. But the pacing—the pacing told her that he was nervous.

So, with an unspoken coordination, Riza and Aelec made their move.

"You make all kinds of friends out in the Fringe," Aelec grunted, keeping his eyes locked on Leonis. "Riza needed a job, so I welcomed her aboard my crew. Now I have a question for you. Do you know what happened to Agent Milli Spectre?"

Leonis practically skidded to a halt. "Come again?"

"The C.B.I. lists you as their Most Wanted suspect in Agent Spectre's disappearance," Riza said. "If we can hear your side of things, it's possible we could help clear your name."

Inclining his head, Leonis met Riza's gaze and asked, "What

authority do you have? You're a civilian, he's former Imperium, and he is... an assistant?" He waved a hand at Golath and continued, "No, he doesn't strike me as such. Perhaps a bodyguard?"

"A friend!" Aelec snapped, his voice echoing throughout the old structure.

A hush ran over the ring of Syters, their eyes widening. Nyri's lips parted in amazement as her short tentacles twitched. Joss wasn't fazed, a frown tugging at his mustache. Leonis, however, raised his eyebrows in genuine astonishment.

"Really?" He resumed pacing, keeping his distance. "In my experience, it takes a considerable bond for a Kygi to befriend another species. But how deep does that friendship go, I wonder?"

Without clicking, Golath stepped forward, his lumbering body shielding Aelec from Leonis. The Kygi hunched slightly to meet Leonis' gaze, and a low clicking emanated from his respirator like a growl.

The Syter leader smirked and said, "Okay, point taken."

"I don't care what you think," Aelec said, stepping out from behind Golath. "I'll ask again. What happened to Milli?"

"She's a friend of yours?"

"Yeah." His lips curled into a snarl. "Now answer the question. My patience is growing thin."

Riza quickly butted in, the rising tension almost palpable. "They were close friends in the Imperium armada. When Aelec found out she was missing, he set aside everything in order to find her. No matter the time nor the cost. His mission... our mission is to find Spectre and bring her home."

"And since she was last seen keeping tabs on your little gang," Aelec growled, "the C.B.I. has a bounty on your head, Ingot. But I'm a firm believer in justice, which is why we're giving you the chance to explain yourself." He paused, then added, "Milli's husband told me that the Syters were harassing her. At work. At home. What in the Void was your problem with her?"

Leonis frowned and looked down at his feet. "That was an unfortunate set of circumstances."

Aelec drew his lips into a thin line. "Explain."

"Please," Riza added softly. "We offered to help clear your name. Please, tell us what happened."

When Leonis didn't answer, Riza pressed further, "If you knew Arenia, then you know that my family stays true to their word. Let us help prove your innocence, at least in this matter."

The older man sighed and ran a hand over his cornrows. At his side, Nyri narrowed her eyes at Riza, but ultimately didn't voice any objections, as did Joss. She had to hand it to the Syters; they didn't try to undermine their leader as he weighed his decisions.

A moment of silence elapsed, punctuated by the emptiness of the old structure. Even Golath's clicking had ceased. Oxygenators were so far back in the mine that they were inaudible, only muffled reverberations came from carried voices.

Leonis cleared his throat and said, "It's true, the Far Syters and the C.B.I. have been hostile towards one another in recent months. Ever since it was discovered that we were old affiliates of the Insurrectionists, the government has been much less tolerant of our protests. There were even a few unlawful raids on some of our warehouses three months ago."

He made a grand gesture to the structure around them. "Hence why we're presently shacking up in this old Foundry. Not many people know this is down here, and even the Caps haven't managed to find it."

"No doubt with the help of those shifter devices," Aelec grunted.

"Yes, the shifters give us exclusive access to the pathways beneath the gravtram tunnels," Leonis said. "But do you really think the Imperium doesn't have technology more sophisticated than these?"

Proffering the disk-like device, he continued, "Regardless, the shifters and the Foundry are only temporary means to extend our stay here on Oais. We've been meaning to leave ever since the Caps started targeting us. Eventually, Agent Spectre was assigned to keep tabs on our holonet presence, restrict our content, and document our activities. That didn't sit well with some of my younger followers."

Leonis groaned, pinching the bridge of his nose. "They thought if they harassed her enough, she'd back off. It was some real nasty stuff they sent her. I have no love for the Imperium, but it was harassment that I would never sanction."

Riza noticed Aelec's hand curling into a fist, his knuckles cracking.

"Yet it happened anyways," Aelec hissed. "She was doing as ordered, and you tormented her for it. There's no honor in shaming someone for doing their job."

"I agree," Leonis said. "That's why I reached out to her to discuss a truce."

"What?"

Riza blinked in surprise. She was dubious of his words, but there was a sincerity to his voice that made her question. For the past day, she'd had the scenario painted firmly in her mind. Leonis Ingot, a radical activist, made enemies with the C.B.I. and ordered his followers to harass Spectre. Then, when Spectre confronted them, it put a target on her back that the Syters made good on in the western docks.

Yet, here was Leonis Ingot. A crusader, yes, but he seemed measured and reasonable. Riza knew all too well not to judge someone by their reputation or the actions of their followers. She'd learned that lesson the hard way with Aelec. She also knew how uncontrollable young activists could be. Arenia had shown her that.

"I wanted her to know that not all the Far Syters were personally against her," Leonis continued. "I wanted to keep our cause civil and legal. I also knew that we wouldn't be able to remain on Oais for long if members of the C.B.I. wanted us in prison."

Aelec perked up, his eyes glinted with understanding. "When she met with you, it was to discuss the terms of your departure."

Leonis nodded. "As long as the harassment ceased and we didn't break the law, she was going to put in a good word with the port masters and get us all off-world."

"And then she went missing," Riza finished.

"It doesn't change the fact that she vanished at one of your protests," Aelec growled, his eyes darkening.

"My followers had no idea she was even there!" he protested. "When I saw the news on the holonet, I questioned each Syter who was there. None were aware of her presence. You can thank Milli's training for that."

An idea sparked in Riza's mind.

"Mister Ingot, how many of your followers were present at the protest?"

"Twenty," he answered quickly, frowning. "Each of my followers has a precision motion tracker in the event they go missing. And I keep daily logs."

"How precise?"

"Its field narrows to a ten-meter radius on their location. Why?"

Riza rubbed her hands together and said, "If you'll give me my terminus, we can check to make sure all your followers were accounted for. Ten meters is a wide berth."

Leonis looked to Nyri and Joss for counsel. Joss shook his head, his posture tensing as he looked at Aelec the way a hunter might look at a rabid traxi hound. The Vitrax, however, didn't object; in fact she smiled encouragingly. Rubbing his beard, Leonis paused before gesturing to the equipment tent.

"Come. I'll let you access your terminus, but only if it's connected to our servers. Can't risk you sending a signal topside."

"Fair enough," she said. "I think this will help prove your innocence."

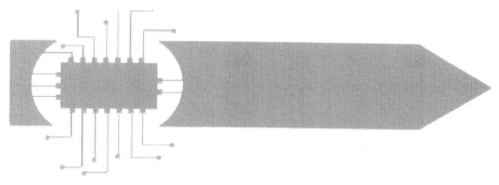

CHAPTER 25

New Skyline: The Western Dockyards, GST: 19:30

"Their signal just went dark!" Myra advised, swiping through holograms on her terminus.

The ever-persistent patter of rain reverberated throughout the cylindrical hallway. Long skylights allowed her to glimpse the churning, black sky that overshadowed New Skyline. They traversed through the enclosed hallway leading to the western dockyards, and it was surprisingly devoid of foot traffic.

Myra sidestepped a pile of abandoned cargocases. Dylis was nearby, his E-rifle equipped and at the ready. Half of his tan face was obscured by shadows, and the dim LEDs almost obscured Rant's black frame—his numerous red eyes glowed like embers in the darkness.

Dylis pushed back his auburn hair. "Try them again. I swear to the Sol, if the Starblades got to them..."

Myra did so, waiting for Aelec to respond though only crackling static emanated from the terminus.

"Rant, are you detecting any disruptions in our area?" she asked, her tentacles flicking nervously.

"Answer: Negative, Master Myra," the droid answered. "This unit interprets this as either a frequency jammer in the gravtram tunnels, or Aelec Xero has disabled his terminus."

"Aelec wouldn't be stupid enough to do that," Dylis said. He kept pivoting as he walked, always ensuring that his back wasn't to any one place for too long.

"I agree." Myra swiped through the holograms before saying, "I can't get a hold of Riza, either. Something's up."

"What a spectacular revelation, Myra," Dylis scoffed. "Here I thought they just turned off their commlinks to bang one out."

She glared at him. "Something else is wrong. You've been on edge ever since the mithium shop, Dylis. What's going on? What aren't you telling me?"

He didn't answer, continuing his militaristic pivoting as he walked through the corridor. When they reached the hub, Dylis entered first, checking each corner in a four-point scan. It took only a few heartbeats, but Dylis' shoulders relaxed and he nodded for her to enter.

As she passed by, Myra saw franticness in his green eyes as they darted around the area. The older human huffed as sweat glistened on his wide forehead. She placed a hand on his firm forearm, an aura of alarm radiated from him like an energy shield.

"Seriously," she said soothingly, "what is wrong? Who was that man in the cam footage?"

Dylis closed his eyes, inhaling deeply as his grip relaxed on the E-rifle. When he opened his eyes, he met Myra's gaze and frowned.

"I should've pieced it together earlier," he mumbled. "When I tussled with him in the hospital. I don't know him specifically, but I know of his kind."

Myra blinked, her lips parting. "The shadow that strikes with the light of a star? I thought you'd never heard of them before."

"There's a ghost story here in the Capital Worlds. A faction that's so good that they've never been seen. Have you ever heard of the Starblades of Argentia?"

She shook her head. "Should I have?"

"Not likely, I suppose," Dylis said, beckoning for her to walk with him. "Even the Outriders only ever heard legends about them. Some even fantasized about meeting one. My mentor, Pyrso Wyri, swore he saw a Starblade in the skirmish between the Imperium and the A.I.L. ten years ago."

"The A.I.L.?" the Vitrax asked, her brow furrowing.

"Anti-Imperium League," he answered, pivoting in the hall. "A lot of terrorist factions have popped up over the past few decades, each with names that get dumber and dumber. Like the *Insurrectionists*. Pfft, c'mon, at least try to be creative."

"And your mentor," Myra continued, "this Pyrso guy. He said he saw one of these Starblades?"

"Claimed to," Dylis corrected. "Why would they send an assassin when an army of galactic super-soldiers were on the job? Makes no sense. Regardless, I used to think they were nothing but ghost stories used to inspire or scare Imperium soldiers. Then, I met someone from Argentia."

Myra's lips tightened into a line as she pondered his words. A surge of recognition entered her mind like a shot of dopamine.

"The fight on Faerius," she breathed, her voice cracking. "When you took your vow."

Dylis nodded. "Yeah. They weren't assassins, at least not yet. But when you meet a fighter from Argentia, you never forget them."

"Stars above," Myra murmured, putting a hand to her forehead. "This situation just keeps getting more and more screwed."

"Best we can do is find Aelec and the others," Dylis affirmed. "If we find Milli, awesome. But if she got on the bad side of some Starblades, then we need to leave that shit alone."

Myra didn't press the matter. Finding their crew was a priority, not locating Spectre. Dylis remained silent as they continued through the network of dockyard hallways.

Eventually, they reached the spot where Spectre had vanished, according to the C.B.I. reports. Myra's tentacles twitched as she felt a spike of alarm. The echo of a terrible deed was etched into the pale carbocrete like an engraving.

She saw the fusionfibers blocking off the entrance to the spot where Spectre had gone missing. The glowing, yellow cords were spaced unevenly and in a sloppy pattern; someone could easily slip beneath them.

Glancing at the schematic Aelec had sent them, Myra stared at the hallway beyond the barricade. "So they picked up Spectre's trail," she said, "and followed it to hangar bay L-three-three-four before following a vent shaft into the tunnels. The spot we lost their signal is two kilometers north of here. What's our plan?"

Lowering his E-rifle, Dylis looked over her shoulder at the schematic. "Hmm. There's no way to get to that spot unless we follow their path or go all the way up to the Rakto District. Shit! We're losing time!"

Dread tugged at her belly. There'd been no sign of the Starblade since Medina General, and her first thought was that he'd ambushed the others. She couldn't conceive of an activist guild getting the jump on Aelec like that. It had to be the Starblade.

A thought came to her like lightning flashing in the storm clouds.

Her eyes scanned the hub, and after a heartbeat she found what she needed. A maintenance console.

Jabbing a finger at it, she said, "Rant, I need you to access the dockyard's network. See if this Na-jima guy parked his ship nearby."

She blinked and the droid was already at the console, extending one of his appendages to link with it. Dylis regarded her with a furrowed brow.

"What in the Void are you doing?"

"If the Starblade got to Aelec and the others, the only way we can find them is by accessing the ship's logs. Stars above, they might even be on the ship!"

Dylis gulped. "And if they're already dead?"

"They won't be! Aelec believes that Milli was taken alive, so I believe Na-jima would do the same with them." When Dylis looked away, she gripped his arm and murmured, "They're still alive. I can feel it, Dylis!"

Dylis sighed, but didn't press the matter. Myra absently ran her fingers through her tentacles as she waited for Rant.

All she could think about was Aelec being attacked by that assassin. While her romantic feelings for him had long faded, she still cared for him as her employer, her captain, and her friend. Golath too, for that matter. The Kygi was like family, and she felt a kindred spirit with him as a fellow nonhuman.

And Riza? she asked herself. *Would I really be upset if anything happened to her?*

She bit her lip as she pondered the thought. A well of shame rose in her chest, and she felt sick to her stomach. Of course she didn't want anything to happen to Riza.

A rapid beeping from Rant drew her out of her thoughts, the droid's head swiveling to face her.

"Declaration: This unit has successfully accessed New Skyline's western dockyard shipping logs. Target Rajim Na-jima was seen exiting an S-fifty-three model freighter that docked in hangar bay L-three-three-six. Subject hangar bay is approximately one hundred and fifty-three meters from our present location."

"Good," she said, "let's pay him a visit."

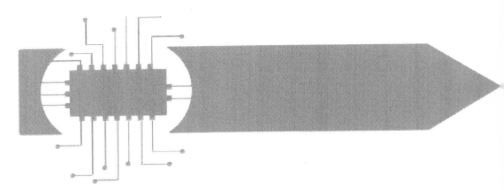

CHAPTER 26

C losing the distance to hangar bay L336, Dylis kept his finger on the trigger of his E-rifle and his mind focused on his nanotech clusters. After Rant had ascertained the target hangar bay, it didn't take them long to follow the dockyard's network towards their goal.

The hub areas were still empty of people—the dissonance of voices replaced by whirring machinery and distant klaxons. Over the eerie sounds, Dylis heard a mechanized voice speaking over the dockyard's commlinks.

"Attention, the western dockyard is presently undergoing mainte-nance routines. Starlane traffic is to be diverted to the southern, east-ern, and northern dockyards while maintenance is performed. Please vacate the premises until twenty-hundred Galactic Standard Time. We appreciate your patience and flexibility."

Dylis snorted at the inconvenience this likely caused the citizens of New Skyline.

You'd think with all the droids available they'd keep each terminal operational and do maintenance throughout the day, Dylis mused. *Guess there's still a few hitches in the Imperium's inner workings.*

It was a strange introspection to make. Ever since the heist at the Golden Spire, more and more things shed an unflattering light on the Imperium. Corrupt governors, brewing system conflicts, apathy towards government agents, nefarious workings even on a Capital World... Things kept whittling away at Dylis' convictions that the Imperium was some grand, flawless empire.

He put those thoughts aside, reminding himself of the mission to cleanse his clan-mark. Penance for his actions on Faerius wouldn't come if he continued to doubt the regime that had bestowed his abilities, family, and home. No, Dylis had to persevere in his quest. It wasn't his job to worry about the foundations of the Imperium.

Right now, his focus was on finding Aelec. He couldn't lose him. Dylis had great adoration for Aelec, but sometimes he felt his age, especially when the younger Outrider rushed headlong into a situation.

Dylis understood more than most why Aelec wanted justice for what happened to clan-Xero, but this was bordering on foolhardy. If he wasn't careful, Aelec would get way in over his head, and possibly killed if the Starblades got to him. He shivered at the thought of what might happen if Aelec brazenly attacked Kuvan with such a gung-ho attitude.

I don't want him to make the same mistakes I did, Dylis mused. *Aelec's clan-mark isn't worth this endless pursuit of justice.*

Rounding a corner of the final hub area, Dylis snapped his E-rifle up. His cheek pressed against the cool metal of the weapon, his eyeline directly along the aiming sights. The subtle pulsing of the fusion ammunition synchronized with the steady beat of his heart.

Myra and Rant were a few paces behind him. It was his duty to ensure their safety, though Myra was more than capable of protecting herself. Multiple times she'd created a pulsecannon with her nanotech circlets, and she'd expressed enthusiasm for wielding a pulseblade.

But it was Dylis' duty as an Outrider to protect her, so he took point.

As the corridor came to an end, light from the hangar revealed the freighter parked within. The S-53 was smaller than the *Erinyes*, its rigid frame was sharp like that of an arrowhead. A conical cockpit extended at the second deck's bow. It was a double-decker vessel, which allowed for ample cargo space.

Perfect for holding captives, Dylis considered.

Stepping into the hangar, Dylis scanned the bay, his E-rifle warm with pulsing energy. He breathed slowly, his lungs straining against the anxiety clamping around his chest. Dylis had been on countless harrowing missions in the armada, but the thought of hunting a Starblade filled him with apprehension.

Dylis looked for any sign of movement. His eyes flicked up to the sage-colored ship then down to the landing struts. He glanced at the repair bay, the fusion coil racks, the cargo containers... even the droid control tower. A Starblade could pounce from anywhere in this place.

Upon seeing no immediate movement, he beckoned for Myra and Rant to enter the hangar. Myra stepped lightly, her finger hovering over the activation key on her circlet. A shadow moved in his peripherals, but it was just Rant walking along the hangar's curved walls.

Dylis continued to pivot, the humidity of the dockyard clinging to his skin. Moments passed as he scanned, and once he was satisfied that they were alone, he finally spoke.

"Rant, scan the ship," he ordered. "I want to make sure he's not hiding in there."

The droid crawled down the wall and onto the hangar floor as effortlessly as an insect. A high-pitched beeping emanated from him, his domed head jerking from side to side.

"Statement: This unit detects no lifeforms aboard registered S-fifty-three model freighter, ID *Concordia*."

"Alright," Dylis grunted, "Let's see if we can crack this girl open. Rant, I want you to manually override the boarding ramp."

Obeying the command, Rant moved beneath one of the ship's six engines and halted at the sealed boarding ramp. It was common practice for ships to have security systems in place to lockdown or shield their ramps from intruders. The *Erinyes*, for instance, had a shield protecting its open ramp which could only be deactivated by their terminus signatures. S-53s didn't have as advanced of a system as an I-0552 freighter, so their ramps simply retracted into the hull until the pilot unlocked the system.

But without those sequences, it would take a top-of-the-line hacker to break into a freighter's boarding ramp. With Riza missing, Rant was the next best thing.

The droid extended two of his appendages, connecting them to a couple conduits. A few grating *clicks* came from Rant's appendages as they rotated. He had to be careful with a manual override; one wrong move could trigger an alarm.

If only Riza was here to block those damned signals, he thought, his eyes darting around the hangar. *Little Miss Hacker made it seem so easy.*

Seconds passed like minutes as the droid worked. Dylis felt a swell of nervousness creeping into his chest as he continued to pivot. His paranoia was getting the better of him; he felt as if eyes were all around him.

A trickle of sweat inched down his left temple. The back of his head itched. His finger twitched on the rifle's trigger.

A *hiss* erupted behind him, and he spun around.

The ramp was open.

Air escaped his lungs, whooshing out like the steam from the ramp's hydraulics. Myra's violet eyes were focused on him, surveying him with a familiar glint of worry.

"You okay?" she asked gently.

Dylis cracked his neck before answering, "Nope. But I'll power through it."

The Vitrax cocked her head to the side, clearly unconvinced. He ignored her, beckoning for them to enter the ship while they still could. Rant and Myra went up first, and Dylis backed up onto the ramp, ensuring that no one was following them. Yet, even as they entered the first deck of the ship, Dylis couldn't shake the feeling that he was under surveillance.

Even when Rant assured him that no cams were active on the ship, Dylis' paranoia followed him like a shadow. What in all the Void could Milli have been involved with that resulted in a Starblade being sent after her? Dylis had hoped by this point they'd be infiltrating the Wasp Nest, not kicking a proverbial hornet's nest.

The inside of the *Concordia* was a stark contrast to the inner workings of the *Erinyes*. They had easy access to the three box-shaped rooms, each connected by a wide threshold. Dylis kept his eyes peeled for any sign of a holding cell.

"Aelec?" Myra called, her voice echoing through the dull gray rooms. "Riza? You in here?"

Her voice carried for a second longer, then there was silence.

The air had a stale chill—goosebumps crept along Dylis' arm. Pale orange LEDs shone from the ceiling, revealing a few cylindrical supply containers along the wall. He checked them quickly. There wasn't any security on the containers, so he opened them with ease only to discover that they were indeed containing supplies. It was a long shot that Aelec, Riza, or Milli were stowed inside a container, but he was nothing if not thorough.

When it was determined that no one was being stashed inside the cargo areas, Dylis moved further into the ship.

The trio reached the final room on the first deck, which was nothing more than a workshop similar to the cargo bay in the *Erinyes*. Tools were lined in neat rows across the benches, organized based on function. A workbench lamp focused on a device at its center, or at least the skeleton of one.

A webbed outline of an arm bracer was on display. It reminded Dylis of what a terminus might look like when stripped down. But it wasn't. Its frame was smaller, the design sleeker, and there were strange conduits near the wrist.

Myra approached the table and ran a hand over the work-in-progress device.

"Any idea what that might be?" Dylis asked.

She shook her head, humming faintly. "Some sort of bracer, perhaps? The mechanics indicate it's not meant for jewelry, but it's not advanced enough to be a terminus."

"Yeah, I figured that out on my own, Detective Myra," Dylis groaned, glancing over his shoulder.

"Because you're just so smart, Doctor Dylis," she snapped, "don't get your undies in a bunch because you're scared of the big bad shadow assassin."

"Screw you!"

"You wish."

Dylis smirked. Intentional or not, the brief bit of levity helped take the edge off as he continually watched their surroundings. And yet, he couldn't relax. The moment he lowered his guard, that's when the Starblade would strike.

Moments later, they found a ladder leading to the upper deck, and Dylis went up first. He slung his E-rifle over his shoulder, a nanotech gauntlet forming in case someone was above them. Dylis poked his head into the next floor and saw nothing.

He narrowed his eyes. *This is easy. Too easy.*

Keeping his nanotech active, he clambered onto the deck, aiming his E-rifle. Myra and Rant joined him, the trio unconsciously formed a defensive grouping as they moved to the cockpit.

The door was wide open, much to his surprise since most pilots would seal it as a preventative measure in the event that someone broke through the vessel's security. Clearly, Na-jima wasn't concerned about the likelihood of someone stealing his ship.

Approaching the dormant terminals of the *Concordia*, Rant extended two of his appendages while Myra plopped into the pilot's seat. Clicks from the droid's appendages seemed louder, echoing all across the ship. Rant beeped once, and the hologram dashboard flickered to life. Myra's fingers were a blur as she accessed the internal data systems of the *Concordia*.

The Vitrax made an exaggerated swipe with her hand as she went through the ship's logs. The motion was almost theatrical, and whether intended or not, the flick of the wrist reminded him of Riza. A realization dawned upon him, like recalling a forgotten dream.

"That's why you're so pissed at Riza," he blurted, unable to help himself.

"What in the Void are you talking about?"

Dylis nodded towards the terminal, saying, "You both have technical aptitudes. Piloting. Hacking. You see part of yourself in her. That's why when she double-crossed us it spurned you the most."

He paused, considering his words, before asking, "Are you worried that you might be capable of that too?"

Myra froze like a morristeel statue. Her fingers hovered a centimeter over the holographic dashboard, her breathing stilling. Rant's domed head swiveled rapidly, his numerous red eyes looking from her to Dylis and back again.

Myra turned slowly to face him. There wasn't fury in her violet eyes. They were soft, reflecting a hint of worry.

"Do *you* think I'm capable of such?" she asked quietly. "If shit hit the fusion engine, do you think I'd hang you guys out to dry to save my own skin?"

He frowned. "Myra," he said in a gravelly voice, "I've known you for almost two years now. I don't know what kind of gal you were before you met Aelec, but from what I've seen, I think you'd hang yourself out to dry to save us."

"See, I want to believe that," she murmured, her eyes still boring into him. "But I've cut and run before."

"From a shitbag alien-sire," he protested. "You did the galaxy a favor by screwing Dalin over."

She looked away. "It wasn't just him I left that day. There were other Vitrax... my friends... that I abandoned. Kari, Moto, Palak... So many other slaves are still with Dalin while I escaped. How is that fair to them?"

Taking a step towards her, Dylis said, "Life isn't always fair, Myra. Not everything can be fixed. But as long as we try to make repairs along the way, then that should be enough."

The Vitrax gave him a side-eye look. "Trying to use a ship metaphor, are we?"

He shrugged. "Figured that was the closest way to your heart."

Myra sniffed, her pink lips curling into a smile. Her fingers tapped one of the holograms, pulling up a data sheet detailing communications sent to the ship. She read a few lines before swiveling the chair to face Dylis.

"What?" he asked.

"Are the Starblades exclusive to the Imperium?"

"Yeah, why?"

She pointed to the hologram and answered, "Then why was this ship chartered from Caavo?"

Words failed him. His jaw opened and closed, sheer bewilderment clouding his thoughts. Caavo was the central hive of the Comitor crime syndicate. Why would a Starblade come from there? Was this a rogue agent? Or was this part of a greater operation that Dylis couldn't see?

A gasp from Myra suddenly rocked him from his thoughts, and her eyes widened.

"DYLIS, BEHIND YOU!"

He spun around, raising his E-rifle. The air before him shimmered in the light of the LEDs, the distortion having the silhouette of a man. The E-rifle wasn't even eye level when a blistering blade of light formed as if in midair. Energy flashed before him, the blade slicing through the E-rifle's firing mechanism, rendering it useless.

The Starblade slashed again, aiming for Dylis' chest. He used the dead E-rifle to deflect the blade's trajectory, let go of the weapon, and kicked the Starblade where his stomach would be.

The cloaked figure stumbled backward, Dylis strained to keep the silhouette in his line of sight. Summoning his full nanotech suit, Dylis felt the cool metal wash over his skin like running water. A pulsecannon formed in his right hand. He raised it and fired.

Just like before, the Starblade formed an energy gauntlet just in time to repel the kinetic wave. Dylis' HUD popped up, and he tried to cycle through the various vision settings to detect his enemy. None of his armor's sensors could pinpoint the Starblade. His face grew cold.

A shimmer of air streaked towards him like a ghost. The assassin tried to keep Dylis pinned in the crowded cockpit. Na-jima had patiently waited for them to reach the smallest room of the ship, where they couldn't retreat. Dylis couldn't let the Starblade get a hold of Myra or Rant, so he rushed forward.

The glowing energy blade stabbed at him again as Dylis created a small nanoshield, colliding with the assassin. Searing pain erupted from his left hand—the energy already cutting through the nanotech. He gritted his teeth as they tumbled to the floor.

He pinned the Starblade beneath one arm and his free hand wrestled with the energy blade, his muscles burning with exertion. Despite his physical enhancements, blistering heat surged through his hand as the energy licked his flesh.

"MYRA, RUN!" Dylis bellowed.

The Starblade shifted beneath him, deactivated the blade in his right hand, and summoned it to his left. The arm that wasn't pinned. Blistering, white hot pain exploded from Dylis' stomach as the energy punched through his armor and sunk into his flesh. The nanotech dribbled like blood as the blade cut through it, the heat cauterizing the flesh with a sickening sizzle.

Dylis gasped. The Starblade yanked the blade free, and stabbed him between the ribs. Another stab. Then another. And another. After the fifth stab, Dylis shouted in pain as he finally pulled away.

Dizziness clouded his mind, and he stumbled backward. Dylis snarled, his focus returning like a jolt of adrenaline. He was an

Outrider. He still had friends to protect, a clan-mark to cleanse, and a wife to see.

I will not die here!

Dylis lunged forward, adrenaline lacing with his enhancements. A nanoblade formed on his hand. He swung wildly at the Starblade, his body feeling sluggish. Instead of slashing where the assassin's head would be, Dylis fumbled and cut nothing but air.

The Starblade made a curving, upward slash—a streak of azure light arced before Dylis' vision. The energy sliced cleanly through Dylis' arm at the wrist, severing his hand.

Dylis was in too much of a daze to feel the full effect of losing a hand. The wounds in his chest dominated his attention. He barely registered the cloaked assassin sweeping his leg out from under him. The floor rushed up to greet him, and his head smacked against the metal. Blackness veiled his vision for a few heartbeats.

When his vision returned, time moved in slow motion. The pulsating energy blade was poised to stab down into his chest, but a violet wave crashed into the assassin. Hurtled across the cabin, the shimmer flew a few meters before a resounding *thud* echoed when he struck the opposing wall.

Myra stepped into the cabin, her arm extended with a pulsecannon. Steam coiled around it. Dylis was transfixed by the Vitrax's ferocious expression; her eyes were alight fury. Her lips curled into a snarl, flashing her sharp canines.

A cacophony of electric *thuds* echoed across the cabin as Myra fired the pulsecannon again and again. Wave after wave of violet energy surged from the barrel, pinning the Starblade against the wall. Dylis felt an iota of pride as he witnessed the Vitrax unleash her wrath within the *Concordia*'s cabin.

Faint crackles of electricity emanated from the silhouette. The Vitrax shrieked in a mix of a battle cry and a shout of frustration as she fired another kinetic wave.

Dylis' eyes widened as tiny, blue lightning bolts arced over the cloaked assassin, and after another wave hit him, the invisibility faded. The familiar gray hood and black armor greeted his eyes.

Just as Myra was about to fire again, the pulsecannon sputtered while sparks flew from its barrel. She'd used all of its fuses. The fog around his mind was deepening, but Dylis knew that this fight wasn't finished. The Starblade regained his balance, effortlessly shaking off the effects of being hit by a dozen kinetic blasts.

Myra took a frightened step back as she tried to get her pulse-cannon to reform. The assassin hunched down, his knees bending for a pounce.

Using the last ounce of his willpower, Dylis summoned the nanoparticles into a nanoblade. The Starblade dashed forward, his energy blade alighting. Dylis aimed where the assassin would be, exhaled, and ejected the nanoblade.

The silver blade soared across the cabin just as the Starblade closed the distance. The tip punched into his chest, and the velocity of the projectile stopped him dead in his tracks. Flipping backwards, the Starblade crashed into the floor and his energy blade vanished.

The assassin didn't arise.

Lowering his arm, Dylis felt the lethargy creeping into his body. Much of his nanotech suit had peeled away, revealing his face, chest, and arms. His modifications were supposed to help negate such effects, but it seemed the Outrider geneticists didn't anticipate him being stabbed and dismembered by an energy blade. His left arm had grown cold, numb. Dylis felt the impending urge to close his eyes and drift to sleep.

Myra knelt next to him, her hands frantically searching him for his wounds. Muffled sounds came from her mouth. Dylis had to focus just to hear her words.

"Dylis!" she cried. "Stars above, your hand! What's wrong with your nanoparticles? Why aren't they healing you?"

"So... tired," he replied, his eyes drifting to look up at the ceiling. "Hard to focus on... on mind commands."

Something smacked him across the face, giving him a surge of focus. Myra reared her hand back to slap him again, but Dylis raised his arm in protest.

"Got it," he groaned. "Got it. One sec..."

With a fragment of mental clarity, Dylis managed to summon his nanoparticles to his various stab wounds and the stump where his left hand had been. Cool tingles came from his wounds as the nanotech dispensed various healing solvents, and the pain slowly faded to numbness.

Grunting in pain, Dylis said, "You wouldn't happen to see my hand, would you? Might need that."

Myra's posture suddenly went rigid, her lips parted, and she sputtered a breath. The numerous tentacles on her head writhed like panicked snakes, and her head arched backwards, a groan escaping her.

Dylis' jaw dropped. What in the Void was happening to her?

Before he could do anything in response, Myra relaxed, though her breaths were frantic. The Vitrax's eyes were wide in an unnerving expression. Strangely, the whites of her eyes had turned into the same deep purple as her tentacles.

She spoke as soft as a whisper, "Dylis, the Starblade. He's... he's going to detonate! Stars above, we're going to die!"

"What are you talking about?"

The cabin was silent apart from the Vitrax's ragged breathing. Nothing happened for a long moment. Then, out of the corner of his eyes, the Starblade stirred.

"Are you kidding me?!" Dylis seethed.

A *thud* emanated as the assassin smacked his hand to the floor. Luminous, blue light swirled around his body—the same energy that composed his blade. Seeming to solidify, the energy created a luminous armor around his body that pulsed to an unseen beat. The light strobed slowly, at first, then grew in tempo.

Soon, the energy suit flashed like a heartbeat. The hairs on the back of his neck stood up. The Starblade was going to explode, and Myra had perceived it moments before.

And he hadn't heeded her warning.

"Ah crap!"

With his last surge of strength, Dylis rolled onto his side and pulled the nanotech pucks from his chest. Tossing them onto the floor, he willed the nanotech to create a nanoshield. A big one.

A metallic *hiss* emanated from the pucks as the white nanotech formed into a shield that grew in size. Expanding like a web, the shield began filling the entire circumference of the cabin. Just as it was about to separate them from the Starblade, the explosion rocked the vessel.

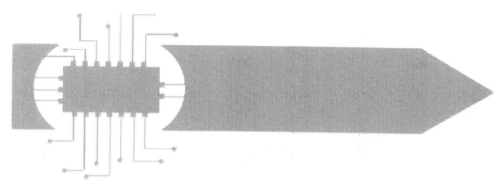

CHAPTER 27

New Skyline: The D.E.F., GST: 19:40

"How certain are you that this will work?" Leonis Ingot asked as he stroked his beard.

Riza blinked, clearing away the stinging that resulted from staring too long at a hologram. With the deft hand of a programmer, she swiped through lines of data, traced symbols, and pressed holokeys.

She stood before the towering, column-like terminal at the center of Leonis' mesh-fiber tent, the system reminiscent of the one inside the Golden Spire vault. Holograms rotated slowly around the central pillar as if orbiting it.

In her peripherals, she saw Leonis sitting on a metal folding chair with one leg crossed over the other. Nyri leaned her hip against a workbench, and Joss stood like a statue behind Leonis.

She took a breath and answered, "Very. I kinda went to the Academy for this sort of thing."

This was her only chance to validate their reason for being here. Riza needed to isolate the various signals of each Syter protester who had been present at the western dockyards on the day that Milli Spectre vanished. If she could confirm their movements, it would provide evidence that the Syters were innocent. It was a long shot, but data didn't lie.

One of the holoscreens passed near Riza, catching her eye. A timestamp on the footage read: *4487.0322, Jan'il Mountains, Nidal.* She cocked an eyebrow. That footage was nearly twenty years old. What could Ingot possibly be looking for during that time?

In the garbled light of the hologram, a team of archeologists were examining a structure similar to the Foundry. One of them put a hand on the glossy metal, waves rippling out like a stone thrown into a pond. At the video's angle, the building resembled a tower or monolith, four sharp pillars extending from its zenith.

The hologram crested around the pillar, moving out of sight, and she knew better than to ask about it. Riza was amazed to see that another building reminiscent of the Domain Expanse Foundry existed elsewhere in the galaxy. If such architecture was present on Oais and Nidal, then what other worlds had them?

A green light blinked on her terminus. Her work was complete. Waving her hand, she sent the data to one of the larger screens.

"Okay," she said confidently. "I've compiled the tracking signatures of every single Syter from three days ago. Even the ones who weren't at the western dockyards. This should be an ironclad alibi."

"It still leaves a possible motive in the air," Aelec grunted from behind her.

She looked back at him. "Motive comes next. Right now, we deal with the logistical proof."

The tapping of bone against stone came from beyond the tent as Golath paced. The Kygi grew anxious being inside the crowded tent, opting to remain outside.

Leonis cleared his throat, his dark eyes reflecting an iota of impatience. Cracking her knuckles, Riza pressed a holokey, allowing the simulation to run its course. Analyzing data and reading the patterns was something she learned in the early semesters at the Academy. Having an eye for detail was crucial.

Minutes passed as she watched the tracking signals of each Syter, which appeared as yellow dots on a schematic of the western dockyards. They were consistently bunched together in the corridor leading to hangar bay L330. Riza hardly blinked; she watched as the yellow blips remained in place during the exact time of blackout. Being thorough, Riza expanded the city's schematic to show all Syter activity.

None were close to Spectre at the time she vanished.

Riza stopped the feed and looked at Leonis, and the older man ran a hand over his cornrows.

Before the Syter leader could respond, Joss spoke up, "That's it? That's your grand way of proving our involvement? Shit, if it were that easy, we'd have done it days ago! The C.B.I. won't buy it."

Leonis shot a hooded glare at him, making Joss lean back. The other escorts similarly shifted uncomfortably as their leader stood from the folding chair. Cupping his chin, Leonis surveyed the hologram footage for a long moment.

"It's the proof we need," he said softly. "A precise tracking of our members at the time of the blackout. The C.B.I. could try to poke holes in it, but these logs give us an alibi the day Milli vanished."

"That still doesn't settle the matter of motive, Ingot," Aelec said, his voice booming through the tent. "This doesn't change the fact that she was still ordered to keep your gang contained, which probably wasn't good for activism. Was it?"

Leonis sighed. "I'll admit, it was a roadblock. But we are not a violent organization. We will defend ourselves, sure. But actively trying to harm government agents when it would hinder our chances of branching off-world? I'd be an idiot to sanction such an act."

Aelec scoffed, crossing his arms. "Sounds like nothing but excuses."

Leonis shot Aelec a gimlet stare and asked, "What is your real issue with us, Xero? I know Milli was your friend, but I think there's more to it than that."

"Yeah, there is," Aelec replied, "I can't stand people like you. Activists. All words and no action from the comfort of your thriving city. None of you would last ten seconds in a real fight. You've never been on the front lines defending your city, or skydropped from orbit, or hunkered in a starship on the verge of destruction."

"Not all of us are war machines, Xero," Leonis growled, meeting the Outrider's gaze. "Some of us would rather save lives, not take them. Build instead of destroy. Secede rather than rebel."

"Secession *is* rebellion," Aelec snapped. "Your disloyalty insults all my fallen brothers and sisters. People who were murdered in the line of duty while you get to sit here and dig in the dirt."

Taking a step forward, he continued, "On Morrigar we have a saying, 'Give someone fuses, and they'll make a ship. Give someone words, and they'll nod their heads.' Words only have so much power in this vast universe. Actions speak louder than words. If you want to see change, then be the change. Shouting about it only makes you look like spoiled children."

Riza swallowed, a shiver creeping down her spine. Seeing Aelec this passionate, this intense, made all other thoughts fade. Her eyes were glued to him, this warrior of mind and body, and she understood him. Aelec had been raised as a man of action, someone whose entire culture was dedicated to bringing peace to the Imperium.

Yet, Riza believed that there was more to bringing prosperity than physical action.

Galactic wellbeing was a delicate balance of technological improvements, social equality, political debate, and militaristic action. It wasn't just one or the other. Leonis wanted to ensure social equality by providing alternate governance for those who wanted it, and rather than resorting to violent rebellion he opted to enact public activism.

Leonis was quiet as he took a few steps towards Aelec, waving for his escorts to remain where they were. The Syter leader wasn't a tall man by any means, and he was nowhere close to having the musculature of the Outrider. He stopped a meter from Aelec, standing tall and with enough confidence to shake the Imperator himself.

"You want to see me put my words into action, Outrider?" Leonis whispered.

Aelec snorted. "You don't have what it takes to challenge an Outrider."

Leonis raised his arm. Aelec's fists clenched, and his footing shifted into the first vestiges of a martial stance. Joss' hand tensed on his E-shotgun. Riza had to intervene.

With a wave of his hand, Leonis pressed two fingers to the nearest hologram terminal, his eyes never leaving Aelec. The holo-screen expanded to show more cam footage, this time coming from inside a temple. *This* temple.

Riza's eyes went wide as Milli Spectre melded into the screen, sitting in a seat opposite Leonis Ingot. The Syter leader was running his hand along one of the strange obelisks, and Riza spotted a time-stamp: *4509.0824.*

"*Thank you for meeting me in person, Agent Spectre,*" Leonis said in the footage. "*I know this has been a hard week for you. If it's any consolation, I've done my best to rein in those ungrateful lowlifes who harassed you.*"

"*It's not,*" Spectre said dryly. "*If you really want to make up for your Parasytes, you'll keep your word and move your operations off-world. I trust that that's still your intention.*"

"*It is,*" he said, inclining his head. "*Nidal has a smaller C.B.I. presence, and the temperateness should help with demonstrating that our cause is both just and peaceful. Ecumens have a nasty habit of jumbling things up.*"

Spectre gave a humorless laugh in response. Leonis scratched at one of his cornrows and continued, "*As long as the C.B.I. doesn't cause any problems, we'll be gone by the end of next week. I trust you have our transport lined up?"*

Spectre nodded, a hologram flaring up on her wrist. *"The O.P.T. Arcadia. Inbound to Oais on forty-five-zero-nine point zero-eight-thirty at local time fourteen-fifty. Outbound manifest is presently off the radar of my agency, courtesy of yours truly. Just be at hangar S-one-one-seven at that time, and there won't be any problems."*

Leonis cupped his chin and asked, *"And I have your guarantee that no C.B.I. agents will be secretly waiting for us?"*

"You've got me here on recordings," she retorted. *"That's enough leverage for me to uphold my end of this deal. See to it that you do the same."*

Standing from his seat, Leonis Ingot approached Milli Spectre and held out a hand. Tentatively, the woman stood and accepted it.

"I'm a man of my word, Agent Spectre."

The image froze as the present Leonis tapped his finger against the holoscreen. Words from the recording reverberated in the tent as all were silent. The tension still hung in the air, but Riza didn't get the sense that it was going to lead to a physical altercation. Aelec's fist unclenched, though he still glared at the shorter man.

"I am not a violent man," Leonis repeated quietly. "I'd do a disservice to myself and my followers by lowering myself to something as brutish as fisticuffs."

"Sometimes you have to actually fight to protect what's yours, Ingot," Aelec grunted. "Luckily for you, this time I won't have to. Seems like we have something in common: reliance on Milli Spectre."

Relief flooded Riza like a cataclysm. Tension faded, the veil of violence lifted, and Aelec met her gaze. His aureate eyes softened as he looked her over, but it was layered—more complex. A hint of uncertainty was in his gaze, as if he was asking her, "did I do the right thing?"

A warm smile spread across her lips. It was stronger than any words she could say to him. He looked to her for support, just as she would look to him for stability. Riza felt the balance of their dynamic swirling with her rising adoration for Aelec. Her heart thundered in her chest, both from excitement and a new sense of longing.

Putting a hand on her hip, Riza said, "Well, now that that's settled, maybe we can work together to figure out who actually ambushed Spectre."

Leonis crossed his arms as he paced in front of the nearest terminal. Joss, Nyri, and the other escorts watched them like morhawks, their eyes barely blinking. The older man hummed as he pondered her suggestion.

After a moment, Leonis said, "I'm not sure what else we can provide on the matter. Apart from the radicals, I don't think Milli earned the ire of anyone else. She steered clear of the Roid Riders, the T.L.M., and the Sons of Levity. Unless there was a faction off-world that she got on the bad side of."

Those words repeated in her mind, and she breathed, "What if Spectre was the target of—"

"An off-world faction," Aelec finished, and their gazes locked like magnets drawn together.

"Do you think…"

"There's no way they could link us to her," Aelec said, his brow furrowing. "She kept the trail clear. All logs and communications were wiped from the holonet."

"Unless she missed one," Riza suggested.

"Or someone tapped in." He turned to regard Leonis once more and asked, "What did the Syter radicals specifically do to Milli on the holonet?"

Leonis scratched his ear before replying, "Most of it was slander via message boards. Some of them sent her threatening videos. Another tried to hack into her home security system to find… undignified footage of her. There was one brief instance where they hacked into her account at the Bureau—"

Aelec snapped his fingers. "That! The one who hacked her work account. What did they do?"

Waving his hand near the holoscreen, Leonis brought up a data screen before answering, "It seems like they dumped some of her message transcripts on the holonet before it was shut down. Those transcripts were only online for a minute or two."

"That's more than enough time for someone to get ahold of them," Riza said, her eyes widening. "What was the date on those transcripts?"

The older man swiped through lines of data and narrated, "Forty-five-zero-nine point zero-eight-thirteen."

Riza's breath caught. *The day of the Golden Spire heist; the day Aelec contacted her to scrub our holonet trail.*

"Shit!" Aelec hissed, running a hand through his long, silvery hair. "Sol above…"

"What are you talking about?" Ingot pressed, crossing his arms. "What happened?"

"No time," Aelec snapped, pointing a finger at Leonis. "You need to give us our weapons. We're heading back to our ship. Now!"

Leonis sputtered, raising his hands defensively. The escorts raised their E-weapons by a fraction. Joss, in particular, was eyeing Aelec like he wanted to shoot him on the spot. The Vitrax brushed some of her short tentacles behind an ear, her expression strangely aloof.

"Alright," Leonis conceded, showing his palms. "Alright. Just give me a—"

An electric *crack* echoed from beyond the tent. All heads snapped in the direction of the sound. Riza's palms grew clammy. Shouting followed, as did the familiar sounds of distant E-weapon discharges. Screams of agony finalized the cacophony of battle.

"What in the Void is going on out there?!" Leonis roared, storming towards the tent's entrance.

Joss held up an arm, barring him from leaving. "Leonis, we need you safe." He turned to one of the escorts and commanded, "Duncan, take these four to check out the disturbance. Then report back. Nyri and I will protect Leonis."

The man saluted and gestured for the others to follow him outside of the tent. Once they were gone, Joss returned his attention to Aelec and Riza, the spite never left his sharp eyes.

Leonis began pacing feverishly; wringing his hands before him.

"Ingot," Aelec demanded, his voice booming. "Give us our weapons, now! We can help repel whatever might be out there."

The older man stopped, heaved a sigh, and said, "Okay, okay. Joss, give them back their things, would you? I won't decline an extra defender, especially an Outrider."

"Leonis," Joss protested. "That's a bad idea. My job is to pro—"

"Your job is to follow my orders," Leonis snapped, moving away from the taller man. "Now, do as I say!"

"Sir, I—"

A crack like thunder split the air within the tent. Riza's ears began ringing, and the familiar bitter smell of a fusion discharge wafted nearby. It took her a long moment to realize what had happened. When she did, her jaw dropped.

Smoke trickled up from Joss' forehead, revealing a sizzling hole in the pale flesh. Riza froze. Aelec raised an arm reflexively in response, trying to shield her. Joss' lifeless body fell face-first into the floor with a sickening *crunch*.

Steam billowed around the length of an E-pistol. The one held by Nyri.

Leonis turned around in a flash, his eyes wide with thunderous outrage. "Nyri. What have you done?!"

Turning her shadowed, indigo eyes to the Syter leader, the Vitrax muttered, "Sorry, Leonis. This isn't personal."

She snapped her arm up, firing an amber blast into Leonis' stomach. Sparks erupted from the impact, and the force of the bolt sent him tumbling over a nearby table.

Riza wanted to scream, but her vocal chords refused to work, her mind struggling to piece together what was happening. Aelec stepped towards Joss' fallen E-shotgun, but Nyri spun the pistol in her fingers and aimed it right at him. Aelec stopped dead in his tracks.

Within the Vitrax's eyes was a cold void, an emptiness that both entranced and terrified Riza. Keeping the E-pistol aimed at Aelec, Nyri gingerly picked up the fallen shotgun. With the practiced hand of a gunslinger, Nyri holstered the pistol and readied the larger weapon. Yet, she didn't shoot.

"Sorry to throw a wrench into your investigation," she declared with a smirk. "But I'm here for you." Nyri inclined her head towards the commotion outside. "They're here for you."

The chill of her words veiled the room like a morning mist. Riza stared down the barrel of the E-shotgun, waiting for the inevitable flash of amber. Aelec gave the Vitrax a hooded look, his knees bending as if preparing to pounce. The Outrider war machine stirred beneath his blazing eyes.

"Don't try it, Xero," Nyri said, patting the E-shotgun. "Outrider or not, I'd prefer to deliver you in one piece. Plus, you don't want Noxia to get hurt, do you?"

"Who in the Void do you think you are?" Aelec demanded, his eyes ablaze with fury.

Nyri gave him a knowing sneer. "The Comitors send their regards."

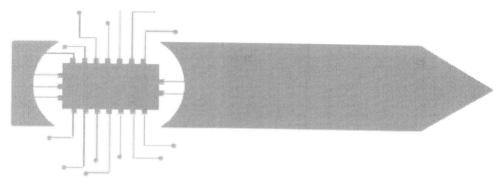

CHAPTER 28

"You work for the Comitors?" Aelec repeated in a half laugh. "You've got to be kidding me."

He couldn't help himself. The frustration, confusion, realization, and amusement all hit him at once. Aelec liked to believe most people in the galaxy had good intentions. But this decision—this oversight on the Vitrax's part—reminded him that there were always assholes no matter where you went.

Standing in the center of Ingot's command tent, Aelec widened his stance, balancing on the balls of his feet. He needed to be ready to lunge at any moment. Unarmed, stripped of his nanotech, and a few strides from the Vitrax, this wasn't an easy trap to escape.

Aelec thought he knew how to read people's intentions, and he felt foolish for underestimating the pink-skinned woman before him. He should've picked up on it rather than fixate on Joss' tough-guy persona. Nyri had expertly used that to her advantage.

"Sorry to disappoint you," Nyri sneered, showing her sharp canines. "Well, actually I'm not. I don't much care what an ex-wardog thinks. You're lucky the syndicate wants you alive. Part of me wants to shoot you and get this over with."

"So why don't you?" Aelec snarled. "Or do you prefer to shoot people in the back?"

The Vitrax chuckled darkly, her short tentacles twitched. She put her back to the wall, raising the E-shotgun to eye-level. Both of those indigo eyes were open, and Aelec saw the echoes of military training. Not from the Imperium, but perhaps a local militia or security force.

He considered his next move carefully. It would be difficult to maneuver in such a tight space, and the only cover was the data terminal. He also had Riza to consider. If he ducked for cover, she'd be exposed and at Nyri's mercy. Aelec would rather face the Comitor's wrath than risk Riza's life.

He could charge Nyri head-on, relying on his enhanced durability to shrug off the fusion damage. Too risky. A solid E-shotgun blast to the heart or face would kill him. No genetic alterations could stop that.

An idea came to him. It wasn't perfect, but it was one that she wouldn't anticipate, nor see. Instead of suppressing the anxiety, he allowed it to release like water bursting from a dam. His breaths quickened, blood drained from his face, and his palms grew sweaty inside his gloves.

Movement in his peripherals drew his gaze, the overturned table stirred. Ingot managed to roll onto his side, a stuttering gasp escaping from the older man. He was still alive, for now.

"Why?" Ingot wheezed. "Why betray us for... for the Comitors? They're slavers!"

"Former slavers, Leonis," Nyri replied. "At least, they will be when I help turn Captain Xero over to them. One Outrider and his C.B.I. friend will grant me full autonomy. And I'll have made an ally of one of the most powerful humans in this universe."

"My C.B.I. friend," Aelec repeated, his face hot with anger. "You're the one who did it. The Syter who leaked her messages."

Nyri sneered. "Ding, ding ding!"

Ingot's dark face lost a bit of color. "We vetted all of the radicals!" he shouted. "You were supposed to be on my side, Nyri!"

"I *was* on your side, Leonis," Nyri said, glancing at him. "Right up until this guy fell into our laps. Outriders bring only death, mutilation, and suffering wherever they go. And here's this one, dumb enough to piss off the Lord Marshall of the Comitors and get a price on his head."

Her grip tensed on the E-shotgun as she finished, "A price I'll get to collect from the Lord Marshall himself."

"How did you know we'd be here on Oais?" Riza asked hoarsely.

"Easy. We baited you here. Once Spectre went missing, we knew it'd only be a matter of time before Xero came to figure out what was up. If I'd had my proper backup in the gravtam tunnels, I would've nabbed your sorry asses then and there."

Nyri let out a dramatic sigh, continuing, "Alas, they're here now. And they're going to cut through any Syter that gets in their way. I can't wait to see the look on the Lord Marshall's face when we bring you to him, Xero."

Aelec scoffed at the absurdity of the situation. A Vitrax voluntarily working with the ultimate scumbag alien-sire in the Fringe. Despite being on a Capital World, the Comitors still owned her loyalty, and she was willing to do anything to obtain her medallion of autonomy. It hinted at desperation.

Gazing upon her, he felt his fury slowly ebbing away as an understanding came over him. It wasn't far off from what he was willing to do for clan-Xero. But Nyri had made an egregious mistake in partnering with the Comitors; they'd just as quickly butcher her as Aelec when this was all over.

Cracking his neck, Aelec took a deep breath and said, "I trust that you know we won't be going easily."

"Make a move and you'll be a fried husk on the floor."

"I'm not going to move." Aelec grinned. "Can't say the same for my friend there."

Nyri's eyes went wide as a familiar clicking emanated from behind her.

Golath surged into the tent at a speed that belied his large frame. The Vitrax spun around and tried to blast Golath, but the Kygi grabbed the E-shotgun and yanked upwards. It discharged with a *crack*, the amber energy impacting a nearby table in a shower of gold sparks.

With another claw, Golath shoved Nyri with a strength that ripped the E-shotgun from her grasp. She tumbled across the floor, her head smacking against the central terminal. Clicking in satisfaction, Golath tossed the weapon to Aelec. He snatched it from the air, cocked it, and aimed it at Nyri. The Vitrax groaned on the floor. One of her tentacles was sliced open, spilling dark green blood.

Adrenaline rushed through Aelec, and he cheered, "Voiddamn! I knew I could count on you, pal!"

Riza gaped. "How... what..."

"Turns out that fear secretes a powerful pheromone that our Kygi friend can easily smell," Aelec explained. "All I had to do was embrace that fear."

She blinked in amazement. "That was really smart," she breathed.

"Thanks," he grunted, winking at her.

Riza returned a smile, then rushed to help Ingot. He pointed her to an emergency autodoc on a workbench across the tent. Riza promptly retrieved the handheld device, using it to stabilize Ingot's gut wound. The bitter scent of antiseptics filled the air.

With a groan, Ingot sat up and put his back to the tent's wall, Riza kept the autodoc pressed firmly against his stomach. Ingot nodded his thanks to Riza, and his gaze slowly darkened as he looked at the Vitrax.

Nyri put a hand to her head; green blood leaked between her fingers. It wasn't a fatal injury, but her dopamine surges would be weaker for some time.

"What did you do with Milli?" Aelec demanded, his grip tensing on the E-shotgun.

Nyri squinted up at him and groaned, "Don't know."

"Did they kill her?"

"No idea," Nyri replied, blinking slowly.

His rage surged forth, and Aelec had to resist the urge to shoot her. Riza stepped up beside him, her eyes alight with azure fire.

Squatting in front of the Vitrax, Riza hissed, "If you don't know where she is, tell us who in the Void does."

Nyri chuckled weakly. "Sorry, sister. You don't scare me. You're a schoolgirl trying to act tough."

Aelec stepped forward and pressed the barrel of the E-shotgun into Nyri's forehead. The motion combined with the warm barrel touching her skin made her wince, her laughter ceasing. Her bravado melted away, fear swirling in her crystalline eyes.

"What about me?" he asked in a low monotone. "Do you think I'm just *acting* tough?"

Nyri swallowed hard. "No. No I—"

"Is Milli Spectre alive?"

An explosion rumbled from further in the D.E.F., drawing his attention. Pandemonium traveled like a whisper on the wind. A feeling of wrongness clamped around his heart, and he knew the assailants were winning against the Far Syters.

"What is happening out there?!" Riza asked, horrified.

Nyri's bluster returned, and she snorted in amusement. "They took her, and now they are coming for you. The Starblades."

Aelec's heart skipped a beat. He felt Riza's gaze upon him, and he could sense her mortification. Color left his face, and true, genuine dread chilled his body. He hadn't felt this way in a long, long time.

"Starblades," he repeated. "The Comitors sent Starblades after us. Impossible. They're supposed to be a ghost story!"

"Oh they're real alright," Nyri murmured, wiping a trickle of blood from her brow.

"Aelec," Riza said, facing him squarely. "What in the Void is a Starblade?"

"A myth in the armada," he growled, trying to accept the reality. "Ghosts from Argentia that perform the Imperator's bidding. Somehow the Comitors have enlisted their services. It doesn't make sense! If the Starblades are real, then they'd be loyal to the Imperium, not the syndicates."

"Unless the Comitors have an ally in the government," Riza noted. "Someone like Veritas Kuvan."

The realization hit him slowly. Rage and fear predominated his thoughts, but Riza's collectiveness pierced through those clouds like the lights of a gravvehicle. Aelec was reminded once more of why it was important to have Riza around. It was because she pieced together something that he should've.

The Comitor syndicate was still in league with Veritas Kuvan, and they'd hired the galaxy's deadliest assassins to hunt him down in retribution for breaking into the Golden Spire.

He should have known that the Comitors' reach didn't end at the Capital Worlds, especially after what he saw on Morrigar. His homeworld had been assailed by a squadron of Comitor droid bombers, massacring his entire clan. He couldn't wrap his head around it; the Imperium was supposed to be untethered from criminal syndicates.

His fear was replaced by a sense of purpose—of protectiveness. It was his duty as an Outrider to defend Riza, Golath, and even the Syters from a threat such as this. Beneath all of that was still the stubborn desire for justice.

The sound of battle grew louder, ringing in his ears like white noise. Nyri was counting on the Starblades to be her backup and eliminate the remaining Far Syters within the Foundry. Aelec's resolve fueled him as he chose his next move.

"Well then," Aelec growled, lowering the E-shotgun. "I suppose I'll have to ask these Starblades where Milli is."

Aelec strode out of the tent, his steps purposeful, vengeful. Golath and Riza followed him. Their worry was like a voice in the back of his mind. Aelec had left Ingot to keep an eye on Nyri, giving him the E-shotgun to ensure her cooperation. He wanted her alive for further questioning after he dealt with the Starblades.

"Aelec, what are you doing?!" Riza protested as she caught up with him.

He didn't answer at first, his stride carrying him around the mesh-fiber tent and towards a cluster of containers near the back.

"I'm going to find Milli," he said simply.

The sounds of violence echoed from outside the shrine and were growing louder. More E-weapons discharged, followed by a strange electrical *hiss* of energy. Stopping next to one of the metal containers, Aelec opened it and retrieved their confiscated equipment.

The nanoparticle clusters clicked into place as he placed them on his arms, chest, and legs. When he was done, Aelec handed Riza her E-pistol and nanotech circlet, then tossed the fusecaster pieces to Golath. The Kygi caught each piece expertly in his four claws, clicking as he assembled the weapon.

A familiar haze crept over his senses as he adorned his equipment; a sensation that plagued him before a dangerous fight. The clan-Elders had referred to it as the warrior's meditation—a state of mind where an Outrider sifted out all distractions to focus on the battle ahead. It was his way of mental preparation, and a method to quell the churning trepidation in his chest.

Aelec was going to have the fight of his life. Starblades were myths even among the Outriders. Based on Dylis' encounter in Medina General, the stories weren't exaggerated about their ability to harness incredible power.

"And if they won't talk?" Riza asked, desperation lacing her voice. "Aelec, stop and think about this! If Imperium assassins are after us, we need to get out of here. We can regroup with the others, flee to Morrigar or somewhere where we'll be safe!"

Aelec sighed as he primed his E-pistol and spun it in his hand. "I won't endanger more of my people, Riza. It's clear that the Comitors' reach doesn't end in the Capital Worlds, especially if they can send Starblades after us. There's no hiding from it. We have to face them."

Riza threw up her hands. "That is a terrible idea! This is so unlike you, Aelec. Where's the brilliant heist planner I met weeks ago? You're smarter than this!"

"I have to do this!" he snapped back. "I've already lost one clan to Kuvan. I won't lose anyone else. Not Milli, not Rant, not Golath, not Myra, not Dylis, and especially not you."

Riza went rigid, a sharp breath drawing past her lips. Her mesmerizing, oceanic eyes locked onto him, shock swirling within.

Aelec instantly regretted his words. He'd *always* had bad timing when it came to relationships. Ida, Myra, and now Riza... The mission came before his feelings, and he cursed himself. Riza was hardly a meter from him, and he soaked in her appearance.

She was so beautiful; her milky skin was tantalizingly smooth contrasted by her silky, black hair. When she shifted, her striped shirt hugged her frame and emphasized her curves. He yearned to be open with Riza, to let her know how much he treasured her comforting persona. Riza Noxia made him want to be a better man.

An image of Milli being tortured by the Comitors overtook his thoughts, and he couldn't abandon her. It was his responsibility as a friend to help her. Even if she was already dead, it was Aelec's duty to confirm and bring the news to Ferris.

His clan-leader, Tolum, once told him that, *There's always another mission, but only so many personal pursuits.*

Aelec summoned his nanotech armor, spreading it across his body from the neck down. The white and blue metal flowed like water beneath his duster. With his eyes still on Riza, he commanded, "I want you to go with Golath and get out of here. I can't risk the Starblades getting their hands on you."

Riza shook her head, scoffing, "Screw that! You don't get to send me away when things start to get dicey. We're a team, Aelec!"

"Riza..."

"I'm staying!" She stamped her foot down and put her hands on her hips. "You need me. You need Golath. We can beat these guys together!"

Aelec met her gaze, and he saw a fiery determination alight within her eyes. He wanted her by his side during this fight, but Aelec would never forgive himself if something happened to Riza.

Stepping close to her, he tenderly gripped her upper arm and said, "Riza, if the stories are true, then the Starblades are nothing like the pistol-jockeys out in the Fringe. It's too dangerous."

"And you can handle it on your own, is that it?" she snapped, her lips trembling. "All this talk of danger, but it's okay if you throw yourself at it? No! You need us!"

She stamped her foot once more, stepping up to him defiantly. Riza would not back down from this, and Aelec admired her even more because of it.

Nodding reluctantly, Aelec said, "Alright. Grab an extra E-pistol and some munitions. You'll need them."

A smile beamed from Riza's radiant face as she headed towards the weapon containers. She put her back to him, her dark ponytail falling to her shoulders. Aelec took a deep breath, turned slowly, and raised his right arm. A chill tingled his hand, emphasized by the guilt slowly building in his gut.

An electric *thud* resounded, and Riza froze. Crystalline electricity sparked around her, and she teetered backwards. The nanotech peeled away from his hand, the low power of the stun blaster fading with a soft whine. Dashing forward, Aelec was quick to catch her, cradling her in his arms.

Riza's eyes were wide, disbelief and rage glaring into him. Golath spun around, hunching defensively. Upon seeing what

Aelec had done, Golath cocked his head to the side. Meeting the nonhuman's gaze, Aelec shook his head and Golath understood the silent command.

He looked down at Riza. Feeling her pressed up against him made him want to carry her off to the ship and leave this mission behind. But the ever-persistent battle raged within him. Duty versus love.

Cradling Riza's head against his chest, Aelec said, "I'm sorry about this. But your captain commands you to get to safety."

Her sweet, earthy scent drew him in. Her full lips parted, and her eyelids drooped. His resolve crumbled, just a bit. Aelec lowered his face to hers, and he kissed her. Lips softer than the finest silk touched his, and a soft moan escaped Riza's slender throat. The kiss lasted mere seconds, but Aelec felt as though a new dawn had arisen. Parting from her was agonizing, his heart yearned for him to remain rooted in that tender embrace.

But as always, duty prevailed.

Riza's eyelids fluttered, unconsciousness taking hold of her. "You," she slurred. "You... son of a..."

"Yeah, I know," he murmured, holding her close. "You can yell at me when I get back."

Riza's eyes were about to close, and she whispered, "Aelec... don't..."

Her head pushed against his pectoral, and she let out a soft sigh. Within his arms, he felt her body go limp as unconsciousness claimed her. Aelec lifted her easily, his enhancements making it seem like she weighed nothing more than a cargocase.

Carrying her over to Golath, he said, "Take her and get back to the ship. I'll draw the Starblades away so that you can get back to the tunnels. Riza's got enough data on her terminus to resolve this investigation, should I get a little held up."

Rapid clicks came from Golath, his head bucking forward.

"Yes, held up would probably mean I'm either dead or

captured," Aelec answered, showing his palms. "But I don't plan on being either of those things. Trust me."

A soft crunching emanated from the Kygi's chitinous plates as he lowered his powerful frame. Almost reluctantly, Aelec put Riza into his waiting claws, and he already missed the warmth of her body pressed to his.

Golath cradled Riza in his upper claws while his lower ones awkwardly held the large fusecaster. Beady, yellow eyes darted from Riza to Aelec, and a song of gentle clicking came from the Kygi. Over the breadth of language, Aelec could feel Golath's acceptance.

Aelec bowed his head and said, "Thank you, my friend. I'll see you when this is all over." He spun around and dashed out of the shrine's main entrance, finally glimpsing the chaos beyond.

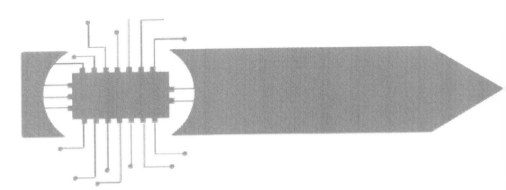

CHAPTER 29

The distinctive heat of raging fires warmed his exposed skin, and the first vestiges of smoke tickled his nostrils. Aelec was no stranger to fiery destruction, and his enhancements allowed him to ignore the fumes as they spread into the Foundry.

Peering through the haze, Aelec saw the farthest structures were ablaze with blistering, blue flames. The inner workings of the D.E.F. were alight and churned out columns of smog as they burned. Black smoke curled all around the Foundry, the frantic *hiss* of air scrubbers meant they were desperately trying to filter it all out.

Aelec felt an iota of nervousness. If the air scrubbers failed, carbon dioxide poisoning would set in quickly, and the inhabitants would suffocate. His own nanotech armor could protect him for an hour, maybe longer, but eventually, he would succumb. *I better make this quick.*

Amber flashes emanated from the pathway before him. Two Syters broke through the veil of smoke, running towards him. One had a hand over his cheap respirator mask, while the other reloaded an E-rifle—the barrel smoking from continual discharges.

Just as he raised his E-pistol defensively, the Syters wheeled around and fired into the blanket of smoke. They pulled the triggers frantically until metallic *clicks* came from the rifles, their ammo empty.

A surge of sapphire light erupted from the veil, its shape reminiscent of an elongated dart. With pinpoint precision, the dart struck one Syter in the chest, right above his heart. Sparks burst from his back, the energy burned right through the combat suit. He collapsed in a heap.

Aelec knew of only one weapon that could perform such a feat: a viperbow.

The second Syter was similarly slain, a gasp escaping him as the dart passed through him. He dropped like a marionette with its strings cut. A shadowy figure appeared from within the veil of smoke.

Summoning a nanoshield, Aelec braced his shoulder against the tall nanotech barrier. His heart pounded in his chest. No more viperbow bolts came from the assassin. Aelec watched closely, his mind sharpening.

Moving like the smoke itself, the shadowy figure moved like a predator stalking its prey. The Starblade inched forward, gray cloak and black armor blending in with the desolation. The hood itself was interwoven into the armor—pieces of mesh-fiber were shredded from past battles. A blank, metallic facemask stared back at him.

Blue fusionfibers pulsed on his left arm, and Aelec noted the crossbow-looking device built into the gauntlet. The viperbow's strings faded as the assassin deactivated the weapon.

Their appearance isn't over exaggerated, Aelec thought, flexing his fingers. *Sol help me.*

The Starblade's black armor was a distinct contrast to an Outrider's white; his regalia was meant to intimidate—to be bold and memorable. This was a warrior you did not trifle with and expect to walk away unscathed.

Pale, blue energy coalesced around the Starblade, forcing Aelec to inhale sharply.

Energy weapons were common, like Kygi plasma whips and Terran fire swords. Yet this weapon stood out like a sun backdropped by a sea of stars.

Twin blades extended from the man's right arm, crackling in the air. Azure mist coalesced over his left hand, forming a gauntlet, then over his shoulder like a pauldron, and finally over his pectoral like a breastplate. This was different from normal invisible energy shields; it only covered specific parts of the Starblade's body, and Aelec knew he had to adjust tactics.

Common energy shields could be disrupted by kinetic blasts from a pulsecannon, or worn down with continual fire from fusion weapons. But Aelec didn't know how his arsenal would fare against a Starblade's energy. He'd need to target the non-shielded parts of the assassin's body.

Aelec aimed the E-pistol directly at the Starblade but didn't fire. He strafed away from the shrine, goading the assassin to follow him. There was only the one assassin stalking him, and Aelec didn't know if there were any more in the vicinity. All he could do was distract the one in front of him.

The assassin gave him a wide berth, like a morcat circling its prey, but followed him.

"Tell me," Aelec called over the crackling flames. "How many of you did it take to capture Milli? Two? Three? Seems a bit sad."

The Starblade went rigid for a moment, and then continued stalking. He remained silent, though Aelec could now see the keen blue eyes staring out from the facemask's slit. Like icy orbs, they pierced into him without any hint of emotion.

"Rumor is that Starblades are supposed to be the best killers in the galaxy," Aelec continued, his finger twitching on the pistol's trigger. "Yet, here you are making a complete mess of the place. I gotta say, an Outrider wouldn't be so haphazard."

Again, the Starblade said nothing, but his steps grew faster, and he hunched slightly as if preparing to pounce.

Aelec gave the assassin a hooded glare. "Tell me where Milli Spectre is, and I'll leave you in one piece," he growled.

Only a few meters separated him from the Starblade, and he was running out of space. Aelec stood his ground, not wanting to get backed into a corner. There were a few meters between him and a Foundry structure to his right, and at least four meters separating him from the shrine on his left. He bent his knees, preparing to move.

"You shall be with Spectre soon enough, Outrider," the Starblade said, his voice deep and grating. Raising his empty hand, he made a fist and shouted, "*Hali!*"

Aelec saw movement in his peripherals; the air shimmered in the shape of a humanoid figure. His eyes widened as he fell right into the Starblades' ambush.

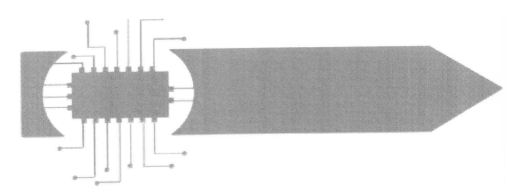

CHAPTER 30

Cradling the slender human female in his lower claws, Golath bounded through the throng of blocky structures. Ancient stone melded into the metal buildings of the Foundry, the violet steel reflecting light from the pulsing illuminations emanating from deeper in the complex. Echoing shouts of pain and violence met his hearing organs, making him click to the emotion of anxiety.

Liberator Aelec had given Golath a mission, and he would not fail.

Over the sweet scent of Hacker Riza, Golath detected the first notes of carbon dioxide that his respirator mask expertly filtered out. Numerous fires churned out black smoke, and it emanated from the Foundry's entrance, meaning he would have to charge through it. His Kygi physiology and respirator would keep him from harm, but Hacker Riza would be at great risk.

Golath clicked to the emotion of fear. He needed to be fast.

He crouched low, made a powerful leap, and soared several meters into the air. Clearing the roof of a short structure, Golath landed on the flat surface and continued running. Keeping Hacker

Riza cradled close to his thorax, Golath leaped again, but didn't clear the roof of the next building. He scrambled, his claws scratching at the ledge before making purchase.

Hoisting them up, he bounded across the elongated rooftop. Firelight shone over the steel structures around him, the growing heat emanating from the Foundry's northern sector—the place he had to go.

To his right and several meters below, was a clearing between the shrine and the machine complex. His eyes caught a familiar figure. Liberator Aelec's hair had an orange glow, like metal reflecting the firelight, and his dust coat waved around his ankles. The human spun his E-pistol between the digits of his right hand.

Golath saw another figure appear from within the smoky thoroughfare. A hooded humanoid wearing sleek, black armor and brandishing twin glowing energy blades stepped forth like a wraith. Liberator Aelec backed away, goading the assassin to follow him. Once the Starblade's back was to Golath, he started moving again.

Straining his legs, the Kygi leaped over the gap between two buildings. He navigated across the taller structures to remain far from the inevitable battle between Liberator Aelec and the Starblade. With the added weight of his fusecaster and Hacker Riza, Golath had to time his jumps precisely.

Sparks flickered from his talons as he skidded across the steel roof. A building nearby collapsed into a blistering inferno. Black smoke plumed, stinging his eyes. The entrance to the Foundry was just a few blocks away; he was almost out. Just a few more leaps and they would be free of the chaos.

Hacker Riza stirred in his lower arms, and his stride faltered. Golath stopped near the lip of the roof and stepped back. The female human's eyes snapped open as she sputtered for breath.

"Golath, what's happening?" she queried in the human Trade language. "Where in the Void is he? I'm going to kill him!"

Clicking to the emotion of awkwardness, Golath shrugged and tried to keep moving. Hacker Riza would not have it, and she squirmed out of his grasp. Flopping to the flat roof, she growled in frustration as she went on all fours. Over the carbon dioxide, he could smell sweat secreting from her skin as she worked the small muscles of her fleshy frame.

"Why would you go along with this?" she hissed, finally looking up at him. "Didn't you swear to protect him?!"

Golath waved his hands, clicking to the emotion of anger. Of course he did not want to abandon Liberator Aelec, but he had sworn to obey the human just as a warrior-priest served the Matriarch. It was not a servitude like the Empyrean-forsaken alien-sires of the Fringe—it was devotion created from his own hearts. Golath obeyed Liberator Aelec because he felt it was the right thing to do.

Hacker Riza groaned, squeezing her eyes shut. "Voiddammit, I hate that I can't fully understand you! C'mon, Golath! You know we can't just leave him! He's our captain!"

She opened her eyes, stood, and grasped one of his forearms. "Golath, he's not thinking straight. You know it! We can't let him throw his life on the line for Spectre! We're his crew, so we need to have his back!"

Golath looked from Hacker Riza to the entrance and back again. He could not disagree with her; Liberator Aelec was who he had chosen to follow in the vast Void. But how would Liberator Aelec react if Golath disobeyed a direct order? Would he break their friendship?

It was in that moment that Golath noticed the similarity of his first encounter with Liberator Aelec. It was like a mirror into their history, but with the roles reversed.

Kyg-nor was firmly under the yoke of the Comitor Syndicate; the Kygi were nothing more than creatures used for entertainment. Golath had been under the gladiator collar for decades, and attempt after attempt to revolt had ended in utter failure. His spirit had been beaten down so substantially that he had entered a defeated trance —staring at the walls and refusing to communicate with the other gladiators.

Even when the Great *Erinyes* had assaulted the coliseum and blasted through the energy field around their quarters, Golath had remained inert. He remembered being unable to click to any emotion; his fiery spirit had shrunk to the tiniest tongue of flame. What was the point of fighting if he was just going to be under the yoke of a new slaver?

Golath remembered that ruined barracks so vividly—the crumbling red stone, the yellow moss that shone with bioluminescence, and the broken racks that had strewn weapons across the sandy floor. One such weapon had been a fusecaster, its multiple chords glowing with green energy.

Kygi carapaces were extremely durable against fusion, plasma, and even projectiles, but a fusecaster bolt was one of the few weapons that could puncture their chitinous plates. The ones covering his thorax were weakest of all. Kygi who chose ritualistic suicide often did so by firing a fusecaster into their hearts—it was the honorable way to end their life.

He remembered kneeling on the sand-covered floor, holding the fusecaster with all four claws. The bolt's conduit was pointed at the fissure between plates, leading directly to his hearts. Golath recalled emitting a tone of clicks, but he could not remember what emotion came forth.

Sadness? Calmness? It didn't matter.

Just as he was about to release the chords, a firm hand gripped the weapon's fusionfibers. Its strength had matched his own, preventing his attempted suicide. Golath's curiosity made him look up from his task, and golden eyes greeted him.

That was how he met Liberator Aelec. Not only was he the one who freed Golath from his shackles, but he freed him from his stupor. He had kept Golath from taking his own life, and for that he would always be grateful.

Now, Liberator Aelec was the one courting death and refusing to leave with his crew. Golath owed it to the human to do what he had done a revolution ago.

If Golath betrayed Liberator Aelec's wishes, it would break their unspoken covenant of friendship. To a Kygi, such a bond was as strong as if they had been born in the same clutch of eggs. This bond would be held by Golath until the Void claimed him, unless the human chose to sever it. Liberator Aelec would be justified in ending their bond if Golath proceeded down this path.

Could he take that risk? The Great *Erinyes* was his home, the crew his family. If he lost them, he would submit himself to the will of the Void.

Golath clicked to the emotion of adoration. Liberator Aelec was his family, and he would not leave him to his fate.

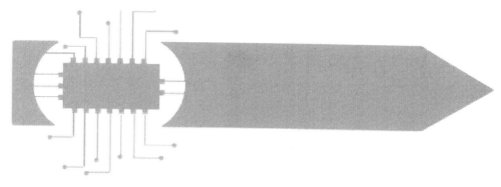

CHAPTER 31

The stealth figure lunged from the rooftop, the air shimmering like a heat wave. Aelec turned his nanoshield into a grappling hook and fired it at the shrine's roof. The hook sank into the stone and instantly pulled him away, the Star-blade mere centimeters from him.

Aelec's helmet molded around his face. He snapped his arm back, and fired the E-pistol at the cloaked assassin. The shots were wild; his aim was thrown off and he couldn't draw a beat as he was dragged through the air.

As he sped towards the shrine's roof, Aelec reached to grab the stone lip. Bright, sapphire light flashed before him. Twin energy blades appeared out of thin air and neatly cut through his nanotech chord.

Aelec barely had a moment to react before crashing into the shrine—his momentum thrown off. His armor took the brunt of the impact, but his vision spun as he fell several meters, smashing into the ground. He landed awkwardly on his side, and the E-pistol flew from his fingers.

Jumping to his feet, Aelec willed the particles in his right hand into a pulsecannon. The second stealth assassin leaped at him again. Warmth touched his palm as the weapon formed, and he fired, intercepting the Starblade. Electricity arced around the figure, the kinetic wave disabling the stealth composites.

The first Starblade rushed forward, and the shimmering form of the third assassin leaped from the shrine. Aelec twisted, forming a nanoshield in one hand while the other transformed into a pulsecannon. His shield intercepted the first, and the pulsecannon fired to disrupt the third. Blasted backwards, the third assassin was revealed. The Starblade flipped and landed in a crouch.

Slicing through the nanoshield like butter, the first Starblade vivisected Aelec's defense and the fragments melted to the ground. When he tried to fire the pulsecannon, the Starblade slashed the barrel off the weapon. Aelec's eyes widened, and he could feel an emptiness in his neural interlace—the shredded nanoparticles were dead.

When the Starblade pulled back for another stab, Aelec stepped to the right. The energy blades missed him by centimeters, and Aelec brought his knee up to the assassin's gut. Summoning a nanoblade, Aelec stabbed at the Starblade's neck, but the angle was too close. A metallic *screech* resounded as the blade glanced off the armor.

The Starblade recovered quickly, making targeted slashes at Aelec's midsection. Aelec used his free hand to block the assassin's arm at the wrist before trying to stab him with the nanoblade. The Starblade smacked Aelec's wrist away, and the process repeated.

Time slowed as he countered; he couldn't let the energy blades touch him. He'd practiced this style of bladeplay with fellow Outriders, and it reminded him of a chess match—each move was precise, calculated. If he was blocked, he'd smack the assassin's hand away and try a different angle. When the Starblade stabbed at him, he had to pivot and swipe the attacking arm away.

It felt like several moments had passed during the exchange, but in reality it had only been a few seconds. Aelec had to move. *Now!*

Pivoting away from another stab, Aelec activated the gravlifts in his boots, soaring a meter off the floor. He blinked, and a few meters separated him from the Starblade. His HUD blared as his fuse levels dropped, and the gravlifts sputtered. He couldn't use them for much longer.

The other two assassins were already dashing after him, firing their viperbows as they ran. Pulsing sapphire darts streaked towards him like beams of light. This time he knew better than to form a nanoshield.

Aelec created another pulsecannon and unleashed a violet wave that intercepted the darts. An electric *crack* echoed throughout the Foundry. White light flashed over his vision, and when it faded, both energy forces had dissipated.

Okay, he thought. *Counter their energy with a pulsecannon. Got it.*

With a Foundry structure nearby, Aelec used his gauntlet to magnetize to the metallic surface. Clinging to the wall, Aelec fired more blasts at the assassins below. The Starblades raised their arms, their energy shields diverted to their gauntlets just as the kinetic waves struck them.

Light erupted, their shields faded, and Aelec released the magnetic field in his hand. Forming twin nanoblades, Aelec let out a snarl as he rained down upon them, intending to skewer the Starblades at their necks.

Clank! Their armor deflected his nanoblades despite the accuracy.

Aelec tumbled once he hit the ground, entangling with the two assassins. They wrestled for control; limbs snapped around wildly followed by the scraping sounds of metal on metal. He headbutted one of the Starblades, making him roll away from the chaos. Aelec tried to stand.

Deep-rooted, scorching pain enveloped his entire bicep, the nanotech armor melting away like molten steel in a forge. Twin, glowing tips punctured through his arm, and Aelec started to lose feeling. He growled viciously, flinging himself off the energy blade. Rolling away from the Starblades, Aelec tried to summon a healing cast over his upper arm, but there was a sluggishness to the nanotech. White metal crept over his exposed arm, the seconds feeling like minutes.

Oh shit! Aelec thought in a panic. *C'mon! C'mon! Don't fail me now!*

He felt the first tingle of healing foams when something struck him from behind. The third Starblade. Scorching pain pierced through his left arm above the elbow. Numbness followed, his arm dangling helplessly. Aelec seethed, baring his teeth.

He still had his right arm. A pulseknife extended from the nanotech gauntlet, and he stabbed into the nearest Starblade. It sank between the crevasses in his greaves, blood leaked from the puncture, and the assassin stumbled backward. Despite the momentary victory, the other Starblade slashed his right arm along the tricep.

Both of his arms were limp, and Aelec's face went cold.

In a last-ditch effort, Aelec twisted around and kicked, but the Starblade expertly stepped to the side. The assassin jabbed the energy blades into Aelec's leg directly behind his kneecap. Shouting in pain, Aelec dropped back to the ground with a *thud*, his nanotech armor a mess of shredded and melted bits. Hot air brushed against part of his face and chest. His body was exposed, the nanoarmor spreading in an attempt to cover his vital regions.

Shadows darkened around him, and he looked up to see the three Starblades. Aelec's eyes drifted to their neck armor. The metal was chipped and cracked. He'd been so close; just one more strike and he'd have killed them.

Aelec felt hollow, empty. It was a sensation he hadn't felt since his first days of Outrider training. Before he had any mastery over nanotech, or pulseblades, or E-weapons... It was the feeling of complete and utter helplessness.

The Starblade closest to him cocked his head to the side and said, "Fairly impressive for an Outrider, but ultimately futile. This is why *we* are the Imperator's Hand, not your kind."

"Imperator's Hand?" Aelec repeated through clenched teeth. "Really? So, what's your specialty with him? A back massage or a reach around?"

An armored boot pressed into the wound on Aelec's upper arm. The numbness faded and was quickly replaced by a blistering pain that was so deep he thought it was in his bone marrow. Aelec's eyes snapped shut in response.

"Insolent degenerate," one of the others hissed. "You are lucky they want you alive. Taking an Outrider apart with a durlux blade is a satisfaction we rarely get to indulge in." The voice was soft, feminine. Aelec didn't realize that one of the Starblades was a woman.

The main Starblade snapped his fingers and ordered, "Bind him. We need to reach the surface."

Squatting next to Aelec, the third Starblade detached part of his gauntlet and affixed it to Aelec's forearm. An electric *hum* came from it, and Aelec felt its vibrations down to his bones. His nanotech armor dissipated entirely—the white metal pooling around him as if in fright from the humming device. Within seconds, he was devoid of nanotech—leaving only his clothes.

A quantum dispenser, he realized, his thoughts awash with horror.

Using all his willpower, Aelec tried to re-summon the nanoparticles, but there was no response. A void separated his mind from the nanotech, and it reinforced his sense of helplessness. Even his physical enhancements were no match for the Starblades.

They were true enforcers of the Imperium.

And they had defeated him.

Still squatting next to him, the same Starblade plucked a few bracelet-like devices from his belt. They snapped around Aelec's neck, wrists, and ankles. Pulsing vibrations came from them, and he knew they were gravcollars. They were extremely rare—usually exclusive to the Imperium armada—and were used on high-value targets.

Beneath Aelec's pain and delirium, he felt a small note of pride.

Just as the Starblade was about to activate the gravcollars, a flash of emerald light blazed around them, and he heard the distinct sound of energy impacting metal. The Starblade lurched forward, pressing a hand against Aelec to steady himself.

The female Starblade jumped to the side as an arrow-shaped bolt soared past. A *hum* of electricity emanated from her as she called forth her energy shield, the azure light dazzled like the crystal shores of Tog. She raised her arm to cover her face as an amber streak smashed into her shield, showering the area with sparks.

Resounding *cracks* of energy erupted from beyond, and Aelec turned his head just slightly to see a welcome sight. Standing atop one of the Foundry structures were Riza and Golath.

The Kygi hunched as his four arms pulled the cords of his fuse-caster, unleashing a salvo of emerald energy upon the Starblades. Riza had her feet planted and arms extended in a perfect firing position as she used her E-pistol like a trained ranger of the Imperium.

Alertness rocked Aelec out of his vulnerable state. He tried to break free of his bindings and join the fight. Numbness weighed down his arms, and his right leg was sluggish. Even without the gravcollars active, Aelec had been systematically broken down so much that it would be days before he recovered.

Aelec cursed himself for not being more far-sighted. Outriders were raised to be weapons of war, but their society reinforced the belief in camaraderie. Success came from working together, and Aelec had foolishly tried to undertake this task alone.

Even the Starblades—the deadliest assassins in the galaxy—worked as a group to disable their target. Aelec had to accept that he was no longer an Outrider first and a captain second. No, he was a *captain* first, and an Outrider second.

It was his duty to work with his crew so that they overcame challenges together.

As the chaos ensued, Aelec couldn't help but grin at Riza even though she was several meters away.

Disobeying a direct order, Aelec thought as he watched Riza fight for him. *We'll make a fine outlaw of you yet, Riza Noxia.*

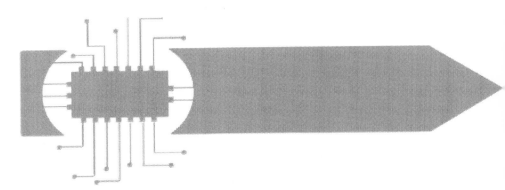

CHAPTER 32

"Golath! You keep up the suppressive fire!" Riza called over the firefight. "I'll get to Aelec and get those binders off him!"

The Kygi clicked in acknowledgement, his yellow eyes focusing on the three hooded figures below them. They stood on a flat roof roughly six meters off the ground, giving them just enough vantage to see where Aelec was and how to place their shots against the Starblades.

They'd arrived moments before, Riza riding on Golath's back as the Kygi scuttled from one structure to the next. Golath's claws pulled at the emerald fusionfibers as if playing a harp, and more arrowhead blasts streaked towards the Starblades. Riza squeezed the trigger of her E-pistol, and then glanced at the drop below. At this height, she'd break her leg if she jumped unaided. An idea came to her.

From her jacket pocket, she pulled out a quantum card and infused her circlet, allowing it to transform into a grappling hook. She'd seen Aelec do it numerous times, so why couldn't she? She tapped her earring, feeling the interlace's link like a soft voice in her head, and commanded it to change. The white metal liquified, molding around her left hand into a bulky device.

She fired the hook into the lip of the roof and leaped off her perch. Her desire to rescue Aelec superseded all caution, and she didn't register the unrefined nature of her grappling hook. The metallic cord whizzed as she dropped, the ground rushing up to meet her. Her heart jolted and the cord ran out, jerking her upward. She winced, her shoulder feeling like it would rip out of the socket. Riza dangled in mid-air for a heartbeat, and then a dazzling dart of sapphire light neatly cut through the nanotech cord. Her stomach lurched as she dropped the remaining distance.

Her boots slammed into the floor, her knees buckled, and a sharp pain shot up her right ankle. Breath was forced from her lungs as she collapsed, her head luckily did not strike the ground. When she tried to stand, the pain erupted from her ankle yet again.

"Shit!" she cried, her eyes watering from the pain. "No, no, no!"

Glancing up, she saw one of the Starblades dashing towards her. His hood fluttered, and energy shined over his left side like a glowing chrysalis. She blinked, and he was just a few steps from her. Twin blades of light extended from his right hand, and he wound his arm back.

Riza let the pain, fear, and anger rush past her lips, screaming as she unloaded several fusion blasts at him. But trying to hit a moving target was like trying to code an algorithm with your eyes closed. Amber streaks exploded into sparks as they struck the ground, silhouetting the hooded assassin.

Riza screamed, "Golath! Help!"

The Starblade's shadow loomed over her. Riza's face went numb, her mouth hanging agape as she watched the energy blades inching toward her. The Void was coming to claim her, and she could do nothing to stop it.

Brown carapace blocked her vision, followed by a prolonged *hiss*. Steam billowed and sparks drizzled. Riza blinked, and Golath was suddenly in front of her. Loud, guttural clicks came from the

Kygi as he shoved the Starblade away, his claws a blur as they fired the fusecaster.

The assassin backed away, but the emerald bolts struck his unshielded side and eviscerated the black armor. A gasp escaped the Starblade as his arm fell away in pieces. A line of green was drawn across his waist, and his torso slid away from his lower half.

As the Starblade fell, the other two fired their wrist-mounted viperbows. Dozens of energy darts struck Golath's carapace, blackening the russet color. Low clicks resounded from the Kygi as he raised his arms, trying to shield himself, but his carapace could only protect him so much.

The barrage stopped him in his tracks, and after repeated abuse, Golath shied away. She had to help him. Rising to one knee, Riza frantically pulled the E-pistol's trigger, the shots streaking between Golath's powerful legs.

Electrical *pings* came from the Starblade's armored shins as the bolts made contact. Taken aback, the assassins staggered backward, the black armor on their shins chipping away. Riza stood despite the screaming pain in her ankle. Putting all her weight on her left leg, she teetered slightly. Golath was at her side in an instant. The nonhuman used one of his arms to help steady her while the others readied his fusecaster.

Riza glared at the assassins and called, "Step away from him! We are citizens of the Imperium. You have no right to harm us!"

One of the Starblades, a male, cocked his head to the side, amusement wafting from his cold eyes.

"You have trifled with powers far beyond your station, Riza Noxia," he said, his voice clear and resounding. "Reach too close to the star, and you will burn. The order of this universe is not meant to be tampered with, especially by the likes of you."

"You mean trying to bring a scumbag politician to justice?" she snapped back. "If a plague spreads through a city, is it not the job of citizens to eradicate it?"

The Starblade shook his head, saying, "Fighting the will of the galaxy is a futile effort."

The Starblades acted in unison, firing their viperbows. Riza tensed and Golath moved to protect her, but none of the darts struck the Kygi. They were soaring past them.

It took her a second to understand what was happening, and she felt an alarming chill run up her spine. Riza gasped and spun around, the projectiles were eviscerating the Foundry structure behind them. Portions of metal crumbled from the onslaught, and after a few more glowing darts sliced through, the structure collapsed.

And they were directly below the falling debris.

"GOLATH!" she shrieked. Her legs refused to work, her body rigid with terror.

The shadow of the falling debris eclipsed her, and all she could do was stare up at it. Riza then felt a pair of claws scoop her under the arms. Golath tried to pull her away, but the floor shook, knocking him off balance and they both tumbled to the ground. Chunks of metal crashed around them, and the Kygi scrambled to protect her with his body. The thud of metal against carapace filled her ears, followed by a series of soft Kygi clicks. Riza cried out in terror.

Dust billowed out, stinging her eyes and making her wheeze. Light faded as more debris piled atop the Kygi, burying them in the remains of the Foundry structure. The last thing Riza saw was Golath's yellow eyes closing tightly before the darkness enveloped them.

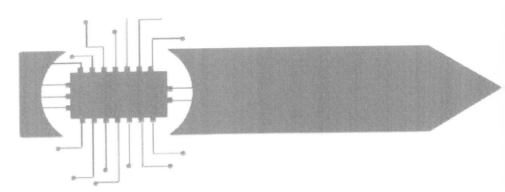

CHAPTER 33

"RIZA!" Aelec bellowed, his haziness clearing as he witnessed the structure collapsing. "GOLATH! NO!"

They were directly beneath the falling debris; Golath wasn't fast enough to get them out of the impact zone. The Kygi fell atop Riza as chunks of pale, violet metal crashed around him. Aelec wanted to leap into action, to summon his nanoparticles and pull them out. No matter how much he struggled, his body wouldn't move.

Aelec was trapped and helpless to save his friends.

A cloud of dust expanded outward in a ring as the structure crumbled, the metal and stone grinding together in an ear-grating cacophony. When the dust cleared, Riza and Golath were nowhere to be found. His heart pounded for several beats, but nothing arose from the wreckage. They were gone.

Staring at the pile of rubble, Aelec felt an unbearable weight on his chest as if buried beneath it. Time slowed, and he was reminded of when his clan had been massacred. Disbelief escaped from him like oil leaking through a crack. It was happening all over again.

Everyone he was close to perished while he survived. He always survived.

Was the Sol punishing him for being born an Outrider? For being born a weapon for the Imperium? The Sol was the god of justice, so was this its way of balancing the universe?

The Starblades hoisted him to his feet, his mind fuzzy with fatigue. One activated the gravcuffs, and his limbs locked into place, his body hovering in midair. The female Starblade grasped his arm and pulled him effortlessly like some twisted, dangling puppet. They led him through the ruins of the Foundry—through the smoke and flames engulfing the underground facility.

A hollowness ate away at his stomach, and he felt sick. A chill ran through his body, and exhaustion tugged at his eyes. The physical and emotional pain created a tempest of agony that kept his body alert and sluggish at the same time. Part of him wanted to shout, and another part wanted him to sleep, to drown out the world around him.

The event replayed in his mind in vivid detail, metal chunks piling atop Golath and Riza as they huddled together. He should've saved them, protected them. Was that not his duty as a captain? They'd disobeyed his orders, returning to save him rather than flee. But they'd done so because of his decisions—his foolishness. He'd been so fixated on rescuing Milli that he'd left his own crew exposed to danger.

Something broke within him. The pain of loss was familiar, but seeing how unceremoniously Golath and Riza perished because of his failures drove him to a new level of shame. He'd been selfish, arrogant, overconfident, and reckless in this pursuit of justice, and it had cost him his friends.

It cost him a loyal and devoted Kygi. It cost him the woman he cared so deeply for.

In that moment, Aelec understood the concept of a tainted clanmark. He'd berated Dylis for years about it, never fully understanding how it weighed on an Outrider's psyche. Now, he felt the true ramifications of bringing shame to his Outrider honor. Failure to protect his crew had tarnished his clan-mark.

It was a subtle thing ever present within his mind, like the vestiges of a nightmare that stuck with you for days on end. Only this nightmare wouldn't fade. No, Aelec would feel this pain for the rest of his life.

Through the haze of fatigue, he was guided through the remains of the Foundry. The bodies of the Far Syter guards were sprawled across the floor, some already subsumed by crackling blue flames. The stench of roasting flesh mixed with the noxious smoke. The Starblades passed by it all as casually as if they were walking through a public marketplace.

He was so tired. It took all his effort to keep his eyes open. Closing them for a moment wouldn't hurt.

Blinking, the scene changed from the Foundry to the corridors leading back up to the gravtram tunnels. He blinked again, and they were walking beneath the gravtram rail in the sprawling tunnels. Aelec could barely focus on anything before closing his eyes and waking in a new location. Exhaustion enveloped him like a blanket as he watched the dim lights pass overhead.

When Aelec closed his eyes for the third time, he felt himself drifting, and he could fight it no longer.

Aelec's eyes snapped open, his lungs sucking in air as if he'd been deprived for hours. A blurry haze of black and blue blanketed his gaze, his eyes trying to readjust. He sniffed, the familiar scent of recycled oxygen tickling his nostrils. Cool, crisp air touched his exposed skin.

A ship, he concluded. *I'm on a ship. But whose?*

As his vision focused, the answer came to him, as did the sensation of hopeless dread.

He was held upright in a dimly lit cabin, a few cerulean LEDs traced along the ceiling. Aelec's back pressed into the metal wall, a set of clamps keeping him pinned. Cold steel dug into the bare skin of his chest, arms, and ankles. He tried moving, but he could only turn his head in this barbaric prison. Soft vibrations came from the clamps, indicating that they had gravcuff reinforcement. More man-sized clamps lined the walls around him; they were all open, save one.

Aelec's heart skipped a beat as his eyes fixated on a shadowed figure bound to the wall. It took his eyes a second to adjust in the dim lighting. Shadows slowly revealed a slender frame, the curvature confirming it was a woman. Her pale skin was tinted navy blue from the LEDs, her black hair melded perfectly with the shadows hanging around her face.

His eyes traced along her right arm. An intricate tattoo flowed from her elbow down to her wrist. Lines and geometric shapes made up the artwork, but at the center was the planetary symbol for Oais.

Aelec had seen that tattoo before.

"Milli," he breathed hoarsely.

She didn't respond. Listening closely, he heard ragged breaths pass through her lips slowly, lethargically. Milli was still alive. Yet, her breaths were labored, sporadic. Aelec tried shifting his shoulders but was unable to find any leverage to escape. He hated being like this—being trapped with no means of helping her. It was like a lake being just out of reach for a man dying of thirst.

He growled, thrashing once more. Where in the Void was he, anyways?

Answering his question, the cabin door slid open with a *hiss*, and pallid light spilled into the room. Aelec squinted. Two shadows moved in his limited vision, and the door sealed shut behind them. The stench of acidic cologne assailed Aelec's nostrils, and he coughed.

Opening his eyes, he saw a man standing like a statue before him, his arms clasped behind his back. The man was exceptionally tall, the top of his head eclipsing Aelec's despite being held up a few centimeters off the ground. He wasn't even wearing platform shoes, just simple brown loafers that contrasted his cream-colored pants. The man straightened his gray, knee-length suit jacket before pulling on the collar of his black turtleneck.

He was an older man; wrinkles webbed out from his eyes and the receding hairline framed his narrow face. His hair was bound in a ponytail. The cabin's lighting made it appear light blue. No... His features became more familiar, and Aelec knew that the man's hair was *dyed* blue.

Anger threatened to burst forth like a broken dam. Everything that had been bottled up for the past two years yearned to be released. Before him was the man who'd set him on this path. The man who he so desperately wanted to bring to justice.

Veritas Zerick Kuvan stood hardly a meter from him. Keen, green eyes stared at Aelec, and a wide smile spread across the man's face.

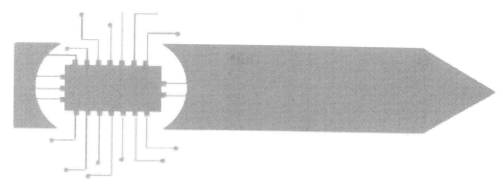

CHAPTER 34

When Riza woke, her vision was blanketed by a veil of blackness. Not a single ounce of light seeped through. It was as if a black hole had swallowed her, and she was now adrift in the nether world of space. The suffocating pressure made her feel like she'd been buried alive.

Wait... She *had* been buried alive!

She remembered the flashing darts of the viperbows eviscerating the Foundry structure behind her and Golath. The vivid detail of crumbling debris entered her mind, and she recalled Golath rushing in to protect her. Chunks of metal piled around them until something hit her in the back of the head.

They'd failed to rescue Aelec; the Starblades had made short work of their crew. If only she'd been with him at the start of the fight. She wanted to hate Aelec for facing them alone, but he only did it to protect them. Now Aelec was captured and Sol knew where they'd taken him. Riza felt a tear leak from the corner of her eye, her breaths shallow and rapid.

She was trapped, and Aelec couldn't save her. His marble face predominated her thoughts; his rough lips against hers. Sol above, he'd actually kissed her. That normally would've excited her, but that thrill was subsumed by anxiety.

Riza wheezed; the air was hot and stuffy, it felt like she wasn't getting enough oxygen. She tried to move, but the pressure increased, and she hyperventilated. This wasn't how she wanted to die!

Her thoughts scrambled for a solution, and she tried to command the nanoparticles but got no response. The interlace was still clipped to her ear, but its voice was faint in the back of her mind. She tried again, but it was like shouting in a void. She felt light-headed, the creeping coldness of unconsciousness threatening to claim her once more. A single thought entered the muddled ruins of her mind.

Focus.

Aelec's voice resonated as though he were speaking in an empty cavern. Riza slowed her breathing, even though it made her lungs feel like they were on fire. Riza focused on the singular thought of wanting the nanoparticles to shift, and the cold metal of the broken grappling hook melted. Breathing deeply, she thought of a command and the nanoparticles gradually formed into a small pulsecannon. While she couldn't move her arm, she could feel that it was outstretched and aiming at a section of debris. A warm thrum came from the weapon as it reached a full charge, and Riza prayed to the Sol that someone would find her.

An electric *boom* emanated from her hand, the kinetic wave bursting forth and blasting through the pile of fragments. She was still trapped, but the pulsecannon had made a sizable hole, allowing light to pour in. Light and smoke. Riza felt a chill, the smog easily flowed into the pile and touched her face. Riza wheezed, and her eyes watered. Her lungs screamed.

Sol above, she prayed, *please not like this! Please!*

Something shifted in the debris. She tried to incline her head, but her body was still stuck beneath a massive metal chunk. No, the wreckage above her was moving. A familiar clicking emanated from above like the suspenseful percussion of a drum.

Golath! She'd forgotten that Golath had shielded her! She wasn't buried under slabs of metal; she was beneath the Kygi. Firing the pulsecannon had loosened some of the slabs around them, allowing Golath to obtain leverage and lift more rubble off them. Using his chitinous back and all four of his arms, Golath pushed, shifting the refuse and relieving the pressure on Riza. She no longer felt crushed, but her lungs still burned from the smoke.

Riza managed to roll to the side and wheezed, "Go... Golath. We've gotta..."

The Kygi clicked gutturally, sounding more like a growl. Metal scraped against stone as dust swirled around them. Golath heaved, but there was still too much refuse around them to escape. His yellow eyes were wide with panic. A shadow eclipsed the light pouring from the blasted hole.

Several figures appeared outside the hole, and muffled shouts emanated from all around. Hands pawed at the slabs of metal, lifting the debris off Golath. Riza squinted her eyes against the smoke, but she managed to pick out some of the Far Syters rushing in to help them. Leonis Ingot was one such rescuer.

Heaving another slab away, Leonis held out his hand for Riza to take and she didn't hesitate. The older man pulled her from beneath Golath, but she stumbled from the pain in her ankle. Leonis steadied her while the others helped Golath. Riza's chest convulsed as she inhaled more smoke, and she felt bile rising in her throat. He pressed a respirator mask to her face, and she took a deep breath, her lungs rejoicing at the crispness of fresh air.

"C'mon!" Leonis shouted. "We need to reach the surface! The Foundry is about to collapse!"

Riza hesitated, her head snapping around to see Golath stumbling from the wreckage and the Syters steadying the massive nonhuman. Relief warmed her heart. She put her weight on Leonis, and he led her into the main thoroughfare towards the exit. Fires blistered within the glossy walls of the Foundry, the ancient metal reflecting the flames like a lens flare.

It felt like an eternity navigating the paths of the Foundry, but they finally found the exit. Passing through the expansive door, they sealed it behind them and followed the narrow corridors that lead back to the gravtram tunnels. At the preordained spot, they used the phase-shifters to open a doorway of energy, and reached the safety of the tunnels.

Riza sat with her back to the slanted wall of the tunnel, a mesh-fiber blanket draped around her shoulders, as she breathed through the respirator. She reached up and traced a finger down the crusted blood running from her hairline to chin, and she blinked away tears, her eyes still stinging.

After arriving in the gravtram tunnels, Leonis had placed a nanotech brace on Riza's ankle, which made it easier to walk. Golath leaned against the wall beside her, resting a claw gently on her shoulder. Three dozen Syters crowded around them. Their faces were soot-stained, and a chorus of coughs echoed in the dim tunnel. Leonis squatted next to a young man, using another crustacean-like autodoc to mend some burns along the man's arm. The bitter scent of antibacterial sprays and healing gels wafted from the device.

Riza was silent as the group recuperated. She just kept breathing into the respirator. Seeking to comfort Golath, she reached out to grab one of his claws and squeezed gently, the carapace rough against her palm. Golath eyed her curiously.

"Thank you," she wheezed through the apparatus, her voice metallic. "For saving me. I understand now why you're so dedicated to Aelec. If I can, I'll repay the favor one day, Golath. I've got your back."

She paused, looking away from him before saying, "I'm sorry I couldn't save him."

The Kygi's grip on her hand tightened. Clicks came from his respirator. They were slow and melodic, like a humming lullaby. Guilt tugged at her stomach. She could feel it working up into her throat like bile. Realizations kept hitting her as she replayed the events in the Foundry. Aelec had chosen to sacrifice himself to protect her, and she hated him for taking that choice away. Yet, she adored his selflessness; she'd felt safe in his arms.

Aelec was an inspiration, something that she aspired to be like. Riza wanted to be efficient with nanotech and capable as a fighter. But the battle with the Starblades was a harsh reminder that she wasn't meant to be a gunslinger like Aelec. She had to find her own path—one of strategy and cunning.

Rushing in headlong with nothing but an E-pistol resulted in exactly what she should have expected. Riza hadn't been raised from birth to kill or harness nanotechnology, so of course she'd failed. Films on the holonet always depicted heroines relying on luck in an epic fight, but any luck Riza had was used to keep her from being crushed by debris.

Luck didn't infer combat skill. She berated herself for not thinking clearly; Riza had been too eager to prove her worth in a fight. The result was laid before her.

An approaching figure snapped her out of her musings. Leonis brushed a few clouds of ash from his cornrows as he stepped up to them. "Do you need another autodoc spray?" he asked, proffering the crab-like device. "There's a few more charges left in this one."

Riza shook her head. "I'm alright. Might need to see a full autodoc after this to check my lungs, though."

"We all do," Leonis agreed, offering the device to Golath. When the Kygi declined, he continued, "You need to get back to your ship. You shouldn't be seen with us now that we're exposed."

She nodded, understanding that the Syters were still public enemy number one and no longer privy to a hidden refuge. Without

Spectre's help to get them off-world, Leonis and his followers had a tough road ahead. But Riza was reminded of the deal Nyri struck with the Comitors. The Vitrax was leaning against the opposite wall with her hands cuffed. A few guards stood watch, though their haggard appearances didn't inspire much confidence.

Leonis saw where her attention was and frowned at Nyri.

"What are you going to do with her?" Riza queried, standing slowly.

"I don't know," Leonis sighed, rubbing his gnarled beard. "Part of me wants to turn her over to the C.B.I. Maybe in exchange for her I can get a pardon for my followers. Nyri got the better of me. She forged her identity, thus allowing a Comitor agent to infiltrate my ranks and aid in Agent Spectre's abduction. Keeping my guild within the law was what I set out to do, but it wasn't enough. Nyri committed these acts under my watch, so I'll need to face the consequences."

Riza stepped toward Leonis and gripped his upper arm. "You can't!" she protested. "Veritas Kuvan is in league with the Comitors, and who knows how far his reach extends. If they find out Nyri failed to kill you and you turn yourself in, the law might not be there to greet you."

Leonis remained silent, his eyes fixated on Nyri. His jaw clenched as he worked through the implications. "You may have a point," he murmured. "If a Veritas is corrupt, then I won't make it to trial. Neither will she."

He ran a hand over the autodoc attached to his stomach, then said, "I'll keep her under heavy watch for now. Perhaps we can get her to talk."

Riza took a deep breath from the respirator, and murmured, "Good luck, and thank you for your help." She handed him the respirator. "We're heading back to the surface."

Leonis nodded, and the pair broke away from the throng of Syters to head back to the southwest. She and Golath moved quickly, though the brace on her leg prevented her from all-out running. They'd lost enough time already. If Aelec had been taken off-world, she had to find their ship's trajectory quickly.

She tapped her terminus, and the hologram appeared garbled, static buzzing within the neon light. The device was cracked, and she swore under her breath. Riza tried swiping through the screens, but the device barely responded. She couldn't access her tracking application.

Another idea sparked in her mind. Swiping furiously through the distorted holograms, she pulled up her commlink and managed to send out a call to Dylis' terminus. Prior to their excursion into the tunnels, Dylis was tracking down the black market mithium dealer, but he kept a tab on Aelec's locator beacon. Chimes emitted from her terminus, but no answer came. She tried again, but the same result caused a knell of panic to arise within her.

Something felt off. Since they hadn't communicated with him for a few hours, wouldn't he and Myra have come into the tunnels after them? Riza gulped. What if something happened to them, too?

No, she thought, her heart sinking with dread. *No, no, no! I can't lose them and Aelec!*

She swiped away the garbled holograms, and focused her attention on reaching the dockyards. One of the first lessons she'd learned at the Academy was to solve one problem at a time. Challenges in life were just like a programming algorithm. Getting back to the dockyards was the first step, then she could worry about finding her crewmates.

Golath followed her without protest, and he even helped guide her to the correct passageway based on their scent trail. Her heart pounded in her chest, amplified by the burning sensation in her lungs. She'd need to spend a few hours in the ship's autodoc to fully heal from the smoke inhalation.

Once back at the ventilation shaft, Riza used the last bit of her fuses to mold her nanotech circlet into a pair of magnetic gloves. Climbing up the shaft was difficult, especially with the brace on her ankle, but the pair soon found themselves clambering into the empty bay of hangar L334.

Reaching the closest central hub, Riza and Golath were following the dockyard corridors when something drew her eye. A few sections down was a churning crowd of people, an ethereal echo of voices resounding in the hallway. Many wore dark suits, and countless flares of hologram lights forced her to squint. They were news pundits. A few surveillance drones hovered above the crowd, their red and blue markings indicating that they were from the police.

Riza drew in a sharp breath. Something had happened in hangar L336, and a sinking feeling kept her rooted to the spot. This along with no sign of Dylis and the others... It was too much of a coincidence.

She and Golath moved behind one of the abandoned cargo containers, the dim LEDs helping conceal them from prying eyes. Leaning her head out, she surveyed the crowd of reporters, their voices growing clearer.

"...Vitrax and her companion are nowhere to be found."

"Local cameras showed them entering the vessel moments before it exploded."

At that moment, Riza felt a piece of her heart chip away. Her back pressed against the container, shoulders slumping as she fought off a surge of exhaustion. Riza couldn't move, uncertainty clouding all rational thought. What was she supposed to do if Aelec, Myra, Dylis, and Rant were gone? She couldn't fly the *Erinyes* on her own, and neither could Golath. How could she hope to bring down Kuvan without the help of the crew?

Tears brimmed her eyes, both from the tempest of emotions and the physical stinging. She put a hand to her forehead; the sensation of hopelessness overwhelming her. There was nothing she could do.

Rapid clicks came from Golath, and he tapped her on the shoulder. She followed his attention, and saw that someone was coming down the corridor opposite the crowd. In the dim lighting, all Riza could see was a feminine figure walking at a brisk pace. The shadows melted away, revealing the familiar glimmer of purple, prehensile tentacles. Her eyes widened, and Myra stepped into the light.

"Riza!" the Vitrax cried out.

Before Riza could react, Myra dashed down the corridor and threw her arms around her shoulders. Myra squeezed her in a tight embrace. Riza was stunned by the display of affection. Pure elation replaced the shock of it, and Riza found herself hugging Myra back as more tears leaked from her eyes.

Pulling herself away, Riza caught a good look at Myra as they stood with their hands on each other's shoulders. A similar veil of grime covered her pink skin, and a trickle of dried, green blood ran down her cheek from a cut beneath her left eye. Myra's leather jacket was singed in various spots and flecked with gray smears.

Spotting Golath, Myra let go of Riza and embraced the Kygi. He used two of his arms to mimic the gesture while the other two patted Myra's shoulders. When she broke away from Golath, Myra joined them behind the cargo container and looked them up and down.

"Stars above," Myra breathed, "what happened to you?! Where's Aelec?"

Riza pressed her fist into her palm, replying, "I'll tell you the whole story later. But Aelec's been captured by the Starblades. Can you track his beacon?"

Flicking her wrist, Myra pulled up a hologram and swiped through a few screens. A moment later it flashed red, and the Vitrax's brow furrowed.

"His signal's out!" she declared. "They likely stripped him of his suit and terminus."

"We need a bigger scanner then!" Riza said, another idea forming. "I need the *Erinyes'* terminal. Let's go!"

The trio broke into a run as they headed away from the crowd in the direction of the *Erinyes'* bay. After a few strides, Myra asked, "So, what in the Void happened?"

"We found the Far Syters in a Foundry beneath the gravtram tunnels, but there was a Comitor agent among them. She betrayed the Syters and summoned the Starblades to clean house. We barely escaped the Foundry in one piece."

"I can't believe this is happening. Both of them are down!"

"Both of them?" Riza's breath caught as the realization hit her. "Where's Dylis?! Is he alright?"

"He's alive," she answered, "but he's not in good condition, Riza. One of the Starblades got to us, too. We almost got their ship's comm data but the Voiddamned assassin suicide bombed us before we could download it."

"The explosion," Riza affirmed. "How did you manage to escape?"

Myra grimaced, her stride faltering. When she recovered, she replied, "Some quick reflexes on Dylis' part. And... err... some precognitive warnings on my end."

Riza's jaw dropped. It was said that older Vitrax had the ability to see future events, but that skill was incredibly rare and only developed in the latter half of their lives. Myra, at only twenty-seven years old, had had her first premonition?

"That's..." Riza stammered, "That's..."

"It's not important right now," Myra said, shaking her head. "What matters is that you and Golath are alive. Dylis is stable, for now, and Rant's keeping an eye on him. The ship's just a few bays down. Hurry!"

Riza felt a weight lift from her shoulders. Not only was Myra alive, but it appeared that a rekindled friendship was on the horizon. It was a small comfort in the chaos that had upended their mission to Oais, and Riza wasn't going to let it slip away.

The shadow of Aelec's capture loomed over the bright spot of their renewed friendship, and time was not on their side. So she ran. As fast as she could.

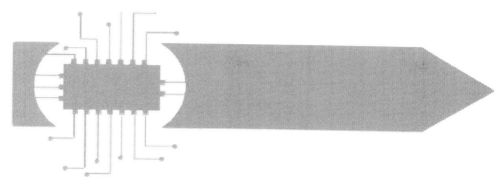

CHAPTER 35

4509.0831 / CW Star System: Picon / 9,537,362.4 kilometers from the planet Oais / GST: 06:55

"Aelec Xero," Kuvan said in a deep, sonorous voice. "Still hanging in there, I see."

Aelec blinked slowly, unfazed by the poor attempt at humor. "Kuvan," he growled, "what have you done to Agent Spectre?"

Kuvan glanced at the unconscious woman and said, "Relax, she just had a bit of a rough tussle with some Starblades. It's not wise to fight against enforcers of the Imperium. Though I guess she's technically also an enforcer for us. Ah, it gets so complicated with sides and factions these days."

"What's the meaning of this?" Aelec demanded. "Why attack Milli? Why go after me?"

Kuvan arched a manicured eyebrow. "You tell me. From what I've heard, you've been a very busy man these last two years. The captain of the *Erinyes*, eh? Never pegged you to be in the smuggling business."

Aelec remained stone-faced, refusing to give any kind of reaction to Kuvan's words. While it wasn't a formal interrogation, Aelec assumed that Kuvan was trying to unearth more details about his exploits. Rage and vengeance surged within him, but Aelec pressed them down. He wouldn't give Kuvan the satisfaction of seeing his outrage.

"Life's hard in the Fringe," Aelec said simply. "I did what I had to do to survive."

"Indeed," Kuvan said, smiling with his bright, white teeth. "Quite the reputation you've obtained out there. Smuggling, thievery, bribery, abduction, assault, murder... All against the syndicates. An impressive feat, though I should expect nothing less from one of my most distinguished Outriders."

"I am not *your* Outrider," Aelec grunted darkly. "Honorable discharge, remember?"

Kuvan snorted. "It's hard not to. What a tragic day that was, the sole surviving soldier of clan-Xero. Must've been tough for you afterwards. Rash decision making wouldn't be too far of a stretch after something like that."

"Watching my entire clan die in a careless bombing run didn't sit too well with me," he said, his gaze locked on Kuvan. "And since it was so blatant that the Comitors were responsible, I chose to give them a little payback."

Kuvan continued to grin—the dangerous, threatening smirk of a man with too much power. It was arrogance incarnate; a vessel to demonstrate how detached one could be if they became too disassociated from the rest of the galaxy. This was a man who believed himself to be untouchable, and was thus amused at Aelec's tribulations.

"Your exploits are quite well known in the upper circles," Kuvan said, his voice oozing with pompousness. "A dashing gunslinger like the days of old. Robbing the criminals and liberating the slaves. You're practically a folk hero, my good Aelec."

"Upper circles," Aelec repeated. "Fancy term for a gaggle of criminals."

"You think me a criminal?"

"I *know* you to be a criminal." Aelec gave him a hard stare. "You're a morcat in mantelope's clothing. A scumbag pretending to be a servant of the people. You can try to fool the rest of the galaxy with your façade, Kuvan. But I know what you really are."

The tall man opened his arms, smiling still. "You're right!" he exclaimed. "I am a scumbag wrapped in the mesh-fiber suit of an Imperium Veritas. But guess what? The galaxy doesn't give two shits. People like me have existed since long before you were born, and they'll keep resurfacing long after you're dead. You want to know why? Because we make the galaxy what it is. Those of us with money and power get to move the pieces on the board so that life continues to function in this Voidspawned universe. For instance, without me, Morrigar's infrastructure would have collapsed, and the Outrider clans would've succumbed to infighting."

He pressed his fist into his open palm for emphasis as he continued, "The galaxy needs men like me, whether the people like it or not. I'm the necessary evil. I can keep the syndicates towed in exchange for a few favors here and there. I've provided the resources to squash rebellions that wanted to shatter the Imperium. And I have ensured the continued prosperity of the Outriders in an age where many want them eradicated for being war machines."

That caught Aelec's attention. His eyebrows raised by a fraction, and he cursed himself for giving it away. Kuvan caught on immediately.

Kuvan tilted his head to one side and smirked devilishly. "Oh yes," he sneered. "Many on Diivoro and Seraphi wondered why the Imperium should have an entire culture of raised-from-birth soldiers. If the nine worlds are unified under the Imperium, what use do we have for these conquering war machines?"

He leaned closer, his acidic cologne burning Aelec's nostrils. "I made sure those questions fell upon deaf ears, Aelec," Kuvan murmured. "I protected your entire race. I gave you purpose against the Insurrectionists. And you repay me by robbing my partners and trying to expose me. Not smart, Aelec."

Kuvan paced towards Milli, wagging a finger at Aelec. "Not smart at all."

"Stay away from her!" Aelec snapped. "She's done nothing to deserve this. You have me. Now let her go!"

Kuvan stopped in front of Milli and glanced at Aelec, his thin eyebrow arching once more.

"Oh, she doesn't deserve this, does she?" the Veritas asked derisively. "Tell me, Aelec, how would you treat one of your Outriders if they repeatedly committed cybercrimes and sold information to some petty thugs in the Fringe? Accepting bribes and purging information from the holonet are Capital crimes. As is conspiring to besmirch a member of the Imperium Veriti."

"She had nothing to do with that!" Aelec snarled through clenched teeth.

Kuvan scoffed, rolling up the sleeve of his jacket to reveal his wrist terminus. The device blinked to life, the neon azure light shone brightly in the dim cabin. Several lines of communication hovered over his arm. Aelec recognized it as a holonet message.

The message he'd sent to Milli.

Kuvan cleared his throat before narrating, "My crew and I require the use of an Imperium-produced starship. One that can properly display a chain code with authorizations to Imperium facilities on Markum."

He glanced up at Aelec, half his angular face shrouded in shadow. "This was sent by you to Agent Spectre, was it not? And seeing as how she didn't report this, it begs the idea that she was in cahoots with your little crew."

The terminus' light blipped out. Kuvan clasped his hands behind his back once more and continued, "Let me guess. Your plan was to get me scared enough to flee to the Wasp Nest so that you could use your stolen access to infiltrate and abduct me. A plan that, shall I say, you'd never have been able to pull off. As it is with any chess match, I wasn't just going to sit around for you to get me in checkmate."

"You sure do like making a lot of assumptions," Aelec grunted, his nostrils flaring. "That's what makes a good politician, right? Talking out your ass."

The Veritas smiled, turning his gaze to Milli. "On the contrary. Making assumptions about people is the best way to narrow down what they might do. Once I heard that data from the Golden Spire had been taken, I made sure to keep a close eye on strange happenings across the galaxy. When the Lord Marshall informed me that you were his prime target, the pieces all clicked into place. The massacre on Morrigar, your military discharge, your exploits in the Fringe, and the subsequent robbery of the Golden Spire gave me an inkling as to what your plans were. When Nyri showed me Agent Spectre's logs, I made the correct assumption that you'd be gunning for me next. But being a ghost in the Fringe and being ex-Imperium would make it exceedingly difficult to apprehend you by normal means."

He reached up to brush some hair out of Milli's pale face. Aelec's eyes narrowed to slits, and he wanted to break the Veritas' hand for touching her.

"So, you admit it," Aelec grunted. "You admit that this was all your doing."

Kuvan shrugged. "What can I say?" he said. "I can give closure to someone who's truly desperate for it. That's your MO, right? It'll be the last comfort you receive before you answer for your crimes."

Kuvan waved his hand dismissively. "Anyway, the Lord Marshall suggested that we find a way to draw you out—put you on our turf. Since Agent Spectre here was your sole ticket to ensuring anonymity and reaching Markum, that was where I chose to strike.

And like the good dog that you are, you came in to try and rescue her."

It all made sense now. Aelec thought that he had the advantage after the Golden Spire heist, but he never considered that the Lord Marshall and Kuvan were still in a partnership. He should've planned for the fact that Kuvan would be alerted to what data had been stolen, and that the Veritas wouldn't just wait for it to resurface. No, Kuvan had been playing his own game, and Aelec had fallen right into it.

"But why wait?" Aelec asked. "Why not just try to capture me the moment I set foot on Oais? Why all the bullshit?"

Kuvan didn't respond instantly, opting instead to run his hand along his pulled-back hair, smoothing it out.

"Apprehending war veterans, even Outriders, is bad publicity," Kuvan explained. "Sure, I could've nabbed you in the dockyard and released a statement on the holonet telling the people of your crimes. But there's always people who see through that kind of stuff. Plus, the Imperator himself might start asking questions. This way, I got you quietly and off the grid while eliminating a few other threats simultaneously."

"My crew."

"Well, yes," Kuvan said in a matter-of-factly voice. "But also the Far Syters. The Starblades cleaned house as best they could. If any Syters escaped, having their asses kicked by the Starblades will have sent a clear message not to trifle with the Imperium. It was a win-win."

Aelec debated asking his next question for fear of what it might mean. Kuvan had made an intricate plan to capture Aelec, but there was still a variable missing from the man's equation.

"How did you know we'd even go for the Far Syters?" he asked.

Kuvan raised a finger and raised his eyebrows. "An acute observation. But all that took was a little goading from my contact in the C.B.I. He gave you the trail to track the Syters, and with Agent Spectre being the bait, I correctly assumed you'd follow it. As to how we knew where you were, your last call tipped him off. Once that was confirmed, it was a simple matter of coordinating with Nyri and the Starblades."

Aelec felt a chill as he considered the implications. He remembered the last transmission he made to the C.B.I., the last man he conferred with...

Oh shit, he thought, making the realization too late. *Director Cormack is Kuvan's contact in the C.B.I.*

Upon seeing Aelec's reaction, Kuvan simply smiled and clapped his hands in a mocking way. "All the pieces clicked into place, eh? It was a fun bit of coordination, I must say. Cormack was the one who assigned Agent Spectre to the dockyard in the first place, making it oh so easy for the Starblades to snatch her up. Sure, he could've given you all the direct path to the Far Syters, but that would've seemed too easy. Misdirection is how a magician pulls off a trick, after all."

Leaning forward, Kuvan examined Aelec before asking, "Now, I've a question for you, my good Aelec. Did you really think your little plan would work?" When Aelec didn't answer, the Veritas kept going. "Did you seriously think that a nobody like you would ever stand a chance against the governor of an entire planet? You've got a serious pair of balls, I'll give you that. But at the end of the day, you're still nothing but a mindless machine programmed by the Imperium. By *me*."

Aelec glowered. "When I get out of these restraints, I'll show you just how mindless I am, Kuvan."

"Aha, I'm sure you would," Kuvan chuckled. "But those gravcuffs are going to keep you nice and secure on our voyage. On the tiniest chance you could escape, you've got no nanotech, you're still wounded, and my friend here would make quick work of you."

He'd completely forgotten about the second man in the room. The familiar hooded figure of a Starblade stood in the corner, the black and gray melded seamlessly into the shadows. White cracks webbed on his neck armor.

"Obaron here has already made short work of you," Kuvan continued. "So forgive me if I'm not shaking in my loafers at the thought of you escaping."

He paused, touching a finger to his pointed chin. "Although," he murmured, "I do like to have all my starlanes covered. So how about this. I know that if you were to try and escape, you'd ensure Agent Spectre was with you. It's why you're here, after all. Well, this should deter you."

A soft *hiss* came from the Veritas's sleeve, white nanoparticles coalescing into a plasma carbine that extended from his right hand. The rectangular carbine thrummed like a revving engine, and Kuvan fired a blistering orange beam at Milli's left leg. Her eyes snapped open; a blood curdling scream of pain erupting from her mouth. Sizzling flesh and crunching bone thundered in Aelec's ears.

He thrashed in his restraints, desperately trying to put a stop to Kuvan's actions. But once again, he could do nothing as someone he cared about suffered. All he could do was watch.

Through the haunting chorus of Milli's shrieks and melting flesh, Kuvan let out an irritated sigh. After a few excruciatingly long seconds, Milli's left leg was vaporized from the knee down, and her screams faded as she fell unconscious. The shock of the deed melted away like ice over a flame, and Aelec glared at the man before him.

"You're not a man," Aelec snarled. "You're a spawn of the Void. A creature so detestable that every human and nonhuman recoils in disgust."

Kuvan snorted in derision. "Scathing, but not very creative. I've been called worse, my dear Aelec. Now, you stay put while we enjoy this little voyage of ours. If you behave, Agent Spectre will be given ample treatment. You could say her life is in your hands."

"I'll kill you for this!" Aelec growled, bucking his head. "After what you did to my clan and my friends... Even if it's the last thing I do. Let's see how talkative you are when my nanoblade is shoved down your throat."

Kuvan continued to smirk at Aelec, his posture as firm as a stone statue. "You'll have to get in line, my young friend," he said haughtily. "But I'm glad to see your Outrider spirit isn't fully broken. That'll make it all the more satisfying when we do break you."

Turning sharply on his heel, Kuvan strode out of the cabin with purposeful steps into the brightly illuminated hallway beyond. Obaron, the Starblade, remained motionless—his cold eyes staring out from the slit in the facemask. A metallic *thud* resounded from the door as it sealed.

Aelec stared at Milli. The young woman's head hung low as she drew in raspy breaths. He felt a small pang of relief. While Milli didn't have any genetic enhancements, he remembered her being tough as morristeel during the skirmishes on Oais. What she lacked in raw physicality she more than made up for in spirit. She fought for her family—her husband. And that was a will that would not be easily broken.

He only wished that he could have spared her from this tragedy entirely. Milli deserved a comfortable life with Ferris, and Aelec had robbed her of that. He cursed himself for making her his exclusive contact to commit the forgeries in the Fringe. It was a selfish decision that left her exposed and at the mercy of luck.

More and more he felt how corrupt and broken his clan-mark was becoming. An Outrider was meant to protect all citizens of the Imperium, and he had failed to do that.

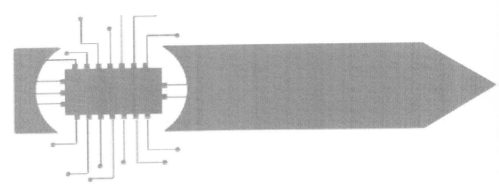

CHAPTER 36

Riza's hand covered her mouth, her expression horrified. She stood in the *Erinyes*' medbay as the sterile, white LEDs reflected off the dark green walls and floor. The smell of antiseptics and rubbing alcohol burned her nostrils. The multi-appendaged autodoc stood like a pillar beside the singular medical bed, its arms working to disperse healing agents on Dylis' body.

Her algorithm for checking outbound ships was still running in the *Erinyes*' terminal, so it would be a few minutes before they got any answers. Riza had made it a point to check Dylis' condition, and she was glad she did.

Dylis was a mess. His injury on Asmodum seemed like a minor

fracture in comparison to the damage he'd suffered here. Presently unconscious, the older Outrider was stripped of all his clothes, exposing his well-muscled chest and arms. Parts of exposed, tan skin showcased a number of old scars and burn marks. He now had several more additions to his collection.

Riza counted five stab wounds across Dylis' abdomen, each one at least ten centimeters in length. White nanoparticles were stuffed into each incision, working to repair the internal damage before sealing the surface wounds. The most notable injury, however, was the stump where Dylis' hand had been, and without the severed limb, he was at the mercy of a regenerator cylinder. The clear, jar-like device was affixed to the stump, greenish-white liquid bubbling within.

Regeneration cylinders were common in the galaxy, but were nearly as expensive as a starship. Even the growth concoction was approximately five thousand fuses per gallon. Myra said that she'd stolen a few containers full of the regrowth mixture during one of their jobs on Asmodum a year ago. Sol above, Riza was surprised more people weren't after the *Erinyes* after a stunt like that.

Steady beeps came from the heart rate monitor, and Riza noticed a few ligaments extending from Dylis' stump. The treatment was working, but it would take close to twenty-four hours before his hand regrew.

Sighing in relief, Riza left Dylis in the capable appendages of the autodoc and Rant as she navigated through the *Erinyes'* corridors. Exhaustion tugged at her eyes. A sensation of lethargy buzzed within her chest and urged her to lay in her bed. So much had happened in the past day, and it was all catching up with her in that singular moment of quiet.

Shaking her head, Riza retrieved a stimulant drink, cracked the aluminum top, and gulped down its contents. The sweetly sour concoction stung her tongue for a moment, but the effects hit her within seconds. Disposing of the can, Riza found Myra lounging on the couch and staring at the main hologram projector.

The glowing blue image of Oais was displayed above the domed device, various lines of data showing the public transit signatures for inbound and outbound vessels. There were hundreds, if not thousands, of ships buzzing around the planet like flies over a ripe fruit.

Despite the sheer magnitude of their task, Riza didn't let it sway her. The algorithm was processing, and she was determined to find where the Starblades had gone.

Myra's left boot tapped rapidly against the steel floor. "Are you sure this thing is working?" she queried.

"Yeah," Riza answered. "Just give it another minute. The biggest variable is when they might've left Oais. I added other variables like voidstream trajectory, crew rosters, and empty cargo manifests to help narrow it down."

The projector whirred as the algorithm processed; hundreds of ship IDs were scanned and discarded for not meeting certain parameters. Riza had hacked into the dockyard's mainframe and managed to connect the *Erinyes'* scanners with a droid flight control tower, providing them with a live feed of Oais' flights.

Myra rubbed her forehead in frustration, asking, "You think they're heading to Morrigar?"

Riza shrugged. "It's possible. They could be delivering him to Kuvan for all we know. But just a few more seconds..." She paced along the greenish-gray floor of the main hold, her chest tight.

Myra leaned forward on the couch, clasping her hands atop her knees as she rocked back and forth. The Vitrax closed her eyes tightly, and it seemed that she was either praying or trying to focus her thoughts. Riza surmised that it was the latter.

If Myra had tapped into her race's ability to have precognitive visions, then it was likely driving her insane knowing that she couldn't achieve the same result. Riza could only imagine the frustration the Vitrax felt, and she hoped that by some miracle Myra would get another vision. Myra opened her eyes and winced.

"Myra, don't strain yourself," Riza said soothingly. "The last thing we need is for you to suffer a brain aneurysm."

"Stars above, I thought I had it again," she sighed, leaning back on the couch. "This isn't supposed to happen for another thirty years. It's supposed to be impossible for a Vitrax to have premonitions until our tendrils lengthen to our lower backs. But if I could just find it again, maybe I could see where our path lies..."

"No," Riza declared firmly. "I need you in one piece. You're the only one who can fly the *Erinyes*, now. *You're* our best shot at catching up with those cloaked assholes."

Myra sighed again, but ultimately acquiesced.

Rapid beeps came from the main projector, and it displayed the results of the algorithm search. Riza's heart sank. There were over two dozen ships heading towards Morrigar that hadn't yielded their cargo manifests, and most were large transports. Common ID signatures indicated that they were Imperium military vessels, and Riza knew the assassins wouldn't hitch a ride aboard those.

She sat on the cafeteria table's bench, her shoulders slouching. Without knowing where the Starblades were really headed, more guesswork would yield similar daunting results. How could they possibly find Aelec?

"Twenty-nine ships populated under those parameters," Riza murmured. "We don't even know if the Starblades are heading to Morrigar. What if they took him to the Wasp Nest or the Mendicant Auditorium? Aelec said we needed an Imperium-made ship to even approach such places, and Milli is still MIA. By the Void, she's probably dead at this point."

Myra stood, placing her hands on her hips as she took a few steps in her direction. Her deep violet eyes shone resolutely. "Then we keep looking," she proclaimed. "There's got to be some factor we're missing. A ship design we're overlooking, or a planet trajectory. There are nine worlds in the Imperium, and only three of them serve military purposes."

"The Starblades," Riza blurted, meeting Myra's gaze. "Where could they have come from?"

Myra's pink eyebrows raised, and she answered, "Argentia! Dylis said the Na-jima guy was from Argentia. That's where they're from."

Riza's face paled, and her lips felt dry and cracked.

Myra cocked her head to the side. "What's wrong?"

"Argentia," Riza breathed, struggling to find the right words. "If he's heading there, then... then...."

"We're screwed," a voice echoed from behind them.

Riza's attention snapped around to see Dylis entering the room on his gravchair. The older Outrider lounged at an awkward angle, ensuring that his dismembered arm was in place. He wore only his loose gray pants; his bare chest was still exposed for them to see the numerous energy blade wounds. A vein throbbed in his temple, and he suppressed a wince.

Myra's fury buffeted. "Get your stubborn ass back in the medbay, Dylis!" she shrieked. "We can't risk the regeneration procedure going wrong! Where in the Void is Rant?"

On cue, a black shape scuttled from the dim corridor and into the main hold, moving seamlessly from the wall to the floor. "Apology: This unit is sorry, Master Myra," Rant said, "but Dylis Wyri would not listen to this unit's instructions to remain in the medbay. This unit is not programmed to harm any member of this crew, and therefore could not stop him."

Dylis waved his good hand dismissively. "I'll go back in a minute, dammit. Just let me speak!"

Myra was fuming, but didn't press the matter. Riza raised her eyebrows. She still couldn't believe he was conscious enough to hold a conversation. Voiddamn, were Outriders hardy people.

Clearing his throat, Dylis grunted, "Aside from the fact that Argentia is quarantined like a host for the Rhodium Plague, it's orbiting a red star and has a weird solar rotation."

Myra scrunched her nose and asked, "Which means?"

"Only a certain sector of the planet is habitable," Dylis explained. "Meaning the only place we could survive is under heavy lockdown and guarded by the Fifth Fleet. In short, that place will be harder to infiltrate than the Golden Spire and Wasp Nest combined."

Riza tugged at her ponytail, her eyes boring into the floor panels of the main hold. Dylis was right; getting into Argentia would be nearly as difficult as breaking into the Imperator's Palace. The *Erinyes* was still damaged, they were short on fuses, and their crew leader was gone. It seemed like a hopeless endeavor.

It wouldn't stop her, though. Aelec was willing to risk everything for them to escape, so they would do the same for him. Plus, Riza owed him a few unsavory words for stunning her *then* kissing her. She analyzed the situation. Planning a mission like this was a lot like forming a terminus algorithm. All Riza had to do was find the right lines of code to link up...

Her eyes lit up as a thought occurred to her.

Glancing up at Myra, she asked, "How much will it cost to leave the *Erinyes* in hangar L-three-one-seven?"

The Vitrax frowned and answered, "Fifty fuses a day. Why?"

Riza stood, wringing her hands. "We reserve our spot for a month. We lack the funds for adequate repairs anyways, so we may as well spend what we have on a secure, public docking area."

Myra's jaw dropped, her expression appalled. "That's fifteen hundred fuses for a parking spot, Riza. Why in the Void would we leave the *Erinyes* for a month?"

"It's a precaution. It may not take the whole month. Aelec said we need an Imperium-made ship to broadcast that chain code, right? So, we focus on obtaining one of those so we have a better shot at getting to Argentia."

"And how do you plan on getting one of those?" Dylis asked, shuffling in his gravchair. "We can't steal one, and we have a fraction of what we'd need to buy one."

The next idea clicked into place just as seamlessly as a terminus coding sequence. Riza couldn't help but smile deviously. Rubbing her hands together, she said, "Oh don't worry, *we* won't steal it."

Myra laughed without mirth. "What do you mean we won't—" She cut herself off, her eyes going wide as she said, "Oh no."

Dylis looked from Myra to Riza, frowning. "What?"

Raising a finger, Riza declared, "I have a job in mind."

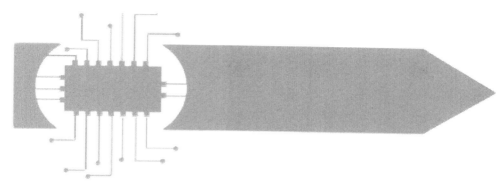

CHAPTER 37

4509.0902 / CW Star System: Tau / Planet: Argentia / GST: 06:20

Two days later, Kuvan returned to the detention cabin, and Aelec thrashed within his captivity harness. He needed to vent his anger, his frustration, and his sense of failure. All he wanted to do was burst free of his restraints and tear the so-called Veritas limb from limb.

His efforts were futile; the gravcollars held him firmly in place. Only his neck managed to buck forth. Aelec snarled like a caged beast, trying to wiggle his way out of the restraints. It was all he could do in the face of doing nothing.

Straightening his jacket, Kuvan tsked in response to Aelec's display.

"Oh how the mighty Outrider has fallen," he sneered. "Thrashing like a nilynx deprived of its morning meal. Clan-Xero did a shameful job of raising you, dear boy."

"Don't you dare use that name, Kuvan!" Aelec spat. "If you sully clan-Xero one more time, I'll—"

"You'll do what?" Kuvan snapped, his cold eyes flashing dangerously. "Nothing. You can do *nothing*, Aelec. No one is coming for you, and there's no escape from this place. So, I shall do whatever I like, last son of clan-Xero."

Aelec glared at the taller man, his gaze hooded. He'd been furious before, but never had he been bloodthirsty. Until now. Even if it was the last thing he did, Aelec wanted to pry Kuvan's tongue out of his mouth before cramming it into the man's stomach.

"One day, I'm going to make you eat those words, Kuvan," Aelec murmured darkly.

Kuvan rolled his eyes and ran a hand along his pulled-back hair. "I'm starting to think that you're all talk and no action, Aelec," he said. "But that will serve you well in this place. The more you talk, the less pain there'll be. Actually... I'm lying. There'll still be pain."

"Where are we?"

The older man clapped his hands as he paced towards Milli's unconscious form, saying, "I'm glad you asked. I always get a little giddy when I touchdown on a different world. Granted, I've visited almost every world in the known galaxy, but still."

Kuvan snapped his fingers, and shadows moved beyond the cabin's brightly-lit door. Aelec squinted, anticipating seeing more Starblades, but he noticed a gold sheen to their suits. The armor was sleek, the shoulder pads sharp, and the gauntlets scaly. Crimson hair protruded from their wide helmets like bright mohawks, and cobalt capes fell from their shoulders. Violet light glowed from the two-meter-long pulsespears they carried.

Aelec's gut sank. These were Arbiters—the personal cadre of the Veriti, High Chancellery, and even the Imperator himself.

Voiddamn, Aelec thought. *Kuvan has a coterie of Starblades and Arbiters. They must consider me a very high-value target for such precautions.*

Metallic *clanks* came from the Arbiters as they marched into the cabin. Two approached the restraints holding Aelec aloft, while the other four leveled their pulsespears at Aelec's throat. He seethed in agitation. Even if he got loose, the Arbiters would cut him down before he could flinch towards Kuvan. So, he didn't resist.

Unbuckling his restraints, the Arbiters relinked the gravcollars on Aelec's wrists and ankles, making him hover in midair. Four Arbiters surrounded Aelec, while the other two retrieved Milli. Obaron, the Starblade, moved from his perch in the cabin's corner to flank Kuvan. The assassin flexed his armored fingers, blue light flickering at the tips.

Clasping his hands, Kuvan said, "We'll be escorting you to the Silent Edict. The Lord Marshall and I have used this place on a number of occasions. Usually to extract info from dissidents like the Insurrectionists or A.I.L. members. We've never had an Outrider here before, so this'll be a fun change."

Aelec inhaled sharply. The Silent Edict was a myth in the armada; a secluded place that was said to be reserved for the Imperium's most damned. It was a place where people were erased. Worst of all, the Edict was rumored to be on Argentia, one of the few planets in the Imperium that was under strict lockdown. Aelec had suspected it was a secret military installation, but it was now confirmed to be one of the most secure prisons in the galaxy.

The Arbiters effortlessly dragged Aelec and Milli through the air, the latter's head was bowed, her black hair cascading over her face. Seeing the nanotech wrappings covering the stump of her leg made his stomach churn. Not with squeamishness, but with infuriated disgust.

He floated out of the cabin and into the intricately ornate pentagonal corridor. Crystalline LEDs pulsed with such a clear light that they looked like glowing crystals, casting glares on the polished floor. Moving deeper into the ship, the glossy floor was overtaken by velvet rugs with patterns of gold and burgundy.

Following the various corridors, he was led to an expansive boarding ramp airlock at least twice the size as the one on the

Erinyes. The Arbiters paused briefly, the steel ramp groaning as it lowered. Bright crimson light illuminated the airlock as it opened to the new atmosphere. A dry, earthy smell wafted from beyond, reminding him of the blistering sands of Pyron.

The boarding ramp thumped against a worn steel platform that was half covered by clumps of crimson sand. The wind blew a continual sheet of filaments into the air, giving the area a hazy look.

Aelec squinted his eyes against the filament-filled wind, his skin already felt dry and cracked. The Arbiters pulled him down the ramp and into the frenzied gusts, their capes snapping wildly in the breeze.

He looked up and saw deep, red clouds splotching the sky above, swirling in strange patterns. Beyond those came an angry glow from the red star that, while lightyears away, looked like it was just beyond the atmosphere. Nearly half of the skyline was eclipsed by the red sun.

"Welcome to Argentia," Kuvan proclaimed theatrically.

Through the haze of blowing sand, Aelec noticed the blocky structures of copper-colored carbocrete extending from the landing pad. Each structure varied in height and width, making the settlement appear like an exotic puzzle. From what he knew of the planet, this was one of many settlements established inside Argentia's habitable zone.

The Arbiters shuffled into a single file line to move through the narrow streets. Orange canopies crisscrossed overhead, preventing the crimson sand from collecting. The continual dry breeze stirred an itch that he couldn't scratch. Aelec hovered between two of the Arbiters, their pace measured as they marched through the barren street. It was a painstakingly slow stride; a nice prelude to the torture he'd soon experience.

After several excruciatingly long minutes, they broke through the main complex of structures. Aelec squinted his eyes against the sandy wind as a portentous sight greeted his gaze. The complex opened into an expansive area spanning several kilometers in diameter. The walls of the surrounding buildings were curved, making it appear as if they were inside a metallic bowl. Hovering at the center of the area was an object the size of a space station: a sphere of metal and light.

The sphere was enormous, at least a kilometer in diameter and close to thirty stories tall. Its white metallic sheen was a distinct contrast to the crimson sky, and fiery orange fissures traced intricate patterns across its surface. Aelec's eyes widened, noticing that portions of the sphere were breaking off and reknitting as if it was an ever-shifting fidget device.

Just like the Foundry, he realized.

Hundreds of security drones buzzed around the sphere like flies zipping around an overripe fruit. Ethereal echoes came from the sphere as it hovered beneath the churning, blood-red clouds.

No one said a word as they approached; not that the colossus needed any introduction.

This was the Silent Edict.

A vast circle of crimson sand was beneath the gargantuan sphere; it was bare of any technology aside from a perimeter fence of yellow fusionfibers. It appeared as though the Starblades sought to keep the ground beneath the sphere in its natural state. Perhaps it was sacred. The legends said that the assassins worshiped the stars themselves rather than the light of the Sol, which no doubt meant many strange customs on Argentia. Customs that he'd never see.

The Arbiters halted on a platform that overlooked the bare section of the complex, Aelec and Milli dangling from their gravcollars at awkward angles. Kuvan and Obaron stood behind them, keeping the pair in their line of sight. A soft *hum* emanated from the platform, and it began to rise into the air directly towards the lowest level of the sphere. A faint gust of wind touched Aelec's face, rustling his silver hair.

Up and up they rose towards the enigmatic structure, a place from a bygone era that heralded his future. As the platform closed the distance, a section along the sphere's side rippled, and the metal opened like the Meridiem structures of Oais. A gaping maw of darkness met his gaze.

Floating helplessly towards the Silent Edict, Aelec could only watch as his fate was taken from his hands and he was ushered into a place of true damnation.

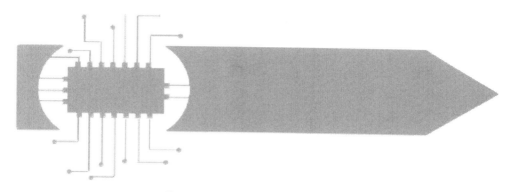

CHAPTER 38

The Northern Dockyards

er fingers brushed along the cool, glossy metal of the starship's hull, and Riza couldn't help but marvel at its design. Contrasting the crescent design of the *Erinyes*, the *Sage's Spirit* was leaf-shaped, with wide curves and a pointed bow. She walked along the stained, carbocrete floor of the hangar bay, following the starboard curve of the vessel.

The familiar rumble of engines filled the air around her, the clear, russet skyline buzzing with activity. Great, lethargic cruisers landed and departed from the dockyard, their engines powerful enough to create gusts of wind from a kilometer away. Riza pulled her leather jacket tight as she continued pacing.

With the *Erinyes* still grounded, Riza needed a new starship to pursue the Starblades. She didn't have time to wait for the *Erinyes* to undergo repairs, and the search had led her to the expansive lanes of New Skyline's northern dockyard. Among the many ships docked in the yard, this YRG-50 was a yacht formerly used by a low-ranking noble here on Oais, which suited Riza perfectly.

Standing nearby with his hands clasped behind him was one of the dockyard salesmen, an older man named Kayd Soren. He smiled under his thick, blond beard as he watched her keenly.

"As you can see, Miss Opaal," Kayd said, "she's in great condition. Newly refurbished with fusion engines that are only four months old. The landing struts underwent maintenance ten days ago, and all holograms had their software renewed. She may be used, but she'll fly as good as a brand-new ship off the conveyor belt."

Riza nodded, her eyes still examining the bronze-colored hull. "New coat of paint, too. And you say that she's been upgraded to hold a crew of thirty?"

"Oh yes," Kayd replied enthusiastically. "We had a few test flights at max capacity, and the *Sage's Spirit* can comfortably house up to thirty-five people."

Patting the morristeel lovingly, she turned away from the ship and faced the salesman. He continued to beam at her, his green eyes squinting in response to another gust generated by a departing ship. Next to him stood Myra, who cupped her rounded chin as she narrowed her eyes at the vessel.

"Nyri, what do you think?" Riza asked, gesturing to the ship. "Is this one to your liking?"

Myra scoffed at the ship—and likely the alias. "It's nothing like our old I-zero-five-five-two; too big if you ask me. I don't see our crew exceeding twenty. And is that a forty-five-twenty comms array?"

Kayd rubbed the back of his head and replied, "It is. But trust me, her signal is as clear as the newer models."

Riza raised her eyebrows theatrically, clasping her hands before her to sell her excitement. Myra, on the other hand, continued to scrutinize the massive ship.

"If we take her as-is," Myra said, "you knock off two thousand fuses. Even for a used model, that comms array should've been replaced two years ago."

Kayd chuckled. "One thousand."

"One point five."

"Best I can do is one point three."

Myra snapped her fingers, saying, "Done. Nice bargaining with you. Of course, Miss Opaal has the final say."

Kayd rubbed his hands together, stepping closer to Riza. "I don't want to pressure you, Miss Opaal," he said softly. "But we do have other buyers lining up. I don't know how much longer I can hold the *Sage's Spirit* for you."

"No need!" Riza exclaimed cheerfully. "I'm sold! Where do I sign?"

Kayd inclined his head, his gelled blond hair shining in the pale LEDs. He waved towards a kiosk at the end of the hangar and said, "Right this way. I'll need your—"

A high-pitched klaxon blared across the hangar bay, the lights lining the walls turning from white to flashing red. Workers within the bay froze, their heads turning in all directions as an air of confusion set in. Kayd looked around frantically, his hands pressed against his temples.

"What in the Void is going on?!" he bellowed over the alarm.

Shouts answered him. Across the bay, near the dealership kiosk, the wide doors burst open, a small detonation sending one of the metal slabs sliding across the floor. Sparks fountained upward as steel ground against carbocrete, the slab stopping centimeters from Kayd's feet. A cloud of pale steam seeped into the bay from the corridor beyond, shadows moving within.

Riza put a hand to her mouth, gasping theatrically as she hid behind the salesman. Myra joined her, exchanging glances with Riza while Kayd blubbered incomprehensibly.

From the steam-filled doorway came several figures, their shapes trailing mist like shredded capes. Dozens entered, each dressed head-to-toe in black, their faces obscured by mesh-fiber masks. Among the assailants was a hulking Kygi shrouded in black wrappings and a Tarantula droid. Within moments, they were upon the trio, circling them like a pack of nilynxes around a fresh kill. E-weapon barrels pointed at them, and Riza was quick to throw her hands up, letting out another gasp. Myra sniffed, but similarly raised her hands, trying not to look at Riza.

"What is the meaning of this?!" Kayd demanded, his voice cracking.

"What's it look like we're doing?" a basso voice answered. "We're robbing you, son. Now, hands where I can see them."

Kayd was last to lift his arms, words stammering past his lips. "Please... please don't hurt us! You... you can take whatever you want."

One of the assailants, a larger man, snorted, "A very poor choice of words, friend. We'll be taking this." He lifted his head towards the *Sage's Spirit* and then inclined his head to the women. "And for leverage, they'll be coming with us too. Don't want you making any stupid decisions, now would we?"

"Wait... You can't—"

The larger man pressed his E-pistol to the side of Kayd's head, shutting him up. Riza's breaths came in frantic flutters as she eyed the group of masked men and women.

"Please, don't let them take us!" Riza pleaded, her voice a little too high-pitched.

"Miss Opaal," Kayd groaned, giving her a sideways glance. "Do as they say."

She gulped but offered no further protest. A pair broke from the group and grasped Riza by the arms, pulling her towards the ship. Myra was similarly escorted away, and the assailants all backed away from Kayd, their E-weapons still aimed at him.

Reaching the *Spirit*'s boarding ramp, the same basso-voiced assailant spoke, "Unlock the ship and transfer access to my terminus. Now!"

Kayd obeyed, flicking one of the holograms towards the assailant, his terminus blinking with neon green light. A resounding *clank* came from the ship as the boarding ramp opened, and the black-clad group ushered them in hastily. The pair roughly pulled Riza into the cargo bay and pushed her up against one of the stacked crates. Ocean blue light poured from the LEDs that were arrayed in X patterns on the ceiling.

Hydraulics hissed as the ramp curled inward, sealing the ship with two dozen people inside. With morristeel walls now separating her from Kayd, Riza's shoulders sagged, and she huffed a relieved sigh. The corners of her mouth tugged into a smirk, and she resisted laughing.

Beside her, Myra arched a brow, her purple eyes wide with surprise. The Vitrax's thin lips parted as she scoffed, "Stars above, that worked?!"

The larger black-clad man pulled off his mask, revealing a chiseled, tan face. His receding auburn hair was a mess. "Let's not toot our own horns just yet," Dylis said, combing his fingers through his hair. "We still need to make it into orbit. Let's move people!"

A few of the others similarly removed their masks, revealing some familiar Far Syter faces. Many began running into the various connecting corridors. Everyone had a role to fill if this plan was to work. Leonis Ingot, his face free of the mask, strode towards her like a man who'd just won the SolarBall.

"I'm about to stream to the holonet," he proclaimed, holding up his terminus-laden arm. "Let's get you two into the main hold. We'll have to cuff you to the seats to sell it."

Riza shrugged, straightening her black jacket. "You Syters sure know how to show a lady a good time." She paused, then added, "Leonis, I still can't thank you enough for agreeing to this."

He waved off the remark. "Thank me later when we're in the voidstream, Miss Noxia. For now, best get back into character."

Riza closed her eyes, melding back into the helpless, quivering hostage role. Her eyes widened, her head constantly swiveled, and her breaths were short, frantic. By the Void, she felt like she was actually having a panic attack as she sold the performance. Leonis' terminus displayed a screen reflecting her image, a red dot blinking in its corner. Metal cuffs and hands shackled her as she was escorted through the pentagonal halls of the yacht. A few Syters were still masked and in view of the recording, shoving Riza with the butt-ends of their E-rifles.

They entered the ship's main hold, though it was more of a lounge than a command center. Couches with plush, white cushions formed a ring around the central hologram terminal. A few Syters ran past her towards the cockpit, their boots leaving prints on the pristine, tan carpet.

Riza was roughly shackled to one of the seats, a Syter aiming his E-pistol at her temple. As long as she played the hostage role well, the Imperium armada would think twice before trying to board the yacht. Riza had dug up the old forged records of Riza Opaal the day prior, ensuring the authenticity of her persona as a naive, fresh-from-school Seraphian.

Leonis spoke over the holonet recording, the terminus modulating his voice as he proclaimed, "We are of the Anti-Imperium League, and we will no longer be tethered to this corrupt planet. I send this message out to the Oais reserves and the armada. The hostages will be executed if anyone approaches the ship. Do not pursue us. Do not hunt us. If you abide by this, then no harm will come to the hostages."

Behind Leonis, Dylis conferred with the other Syters, pointing at the connecting corridors. "I want Rant, Igor, and Maze working to mask our voidstream drive signature," he ordered quietly, waving a hand at a few others. "Ryker, Izzy, create an inbound manifest for our destination."

Riza felt the first vibrations of the yacht's fusion engines, the opening percussion that heralded their departure. That vibration grew into an all-out rumble, her teeth chattering as the *Sage's Spirit* achieved liftoff. A long viewport across the main hold looked out on the passing skyscrapers, the wisps of russet clouds, and then the dark expanse of space. A bombastic, electrical whirring echoed from deep in the yacht, the voidstream drive powering up.

Beneath her mask of terror, Riza marveled at the show she managed to create; the job she'd planned. For a heist this size, Golath and Dylis couldn't shoulder the hijacking alone, so they'd struck a deal with the Far Syters. Desperate to get off-world after the loss of the Foundry, Leonis and his followers had agreed to hijack the ship in exchange for being dropped off on Faerius.

When the drive's whirring reached a fevered pitch, Leonis turned off his terminus and strapped into his seat. The others emulated the action, the whirring went silent for a few seconds, and the ship lurched into the voidstream tunnel.

With the *Sage's Spirit* between worlds, Leonis stopped the recording, and a chorus of cheers echoed throughout the ship. Riza and Myra were uncuffed from the seats, the Vitrax storming towards the cockpit. Nearby, Golath pulled off his numerous black wrappings, patting her on the shoulder with a free claw.

"We did it," Leonis breathed. "Sol above. The armada obeyed our demands."

Riza rubbed the red marks on her wrists. "You all need to be ready for the drop-off on Faerius. It'll be a tight window. And you're positive Nyri didn't know the whereabouts of the hideout?"

He shook his head. "Only I know of its exact location. She can squawk to the C.B.I. all she wants, but it won't matter." Leonis paused for a moment, then added, "I must say, your generosity to me and my guild is unprecedented. How can you trust us so easily?"

Riza drew her lips into a thin line before answering, "Because I have no other choice. Am I worried about duplicity? Of course I am. But the way I see it, you need us just as much as we need you. You guys are protesters, not terrorists."

"And now we're hijackers," Leonis pointed out. "As well as fugitives."

"It's not a perfect scenario," Riza admitted, "but you know this was our best chance to get you off-world. It was either this or leaving you at the mercy of the C.B.I."

Leonis' gaze wandered over the bustling Far Syters. Beneath his graying beard, a frown tugged at his lips. She had offered them the lesser of two evils, and it was certain that the Imperium would hunt them when the dust settled.

She was reminded of something Arenia once told her, *It is better to die flying in the Void than live behind a lasergate.*

Bowing his head in acceptance, Leonis stepped away from Riza, but stopped short. Looking over his shoulder, he asked, "You're sure you want to go to Argentia afterwards?"

Riza nodded.

"Why do you care so much about Xero? I understand loyalty, but what you're planning to do is short of insanity. Why risk the wrath of the Imperium for one Outrider?"

The question hit her as if she'd been thrown into a voidstream portal, her mind floating amongst the stars. The answer was both simple and complicated. Everything came crashing down upon her —her exhaustion, her uncertainty, and her fear all jumbled together. Leonis' question burned within her mind. Why risk everything for Aelec? He was her captain, sure. An employer, yes. But that didn't entitle him to such steadfast devotion.

No, it was Aelec's character that had earned her loyalty, her trust, and her compassion. He had the best parts of the Fringe and the Imperium—a man of principle, craftiness, quirkiness, and fidelity. He was firm and tender, exactly like their kiss. Aelec was what men should aspire to be.

Aelec was her leader. Her friend. And that was worth flying into the maw of a singularity.

Placing her hands on her hips, Riza declared, "Because he's my captain. And I'm going to save him."

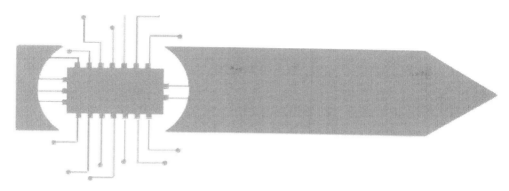

EPILOGUE

"The Void sure is full of wonders, huh?" Esean noted as he gazed up at the marvelous structure.

Despite the frigid chill of the mountainous tunnel, the fiery excitement pulsing in his veins kept him warm. At the age of nineteen, Esean could hardly keep still, his energy warding off the effects of the world. Plus, he could shrug off the occasional discomfort in favor of his passion.

Esean's passion was archeology.

Standing on a landing grafted of purplish-black stone, he observed the grand staircase leading towards a shrine at the zenith of the mountain cavern. The cave was enormous, larger than anything he'd ever seen, especially one concealed within Faerius' mountains. Neon green lights dotted the darkness, while the stairs were illuminated by the crawler.

His team had spent months working on this site, and the first vestiges of ancient Meridiem architecture protruded from the mountainside. Little did they realize that it was merely the first half of the entire structure. Geological reports indicated that millennia of shifting tectonic plates had split the structure in two, forcing one half toward the surface while the other dwelled within.

Looking over his shoulder, Esean saw his team bustling around the cave crawler. Kortni and Manny pulled out some survey gear while Tagg checked over his E-rifle. Of their group, Tagg was the only one with combat experience, though it was only because he took firing lessons at the Umber Academy.

Tagg slung the rifle over his shoulder and said, "Yeah, it sure is full of old shit. And it always begs the question of 'why haven't we discovered this already?'"

"It's because we're always distracted by the next best thing," Kortni called, placing some tools in her belt loops. "Humans are like goldfish. We see one thing, think it's cool, but then bam! Shiny object draws our attention."

"You sure that's not just you, Kortni?" Manny joked, hefting one of the surveying tripods.

Punching him lightly in the shoulder, Kortni snorted. "Whatever you doof. But my point's proven. Here we are, barely a year graduated, and we're already gawking at the next shiny thing."

"Doesn't seem too shiny to me," Esean said, holding up his terminus to record footage. "C'mon. Let's see what's inside."

His heart pounded as excitement propelled him up the old steps, his team right behind him. Their footsteps echoed throughout the vast cavern, sounding like the beat of a Morrigarian alternative rock song. Up and up they climbed, Esean's confidence outshining his concern for traps or other dangers. He was an explorer; he had to know what the Meridiem might've sealed away.

He checked his terminus. The hologram was recording footage but a few red bars were blinking. It wasn't connected to the holonet.

Even after adjusting some of the settings, the device refused to broadcast.

"Dammit!" he cursed. "There's terrible signal up here. It won't let me stream to the holonet."

Kortni shrugged. "It'll record for your personal files, though. You can upload it later."

"I guess so," he sighed.

This was Esean's first expedition since graduating and leaving Oais, and he wanted to show off his work. Being independent and unsanctioned meant that he had to claim his discoveries quickly.

Reaching the shrine's peak, Esean's jaw dropped. Grand columns of glistening variium held up the pointed zenith, portions rippling like the waves in the ocean. Fissures within the purplish metal were devoid of light. *Strange.*

"Ain't this something," Manny breathed, setting the tripod down and activating a few probes. "How old do you think it is? One, two millennia?"

"Older," Esean said, running a hand along the cold metal. "In Meridiem Studies we learned that variium remains in motion and illuminated for at least two thousand years. The lights are dead here, and the metal is barely transforming. I estimate it's been here at least three millennia."

"Voiddamn," Kortni murmured. "What were the Meridiem doing on Faerius three thousand years ago? I didn't know they'd unlocked interstellar travel at that point."

"The records don't go back that far," Esean explained, "and even modern Meridiem don't know their full history. Whatever happened on M'ras practically eradicated their entire culture. It's difficult to discern whether this shrine was built before or after M'ras' shattering."

Tagg grunted, rolling his eyes. "So long as it doesn't jump out to eat us, doesn't matter how old it is."

Esean sighed—he didn't feel like arguing with the amateur mercenary. Instead, he and his team went about their work to survey and document the entrance to the shrine. Manny pointed in various directions, and the floating probes hovered in designated spots for surveying. Kortni used a plasma pick to scrape samples from the floor.

Esean raised his arm higher, neon blue light reflected off the glossy variium walls and faintly illuminated the inner chamber. He hadn't ruled out the possibility of old traps still existing, so he took a few careful steps into the room. Esean shined his light all around the area. Nothing seemed out of place.

Concentric rings were inlaid on the floor like a whirlpool; the floor indented every half meter. An obelisk of pure black jutted up from its center, and Esean wasn't sure whether it was stone or metal. His eyes flicked upward. The domed ceiling was painted with the mural of a Meridiem figure towering over a horizon. The image's six-fingered hands were splayed wide in a welcoming gesture, and the cat-like eyes were comically wide.

What drew Esean's attention, however, were dozens of detailed, box-like devices forming a crescent over the Meridiem. Esean scratched his chin. He'd studied Meridiem history during his time at the Umber Academy, but the records never mentioned these box-like things.

Focusing on the obelisk, Esean approached, and with every step the air grew warmer. It was like approaching a fusion generator that was on low power. He closed the final meter, and the air around the obelisk shimmered. Esean scanned it with both his eyes and his terminus. The device beeped, flashing red as no data populated.

Odd, he mused as he reached out a hand. *It looks like nothing more than a pillar of obsidian. How can there be no info on it?*

Esean's curiosity got the better of him. He lived by the creed 'nothing ventured, nothing gained'.

His bare palm touched the obelisk. A prolonged *hiss* emanated from within, and a gust of wind pulsed outward. Like a shockwave, it expanded, passing beyond the entrance. A second later, the air was still. A weak moan, dry and electronic with numerous metallic *clicks*, emitted from the obelisk. Esean took a step back, his enthrallment quickly replaced with terror. He should run; he should be anywhere but near this device. Yet he couldn't pull himself away from it.

Glowing lines of orange traced in strange patterns along the obelisk as the heat grew more intense. Mechanical groans resonated from the fissures and the black material peeled away, revealing a compartment within. Brilliant, orange light forced him to squint.

"Sol above," he breathed, keeping his terminus raised. "I can't wait to send this to the holonet!"

Within the illuminated interior of the obelisk was the outline of something rectangular. Esean leaned forward and saw that it was a sheet of glossy metal the size of an average textbook. The silver steel rippled as if it was breathing, its face engraved with lines of golden glyphs. Esean's eyes lit up. He recognized those symbols from his studies at the Umber Academy. It was ancient Meridic.

"Hey guys!" Esean called, his voice cracking. "Get in here!"

Tentatively, Esean grasped the device and pulled it from its resting place. The steel was pleasantly warm to the touch. It rested in his palm as tenderly as a falling feather. Testing a theory, he released his grip. The sheet remained in place, bobbing in the air.

Checks out, he thought, *Meridiem technology can sustain perpetual anti-gravity stasis. But these glyphs aren't based on common Meridic, I'll need a proper linguist to help translate this stuff.*

Yet there was one glyph that he recognized, which translated to *Tablet of the Spatium*. Well, in common Meridic it probably meant *Spatium Tablet*.

"Remarkable," Esean breathed. "Guys, have any of you ever heard of a Spatium Tablet before?"

His voice echoed throughout the shrine, and silence answered him. Esean frowned. He'd called for his companions a minute ago. They weren't so far away that they couldn't hear him. Grasping the Spatium Tablet once more, Esean turned towards the shrine's entrance. His eyes narrowed in the dim lighting, but he saw the distinctive glow of Manny's terminus.

Perhaps this was a prank; a way to get him riled up. He wouldn't put it past Manny and Kortni to do something ridiculous. Esean walked towards the entrance, but he noticed that all the lights were stationary—there wasn't an ounce of movement.

An iota of fear crept through his body, the excitement vanishing like a puff of smoke.

"Guys?" he called, keeping his terminus raised. "This isn't funny!"

The pounding heartbeat in his chest reverberated into the Spatium Tablet clutched in his hand—the metal rippled in tandem. The shrine, the cavern, perhaps the entire mountain had fallen eerily silent. Esean couldn't even hear the humming engine of the crawler.

Passing through the arched entrance, Esean glanced about the upper landing and froze.

Tagg, Kortni, and Manny laid upon the landing, their bodies motionless. There was no blood, only a distinctive, cauterized slash in the center of their backs. His team was sprawled across the landing, dead.

Esean felt his face grow cold, and his fingers let go of the Spatium Tablet. He didn't understand. They were alone in the cavern. No one else was around.

How?! he screamed internally. *How could this have happened?*

The air carried a soft, electrical *hiss*. Esean spun around and saw twin blades of pure energy lunging towards him. He raised his arms instinctively. Blinding, searing pain erupted from his left pectoral as the energy sunk into his suit, easily slicing through the flesh, and puncturing his heart.

Esean didn't scream, only a coarse wheeze escaped his lips. The energy blade lingered within him for what felt like an eternity, and then it was gone. Feeling left his legs as his knees buckled, and his body crashed against the ground with a *crunch*. He was still lucid, but his mind grew muddled.

The air in front of Esean shimmered, lines of electricity arced around a humanoid figure. A hooded man melded into existence, shadows enriching the black armor that covered his frame. Piercing blue eyes stared out from a slit in his facemask.

"Who—" he wheezed, unable to move. "Why—"

The assassin said nothing; he squatted next to Esean and unhooked the terminus from his limp arm—the device was still recording footage. Raising it to eye level, the man paused the recording and swiped to see how much had been documented.

After a moment, he extended his arm, a terminus lighting up from within the armor. The holographic screen was backwards to Esean, but he managed to pick out a string of words: *Holonet Signal Blocked.* Esean's eyes widened.

It wasn't a lack of signal, he realized. *He was jamming us the entire time.*

Standing, the assassin dropped Esean's device on the floor, his boot following atop it. Esean groaned as the terminus buckled under the assassin's boot, glass and bits of metal breaking away as the hologram faded.

A chorus of electric crackles emanated from around Esean, more figures appearing out of thin air. Three similarly garbed assassins stood near each of Esean's fallen companions. They all looked the same, with their armor and hoods, but the one standing above Tagg's corpse wore a detailed facemask. Lines of violet outlined the cheekbones, and a gold strip flowed from nose to mouth.

Esean's vision grew dark as the sensation of weightlessness overtook him. He was moments from death's door; the Void would soon claim him. Yet his academic fascination caused him to observe the assassins as his final moments ran out.

The marked assassin approached and grasped the Spatium Tablet with both hands, bowing his head. Electronic *hums* and *clicks* came from the device as if it were greeting its new bearer.

Another assassin approached, bearing a white briefcase inlaid with metallic seals. Carefully, the assassin placed the Tablet into the container, and a *hiss* of steam emitted as it sealed.

"Get this to the Imperator at once, *aljiwali*," said the marked assassin.

The other one bowed, saying, "As you command, Starmaster."

Looking from Esean to the entrance to the cave, the Starmaster declared, "The rest of us shall destroy the crawler and seal the tunnel. May this be their burial place."

Bowing their heads, the assassins walked down the grand staircase, heading towards the bottom of the structure. Turning his back to Esean, the Starmaster followed his companions. The last thing Esean saw was the gray hood disappearing into the darkness.

That same darkness swallowed Esean.

END OF BOOK 2

DID YOU ENJOY?

"IMPERIUM"

Thank you for reading *Imperium*. Please consider leaving an honest review on Amazon and/or Goodreads because these are incredibly important for independent authors. Reviews help readers who are considering this book, but it also provides valuable feedback to the author.

Thank you for your support!

ACKNOWLEDGEMENTS

Another one bites the dust. If you haven't noticed, I tend to let my full quirkiness shine through in the Prefaces and Acknowledgement sections of my books. So here's my unfiltered thank you for reading this entry of *The Outrider Saga*! As an indie author, your interest in reading my work is enough to make my day brighter. This is a hard road, but when I see people enjoying these stories it fuels me to keep going.

Time for the shoutouts. I would like to thank my wife, Megan, for six wonderful years together and for constantly saying "okay" to my indie author plans. No qualms or objections. Just pure support. I love you mostest.

A big thank you to Nadia, my cover artist from MiblArt, for her incredible work on *Imperium*'s design. It's my second favorite cover of my books thus far! A huge thanks to Katherine D. Graham for doing a copy edit in record time. I'm also extremely grateful for my formatter, D. M. Sonntag, who deals with all of my eccentricities both good and bad like a pro.

I always need to give thanks to my parents and brother. Sci-fi may not always be their preferred books to read, but I'm always keeping my fingers crossed. An extended shoutout to the Romeos, Kalwickis, Butlers, Mottingers, Austins, Robbins, Crockers, and Farleys. Though I don't see you all as often, the bonds of family never waver and I always love our time together.

A huge shoutout to my beta readers. Ciara Hartford, your unconditional support (and love for Dylis) is encouraging, especially when I have my rough days. Amanda Auler, you might think you were being harsh, but your feedback pushed me to be a better writer. I prefer honest critiques over false praise. To JWS, I'm glad I didn't have as many technological hiccups as in *Erinyes*, and I hope this story eventually grows on you like *Empire Strikes Back*.

To my ARC team, Luke Courtney, Devon Gambrell, S.E. Schneider, Michaela Fallstick, Nicole MCN, Janine Batiste, S.L. Martinez, Andrew Bast, Richard Holliday, Cinder Ackerman, Tara Smith, Tiffany Ewald, Theresa Hayden, and Stephanie Mansaur, you all are incredible and this launch wouldn't be what it is without you. A successful book release is all thanks to your efforts. Thank you so much for your dedication, and I hope you enjoyed this story!

Finally, I must once again thank you, the reader, for giving this indie sci-fi story your time and attention. I am always open to your praise and criticism alike, so do not hesitate to nudge me on social media (as long as it's appropriate).

More projects are incoming, and I hope you're ready for *The Outrider Saga* Book 3 in the near future. Blessing to all!

INDEX: TERMINOLOGY

ACTLE: a large, flying reptile native to Morrigar.

ALIEN-SIRE: the owner of an alien plantation in the Fringe Territories.

ALJIN: a style of hooded armor commonly worn by the Starblades of Argentia. The sleek, black armor covers the entirety of the Starblade's body, while a long, mesh-fiber hood is integrated into the pauldrons.

ALJIWALI (TITLE): the name given to Starblades who have achieved the rank of Keeper of Holy Rites.

ARBITER: the personal guard for members of the Imperium Veriti, High Chancellery, and the Imperator himself.

AXI-1200 (YACHT): a medium-sized yacht used by high-ranking members of the Imperium. AXI-1200s are known for having a design resembling manta rays.

BAC (DRINK): a dark whiskey-bourbon from the planet Terras.

C-57 (SNUB FIGHTER): a sleek and elegant starship used for escorts over the planet Sath. Commissioned by SecuriTrax, C-57s are a one-man snub fighter that resembles the shape of a falcon in mid-dive. However, C-57s are often in need of repairs due to their high speeds, thus are outfitted with Tarantula utility droids.

CARBOCRETE: a composite building material that is a combination of concrete and carbon fiber. Due to the bonded molecules in carbocrete, the substance is far more resistant to wear and tear.

CARGOCASE: a sizable luggage carrier often used by people traveling via public shuttles. One cargocase can carry six full outfits.

CHAIN CODE: a data sequence used by members of the Imperium armada to authenticate their rank and ship ID. These sequences can be downloaded to terminals and transmitted via ship IDs.

CLAN-LEADER: the elite-most warrior among an Outrider clan, and one who has forsaken the use of nanotechnology.

CLAN-MARK: a spiritual concept of an Outrider's character, a creed that encapsulates their honor, integrity, and determination.

CLAN-PRODIGY: the chosen apprentice of the clan-leader in Outrider culture.

DATACHIP: a fingernail-sized device used to store or upload computer data.

DOMAIN EXPANSE FOUNDRY: a prototype "living machine" of the First Human Expansion. The technology was developed by the

Domain governance of Terras and was shipped off-world during later ventures into space. These Foundries were designed to harvest natural resources and convert them into building supplies at an exponential rate to expedite the colonization process.

DURLUX: a hard-light weapon used exclusively by members of the Starblade Order of Assassins. Conduits integrated in the Starblades' gauntlets use particle dilators to convert light mass into a hard-light object, commonly a blade. This method was enhanced to create projectiles, shields, and armor that could be summoned and dismissed at will by the Starblades. Mastery of durlux weapons is known as the Way of the Starblade.

ECUMEN: a world-spanning city.

E-WEAPONS: a standard pistol, rifle, shotgun, or turret that fires concentrated rounds of fusion energy. E-weapons use compact-channel linear accelerators to fire a fusion "slug" from the weapon's extended barrel. Within E-weapon barrels are twin conducting rails that accelerate the fusion projectile via electric currents.

FLORIC (DRINK): an alcoholic liquid of green color that has a sweetly-sour taste, often preferred by the Kygi species.

FUSE: a term used for the standard unit of quantocurrency used in the Fringe Territories and the Capital Worlds. A single fuse is enough to purchase a week's worth of rations. To some members of the galactic community, the more accurate term is 'planck'.

FUSECASTER: a large, multi-cord crossbow with strings made from emerald fusionfiber. This weapon is a common firearm used by the Kygi species.

FUSIONFIBER: a concentrated beam of energy that can be used like a cable or cord.

GRAVBIKE: a one to two-person vehicle that utilizes gravlift engines to hover off the ground and accelerate to a speed of up to two hundred kilometers per hour.

GRAVLIFT: a device that creates negative gravity fields which push against a planet or ship's gravitational field. Gravlifts are often used as a propulsion mechanism for starships as they lift off from the ground, but they are also used to power elevators.

HIGH CHANCELLOR (TITLE): a representative of a star sector in the Imperium who oversees the planetary Veriti and reports directly to the Imperator.

HOLONET: the galactic-wide news source.

HUSK-RACER: an amalgamation of gravbikes linked up with bulky, hodge-podge fusion engines. Husk-racers are used for the dangerous and thrilling sporting event, husk-racing. The goal of the sport is to last the longest in a racing sprint since husk-racers are not built for extended flights.

I-0552 (FREIGHTER): a common cargo freighter used by Solar Industries in the Fringe Territories. These vehicles are pincer-like in shape, have a circular hull, twin cargo mandibles that extend from the bow, and a cockpit set between the mandibles. I-0552s are outfitted with twin fusion cannon batteries, a voidstream drive, and two fusion engines.

IMPERATOR (TITLE): the supreme commander and ruler of the Sol Imperium.

KYGI (SPECIES): a race of insectoid creatures from the planet Kygnor. The Kygi average around two meters in height and have a brownish-gray carapace that covers their body. They have four arms, mandibles over their beaked mouths, and beady yellow eyes. Kygi cannot survive in oxygen-rich environments and require a respirator. Due to their physiology, Kygi can survive up to two hours in the vacuum of space.

KYHARP: a musical device played by members of the Kygi species. Kyharps are similar to human harps, but they have countless more cords and bows to accommodate the four hands of a Kygi.

LORD MARSHALL (TITLE): the leader of the Comitor crime syndicate and the overseer of all alien-sires.

MANTELOPE: a species of bovid native to Morrigar.

MEDALLION OF AUTONOMY: a metallic visa that acts as a writ of independent citizenship for aliens in the Fringe Territories.

MERIDIEM (SPECIES): a race of humanoids from the planet M'ras. The Meridiem are tall and thin, with pointed ears and pale, smooth skin on their faces and chests. Their backs, legs, and arms are covered in reptilian brown scales.

MESH-FIBER: a flexible, net-type fiber commonly used to make clothes. Mesh-fiber is fabricated from morristeel, nylon, and polypropylene.

METHANE (GAS): an odorless, colorless, and flammable gas that can be mined from the asteroids in the Xionic Belt. Due to the decay of natural materials inside the asteroids, pockets of methane are common in the space rock. Methane is used to fuel electricity.

MITHIUM: a special (and highly secretive) alloy used to graft quantum cards. The alloy is under the strict control of the Ruby Dawn Baking corporation and is not disclosed to the public. What is known about the alloy is that it is light, flexible, and highly durable. Mithium often comes in a shade of violet.

MOD-PILL: a common nanotech pill that has modafinil and placebo mixtures to boost cognitive thinking.

MORCAT: a species of feline native to Morrigar.

MORHAWK: a species of avian native to Morrigar.

MORRISTEEL: a metal ore that can only be found on Morrigar. This rare metal has the unique property of having both covalent and metallic bonds, making it malleable to shape while resistant to energy discharges by dissipating electrons on its surface. Because it has the strongest atomic bonds in the known universe, morristeel is a coveted alloy in the Sol Imperium and is used to make weapons, armor, and vehicle hulls.

NANOPARTICLES (COMMON): a cluster of billions of miniscule nanites that are commonly integrated with modern technology like terminuses, hologram pucks, fusion engines, gravlifts, and void-stream drives.

NANOPARTICLES (PURE): a cluster of billions of minuscule nanites specifically used by Outriders that can be combined to create pulsecannons, blades, grappling hooks, healing solvents, utility items, or a full suit of nanotech armor.

NANOTECH (ARMOR): a suit of armor with the ability to rebuild, reshape, or redesign itself within seconds of activation. Primarily used by Outriders, the nanotech armor resembles an organic-like muscular exoskeleton which is stronger, more agile, and more flexible than most combat suits.

NILYNX: a species of feline native to Nidal.

NORA, CLAN: an Outrider warrior clan from the planet Morrigar.

OUTRIDER (RACE): a race of enhanced humans from the planet Morrigar. The Outriders are almost the pinnacle of human attributes with lean muscles, quicker reflexes, and greater durability. A side effect of certain Outrider genetic enhancements causes some of them to have golden eyes and silver hair.

PASSBALL: a common sport played in the galaxy.

PHASE-SHIFTER: a device that is able to turn a portion of any surface impalpable and transparent, allowing matter to pass through.

PLASMA (CARBINE): a large firearm that emits a condensed beam of plasma energy.

PLASMA (CUTTER): a device used by Techno Mining to cut through the outer shell of asteroids. Plasma cutters are intense enough to burn through most substances, even morristeel.

PLASMA (GRENADE): an explosive device that utilizes superheated plasma.

PUCK (HOLOGRAM): a portable, cylindrical device used to display a hologram.

PULSEAXE: a variant of the pulseweapon arsenal that takes the shape of an axe. The electric pulse emitter is installed on the "eye" of the axe so that the energy envelops the blade from "toe" to "heel".

PULSEBLADE: a variant of the pulseweapon arsenal that takes the shape of a short sword. The electric pulse emitter is installed in the "rain guard" of the sword so that the energy envelops the blade along its "edge" to the "point".

PULSECANNON: a variant of the pulseweapon arsenal that can be used as a firearm. Commonly used by Outriders (though anyone with nanotech can use it), these weapons emit an electric pulse that fires from the cannon and expands into a small shockwave.

PULSEHAMMER: a variant of the pulseweapon arsenal that takes the shape of a hammer. The electric pulse emitter is installed in the "cheek" of the hammer so that the energy envelops the hammer's "face" and "peen".

PYRON (RACE): a species of humanoids native to the planet Pyron. They are known for wrapping themselves from head to toe in tan or brown robes while wearing face masks or goggles. The garb is a result of the Pyrons shading themselves from the blistering sun of their homeworld, and it's a tradition they carry even on temperate worlds.

QUANTUM CARD: a palm-sized card made out of mithium that has the ability to siphon or distribute quantum energy. The mithium cards are made up of antimatter storage devices, which have a quantum containment field, thus allowing for contact distribution of quantum energy. Quantum cards can contain up to 5,000 fuses before overloading.

QUANTUM DISPENSER: a device that emits ultrasonic frequencies that cause clusters of nanoparticles to separate.

QUANTUM DISINTEGRATOR: a device that emits an ultrasonic frequency powerful enough to atomize nanoparticles.

QUANTUM SCALPEL: a medical scalpel that has the ability to generate an electrical field around clusters of nanoparticles and compels them to coalesce into a single mass for extraction.

QUANTOCURRENCY: a form of economic exchange involving the distribution of quantum energy for goods and services. Quantum energy is used to directly power all nanotech in the galaxy, making it the most valuable item in the galaxy. Quantocurrency is used by all members of the Capital Worlds and the Fringe Territories, since the cash industry went extinct in the year 4021. The way the system works is that quantum cards are created by the R.D.B. and distributed across the galaxy. Cards contain a specific number of quantum energy fuses and can be built upon or distributed via the card's containment field. Empty cards can be refilled, but they can only hold 5,000 fuses or risk overloading. Fuses are used to power the nanotechnology which has been incorporated into most modern technology.

S-53 (FREIGHTER): a small freighter that is commonly used for smuggling.

SILENT EDICT, THE: an installation on Argentia that serves as the Imperium's max-security prison. The oldest structure on Argentia, the Silent Edict is reserved for their most dangerous criminals. Combined with the planet's limited habitability, the prison has been made infamous for being completely impenetrable and inescapable. The Silent Edict is one of the few ancient variium structures utilized by the modern galaxy, excluding the decommissioned Foundries, shrines, and monoliths. As with all Meridiem structures, the variium plates along the Edict's surface will ripple, sometimes breaking off to reknit onto different portions of the facility. This serves as a way to keep the structure in a constant state of repair and reinforcement, ensuring that time does not erode its infrastructure.

SOL, THE: the universal god of the sun, justice, law, and war. A common phrase in the galaxy, "Thank the Sol", is often used in moments of celebration or reflection.

SPATIUM TABLET: a sheet of glossy metal the size of a book. The silver variium is engraved with golden glyphs of the Meridic language.

SPICE: a chemical intoxicant that is created from plants native to the planet Caavo. A combination of plant nectars and hallucinogenic compounds resulted in the creation of spice.

STUNSTICK: a melee weapon often used by law enforcement to stun targets.

TARANTULA UTILITY (DROID): a spider-like droid that is manufactured on the planet Sath.

TERMINUS: a wrist-mounted bracer with a built-in holographic terminal.

TOGRIAN (SPECIES): a species of tortoise-like sentients from the planet Tog.

TOGRIED (EGGS): an egg that has been boiled in a mixture of soy sauce, butter, and mayonnaise. This is a delicacy often cooked by Kygi chefs.

TRADE (LANGUAGE): the intergalactic standard method of communication.

UNI-MODULATOR: a universal modulation that can be installed within a terminus to block any frequency emitted by a transmitter. These are often used to block alarm frequencies.

VAKAMA: a skirt worn by male warriors on the planet Terras. The vakama is secured with six straps: two in front, one on each side, and two in back. Vakamas are often worn with silk robes tucked in at the waist.

VANKIR: a rhinoceros-like creature native to the planet Asmodum. Vankirs can reach up to two tons in weight, and are often the size of a small starfighter. The beasts are regularly hunted for their ribs, meat, and marrow.

VARIIUM: a metal used by the Meridiem which has the ability to shift at will. Variium alters itself to naturally combat the effects of erosion. Studies show that it can remain in motion and illuminated for at least two thousand years.

VERITAS (TITLE): a governor of a single planetary system in the Sol Imperium.

VIPERBOW: a rare energy weapon often used by members of the Starblade Order of Assassins.

VITRAX (SPECIES): a humanoid species from the planet Sath. The Vitrax average between five and six feet in height, have pink skin, and violet eyes. Males and females have different physical traits. Female Vitrax have long, prehensile tentacles that protrude from their heads like hair and skin with a lighter shade of pink. Male Vitrax are bald, but have smaller tentacles protruding from their chins like goatees, and have skin that is a darker shade of pink. Vitrax have a unique biological feature that allows their tentacles to secrete increased amounts of dopamine into their brains, which gives them hyperawareness.

VOID, THE: a common slur in the galaxy. The Void is the equivalent of damnation, so most species universally view it as such. However, some species and religions make the Void out to be something ethereal.

VOIDSTREAM: a dimensional pathway that is used for faster-than-light travel between planets. The voidstream is a series of "tunnels" that connect planets, asteroid fields, and stars by gravity. Void-stream drives open a portal to allow ships to enter the voidstream tunnel, where the pilot (or navigational terminal) navigates until they exit through another portal at the desired destination.

WORM, XIONIC: a massive invertebrate creature that resides within the asteroids of the Xionic Belt. A gigantic class of helminths, Xionic worms have translucent skin, bio-luminescent organs, sensory antennas, and thousands of rock-grinding fangs. They can reach lengths of up to one kilometer.

WYRI, CLAN: an Outrider warrior clan from Morrigar, and the kin-clan to clan-Xero.

XERO, CLAN: an Outrider warrior clan from Morrigar and the kin-clan to clan-Wyri.

YRG-50 (YACHT): a sleek yacht used by lower-class nobles in the Imperium. The YRG-50 is well-known for its precise symmetry, polished floors, and dazzling LED lights.

ZAPAAK: a common card game played in cantinas, often for betting purposes.

INDEX: PLANETS & SYSTEMS

DIIVORO (TAU SYSTEM): the capital of the Sol Imperium and an ecumen that has been stripped of its natural resources by the voracity of its population. The Meridiem term "Diivoro" has been said to translate to "pearl" in Trade, but some linguists believe the term literally means "wasteland".

FAERIUS (SIGMA SYSTEM): the largest agricultural planet in the Capital Worlds. Homeworld of Fiona Wyri.

MARKUM (TAU SYSTEM): the central military operations planet that is referred to as the "Wasp Nest". Markum is often used as an emergency center for the planetary Veriti, and even the Imperator himself.

MORRIGAR (BETOPA SYSTEM): the homeworld of the Outriders, mainly a rural planet with three hundred major cities for military and space faring, but the most valuable aspect of the planet is its ore mines. Morristeel is one of the most versatile metals in the galaxy, and one of the strongest substances in mass production. The metal is primarily used to create nanotech armor for Outrider warriors. Each clan would have different markings engraved in the metal. The Betopa system is four lightyears (two days) from the Tau system. Homeworld of Aelec Xero, Dylis Wyri, and Zerick Kuvan.

NIDAL (PICON SYSTEM): the primary leisure planet of the Capital Worlds, often referred to as a planetary vacation resort. The Picon system is five lightyears (two days) from the Tau system. There is less than one lightyear (fourteen hours) between Nidal and Oais.

OAIS (PICON SYSTEM): the advanced educational planet for the upper-class citizens of the Capital Worlds. Oais is a full ecumen; the city encompasses the entire planet, but is divided into specific sectors based on educational proficiencies. Homeworld of Milli Spectre, Ferris Spectre, and Leonis Ingot.

SERAPHI (SIGMA SYSTEM): the educational planet used for lower and middle-class citizens of the Capital Worlds. Seraphi is more of a rural world with a few cities as opposed to being a full ecumen. Homeworld of Riza Noxia and Arenia Noxia.

[FRINGE TERRITORIES]

ASMODUM (VADKAIL SYSTEM): a temperate planet with deep underworld connections, and the headquarters of the Black Eye arms dealers. The main settlement on the planet is referred to as Husky Dawn. Its moon is called Tepht. The Vadkail system is ten lightyears (four days) from the Tau system. There are five lightyears (two days) between Asmodum and the Xionic Belt.

BIIRAS (DORANDA SYSTEM): the headquarters of Solar Industries and an ecumen planet. Referred to as the "Bleeding World" due to the bloody color of its plants, and also because of the corporations bleeding the planet dry of its resources. The metropolis cities are referred to as Sectors Blue, Red, Gold, and Silver, and they are divided based on their hemisphere location. The Doranda system is eight lightyears (three days) from the Tau system. There are three lightyears (one day) between Pyron and Biiras.

CAAVO (AERON SYSTEM): the headquarters of the Comitor Syndicate, and an ecumen planet. The planet is an amalgam of junk yards, sewage systems, construction sites, factories, and grimy entertainment modules. The only quality structure on the planet is the Golden Spire—the command center of the Comitors. A place of wealth, debauchery, and high security, the Spire is the hub of economic stability on Caavo. The Aeron system is eleven lightyears (four days) from the Tau system. There are two lightyears (one day) between Caavo, Tog, and Kyg-nor.

KHORRUS (NIRAMIS SYSTEM): a planet on the outer quadrant of the Fringe, and the closest system to the border of the Capital Worlds. Primarily used as an extensive starport, Khorrus is the easiest voidstream jump point in the Fringe to reach the Capital Worlds. The Niramis system is seven lightyears (three days) from the Tau system. There is less than one lightyear (fourteen hours) between Khorrus and Sath.

KYG-NOR (AERON SYSTEM): a desolate planet, and the homeworld of the Kygi race. Kyg-nor is the site of a geological disaster from millennia past. The ancient Kygi discovered a device buried deep within their planet—a tablet—which allowed them to manipulate evolution on their world. The natives used the device to reach peak physical forms (wings, carapace, multiple appendages, keen senses, and durability in different gaseous environments). However, the mystics delved too deep into the secrets of the tablet and tried to terraform their planet to make it more abundant with resources. Not able to wield the true power of the device, the mystics inadvertently scorched their planet's surface, split the planet in half, and corroded the atmosphere. Homeworld of Kuanishu-Zaskari-Aka-Kup-Golath.

M'RAS (SOL SYSTEM): a desolate planet located in the outer rim of the galaxy which is rumored to be the origin of the Meridiem race. The Sol system is fourteen lightyears (five days) from the Tau system. There is less than one lightyear (twelve hours) between Terras and M'ras.

PYRON (DORANDA SYSTEM): a desert planet that neighbors Biiras.

SATH (NIRAMIS SYSTEM): a tropical planet with a large host of alien-sire plantations, and the headquarters of SecuriTrax. Sath is the homeworld of the Vitrax species. Homeworld of Myra'etoileur and Nyri'coutanir.

TERRAS (SOL SYSTEM): a temperate planet at the edge of known space which is rumored to be the origin of humanity. In ancient history, the first colonization of humanity was referred to as the Domain on Terras. The Domain encompassed the entire continent of Pan'gea, and sent expeditions into the stars to spread humanity across the galaxy. A cataclysmic event nearly wiped out the population and set the planet back countless centuries. Terras was labeled as uninhabitable by the rest of the galaxy until the Galactic Standard Year 4470.

TOG (AERON SYSTEM): a tropical planet of the Togrian race, and the origin of husk racing.

XIONIC BELT (VADKAIL SYSTEM): an expansive asteroid field between Asmodum and Caavo. Under the control of Techno Mining, the Xionic Belt is famous for its methane-filled asteroids that are often mined. The asteroid field is also infamous for the giant space worms that burrow in the larger rocks and attack spaceships.

INDEX: ORGANIZATIONS

ANTI-IMPERIUM LEAGUE, THE: a terrorist faction based on Nidal. Established in 4499.0820, this group rose to prominence as a result of the entertainment glorification of the Imperium on Nidal.

BLACK EYE, THE: a group of arms dealers on Asmodum. Low on the crime food chain, the Black Eye operatives stick to smuggling and arms trafficking on Asmodum to avoid the wrath of the Comitors. The guild is run by an individual known only as the Sire.

CAPITAL BUREAU OF INVESTIGATION: the central government police force across the Imperium. Each of the nine planets has their own C.B.I. headquarters and garrisons, though their numbers are often spread thin due to low recruitment.

CERATA, THE: a large group of pirates and outlaws in the Fringe Territories. The Cerata often operate aboard pleasure yachts or frigates to provide an upstanding public reputation to conceal their illicit activities.

CHURCH OF SOL, THE: a religious order that has spread throughout the galaxy, and one that is worshiped by many species. The Church worships Sol, the universal god of the sun, justice, law, and war. Initiates go through four grades: Erinyes, Panther, Courier of the Sol, and Sage. The series of initiations involves passing through either four gates or climbing four ladders, each of which increases in difficulty. Mythology states that the universe was lifeless until Sol was born of a meteorite, which is why damnation is often referred to as the Void.

COMITORS, THE: the leading crime syndicate in the Fringe Territories. Operating from the planet Caavo, the Comitors ensure lawlessness in the Fringe and conduct shady dealings in assassinations, smuggling, extortion, and slavery.

FAR SYTERS, THE: a guild of socio-political activists that rose to prominence on Oais in the wake of the Insurrectionist War of 4507.

INSURRECTIONISTS, THE: a large-scale resistance faction that was established on Faerius. Numerous officials and agriculturalists grew disillusioned with the Imperium's taxation of their products, which led to the formation of the rebellion. The Insurrectionists wanted to claim the agricultural planet for themselves and separate from the Imperium, which prompted an aggressive military response from the Imperator. After the battle in Amarack City, the Insurrectionists hijacked numerous Imperium ships and fled the planet, spreading their cause to many of the other Capital Worlds. In 4507.0730, the Insurrectionists fled to their final bastion on Morrigar, where they were swiftly defeated by the local Outrider clans.

RUBY DAWN BANKING: the central banking company based in the Capital Worlds. The R.D.F. is in charge of the production and distribution of mithium-grafted quantum cards that are used for quantocurrency. While the bank operates primarily in the Capital Worlds, some subsidiaries are based in the Fringe Territories to monitor the distribution of mithium. The R.D.F. headquarters is on Diivoro, and they mine asteroids in the rings around the planet for deposits of mithium.

SECURITRAX: a small-time, private orbital defense force over the planet Sath. Created by the alien-sire Pax Dalin, SecuriTrax serves as the private army protecting the planet's numerous nonhuman plantations. Sire Dalin often fills the ranks of the defense force with his own Vitrax slaves, promising them a medallion of autonomy if they serve five years in SecuriTrax. The defense force is known for utilizing C-57 snub fighters, models that need persistent repairs done by Tarantula droids while in orbit.

SOL'S RESISTANCE ARMY: a minor terrorist organization that arose on Oais. In 4503.0314, the S.R.A. was trying to indoctrinate citizens in the more archaic beliefs of the Fringe Territories. Extortion, kidnapping, arson, slavery—all the barbaric customs that the syndicates practiced—were being introduced to the Oais citizens, and the Imperium would not tolerate that. When attempts at negotiation failed, the S.R.A. began openly attacking sectors across the planet, thus prompting a military response.

SOL IMPERIUM, THE: the central governance of the Capitol Worlds. Led by a race known as the Meridiem, they elicited a galactic expansion thousands of years ago to spread their knowledge to other worlds. After their great expansion into the galactic arena, the Meridiem formed an interplanetary alliance with nine worlds to form the Sol Imperium. The Imperium operates as a democracy, with an elected Imperator ruling over the High Chancellery and Veriti Council.

SOLAR INDUSTRIES: a major tech conglomerate in the Fringe Territories. They develop more affordable technologies and are in competition with SunTech.

STARBLADE ORDER, THE: an order of assassins on Argentia. A fanatical group of assassins, they outsource their services to anyone in the Fringe Territories or the Capitol Worlds. The Starblades view themselves as crusaders tasked with eliminating the wretched people of the galaxy. By their creed, "The Star is light, but it is also death".

STARLANE EXPRESS: an intergalactic shipping industry based on Oais. One of the largest shipping conglomerates in the Imperium, Starlane Express is responsible for building cargo transports and leasing containers to respective customers. The company ships anything from textiles to weapon parts, and their morristeel containers are painted a dark pink with white letters.

SUNTECH: the primary technology corporation in the Capitol Worlds and contracted with the Sol Imperium. SunTech develops tech like hologram pucks, navigational charts, droid memory units, security systems, starship terminals, and wrist terminuses.

TECHNO MINING: a smaller corporation in the Fringe Territories that specializes in distributing methane gas mined from the Xionic Belt asteroids. Techno Mining acquired the mining rights from the Comitors and has exclusive claim to the Xionic Belt.

EXTRAS

READ ON FOR A SNIPPET FROM

EDICT

THE OUTRIDER SAGA BOOK 3
BY MATTHEW ROMEO

Coming soon...

EDICT

THE OUTRIDER SAGA BOOK 3

She stepped into an endless tunnel of darkness. The fear of the unknown made her palms grow clammy. It was a natural tunnel, carved out from the crimson rock in concentric rings like a drill had burrowed into the earth. But the jagged edges, the stalactites, and uneven floor indicated that time itself had been the drill.

Time both buried and unearthed the secrets of the universe.

Myra stared into the darkness, her Vitrax eyes only able to see a few meters in front of her. She couldn't feel anything from the air around her; it was neither hot nor cold. No wind, no gusts, no whispers coming from the darkness. All was quiet, and it sent shivers down her spine.

She wasn't certain how she'd ended up in this tunnel, her memory was veiled like fog obscuring a lane of gravtraffic. Yet, she wasn't surprised to be here; she had a feeling that this was where she was bound to end up. But that simply added to her sense of panic.

How did I end up here if I know I'm supposed to be here? she wondered. Her thoughts echoed loudly as a result of the utter silence.

The familiar chilling rush of dopamine hit her brain, excreted from her tentacles in response to the lack of sensations. Perhaps if she honed her focus, her senses would be heightened to pick up something. Anything.

Yet, nothing came of it.

Running her tongue over her sharp canines, Myra rolled her shoulders as she took a hesitant step forward. Her step was light, thanks to the graceful physiology of a modern Vitrax, but the footstep created an unnaturally loud *thud*. It echoed within the rocky walls, resonating further into the darkness before her.

Myra froze, her face growing cold. Was the sound enhanced because of her dopamine surge? No, it never affected her to that degree. This was a result of the strange cavern.

She gulped, hesitantly taking another step. The same echo cascaded down the tunnel. This time, it was punctuated by another sound.

A wet, fleshy *thump* answered the call of her footsteps. Myra's eyes widened so much that she feared they'd pop out of her skull. Cold sweat slicked her palms. Never in all her life had she heard something like that.

She remained there like a morristeel statue, afraid to even breathe. Silence permeated the cavern until another fleshy *thump* came. Next came the nightmarish sounds of deep, guttural growling combined with clicking, which reminded her of Golath. It was a haunting vocalization that triggered her deepest, darkest level of fear.

Myra wanted to run, to hide, to be anywhere but in that spot. Yet her legs had turned to steel, and even when she closed her eyes, she could see the cave around her. There was no escape.

The thumping and growling grew nearer; it was just beyond the veil of blackness. Something moved just beyond her sight, and her heart felt like it was going to leap out of her chest.

A large hand slapped against the ground a few meters in front of her, with talon-like nails digging into the rock. The joints bent backwards, indicating it was a quadruped. The flesh was marbled a sickly shade of tan and gray, like a rotted corpse. The digits were in all the wrong places; three extended from the hand, while two protruded like spines from the wrist. Long, fleshy tendrils grew out from the top of the limb. Myra's stomach churned.

Myra's gaze traced up the monstrous limb as it melded with the darkness, and she thought she saw the faint glimmer of bioluminescence. Three small orbs of dark green light peeked through the darkness, and a head-splitting screech thundered in the cave.

The screams seemed to meld into her own voice, and she felt her head smack against something metallic.

Her eyes snapped open. She wasn't in a terrifying cavern; she was in her bunk. Cold sweat beaded her forehead, mixing with the growing burn of a fresh bump from hitting her head. The tentacles on her head wriggled in response to her churning emotions.

Rubbing her forehead, Myra steadied her breathing as she rotated on her bunk, feet touching the steel floor.

Was that a dream? she wondered as the pain subsided. *It seemed so real. So vivid.*

It had a familiar sensation to it as well. Unlike a lucid dream, Myra could remember the exact details of what she'd seen in that cave. There was nothing fuzzy in her mind when she thought about the stalactites, the tunnel, the lack of wind, or the haunting sounds of the creature.

No, she'd experienced this before back on Oais, when her life literally flashed before her eyes. This was a precognitive episode. This was foresight.

TO BE CONTINUED

OTHER WORKS BY
MATTHEW ROMEO

THE MAVEN KNIGHT TRILOGY

THE OUTRIDER SAGA

UPCOMING...

THE OUTRIDER SAGA

EDICT

MAVEN KNIGHT STORIES

THE HOLD OF DESTINY

ABOUT THE AUTHOR

 Matthew Romeo is the self-published author of *The Maven Knight Trilogy* and *The Outrider Saga*. He graduated from Randolph-Macon in 2014 with a B.A. in Communications. He is a former Brand Ambassador for The Writer Community of Instagram and a frequent speaker on a variety of writing podcasts. His hobbies include writing (obviously), drawing, martial arts, video games, tabletop role-playing games, and copiously editing his work. He lives in central Virginia with his wife, and he works full-time while writing his next novel.

You can find more about him at www.themavenknight.wixsite.com
Instagram @author_matthewromeo